UNDER *the* JEWELED SKY

ALISON McQUEEN

sourcebooks
landmark

Published by Sourcebooks Landmark, an imprint of Sourcebooks, Inc.
P.O. Box 4410, Naperville, Illinois 60567-4410
(630) 961-3900
Fax: (630) 961-2168
www.sourcebooks.com

Library of Congress Cataloging-in-Publication data is on file with the publisher.

Printed and bound in the United States of America.

VP 10 9 8 7 6 5 4 3 2 1

Long years ago, we made a tryst with destiny,
and now the time comes when we shall redeem our pledge.

Jawaharlal Nehru
Midnight, 15 August 1947

In loving memory of my father, John Farrell

*1957

Wiltshire, England

A wooden trellis, heavy with summer jasmine, lined the low doorway of Ranmore, a sunken cottage dating back to the English Civil War. Sophie pinched off a tiny flower head, bruising the petals in her fingers, and brought her hand to her nose, taking in the sweetness. She looked at the knocker, a cold brass ring hanging loosely from a lion's mouth, and remembered how she had tried to polish it once years ago with wads of cotton soaked pungent with Brasso. It hadn't done any good at all, dulling the dark patina without resurrecting its shine, and the polish had dried into the tiny crevices which she had then scrubbed at for hours with an old toothbrush. A whole afternoon wasted, but occupied.

Her hand reached up, two sharp raps clattering out of the lion's mouth into the empty street. Movement came from inside. The door opened, and Sophie's heart caught in her chest.

"Hello, Mother," she said.

Sophie steadied herself, remembering to breathe, shaken by the sight of her.

The initial shadow of stunned shock on her mother's pale, bloated face passed quickly. She stood, rooted to the spot, and declined to smile.

"It's been a long time," Sophie said.

Her mother looked her up and down, eyes raking over her. "I always knew you'd be back."

The two women stared at each other. Veronica Schofield's figure had broadened appallingly over the last decade, her hips a good deal heavier than any woman should carry, her waist a thick bulge of disinterest beneath the floral-print house dress that had seen better days. She had cut her hair off too, the neat bun she used to wear now replaced with a short, stiff permanent wave, run through with a great deal of gray, rinsed an unnatural shade of blue.

"I'll understand if you would prefer that I left," Sophie said. Her mother looked at her impassively.

"No. I won't do that." She stood aside, one hand on the door, and allowed her daughter to pass.

Inside, the cottage unfurled its dim cloak of claustrophobia, the same oppressive dark furniture pressed into the cramped corners, the same cold flagstones that had felt generations of footsteps come and go. Sophie followed her mother into the kitchen, the air tainted by last night's supper, or today's lunch perhaps, a faintly stale aroma that might have been boiled cabbage or thick, salty gravy. The crucifix above the doorway had slipped partially from its nail and hung at an awkward angle, as though about to fall.

"Where's Granny?" Sophie asked.

"Dead," her mother said, turning her back on her. "Seven years ago."

"Oh." Sophie shifted. "I'm sorry to hear that."

Her mother smiled thinly, lifting the heavy lid from the hotplate on the wood-fired range, sliding the kettle on to it. "Are you indeed?"

Sophie sat at the table, the low ceiling bearing down on her. "What happened?"

"She died," her mother said flatly. "That's what happens when old people have their lives torn to pieces. At least I was here to care for her. Thank God she had a daughter she could rely upon." Veronica Schofield busied herself, warming the teapot, setting out cups, and making much ceremony of unnecessary quarter plates and a fussy arrangement of plain arrowroot biscuits. "Still, that's all done with now. We won't dwell on it."

"You might have let us know," Sophie said.

"Whatever for? It's not as though you would have come to the funeral, is it?"

"That's not what I meant."

"And how was I supposed to know where you were anyway?"

"You've always known where we were."

"Of course I haven't."

"The letters from your solicitor never had any trouble finding us."

"That was different," her mother said, turning her back on her daughter again, watching the kettle boil. "There were matters to be settled."

"And once they were settled? What then? I never heard a word from you."

A silence fell over the kitchen, Sophie feeling an unexpected tug of sadness at the loss of a grandmother she had never felt quite belonged to her. Granny Gasson had been a distant woman, her husband's name etched into the village memorial where she would lay flowers on his birthday each year in the absence of a grave. Only once did she come to visit them at their house in Islington where Sophie had grown up, saying that she couldn't abide the journey or London's filth. Nor did she invite them to Ranmore until the war forced her hand. Sophie had but one vague memory of that first meeting with her grandmother, a fleeting childhood moment that couldn't have lasted more than two hours, involving a homemade cake served silently while she sat awkwardly and tried not to fidget. Then the war came, and before Sophie knew it, her father had been whisked away from them along with every other able-bodied man in the street, and she and her mother had been ordered to get out of London. They had thrown dust sheets over the furniture before boarding a train at Paddington and moving into the cottage with Granny. They would be safe in the depths of Wiltshire. There was nothing there to bomb.

Sophie's grandmother had turned out to be pleasant enough, although she clearly preferred solitude and generally kept her affections to herself. Her mere presence was all that Sophie had needed, the silent witness with whom she could sit when her mother's temper frayed. And now she was dead. Sophie looked around the sunless kitchen and sighed to herself, thinking of her grandmother having gone to her grave after hearing heaven only knows what about her only grandchild. It left her heart heavy, and she felt ashamed. All the way here on the train this morning, she had assumed that Granny would still be around, a white-haired old lady sitting in the garden perhaps, on a comfortable wicker chair with a knitted blanket across her knees. Sophie hoped that her passing had come to her without pain or suffering, returning her to the husband she had missed so much.

"That's the way you wanted it, dear." Veronica Schofield spooned a short measure of loose leaves into the pot and took the kettle from the stove, wrapping the handle with a thick cloth. "When I left India, it was perfectly clear to me that you would choose to stay with your father, so I thought it best to leave you both to it." Boiling water steamed from the spout. "I was made quite ill with it all and I didn't have the energy to argue with either of you."

❧❀❧

Veronica Schofield stole a glance at her daughter's reflection in the small mirror set into the dresser. She'd always known Sophie would come back eventually, tail between her legs, and had spent many an evening staring hypnotically into the blackened window of the small wood-burner in the tiny sitting room, wondering what she would say when that day finally came, rehearsing her responses, turning each one over in her head. Children know nothing of the suffering that is born of raising them. They run around oblivious, sucking every ounce of life from their mother without a single care for the destruction they wreak. It was a thankless task, yet she had done her best and she would not be made to feel one iota of remorse for the actions she had taken. She had given of herself quite enough, to no avail, raising her child in the fear of God, for all the good it had done her.

Mrs. Schofield stirred the leaves and lidded the pot, then hung the cloth over the range, glancing at her daughter as she did so. Sophie seemed respectable enough, she supposed, and she had kept her figure by the looks of it. No wedding ring, she noticed. But that was to be expected after what had happened. As much as it had served as a just punishment, Mrs. Schofield couldn't help but feel a little sorry for her daughter, for the mess she had gone and made of her life. She would be twenty-eight now, which was almost thirty, and everybody knew that thirty was too old for any family-minded man to settle upon. She turned from the dresser's reflection and approached the table.

"I suppose you've come all this way to blame me for your woes, expecting me to pick up the pieces." Depositing the cosied teapot on the table, she sat solidly on a chair, pouring for them both.

"Not at all," Sophie said. She felt tired suddenly, drained, as though someone had siphoned her blood. The sharpness of her mother's voice. It brought it all back.

"And you needn't bother to offer me your apologies either," her mother said. "What's done is done and there's no point in raking over old coals."

"That's not what I came here for."

"Well it certainly took you long enough, didn't it?"

"Sorry," Sophie said.

"Never mind. I suppose it's all water under the bridge."

"Yes. I suppose it is."

"No husband, I see." Her mother slid an upward glance toward Sophie's left hand.

"No."

A long minute passed, cups filled, too hot to drink.

"I haven't any cake to offer you. I don't bother with baking any more. There doesn't seem to be much point now that I'm on my own." She paused for a moment, as if waiting for Sophie to commiserate with her. "I suppose I could pop along to the baker's if you'd like something."

"No, thank you."

"Watching your figure, I expect." She cast Sophie a short smile. "You're looking well enough, although I have to say that lipstick is rather severe." Sophie found herself pressing her lips together, as if to minimize their offense. "Marriage isn't for everyone, of course. I might have stayed unmarried myself had I known what would be expected of me."

Sophie looked at her mother wearily.

"Was it really so terrible?"

"I always did my best for you, and for your father." Veronica sat with her tea, cup hovering before her mouth. "Nobody could have blamed me for leaving. I'd rather have died than stay in that godforsaken place."

Sophie sighed inwardly. This was exactly what she had wanted to avoid. Or perhaps it was precisely what she had needed to test, to see if it had been her imagination, the misery her mother broadcast like seed to the wind. It had seemed like the right thing to do yesterday, as she sat with her monumental decision, that she should finally make the journey she had put off for so long and reconcile with her mother, that she should clear the air and tell her of her news in the hope of encouraging a new beginning. Surely they could salvage something from the wreckage of their relationship? She knew how difficult it had all been, but in spite of everything, she had missed her. She had missed having a mother.

"I always knew it would come to no good." Mrs. Schofield spoke into her teacup. "After everything I did for him, all those years of sacrifice thrown back in my face."

"That's unfair."

"Unfair? I'll tell you what's unfair." The cup clattered to its saucer. "It's unfair to have to go through the humiliation of divorcing an adulterous man after taking solemn vows in the presence of God! He never should have asked it of me."

"He wasn't adulterous."

"Oh yes he was, and everybody knows it."

"You were never happy together. I don't know why you married him in the first place."

"Happy?" She smiled coldly. "Happiness has nothing to do with it, my dear. I did my duty, to you, to your father, and to my mother, and what thanks did I ever get?"

A gulf of silence opened up between them again. Sophie stared at the table, scrubbed clean with a heavy brush as it had always been, its dry wooden surface yearning for a lick of linseed oil and a soft cloth.

The divorce had ruined her father. Against everyone's advice, he had insisted they bring the whole sorry business to a close, offering to grant his estranged wife anything she wanted in settlement, just to get it over with quickly. At first, her mother had refused to even consider it, reaching conveniently to her religious beliefs while Sophie's father dug deeper and deeper, signing everything away from a distance of seven thousand miles. When there was nothing left for him to give, Veronica capitulated, and he provided her with irrefutable evidence for a petition by admitting to a fictitious adulterous affair. She would not lose face, he promised her, and she could tell people whatever she wanted. It had seemed to him the most honorable solution, to create one final act of deception that would end it all with as little fallout as possible. He hadn't cared what it cost him, only that he be free of her, released from the specter of misery that had been his constant companion for twenty years. Sophie was not supposed to have known about any of it, yet she had seen the lawyer's letters while tidying her father's study, his chaotic approach to paperwork far too haphazard to keep secrets safe for long. Her heart had bled for him as he signed away all that was his and told her not to worry.

"Let's not argue," Sophie said.

"No. Let's not." Her mother pushed her teacup away. "There's no point in crying over spilt milk, and I won't turn you away now that you've finally come back, although I expect plenty of mothers would. You can have your old room. I keep the sewing machine in there nowadays, but you can move it to the little bedroom if you want to." She got up from the table and went to the sink. "But I won't have you idling around. They're looking for seasonal workers up at Hawthorn Farm. There's a notice about it in the post office window. Mrs. Milner will be bound to have something to tide you over until you find your feet."

"Mother…"

"I suppose I shall have to think of something to say to the neighbors now that you've turned up out of the blue, and don't expect everyone to take to you straight away either." She kept her eyes fixed on the sink, rinsing out a milk bottle already clean, setting it on the drainer. "They know very well the mill I've been put through, being left high and dry. It's taken years for me to restore my dignity. People were very sympathetic, but the idea of a woman being divorced made some of them very uncomfortable indeed. It was months before I could show my face in church."

"Mother," Sophie said. "I came here to tell you something."

"I should have thought about it before. Where else were you going to end up? There was a time when I wouldn't even have answered the door to you. Nobody knows the ins and outs of what happened, and I won't have it mentioned either. I've had quite enough of people gossiping behind my back."

Sophie watched her mother as she fussed with the tea towel and knew that there was no point in continuing. Nothing had changed; nothing at all. The intervening years had lent her mother only a headful of gray hair and a calcified perspective. The same feelings of dread pulled Sophie down like a lead weight, the air sucked from the room.

Outside, the rain had begun. Not like the fat, warm droplets that spattered a deafening percussion against tropical rooftops under an Indian monsoon, but the persistent drone of a half-hearted English drizzle tap-tapping against the window panes. Her mother saw the taxi draw up outside and peered out of the window, holding back the lace curtain.

"Hello?" she said. "What on earth is that doing there?"

Sophie rose quietly from the table and picked up her handbag. Her mother turned quickly toward her. For a moment she stood frozen, silent, and looked at her daughter strangely, as though confused. Briefly, Sophie thought that she saw something pass across her mother's face, something that seemed almost like panic.

"Sophie?"

Sophie faced her mother. There were so many things she had come to say. She could feel them rising out of her chest now, the words all but forming on her lips, yet only two came out, exhaled softly, without expression.

"Good-bye, Mother."

Sophie walked out of the door, not bothering to close it behind her, not once glancing over her shoulder as her mother called her name.

·1947

The Maharaja's
Palace, India

1

There are those who like to think that the British once ruled India, but this is not so. Truth be known, they barely commanded half of it, the rest belonging to the princes and nizams, the maharajas and maharanas. Over six hundred princely states of varying sizes remained regally detached, behaving as independent, autonomous kingdoms. Some flourished under great rulers who spread peace and prosperity, dispensing protection and justice to their subjects in unequal measure. Others struggled along under tin-pot rajas who adopted hedonistic lifestyles and cared nothing much for their people. Renowned for trying to outdo each other with legendary acts of excess, many drank themselves to death in the process, purchasing Rolls-Royce motorized elephants a dozen at a time while their people starved. Some rulers were tyrannical, others saintly, but most fell somewhere between the two extremes.

Within these princely states, great palaces were built. Among them were those that rose from the plains, carved from gigantic stone slabs and constructed with such precision that they had no need for mortar. Others were set within enormous fortresses, perched on mountainous terrain, their ramparts stretching to the horizon and back with towering minarets crested with golden turrets. A palace might even be seen to float upon water, casting its reflection amid a lake of lotus flowers, appearing as a shimmering mirage through the morning mists. Each palace was the statement of its ruler, an embodiment of their wealth and godliness. The greater the riches and power, the more impressive the construction. Some royal households required five thousand staff to run them, others as few as seven hundred. Astonishing grandeur could be taken as a given. It was merely a matter of scale.

Born into a life of luxury, many maharajas had been reared to believe themselves demigods. Whether old or young when they assumed authority, they often did so whimsically. Self-indulgent, idle lives brought on old age quickly, a trait often passed down the bloodline, with certain dynasties famed for their early deaths and epicurean misrule. This maharaja was not quite so self-obsessed, but even here, in a lesser-known principality overlooking the dry plains that stretched down to the delta, his kingdom shall remain anonymous, for the family survive to this day, and no passage of time could be long enough to intrude upon the privacy of a royal dynasty. No records were permitted, not even an image of the palace itself, photographed only as a reflection in a mirror, lest any part of the Maharaja's greatness be captured and carried away by the camera.

His Highness was renowned for his penchant for pomp and ceremony, with a great deal of inconvenience thrown to his staff for good measure. His entourage was rarely fewer than thirty in number: ministers of the state government, sometimes the dewan himself, a handful of nobles of varying importance, perhaps a guest or two who might happen to be visiting the Maharaja at the time. They would travel like the great nomadic caravans of the Arabian deserts, under the watchful eye of the head of the household, who would orchestrate the aides-de-camp, the chefs and valets, the guardsmen and bearers, the maids and sweepers.

Reputations were lavishly displayed, and it was not unusual for the Maharaja to change his mind over the most complex of arrangements, sometimes several times in one day, throwing the palace into skittering uproar, instigating packing and unpacking, keeping everyone waiting for days on end. Trains were summoned and left idling at the Maharaja's private railway halt for weeks, guards assembled, the engine keeping up steam and His Highness nowhere to be seen. When he did eventually appear, everyone in his presence would stoop down and touch the ground three or four times and then salute with both hands to their foreheads. But the Maharaja was far too exalted to notice their greetings, such was the insignia of his greatness.

The British among the Maharaja's staff did not stoop to the ground, of course. They would bow, or curtsey, just low enough to exhibit their respect without kowtowing to the point of humiliation. The Maharaja preferred that certain positions be held by Britishers, and insisted upon an English comptroller, responsible for ordering and maintaining stores and overseeing the general running of the palace, a fleet of lesser staff beneath him. The Maharaja's military secretary was British too, charged with keeping the buildings in pristine condition, supervising the running of the grounds, and acting as an hotelier in seeing to the accommodations of the constant flow of guests, their daily banqueting arrangements and entertainments. Below the military secretary were the aides-de-camp, the ADCs, who would be assigned to attend to distinguished visitors, meeting and greeting, acting as envoys for the Maharaja, who had not yet perfected the art of being in two places at once, despite his godliness. The Maharaja also required the services of three doctors: two western, and one Indian ayurvedic for those of his household who remained mistrustful of the modern ways, himself included. Only the ayurvedic appreciated that the Maharaja's bodily apparatus and digestion were not the same as ordinary people's because he was an aristocrat.

Dr. Schofield had arrived to replace the outgoing Dr. Castle, whose services had been dispensed with after an unfortunate business with the Second Maharani. Bill Castle had served as a field medic in the Japanese theater of war, and had met George Schofield in Kohima, in the far northeast of India, in 1944, shortly after being shot. Schofield had pulled the bullet out of his shoulder and patched him up just nicely, and the two doctors had become firm friends. After the rumpus with the Maharani, the palace's senior physician, Dr. Reeves, had scratched his head and wondered aloud where on earth they were going to find a replacement, given the short notice and the nature of India's current situation. Bill had immediately suggested the position be offered to his friend Schofield. Judging by the most recent letter Bill had received, things hadn't worked out too well for George since he'd demobbed and gone back to Blighty. A stint in India might be exactly what the man needed, and there was a very comfortable living to be had out here, if one could put up with the Second Maharani's endless dramatics and imaginary ailments. A telegram was dispatched at once.

❦

Things had been pretty grim after the war for Dr. Schofield. While his wife and daughter sat out the Blitz in Granny Gasson's cottage in Wiltshire, their street in London had been bombed. Nobody was killed in the raid, but a few days later, the Luftwaffe managed to wipe out four of their neighbors in one fell swoop.

Their street half obliterated, there was nothing much for the Schofield family to stay for, so when the telegraph came early one morning, George Schofield had made the decision before he had tapped the top of his soft-boiled egg. Sophie had finished with school. There was no point in her staying on for further exams. With all the upheavals of the last few years, it was unsurprising that her results had been so disastrous, adding to the general air of gloom that had settled upon the family once the war had blown over and he had returned from overseas. So India it was for the three of them, in the grandest possible style, and Dr. Schofield was determined to make a success of it, despite his wife's protestations. Veronica would come round soon enough. It was only natural that she had become so very out of sorts, particularly after his long absences, but he had hoped that things might have improved between them by now. Sophie had been badly affected by it all too. They would be able to make a fresh start here, to leave the past behind and to become a family again, and that was all that mattered to him.

☾☉☽

Sophie crossed the blue courtyard, the high yellow sun bouncing shining rays through the water dancing in its fountain. She found the heat exhilarating, adoring the way it seeped right through her, warming her bones. Her mother had told her to stay out of the sun and to cover her skin and wear a hat whenever she went outside. Sophie's head was bare. If questioned about it when she returned, she would say that she had forgotten her hat or pretend that she had remained indoors.

Through the courtyard, past the first row of pillars, Sophie turned left, determined to find the ADC's room. She was not entirely clear on the directions, the palace being a very confusing place, but she had needed to get out of their apartments. Her mother had been tetchy with her all morning, and Mrs. Ripperton, wife to the first ADC, had told Sophie that she was welcome to stop by there any time for a cup of tea and a chat. Sophie had tried to find it yesterday, but had become completely discombobulated and had ended up in a huge billiard room hung with dozens of hunting trophies and carved, silver-mounted elephant tusks. Not that she minded her accidental detours in the least. The palace was like a vast wonderland of exotic treasures, and she thought that even if she died and went to heaven, it could never be a paradise such as this. She had even had a maid for a short while before her mother had dismissed her, insisting that her presence was an unnecessary and vulgar indulgence that would give Sophie ideas above her station and turn her into a sloth. Her own maid Veronica Schofield had retained, a young woman she kept at arm's length and made no attempt to communicate with other than to point and bark single words of instruction that the poor girl had no hope of comprehending.

As a child, Sophie had marveled at the sight of fairy-tale castles
of the sort illustrated in books like *Sleeping Beauty*, but they were
nothing in comparison to this. She could scarcely conceive of the
imagination that could have built such a wonderful sight. It seemed
to her as though it had risen miraculously out of the vast landscape,
bringing with it all the gold and silver and precious stones that the
earth could yield, setting them into the very walls. And the size of
it! Although she had been assured by their bearer that it was quite
modest in comparison to the great palaces of the more famous
princely states. When they had first arrived, she had asked him how
many rooms there were and had been told, quite simply, hundreds.
Whether or not this was true, she could not say, as she had quickly
discovered that there was a great tradition for exaggeration here.

Sophie was glad to be away from England, away from the mal-
aise of a life that had felt like darkness closing in around her. The
move had come just in time. She could not have gone on like that
indefinitely, treading water day by day, longing for the year to turn
when she could finally leave home and make her own way in the
world. Each year had felt like an eon, as though she were treading
the boards in the same old theater, going through the motions of
an endless dress rehearsal that might never see its opening night.
On the morning of her eighteenth birthday, the milestone she had
been waiting for, her mother had refused to acknowledge it, insisting that her coming-of-age was still a full three years away. Sophie
would not step out of their sight until she was twenty-one, for
that was the way it had been for Veronica, and she saw no reason
why it should be any different for her daughter. Sophie's heart had
sunk, but then they had come here, on a first-class ticket, and the
dark clouds that held over her had lifted.

Sophie followed the bleached stone pathway, retracing her steps
from yesterday, thinking that she should turn right at the second
fountain, not left. If she went straight on, the path would eventually split and lead on to the formal Moghul gardens that stretched
out before the palace, and she had already been that way. She made

a mental note of her position and wondered just how long it would take before a person learned their way around the place properly. Months, she expected. Rounding a corner, a sweeper jumped to attention, startled by her sudden appearance, and stepped off the path, making way for her.

"Namaste!" she said. The sweeper mumbled beneath his hat and bowed to her as she passed. Sophie bit the inside of her lip and tried not to smile. That was about the hundredth time someone had bowed to her since they had been here, and she would never get over the thrill of it. It made her feel like royalty.

Turning right at the next fountain, she followed a cloistered walkway, decorated with gods and goddesses hewn into the walls. She passed them without stopping, feeling relatively confident that she would be successful in finding her way today if only she could keep her wits about her and concentrate on where she was going rather than being distracted every few yards by some new curiosity. The palace was filled with them at every turn, from the translucent carnelian flowers inlaid into the stone paths, to the endless corridors lined with miles of fine rugs and chandeliers and treasures of every description.

Without realizing, Sophie wandered deep into the palace's maze, staring up at the paintings, marveling at the ornate carvings, barely noticing how far she had ambled. Before she knew it, she was hopelessly lost. The unmistakable sound of voices came toward her; women, their tuneful language scattering through the echoing corridor, gay laughter, a delicate tinkling of tiny bells. Sophie stood rigid, not daring to breathe.

She looked around, panicked, fearful of what would happen should she be caught. Nobody was allowed to see the palace women. *Nobody.* It was one of the rules that had been emphasized before they had even set one foot across the threshold. The women belonged to the Maharaja, and once they became his possessions, they were locked away for life, never to be seen again by anyone outside, shielded behind the fretworked portals of their private

inner sanctum, the *zenana*. Men had been killed for attempting
to set eyes on a maharani, and there were stories of how their
male slaves were blinded and castrated so that they might serve the
women without seeing or feeling. Thinking quickly, Sophie threw
herself into the shadow of an alcove, flattening herself against the
cool stone wall, praying that they would either overlook her or pass
the other way. The voices neared, the agony of every long second
stretching out like an eternity as she waited there, heart leaping
about in her chest. She looked around in desperation, wishing that
the wall would just open up and swallow her.

෴

There are a thousand places to hide in a palace, if you know where
to look. Jag knew every stone of it like the back of his hand, having been born within its confines and raised there since infancy,
being mothered by all the womenfolk of its servants' quarters, who
greeted him tenderly and spoiled him with sweets. He had never
known his mother, never seen her likeness, although his father
would sometimes compare her to a figure in a painting, or tell the
stories of when they were young and happy in their faraway land,
before he was born. Jag imagined it all, until every moment of it
became as embedded in him as a true memory, gathered by his
own *jiva*, from the days it had spent walking on this earthly plain.

Jag had been permitted to wander wherever he wanted as a
boy and had even been encouraged to play with the Maharaja's
children on occasion. But to play with them had proved impossible, as there was nothing even remotely normal about them.
Of course, they had thought of themselves as perfectly normal in
their fine clothes and gilded cockades, which made matters even
worse. There was nothing normal about a child being saluted
at every turn and having their every whim fulfilled since the
moment of first breath, or stepping in and out of the palace gates
just for fun, forcing the royal buglers to trumpet their arrival

again and again. There was nothing normal about being given a pet leopard cub for your seventh birthday, or shooting your first tiger at twelve. There was nothing normal about any of it, unless you were a prince or a princess, and Jag was neither of these things. He was the son of a servant, an important servant he liked to think, but a servant nevertheless.

As Jag grew up and the Maharaja's children were sent off to study in the great schools and universities of Europe and America, he had missed them not one little bit, keeping to his own studies, diligently following his father's advice that he should take whatever education he could from this brief part of his life and grow up to be a good man, to honor the memory of his mother. When he was not studying, he would work, in some part of the palace, its outbuildings, or its sprawling grounds, doing whatever his father required of him. His was a busy life, his father cautious of the risks of idleness, allowing little time for his son to wander from the righteous road of useful purpose. It would be his passport to a good life, his father frequently reminded him, for he was soon to take his place in this world as every young man should.

Pinned against the wall, Sophie became aware of a small movement. A door she had not noticed, set into the marble behind her, opened the tiniest crack. She braced herself for her imminent discovery, her heart flying into her mouth. The door opened an inch further, and from the darkness, a pair of green eyes appeared, set into the smiling face of an Indian youth of about her own age. She looked at him in desperation. He lifted a finger and pressed it to his lips. Opening the door a little further, he stole a brief glance into the corridor, jerked back quickly, and beckoned Sophie inside. Silently, gratefully, she slipped into the gap. He pulled the slab of marble closed and slid open a hatch, revealing a delicately worked panel, a shaft of light flooding into their hidden chamber, patterning the wall behind them in a bright lattice of lace-thin lines. He stood back and gestured Sophie toward the small window, inviting her to enjoy the view. The voices grew louder as the women approached, the music of heavy jewelry jangling with each step, and then, like a painting floating into view, Sophie caught a glimpse of the first Her Highness and her entourage.

She had never seen such finery in all her life. Not even in books and picture magazines. Not even in the museums and galleries her father had taken her to as a child. They moved as one, like a bird of paradise, aflame with color, their movements as graceful as a company of dancers, wrists laden with thick golden bangles, fingers and toes adorned with jeweled rings. Their saris shimmered in the softened light, drifting cloudlike around painted faces, and through the ancient fretwork panel crept invisible tendrils of exotic perfume, rich and heavy. On they glided, this glorious sight, along the corridor of treasures and the miles of cashmere rugs, past the sculptures and the paintings, the music of their voices fading with their disappearing figures. Sophie stared out through the panel, mesmerized, and felt as though she had just witnessed a spectacle that no eyes before hers had ever seen. Soon the corridor became quiet again. She turned to the youth, who was now little more than a dark shadow behind her.

"*Aap ki merbani,*" she said awkwardly, tripping over the impossible words she had tried so hard to embed.

"You are welcome," he replied.

"You speak English?" After struggling along with the servants for the last fortnight with nothing but a hopelessly inadequate phrase book to help her, a tiny and rather useless volume entitled *Hindustani Without A Master*, giving instruction on phrases such as *the boat is sinking* and *do you sell socks*, Sophie didn't even attempt to mask her surprised delight at finding somebody she could actually talk to. She stared at him, astonished.

"Wait for a little while," he said to her, his face opening into a big smile. "Your eyes will soon get used to the darkness."

Sophie did as he said, the dimness around them slowly revealing itself as a series of uniform shadows along a walkway that ran as far as her eyes could make out. "Come," he said. "We go along here." He led the way carefully along the narrow passageway, checking for her constantly behind him.

"Where does it lead to?"

"Anywhere you want to go. The palace is full of hidden passages and secret chambers."

"Who uses them?"

"No one. Not any more. They used to be used by the servants, who were supposed to remain invisible, but that was in the old days, maybe hundreds of years ago. Most of them have been forgotten now."

Sophie followed tentatively behind him, barely able to see her feet, one hand trailing along the wall to orient herself. His footsteps slowed and halted.

"Stop here for a moment," he said. "I want to show you something." There came the sound of a match striking, bursting a sudden flare of yellow light into the darkness, illuminating his face. "Look." He held the flame near the wall, revealing ancient marks scratched into it. "These are hundreds of years old."

"Who made them?"

"I don't know."

Sophie stared in wonder, reaching out a finger to trace over a faint line of script. "What does it say?"

"I don't know. It is written in dialect."

The match burned down and went out, plunging them into darkness again.

"This way," he said, making off once more. Sophie followed gingerly, her eyes readjusting to the gloom, through which she could just about decipher the vague shape of him before her. They came to a junction, two doors set into the walls, demarcated by the slender white outline of light that seeped through the tiny gaps. "We go this way," he said.

By the time they reached their destination, a door at the end of another long passageway, Sophie was thoroughly muddled. The youth turned to her in the shadows, sliding back the panel behind another fretwork hatch. He peered through, listening intently for a while.

"There's no one here," he said, and pushed the door open.

Together they emerged into a tranquil courtyard of black and white marble, where, in a flood of blinding sunshine, steps led down into a classic Italianate water garden, an oasis, lush with fragrant flowers, heavy blooms laden with perfumed petals, timid orchids clinging to the trunks of nimbu trees, peeping through. In the center of it all sat a lotus pond, the gentle sound of water trickling from pool to pool, surrounded by rising columns replicated from a leather-bound architectural volume in the Maharaja's library, garnished with Rajput designs. A heavenly scent hung unwavering on the still air. Sophie's mouth opened, speechless. She saw that he was looking at her. He seemed pleased.

"I'm Sophie," she said, putting out her hand. He looked at it, but did not take it.

"My name is Jagaan Ramakrishnan." He introduced himself with an unintelligible tangle of words and a small bow. "But you can call me Jag."

"How do you do?" Sophie attempted a short curtsey, unsure of the correct mode of salutation for someone who refused to shake hands. "You live here in the palace?"

"Yes." He hesitated. "Well, not quite in the palace as such. We live in one of the staff quarters, behind the *pilkhana*, the elephant house. My father is one of the Maharaja's bearers."

"Really? Have you ever met the Maharaja?"

"Oh yes. Many times."

"What is he like?"

"Fat." Jag ballooned his arms. "And very wealthy."

"I can see that." Sophie gazed around the water garden, the walls ornamented with pretty alcoves decorated with arabesques of different-colored stones. "I never quite believed that places like this really existed."

"We have lots of palaces in India. This one is not so grand. There are many others that are far bigger."

"Are we allowed to be in here?"

"No," he said, laughing quietly. The water garden was not a place that one could enjoy often, being a favorite spot of the Second Maharani. Any area that she wished to visit would be evacuated well in advance and attended only by her ladies-in-waiting so that she should not be observed by anyone unauthorized or unworthy of her presence. "But I thought you might like to see it. It's very pretty, isn't it?" He detected a glimmer of concern in Sophie's expression and felt a pang of worry. "You won't tell anyone, will you?"

"No!" Sophie said. "Of course not." She thought for a moment, unsure of what she should do, given these unexpected circumstances. "I hate to think what might have happened if you hadn't come along and rescued me like that. It's just that I…" She broke off. Her mother had been quite clear that she was to stay away from the Indians and she was not to speak to the servants unless she was asking for something. It was too ridiculous for words, yet Sophie did not disobey her mother lightly. She looked at Jag. "My father is the new doctor. Dr. Schofield. I was trying to find my way to the ADC's room, and the next thing I knew I was lost again. We've been here for a fortnight, but still I keep taking wrong turns or going round in circles."

"It's not so complicated," Jag said. "All you have to remember is that it is like a big square, with lots of other squares inside it and around it."

"Right." Sophie nodded as though she understood, because she didn't wish to appear stupid.

"It has been added to quite a lot over the years, with extensions being built and alterations being made by the various maharajas, but it all links up. You just have to keep your direction in mind and you will not get lost."

"Thank you. I will try to remember that."

"So, you are doing something important in the ADC's room?"

"Oh no, no, not really. Mr. Ripperton's wife, Mrs. Ripperton, she said I could pop in there whenever I wanted to, and I didn't really have anything else to do today, and I was…" She trailed off again, not wanting to say that she was feeling bored and lonely, or that her mother was not speaking to her, and that she didn't know what to do with herself. "I was hoping that there might be some other young people here that I might make friends with, but it seems that I'm the only one. My mother thinks I should be volunteering at the Baptist mission every day." She frowned a little and chewed the corner of her lip. "It's been a little bit difficult, getting used to somewhere new, especially when there's no one to talk to."

"You can talk to me if you want to," Jag said with a half-hearted shrug. "I don't mind. I like speaking English."

Sophie looked at him again. He had the most extraordinary eyes she had ever seen, deep green, like jewels. It was the first time she had ever really looked into an Indian face, seeing the sculpt of high cheekbones, the richness of the color of his skin, the whiteness of his teeth, the jet black of his shining hair. Tall and slender, with an easy, fluid grace to his movements and a gentle manner, this was not what she had expected at all, not after everything her mother had said about savagery and ignorance.

She wondered if she should say anything, if she should mention what her mother had told her, but it seemed so wrong. Anyway, why shouldn't she talk to him? He was nice, and he had saved her skin, and so what if he was Indian? They were in India, after all, so who else was she supposed to make friends with? Her mother would be furious, but that would be nothing new. Everything Sophie did was wrong anyway, and she had grown tired of the constant criticism of her endless misdeeds in her mother's eyes. Before she could stop herself, the words tumbled out.

"My mother said that I'm not supposed to make friends with the servants."

Sophie hoped that her term, *to make friends*, would sound less offensive than the outright declaration that she wasn't allowed to even speak to them unless she had to. Jag stepped back from her and looked at the ground. Sophie sensed immediately that her words had been hurtful, and she wished that she could snatch them back, saying quickly, "But she's been in a bad mood ever since we got here and we've never been to India before, or rather, my father has, but we haven't. She didn't even want to come, but my father said we had to."

"It's all right," Jag said quietly. "I do not want you to get into any trouble."

"Don't be silly." Sophie decided to brush her concerns aside. "Just this morning I was wondering how I was going to manage being stuck here for six whole months when there was nothing to do and no one to talk to, and now look. Here I am, in this lovely garden, standing here and talking to you. I have even seen one of the maharanis today!"

"You must do as your parents tell you," Jag said.

"Do you always do as your mother says, even if she is wrong?"

"I do not have a mother. She died when I was born."

"Oh!" A blush came violently to her cheeks. "I'm so sorry. I didn't mean to…"

"Please, do not apologize. You didn't know, and I am not sad about it. I never knew her, so I never missed her."

A pause hung over them, Sophie suddenly feeling as uncomfortable as he looked. "I'm sorry," she said. "About what I said about not making friends with the Indians."

"Servants," Jag said. She looked at him. "You said servants, not Indians."

"Oh." She squirmed under her embarrassment. "Sorry. Now I've offended you even more."

"It's OK," he said. "My father wouldn't want me to make friends with you either."

"Why?" Sophie said, feeling suddenly indignant. "Because I'm English?"

"Yes. And because you're a girl. It is indecent."

"*Indecent?*"

"Of course! Everybody knows how you English girls all have hundreds of boyfriends and go out dancing and drinking and seeing the pictures in the dark without a chaperone. An Indian girl would not even be permitted to speak to a boy, let alone to make friends with them."

"Well that's just ridiculous."

"Ridiculous or not, it is the way of our traditions."

"And do you agree with it?"

"It doesn't matter if I agree with it. It is the way it is."

"Hmph." Sophie perched herself on the edge of a balustrade, thinking. "You know, what you said is not true. My mother would go mad if I had ever had a boyfriend, so don't you go thinking that all English girls are like that. We are mostly very prim and proper." She found herself straightening her back, sitting more upright as though with a book on her head. "She can be a bit difficult about things." Sophie reached a hand to one of the plants, touching the leaves. "My father said we needed a change. That's why we came out here. We were all miserable back in England, what with the shortages and bombed-out streets. This was supposed to be a fresh start, but I think my mother had decided not to like it before we had even left London."

"Your father is right," Jag said. "Change is definitely a good thing. Take my country, for example. India has been waiting for change for generations, and now it is finally coming. The date of independence will be declared very soon, and India shall have her freedom once more. My father is very excited about it. There will be many celebrations, and many changes."

"So I've heard," Sophie said. "But aren't you worried about all that?"

"Worried? Why should I be?"

"They say there is going to be lots of trouble and that the politicians are still arguing about who will be in charge."

"There won't be any trouble. Believe me. And what do politicians know? They are just puffing hot air and trying to make themselves look important in the newspapers because they all want to be the first president of the new independent India. Why should there be any trouble when we are finally getting what we wanted and everyone wants the same thing?" Jag stopped, holding out a silencing hand, listening intently. "Quickly," he said. "I think someone is coming."

Sophie stood up and followed him to the doorway, the hinged slab of white marble sinking invisibly back into the wall as he closed it behind them.

"What now?" she whispered, waiting for her eyes to adjust.

"Do you want to see some more of the palace?"

"Yes, please." She nodded, her heart beating a little faster.

"We'll go this way," he said. "It becomes steep and narrow a little way ahead, so be careful."

"Wait! I can't see a thing!" Sophie reached out into the darkness, found the looseness of his cotton sleeve, and hung on tightly.

The First Maharani slept badly that night, unable to escape the uncomfortable feeling that somebody had been watching her.

2

"Do you know what she tried to have me do yesterday?" George Schofield gouged his spoon into the rice. "Leeches! Leeches, of all things! Can you believe that?" Mrs. Schofield didn't reply, so Dr. Schofield continued casually to his daughter instead.

He had given them his usual blow-by-blow account of his trials over supper last night, but he chose to reiterate himself to his wife, as if to impress upon her the enormity of the daily burdens placed upon him. It was part of his role as husband and father, to put himself out in order to rise to his responsibilities, thus deserving his wife's respect, if not her affection. If she had had her way, they would all sit and eat in morbid silence once grace was over, sipping plain water, concentrating mutely on their plates. It was one of the changes he had insisted upon after the move, saying that Sophie was far too old for that sort of disciplinarian nonsense, as indeed was he. It wasn't normal to suffer a complete lack of social intercourse while breaking bread together, and he'd said there was no need for Veronica to continually behave as though it were the Last Supper every time they sat down to eat.

"Likes the sight of her own blood. The more dramatic the better. I told her I wouldn't do it. Not in a million years. We're not in the dark ages, for heaven's sake. If that's the kind of treatment she wants, she can go and try her luck with Dr. Patel."

"I don't know why you bother with any of them," his wife said. "Damned savages." She turned to her daughter. "And as for you, Mrs. Ripperton spent half the morning searching high and low for you. She was under the impression that you were supposed to be going to the mission this afternoon."

"I was in the library," said Sophie quickly. And so she had been, at least for a few minutes, long enough to snatch a book in evidence of time well invested, rather than the hours she had spent creeping around the palace with Jag again. He had taken her all over, showing her his favorite places: the marble piazza enclosing the orange garden, the formal staterooms, the flower house, the Maharaja's private study, the ice house dug deep into the earth. Sophie learned that not one stone of the palace had been placed without consulting the highest of authorities, the palace's very site and position dictated by astrological considerations. She and Jag had arranged to meet again tomorrow morning. The Maharaja was in residence, and Jag had promised to show her something very special if she could get up at the crack of dawn and sneak out early enough.

"Well still, you should be ashamed of yourself," her mother said. "It really was most rude of you. Next time you make an arrangement, you must stick to it. You'll have to apologize to her tomorrow and make your excuses. How many times must I tell you to make the most of your time here rather than mooning around in a sulk?"

Veronica Schofield took up her glass in agitation and drank a little water. George had had no right to drag them all out here, him and his fine ideas. She had always known that she would dislike India. It was a filthy place. Thankfully they would not be here for long, six months, and she had supposed that the experience might be of some value to Sophie in years to come, that someone might be interested to know that she had experienced India before the place was ruined. It had sounded quite grand when he presented the prospect to her, and indeed it was, in a pagan sort of way. They had been allocated apartments on arrival, a sumptuous suite of rooms with their own kitchen and a full complement of staff. Entirely against the grain of her staunch beliefs, Mrs. Schofield had become used to the luxury with alarming ease, although she would never admit to it, of course. It was the people she couldn't abide. Not a single God-fearing Christian among them.

She put her fork down decisively, her glare pinned on her daughter. "You should go and help out in the ADC's room tomorrow and improve your typing skills. At least then you'll come away with something useful when we leave."

"What rot!" her father said. "You get in amongst it, my girl, and do whatever you want. You're a young woman now, and it's important that you have a ready store of engaging conversation when you get home and start stepping out. Just imagine the stories you will have to tell!"

Sophie sat and thought about the only story that mattered, and she would never tell it to anyone, for it belonged to her, and it had only just begun.

⚜

A brown, stick-thin man moved around the palatial room, its ceiling embedded with glinting fragments of mirror. He was naked but for a yellowed threadbare loincloth, made of homespun, tied about his skin and bone, the symbol of deity marked on his forehead, perpendicular lines of white powder, sandalwood paste smeared on his arms and chest.

"Who is that?" Sophie whispered to Jag.

"The Maharaja's holy man. He is going to perform a ceremony for the Maharaja."

The priest began to draw on the marble floor, chalking a diagram in thick lines, marking out a grid that looked almost mathematical in its accuracy. Into each corner he placed a coconut, before arranging a number of other things within the space he had demarcated. A vessel of incense, a brass bowl filled with water, a dish of mangoes, not ripe and tight-skinned but shriveled up, a bowl of bright yellow flowers, and a piece of cloth. In the center

he set down a statue of a goddess on a salver, the figure so small
that Sophie could not tell whether it was made of brass or silver,
or even gold. Next to it, the holy man placed a sacred papyrus and
a small brass bell.

"Look," Jag whispered. Sophie craned into the panel. A rotund
man, of no particular height, as wide as he was squat, came into
view. A servant stepped forward to remove his gown, a heavy silk
coat of sorts, white, with no visible embellishment. Beneath the
gown, the Maharaja wore only a plain loincloth, which Sophie
thought would have to be about the size of a bedsheet to accom-
modate his girth. The Maharaja sat on a large cushion, set upon the
marble floor, at the head of the chalk diagram.

Lighting the bowls of incense with a thin taper, the holy man
began to chant, circling the space, punctuating his prayers with a
ring of the bell, waving the ritual papyrus over the Maharaja's head
each time he passed him. Sophie watched, spellbound, as the holy
man went on ringing his bell, sprinkling water, reciting liturgies,
the Maharaja sitting there in a trancelike state. After what seemed
like a very long time, the priest's chanting slowed to a single note,
low and resonant, filling the whole room. The bell rang once
more. He stopped, pressed his hands together, and bowed down
low. The Maharaja stood, his servant stepping forward to cloak
him, slipping the gown up and on to his thick shoulders before
bowing and sliding back. The Maharaja bowed to the holy man,
then turned and disappeared from view, leaving the priest to gather
up his paraphernalia.

Wide-eyed and smiling, Sophie looked at Jag and pulled
a bemused expression. Jag put his finger to his lips and nodded
his head toward the darkened corridor, moving off too quickly.
Unable to see a thing, Sophie reached out instinctively, and slipped
her hand into his.

3

In sharp contrast to the palace's opulence, Jag and his father shared one small room in the servants' quarters, a collection of uniform low-level buildings set at the very periphery of the palace compound, intended to house the imperative staff in a manner convenient to the Maharaja. Not all the servants lived within the grounds. Many relied on the ramshackle dwellings that had sprung up in haphazard fashion, sprawling across the town that had grown up nearby. Jag's father's hours were long and unpredictable, often taking him away for extended periods when the Maharaja traveled the country, but never when he went overseas, as he did increasingly often, particularly when there was trouble afoot. Jag's father would not cross the black water, and this the Maharaja accepted. For a devoted Hindu, to leave India's holy soil would cause untold offense to the gods, rendering the soul irredeemably lost. The Maharaja got around this by taking as much of his homeland with him as he could, in particular the great silver carriers that would be filled with water brought down from the sacred Mother Ganges. This way he could continue to perform his devotional ablutions without offending the deities, no matter if he was in Patna or Paris.

Jag had spent the morning at the elephant house, washing out the stalls. There was talk that the animals would soon be sold off or sent to zoos, with perhaps just one or two being retained for the sake of posterity. The contents of the *pilkhana* were testament to a bygone era, of elephants caparisoned with giant silver howdahs and gilded jewelry encrusted with precious and semi-precious stones,

huge anklets adorning their painted feet, jeweled plaques on their
foreheads. There were trappings for other animals too, the horses,
camels, and bullocks used to draw the ceremonial carts. The paraphernalia in the *pilkhana* required constant cleaning, a routine that
had continued despite the likelihood that, once the country was
reborn, it might never see the light of day again. The thought of it
had saddened Jag, that such ancient splendors should have to fade,
but there would be no room for them in the new India, the India
that would belong to its people.

Sophie's voice broke into his thoughts.

"If you could change one thing in the whole wide world, what
would it be?"

Sophie dangled her feet in the pool beneath the fountain in
the orange garden, Jag sitting propped up against the wall behind
her, facing the other way, lost in thought as he so often was, his
long legs stretched out on the brief lawn laid out before him in a
neatly clipped circle. No one would see them here. The garden
was completely walled in and not overlooked at all: no windows or
walkways, no panels or spy holes. Nobody ever went there, except
the *malis*, but only in the early mornings, to tidy and water and
take whatever fruit had been ordered by the kitchens.

"One thing?" Jag said.

"Yes."

"Hmm." He thought about it. "I think it would have to be that
my mother was still alive, so that my father would be happy."

"Oh," Sophie said, disappointed that he had chosen something
so solemn.

Jag looked up at her, watching her shuffle her feet in the water,
her head tilted to one side. He sensed that his answer had not satisfied her.

"Or I would make it that I had been born rich, like the Maharaja,
so that I could spend my time reading great books or entertaining
important friends with pig sticking and tiger hunting."

"Where has he gone to this time?"

"To Simla," Jag said, "to talk to the Viceroy about the arrangements. Some of the other Maharajas have gone too. They're worried about what will happen to their kingdoms after independence."

"Simla. I've heard of it. It's supposed to be very nice there."

"It's where the government goes in the summer. Delhi is much too hot for them. It boils their brains."

"Do you know when he'll be back?"

"In another week, perhaps. It's impossible to say. He's always changing his mind."

"You must miss your father when he's away."

"I used to," Jag said. "But now, it is different."

"How do you mean?"

Sophie knew exactly what he meant, but she wanted him to say it aloud.

Since his father had gone, they had been as thick as thieves, giving no mind to the time or the arc of the sun as the days came and went. When his father was around, their adventures were restricted to a few stolen hours whenever he could get away. They had taken to hiding notes for each other, tiny slips of paper, folded tightly and pressed into the gap between the stone slabs beneath the enormous marble urn by the path that led to the formal gardens. The area around it was high-planted, with towering palms surrounded by lower shrubs of fragrant hibiscus and showy pink bougainvillea. Sophie checked their secret postbox several times a day, in the hope that she might find a message telling her where they could meet and when. It was difficult for Jag to get away sometimes, as there was always something his father wanted him to do: attend to a chore somewhere or copy out long passages from books which his father would cast his eye over briefly before throwing away and setting him on the next one. Sophie would have been furious if any parent or indeed teacher had done such a thing to her, and she said so, but Jag didn't seem to mind. His father expected great things of him in the new India, and his education would lead him to a better future, where he could be a man

without a master, if he worked hard enough. One day he might
even have servants of his own.

"You ask too many questions," Jag said slyly. "You know why
I like it when my father is not here. It is the same reason why you
like it."

Sophie laughed, the game over.

"What about you?" he asked.

"What?"

"If you could change one thing in the whole world, what
would it be?"

"I don't know really," Sophie said. "Right now, I'm happy
with the way things are." As she said it, it dawned on her that
this really was the first time in her life that she had ever felt truly
happy. She leaned back and looked down at him sitting beneath
her, smiling up at her, and they sat like that for a while, keeping
their thoughts to themselves. Jag dropped his head and picked at
the grass, splitting a blade open with his thumbnail and putting it
to his lips, blowing hard, trying to get a squeal out of it.

"You shouldn't sit on the grass," she said.

"Why not?"

"Snakes."

"They only bite the English." He tried again, a feeble squeak
coming from the blade.

"Seriously. Please don't sit on the grass. It's dangerous."

"If you insist." He pulled himself up by the elbows and sat on the
edge of the fountain with her. "But you'd have to be very stupid to
get bitten by a snake. They're afraid of people. A snake would only
bite you if you marched right into it and took it by surprise. It's not
the snakes you have to worry about. It's the scorpions."

"Scorpions?"

"Very nasty," he said, putting the blade of grass to his lips again.
"And they're not afraid of people at all. They're not afraid of anything. If one of those stings you, you've had it." He blew another
squeal, this time much louder.

"Really?" Sophie's eyes darted to the ground, and she slipped her feet out of the pool and tucked them beneath herself tightly.

"Oh yes. You are sure of a long and painful death, with hallucinations and convulsions and your whole body on fire. And there is nothing anyone can do to save you, not even a doctor like your father. So you had better be careful."

"That's horrible."

"Very horrible."

"Do you know anyone who has died from a scorpion?"

"Oh yes. It happens all the time. People are always treading on them and dying. It usually happens when they get out of bed. Scorpions like to hide in people's slippers while they are sleeping, and of course the poor person gets out of bed with bare feet, and the next thing they know…" Jag tossed his head casually and flicked the blade of grass aside.

"No!" Sophie stared at him. "You're making it up!"

"No, I'm not. Hey! Look at that!" Jag bent swiftly to the ground and picked up a stray pebble, partially hiding it in his hand. "It's a scorpion!"

Sophie shrieked and flew up from the fountain's edge, snatching up her shoes and running for the path. Jag ran after her, hand outstretched, waving the pebble and laughing wildly.

❦

Fiona Ripperton fanned herself as she walked back to her apartments, thinking that she might have a gin and tonic when she got there. She had given up trying to find Sophie. It was a lost cause.

Mrs. Ripperton had come out to India when she was not much older than Sophie was now, and was under no illusion that the girl would be entirely at sea without her guidance. Mrs. Schofield didn't strike her as a particularly maternal sort. A prickly woman, unaffectionate with her family, far too Christian and quick to find fault with her daughter. Fiona Ripperton had always dreamed of having a girl to fuss over rather than the son who had sucked them dry. Oh, she loved him, of course, they both did, but there has to come a time when a mother's devotion wears a little thin in the face of a committed wastrel. He was his wife's problem now, a nice Canadian girl who couldn't have known what she was getting herself into. Mrs. Ripperton was in no doubt that Michael had married her on the double-quick so that he could sail away from all the debts and bad feeling he had left in London. Silly boy. They had known they were fighting a losing battle before he turned twenty-five, but what could one do? They threw good money after bad before finally cutting the apron strings on his thirtieth birthday, much to his umbrage. If she could have had her time again as a mother, there were a hundred things she might have done differently, but then, she had finally conceded to herself, the results would probably have been the same. Mrs. Ripperton had come to the firm conclusion that some people were just born that way, and that there was very little one could do to alter the pattern laid down by the Creator. But if she had been too loose a parent, then there was one thing of which she was certain. Mrs. Schofield had been far too strict. Sophie was as timid as a mouse in her mother's presence. It was all quite at odds with the bright, cheerful girl who popped her head around the door of the ADC's room, volunteering to fetch the tea or to lend a hand with the escalating heap of filing. Popular as sixpence she was, and clearly adoring of her father. Yet the moment Mrs. Schofield appeared, she would shrink into the woodwork, barely uttering a word. Too much mothering, Fiona Ripperton said to her husband sometimes, venturing an opinion about how much better a job she would have done of raising a daughter, had they been blessed with one.

As her self-appointed guardian angel, Mrs. Ripperton would see to it that Sophie was saved the misery of having no one of her own age to talk to. Decidedly young at heart, she contrived to overlook her sixty-two years and made a point of seeking Sophie out whenever she could and sticking to her like glue, taking her to help out at the Baptist mission, jollying her along and slipping into nonsensical juvenile banter, at which she felt she was particularly gifted. The thought of the poor girl being stuck in the company of her parents and the other palace cronies filled her with a crusading sense of purpose. There were no other young people here, which, in her opinion, had been a dreadful oversight on the part of her parents. If Sophie had been her daughter, she would have taken the time to present her properly at a coming-out party rather than extracting her from all lively society and cooping her up in this great mothballed mausoleum. It was no place for a youngster on the cusp of womanhood. What on earth must the Schofields have been thinking? Still, everybody knew that they would be moving on soon, and there was plenty of time for Sophie to go and kick her heels up in London and find herself a nice young man.

They were supposed to go to the mission this afternoon, and Mrs. Ripperton had called at the Schofields' apartments an hour ago, only to be told that Sophie had gone off to the library. Fiona hadn't mentioned anything about their loose arrangement, not after the last time, when Mrs. Schofield had behaved as though her daughter had run somebody through with a sword. Instead, she had sat and taken tea with Veronica, even though the woman hadn't had an ounce of conversation in her. Afterward, she had gone to the library, but Sophie was not there either, and she hadn't been seen in the ADC's room since Tuesday. Mrs. Ripperton couldn't help but worry. She hoped that Sophie wasn't hiding in a corner somewhere, mopping buckets of tears and wishing that she were back home. Wherever she was, finding her had proved quite impossible. It was as though she had simply vanished into thin air.

It was hot today. Perhaps Mrs. Ripperton would make the gin and tonic a large one, then take a little lie-down.

Sophie came bursting around the corner, running as though her
very life depended on it, shoes dangling from her hands, the expression on her face close to hysterical.

"Sophie!" Mrs. Ripperton rushed toward her. "Whatever's
wrong, my dear?"

Sophie came to an immediate, skidding halt, her face flushed
red, breath coming hard. She stared wide-eyed at Mrs. Ripperton
before glancing quickly over her shoulder. There was nobody
behind her, just a quiet, empty path. Mrs. Ripperton clutched
Sophie's elbow and steadied her.

"Are you all right?"

"Yes." Sophie snatched her breath for a moment, looking
down at herself, dark spots of water on her dress, her feet bare.
"Yes, I'm fine."

"What on earth have you been doing?" Mrs. Ripperton ran her
eyes up and down the girl's somewhat disheveled figure.

"I..." Sophie tried to think of something to say that wouldn't
sound utterly ridiculous. "I thought I saw a snake."

"With no shoes on?"

"I..."

"Have you taken leave of your senses?"

"I was hot," Sophie said. "I took my shoes off and put my feet
in the fountain."

"Oh!" Mrs. Ripperton didn't quite follow. "So where was the
snake? In the fountain?"

"No. I mean, I was sitting there and I thought I saw one in the
grass, and..."

"You really should have put your shoes back on first. Dearie
me." Mrs. Ripperton clucked to herself. "Look at the state of you!"

"Please don't tell my mother," Sophie said. She looked around
nervously again. There was no sign of Jag. "I told her I was in the
library. She doesn't like me wandering around. You won't say
anything, will you? She'll be awfully cross if she thinks I've..."
The poor girl looked stricken.

"Not a bit of it, my dear." Mrs. Ripperton took hold of Sophie's arm and tucked it firmly into her own. "Mum's the word. Now come on. Let's go and get you tidied up a bit, shall we? We can have tea in my apartments, and you can tell me all about it. A snake, eh? How tremendously exciting."

4

August arrived, the oppressive heat adding to the cloying air of heightened tension. The plan had been announced two months ago, at the beginning of June, that India would be divided into two dominions. At first, nobody believed it. They were calling it a *partition*, and the nation would be split in two. Sophie had read about it in the newspapers. The Congress Party had called for a single country, the voices of Mahatma Gandhi and Jawaharlal Nehru pleading for a harmonious land, united in its many glorious differences. But the leader of the All-India Muslim League, Muhammad Ali Jinnah, had demanded a separate Moslem nation, and he would not budge. Negotiations ground to a halt, the two sides coming to a stalemate, and Jinnah was granted his wish.

Many of the Moslem staff had gone already, making their way to their new lives in the new lands, even though the Maharaja had decreed that no one should feel compelled to go unless they wanted to, and that they could be assured of his protection while they lived under his care. Yet the servants had left in droves.

Jag's father would stay, for he was a Hindu, with many years left to serve before asking for his retirement. When that day came, he would return to Amritsar, to live out his old age with his family. They were not his immediate family by blood, but those of his beloved wife, who had left a sister there. The sister lived in a modest house on Kim Street, where her husband ran a small business making shoes. That much his father remembered, although the finer points of his recollections had faded until he was not so sure of the details, such as the color of the door.

Jag knew that it was his father's destiny to return to his home city one day. He talked about it all the time. They would travel there together, father and son, and reestablish old family ties while Jag passed his matriculation and began his adult life, fixing another generational rung on the ladder of his forebears. His father spoke of it often as they sat together in the evening, talking man to son by thin lamplight after washing and performing their *puja*. Jag's father would secure his pension before making his final journey, compensation from his master after a lifetime of devoted service intended to sustain him through his weakening years. For that, he was prepared to wait, for without it, he would be sure to face an old age filled with nothing but hard work and penury.

Jag thought of all this as he washed their clothes, soaping them for far too long, distracted by the mire of worries that kept him awake night after night. He wanted things to be different. He wanted to be able to make his own choices and walk his own path. He was tired of hearing his father's plans for the future. What about *his* future? What was he going to achieve by being dragged off to Amritsar? Three months. That was all she had left. August, September, October, then she would be gone. She had said that they might stay on until Christmas, but what good would that be to him? He knew what he wanted now. He wanted to be able to walk with her, side by side, without hiding in the shadows and sneaking around like criminals. They weren't doing anything wrong, yet he could not even imagine what the consequences would be if they were to be found out.

Jag pulled at the water pump, venting his frustration as he worked the handle hard, filling the trough to rinse the clothes he had come to despise. He hated wearing these things, these simple cottons that marked him as different from her, different from *them*. He should be able to wear a shirt and a tie, and smart trousers with a jacket, to show that he was educated and respectable. He could

read and write as well as any man, and he had a natural gift for
mathematics. Equations, multiplication, long division. There was
no problem he couldn't solve. Except this.

That is the trouble with this country, he thought. You are born
to your status, to your given caste, and once you have come into
its being, you can never leave it, never move up and be seen as
better than the life you were birthed into. It was wrong, and once
India had been freed, it would have to change. Even Gandhiji
himself had said so. He had been moved to speak out on behalf of
the Dalits, the Untouchables, saying that every person who sought
to perpetuate the lowliness of that rank without hope of release
should hang their heads in shame.

Jag's father had returned with the Maharaja three weeks ago,
and Jag had barely managed to get away for a moment since then.
There was too much work to be done. So many people had left,
and the bickering had already started about how the extra duties
were to be divided among the palace's diminished manpower. To
make matters worse, his father had announced joyfully that he
would not be accompanying the Maharaja when he went to Delhi
for the independence celebrations. The Maharaja would take only
six bearers with him, and his father would be permitted to stay
behind, to be with his son so that they might welcome India's new
dawn together. Jag had joined in his father's happiness, hugging
him hard while swallowing his disappointment.

He pummeled the clothes in the water trough before hauling them out and wringing them tightly until his knuckles turned
white, hands hurting. If he did not see her soon, she would forget
about him, and he would be left behind, bereft. Had he been a
son of the Maharaja, with fine clothes and big certificates from
fancy schools and universities, he would be able to march right up
to her in front of everybody and ask if she would like to go for a
drive or for cocktails. The British always had cocktails, and so did
the Indians as far as he could see, at least some of them did, the
ostentatious ones who came to visit and went on shooting parties

and such like. He had seen them, him peering out from hidden panels, watching them fawning around the Maharaja, who, admittedly, stuck to the fruit juices and never touched alcohol. It wasn't right that Jag should be in this position, that he should somehow be made to feel that he was not good enough or did not deserve to become the kind of man he intended to be. He did not want to clean out the elephant stalls and wash clothes and copy pages of obsolete texts when he already had so many ideas of his own. Important ideas. He would find a way to change things, to show his father that the world was a different place now and that he was no longer a boy who must be corralled into the same pen as his ancestors. He wanted more from his life, more than he had ever imagined possible. Above everything, he wanted her.

Inside the palace, whispers traveled the corridors on a matter even more alarming than the day's politics. The source of the trouble came as no surprise to anyone. The First Maharani was up to her usual tricks, this time spreading malicious gossip about the Maharaja's new bride, saying that she looked like a monkey and that the Maharaja had been tricked into the arrangement. All this and more she shared with her ladies-in-waiting while her maids enrobed her in a brocaded sari of Benares silk and placed the heavy bangles on her wrists. By the time she had finished dressing, every one of her servants knew that the Maharaja's intended was covered in fur, and that she had been born that way as a result of an ancient curse in the family's bloodline. The fur had been painfully threaded from her face and hands so that her image could be taken and shown to the Maharaja, but by the time of the wedding it would all have grown back. The comb had become still in the hands of her maid as the First Maharani speculated on the moment His Highness would glimpse his new bride, saying that he would probably die of a heart attack when he realized he had taken a monkey as a wife.

Then her own son, the Maharaja's firstborn, would accede to the throne, and she, as Dowager Maharani, would have wife number three paraded through the streets naked like a zoological exhibit. Not that she had ever seen her, of course, but nobody ever took any notice of such immaterial details, particularly not in the *zenana*, where the women of the palace remained in *purdah*, locked in a deathly monotony of confinement, peering at the world through delicately latticed portals. Each of the maharanis had their own apartments, with their own complement of staff, trained in the nature of their particular foibles. The First Maharani, for example, liked her food rich and sweet, and her chef had perfected all her favorite dishes during his years of service to her. The Second Maharani, on the other hand, never ate meat and only rarely ate fish. Naturally, her chef was very thin.

News of the monkey bride spread through the palace like wildfire, first through the *zenana*, causing the Second Maharani to faint dramatically into the waiting arms of her maid. The screams of anguish from her ladies-in-waiting could be heard all the way to the durbar hall, closely followed by the rushing of feet bearing a message for Dr. Schofield to come straight away.

"Describe to me her symptoms." Dr. Schofield spoke through the pink alabaster fretwork, his face respectfully averted from the hidden lady-in-waiting who relayed his instructions from voice to voice from behind the screen. He waited patiently for the reply to come, knowing that it would take some time and would probably make no sense at all when it did eventually arrive, thirdhand. This whole process usually took about an hour, sometimes two, depending upon the Second Maharani's need for attention that day.

"She is feeling very weak," the lady-in-waiting reported.

"I see," Dr. Schofield said. "What is her pulse rate?"

Another long pause followed.

"It is very faint and irregular."

"I see."

Dr. Schofield knew that this was not the case, and that the Second Maharani would be lying there on her splendid bed, issuing symptoms to her ladies. Dr. Schofield had gradually learned the ropes over the course of his first month at the palace, most of it passed down through the jungle telegraph. Initially he had declared to the ADCs that he could not possibly be expected to carry out his duties with any efficacy if he was to be prevented from actually seeing and examining a patient, but that was declared impossible. Both Her Highnesses observed strict *purdah*, and seeing as the good doctor was neither related nor married to either of them, he could take it on reliable authority that he would never lay eyes directly upon them. His first reaction had been to resign his post rather than run the risk of accidentally killing one of them through misdiagnosis, but he was soon persuaded to stay when the Maharaja presented him with a gold cigarette case and assured him that they would of course make an exception if it were ever thought that either of Her Highnesses were in any serious danger.

Dr. Schofield had come to learn that there were rarely any real ailments in the *zenana* apart from a good deal of bickering and the occasional bout of indigestion. In this instance, he was already convinced that there was nothing much wrong with Her Second Highness except an acute case of having her nose put out of joint. A century and a half of British rule had been largely irrelevant to the princes, yet all this had changed in the run-up to independence, as the rulers came to recognize that their states must integrate with one dominion or the other, either with India or with the newly formed Pakistans, East and West. Making up almost half of India's territory and people, the new nations would be a hopeless patchwork that would never hold together without the princely states. Negotiations were opened and complicated agreements drawn up, and the six hundred princes signed their states away, to India in the main, the rest to Pakistan, bringing down the curtain on centuries of feudal rule. In compensation, the princes would each benefit from the granting of a privy purse, set at a fraction of their state revenues, and few were in any doubt that the time might well come when the royal families might disappear altogether, given their reduced circumstances. It was no wonder the Second Maharani was feeling unwell. Not only had the Maharaja announced his intention to take a third wife, but if the rumors were to be believed, they would soon be shrinking their grand household and selling off the family silver.

Dr. Schofield continued patiently through the screen. "And what is her temperature?" This was his favorite question of all, as the women in the *zenana* clearly had no idea about the correct temperature of the body. On past occasions he had been told variously that her temperature was fifty degrees, two hundred degrees, and almost every nonsensical number in between. After another long wait, the answer came.

"She is as cold as ice!"

"How is her breathing?"

"It is fast and shallow."

"Is there any rash on her body?"

It seemed like an eternity before the Second Maharani decided whether she had a rash, by which time Dr. Schofield had taken a seat beside the screen and begun to look through his book. It reassured the women of the *zenana* that he was carefully checking the indications of each symptom, weighing up the severity of the Second Maharani's condition before delivering his diagnosis. This particular volume was entitled *How Green Was My Valley*, and the doctor had found it hard to put down since finding a signed copy tucked away on a shelf in the Maharaja's library. He made sure to frown occasionally, pinching his chin in thoughtful manner, nodding at the page.

"There is no rash," the lady-in-waiting relayed.

"I see." Dr. Schofield read to the end of the passage, then snapped the book shut. "Hmm," he mumbled, then got up from the chair and paced around a little before opening his bag and taking out a bottle of plain aspirin adorned with a fussy handwritten label. "Tell Her Highness that she is suffering from vanucitis. She requires complete bed rest, and she is to take one of these every morning for five days. Then she will be as right as rain."

The lady scurried back to her mistress with the precious nostrum, another of the doctor's miraculous cures, proof in itself that the Second Maharani was indeed most unwell, which was all that she wanted.

5

The Maharaja was away with his entourage, attending the formal celebrations in the capital at the personal invitation of the Viceroy, leaving the depths of the palace deathly quiet. Sophie had been careful to check that the water garden was deserted before she dared to enter its hidden cloister. Not that anyone would be likely to object to her presence today if she were to be caught. There were far more important matters at hand. Today the world was going to change and the whole palace seemed to shudder at the sense of unknowing that pervaded every corner.

Preparations for the evening were well under way, following the Maharaja's instructions that the entire household should carry an indelible memory of this historic event, culminating in a grand fireworks display at midnight to mark the very moment when the shackles were broken. With any luck, the rains would break off long enough for everyone to enjoy the spectacle without getting a soaking. The odds were roughly in their favor, the monsoon across this arid tract of India tending to be relatively well-tempered, delivering frequent brief showers that gave little relief to the parched landscape rather than the endless downpours that drenched the southern tropics and the high regions of the far north. The rainy season would be over soon anyway, ushering in long, hot days, dry winds blowing in from the Thar Desert.

Sophie sat at the edge of the lotus pool regarding her watery reflection and wondered about her appearance. She had asked her mother once, in an unguarded moment, if she thought her pretty, to which her mother had scoffed and proclaimed that vanity was sinful. Veronica Schofield had always dismissed the very idea of beauty and said that to give it any credence was shallow. There were far more important things in life. Beauty was for those people who could afford it and, in her opinion, was invariably bestowed upon those who had little else to offer. The way that her mother had spoken, Sophie had felt utterly ashamed of herself and had wished that she had kept her mouth shut. But it was hard for her to dismiss the question, especially in a place where beauty was so highly prized.

Gray clouds began to drift across the slab of sky above the water garden, dimming the glare on the pond's surface. They would gather thickly soon, in an hour perhaps, and the afternoon's rain would roll in. Not yet, though, thought Sophie. She could sit for a while longer before the downpour started, and she had nothing else to do anyway. She hadn't felt like resting as her mother had insisted. There was far too much going on. Her mother always rested in the afternoon these days, although Sophie knew this to be just a convenient excuse for her to take herself off and not speak to anyone.

Jag followed the catacomb of secret passages that led to the water garden. With the palace so quiet today, he knew that this was where he would find her. They had stopped leaving the notes for each other. It was too dangerous. On one occasion, he had seen one of the sweepers hanging around on the corner by the big pair of urns, watching Sophie examine the stone slabs while he pretended to sweep an already clean patch of the pathway. There were eyes everywhere, looking for trouble, carrying tales to fan the flames of discontent.

Sophie knew the secret passages now and could make her way without Jag's guidance. She liked to sit in the lip of the farthest pavilion window in the corner of the courtyard, the seats inlaid with black and white marble, giving the impression that they were larger than they were. It was the best vantage point in the whole garden, catching the reflections of the lotus pool, shafts of light throwing dappled patterns on the painted ceiling of the cloistered walkway that surrounded it.

Jag dawdled along the dark, narrow tunnel, his insides uneasy, doing his best to quell the nervousness that churned within him, deep down beyond his understanding. He had been feeling like this for weeks, yet had been unable to share his thoughts with Sophie. This in itself had caused him misery. They always told each other everything, no matter what. They could be trusted to keep each other's secrets. Until now. Just lately, Jag had been unable to find the words, his grief all-consuming. Tonight everything would change, and soon they would be parted.

Sophie dropped a pebble into the lotus pool and watched as her undefined features disappeared in soft ripples across the water's surface. Perhaps he was not coming after all. In that instant she felt unutterably sad, remembering the times they had shared in the beginning, thinking about how they used to talk of so many things. There was nothing in the whole world that she couldn't tell him, and they had spent countless hours sharing their hopes and dreams for the future. It used to be one of their favorite games while they explored together like thieves in the night, stealing through the dimness, watching silently from behind long-forgotten panels set into the palace's ancient history. They were invisible, silent as the spirits, moving like a whisper in the walls. In their hidden world of darkened corners, they would describe to each other the lives they would carve for themselves, the houses they would live in, the people they would know. With Jag she felt free. She would forget herself, the pair of them locked in conversation, fascinated

by anything and everything the other had to say, the hours sliding past too quickly before one of them had to go, the day's great
discussion left unresolved, ready to pick up again the next time.
They told each other everything, each time with another detail
set further into stone, peering into their imaginary crystal balls and
deciding what their futures would hold. But then the future came
too quickly, and before they knew it, it was upon them in all
its terrifying reality. So they stopped talking about the future. It
wasn't fun any more.

Along with the future, there were other things they stopped
talking about too. Their deepest secrets, once so light and free that
they could be hung out in the midday sunshine like drying cottons,
now sat tucked away deep inside. Sometimes Sophie didn't know
what to think, or how to feel, and would wander around in a daze
while she tried to make sense of it all. There would be no point in
trying to explain herself to Jag, no matter how she longed to. Their
differences were far too great. How could he possibly understand
what it would mean for her when all this finally came to an end?
She couldn't bear to think about it, fearful that she would never fit
in anywhere else now that she had had a taste of this magical land.
The prospect of going back to England was just too awful. She
didn't want to leave India. Moreover, she didn't want to leave Jag.

The lotus pool became still, ripples dispersed, the water's surface a mirror once more. Sophie leaned forward to look at herself
again and saw Jag's reflection appear behind her. She turned and
smiled up at him, and wished that her eyes were the same color as
his, like tourmalines born from the rich red earth, handed down
through generations, a legacy of his ancient tribe. Sometimes she
could barely bring herself to look into them, such was their weight.

"I thought you weren't coming," she said.

"I had to help my father with something," he lied. And there it
was again. The strange awkwardness that settled so easily between
them now. Jag sat at the pool's edge, a little distance from her.
"Are you looking forward to the celebrations?"

"I suppose so," she said. Her brow twitched and she returned her gaze to the lotus pond. "Do you think everything will feel different tomorrow?"

"I don't know. It feels different already."

"I expect I'll get stuck with the Rippertons," she said, throwing in another pebble. "I've never known a woman who goes on so much. It's no wonder nobody else will ever sit with her. Will you be at the party too?"

"Yes," he said. "But separately from you, and away from the women."

Suddenly determined, Sophie turned to him. "Then we should meet later, just the two of us." She stood up. "We'll watch the fireworks together. It can be our own special memory of this day. I'll sneak out. Nobody will notice with all the hullabaloo. They won't even know I'm gone."

❧❀❧

"Well! Don't we all look quite the picture?" Fiona Ripperton, resplendent in a billowing black silk gown pinned into submission with a heavy detail of jet beading, bumped Sophie conspicuously with a heavy hip and encouraged her to admire the spectacle. "Isn't it wonderful to see everyone all dressed up?"

Mrs. Ripperton squeezed Sophie's arm affectionately and nodded toward a group of servants gathered in a corner, dancing with abandon to the orchestra. "It seems that some of our Indian friends are quite beside themselves with excitement! Rip says that they shouldn't touch alcohol. It doesn't suit them. Our bearer has been drunk as a lord since breakfast. Heaven only knows where he is now. Probably passed out behind a bush somewhere. They have a different constitution from us." She patted her nonexistent waist lightly. "They just can't handle drinkies. Ah!" Spotting a tray of champagne approaching, she waved enthusiastically at its bearer. "Excellent! Just what the good doctor ordered!" She took two and handed one to Sophie, discarding their empties. "Let me tell you, young lady, this will be the party of the century! It's not every day that one is able to stand at the very altar of history and witness the birth of a new nation, so bottoms up!" She tucked into her glass and encouraged Sophie to do the same. "I expect you to enjoy every moment, and one day, when you're a very old lady like me, you'll be able to tell your grandchildren all about the time you danced the night away in a mahajara's palace!" She swung her substantial hips a little to the music.

The evening dragged on interminably. Nobody wanted to feel left out, and the rounds of speeches and announcements went on for what seemed like an age, with toasts proposed for this and for that and glasses raised one after the other. Sophie began to feel light-headed, unused to the champagne, swept along with the swelling crowds gathered in the durbar hall. The jubilant Indians seemed quite overcome, clasping each other in happiness, some chanting *Jai Hind! Jai Hind! Long live India!*, whereas the Britishers seemed all at once strangely uncomfortable, as though fearing that every brown face in the room might turn against them as the Union flag was lowered for the very last time. As the clock urged toward midnight, every wireless set that could be gathered was tuned in to All India Radio to listen to Nehru's broadcast to the nation. Voices hushed, tinkling glasses were silenced, and Sophie slipped quietly away.

⚜

Outside, the rain had stopped, and for a moment the clouds parted, casting a lamp-bright moon on the surface of the lotus pool. From beneath the wide leaves settled low to the ground, frogs sang to one another, insects humming through the heady evening jasmine, the nighttime alive.

"Look." Jag pointed up to the sky, to the tiny white clustered con-stellation overhead. Sophie followed the line of his outstretched arm.

"The Seven Sisters," she said.

"No," he replied. "They are the six sisters. The seventh, and wisest, married the star that sits there, in Ursa Major." She stood close to him as he pointed to the heavens again. "Up there, beside the one that twinkles at the joint where the handle meets the saucepan. Look closely. There is another star there." He waited as her eyes searched the darkness. "The story of that sister is traditionally told to couples on the day of their wedding." Jag felt embarrassed suddenly, lowering his hand and turning away. He left the stars to the sky and sat by the lotus pool. "We should offer each other congratulations," he said.

"I should be congratulating you really," replied Sophie. "It's your country. I expect you're glad that the British are finally out."

"It won't matter when we are old." He smiled at her. "I doubt anyone will remember or care any more." Jag became quiet. "But nobody will ever do that to us again. India will be far too great a country, even for the mightiest of conquerors."

"In that case, I shall offer you an early apology on behalf of my King." Sophie made a small, unsteady curtsey.

"Apology accepted." Jag took a bow.

"Then let us shake hands and be friends." She offered her hand to him formally.

Jag took it, and in that moment, Sophie felt something give way inside her, a shift from deep within. She looked down at his brown tapering fingers, seeing her own, pale and delicate in his hand, the two of them all at once reluctant to let go at this moment of transition. She heard her heart beating.

"I will remember this moment all my life," she said quietly.

"So will I."

Together they sat, hand in hand, watching the mirror surface of the pool.

"Jag?"

"Yes?"

She hesitated. "Do you think I'm pretty?"

He looked at her hand in his, appearing to gather his thoughts. "No," he said. "You are not pretty at all." He glanced up at her. "You are beautiful." His smile faded, and he looked away.

At the stroke of midnight, a stream of fireworks flew up into the blackened sky, exploding into a vast cascade of brilliant, glittering shards, lighting up the water garden, the magical spectacle reflected in the lotus pool. Sitting at its edge, it was as though the fireworks were above them and below them all at once, suspended in space as the colors burst out and around them in a shower of stars. Sophie reached her hand to the pool and touched its surface with the tip of her finger, sending the fireworks scattering across the water. Without warning, her eyes brimmed with tears. She turned to Jag, overwhelmed, and kissed him.

She felt his arms around her, beneath her, above her, her body dissolving, her dress open. He glimpsed her alabaster skin and looked away, his throat tight. His eyes came upon her again, her body, a flash of moonlit shoulder, a Grecian pose almost, as she stood in her petticoat, her dress now a pool of silk on the cool marble slab. He stared at her, on fire, his love so overwhelming that he might swallow her whole, his shirt over his head and aside, his pajamas loosened and thrown. She stopped, silent, and saw his beauty, feeling his warmth, and oh, his lips upon hers. They kissed again, a kiss like no other. She could no longer tell where he began and she ended, the two of them molten, liquid. He felt his body on fire, the fire of life, the first fire ever known to mankind. She felt her heart give way, the world shifting from here to the ends of time, to the moon and stars and the universe that holds them. Jag watched her shiver in his arms, and then there was nothing but ecstasy.

Above them, the stars had disappeared, shrouded beyond the veil of smoke thrown out from the fireworks that cloaked and bittered the night air.

✤ 1957

London

6

T he tiny flat in Kendal Street held a permanent unpleasant stickiness in the air, both from the hand-laundered delicates that hung dripping from the line above the enamel tub in the bathroom and from the poorly ventilated kitchen, its bottom window painted shut. Sophie's latchkey clattered on to the table as she pulled off her coat and hung it up. A hearty aroma filled the flat, reminding her sharply of her emptiness, having eaten nothing since the tea and toast she had forced down in the station cafeteria that morning.

"Sophie? Is that you?"

She called hello and made her way down the narrow hallway to the kitchen, where steam ran freely down the sash window, fogging the grim view of the red-brick building not more than ten yards behind theirs.

"Where on earth have you been?" Margie dusted clouds of loose flour from her hands and pulled her apron over her head, throwing it aside, blind to the mess she had made as always. "Lucien turned up on the doorstep three hours ago and said you'd stood him up for lunch. He was mighty upset about it. Have you two had a tiff or something?"

"Hardly." Sophie slid the silk scarf from her neck and sat at the table.

"What's the matter with you?" Margie rinsed her hands under the tap, tinny music escaping from the transistor radio perched precariously on the shallow ledge above the sink.

"Nothing."

"Then why the long face?"

"Oh, I'm just feeling a little under the weather." Sophie looked up and managed a smile, shaking off the awfulness of the day. "What are you making?"

"Meat and vegetable pie," Margie said. "Got a bit of scrag end from the market. Mind you, there wasn't much left of it by the time I got all the gristle off. Want to give me a hand with the spuds?"

Sophie rolled up her sleeves. "Pass them over."

Margie spread a sheet of newspaper on the table and tumbled a small pile of potatoes upon it before seating herself and setting into one sharply with a knife, watching closely as Sophie picked up a muddy clod and inspected it.

"All right," Margie said, paring out a sprouting eye. "Let's have it. What's he gone and done this time?" Sophie didn't bother to look up.

"He's asked me to marry him."

"What!" Margie sprang up from the table, hand snatching out to silence the radio, almost knocking it over. Sophie began to peel, her knife moving slowly, concentrating hard. If she got the peel off in one single unbroken coil, it would be a sign, she decided. An omen of some sort. Margie stared at her. "What did you say?"

"I told him I'd think about it."

"Well, blow me down." Margie shook her head incredulously. "That's a bit of a bolt from the blue, isn't it?"

"I'm as surprised as anyone."

"When did he ask you?"

"Sunday."

The peel dropped from the potato, the coil complete. Sophie picked up another and began again.

"*Sunday?* Why on earth didn't you say anything?"

"Like what?"

"Crikey, Sophie! I don't know!"

"I think it took four days to sink in."

"I wish you'd told me." Margie sat down, cheeks high with color. "I can't believe it. You've only known him since…" She thought for a while.

"Five months."

"You're not…"

"No!" Sophie smiled. "Of course not."

Margie sat back and exhaled, the two of them allowing their thoughts to percolate for a while. They had met a handful of years earlier when Sophie first arrived in London, sent off by her father, who had insisted she should strike out and see something of the world rather than fussing over him and hiding from life in an untidy house perched amid the Nilgiri Hills in India's far south. A blessed sanctuary it had been, for both of them, and she would have stayed quite happily. There was no lovelier place on earth. Sophie had turned twenty-four that year, just as the winter fogs were beginning to lift from the forest-bound peaks, and her father had become restless, closing himself off in his study where she could see him from the gardens, leaning back in the big leather chair behind his desk, hands poised against his chest, fingertips pressed together while he stared at the ceiling for hours. He had not discussed what was on his mind, but Sophie had sensed it from his manner, the way he seemed to be distancing himself from her. There had been no arguing with him, and part of her had known that the time had come for her to go. She had lived with him for five years, and now she had lived with Margie for four. It had not escaped Sophie's notice, this habit she made of clinging on, as though afraid to let go.

It had been such a wrench, her sense of loneliness at times so profound that there were days when it was almost too much to bear, rainy afternoons spent alone in the cinema, trying to appear easy in her own company. There was no lonelier place than a crowded city. You could die in your bed and no one would miss you. You might just as well be a ghost; but for your remains, there would be nothing to say that you had been here once, to live a life overlooked.

Sophie had taken a room at Mrs. Stanton's guest house off Queensway in Bayswater, a ladies-only establishment where the doors were locked tight shut at ten-thirty sharp and no male visitors were permitted one step further than the residents' sitting room, and even then only for the briefest of stops, usually to collect or deposit a guest, some of whom had been there for years. The rooms were clean and functional and the women pleasant enough, although the older ones tended to keep to themselves, sharing tales of having had their lives turned upside down by the war. After doing their bit for king and country, they had then been expected to give up their jobs and return to the kitchen the moment their menfolk came home. For some, it was too much to ask, that they should rinse away any notions of liberation and go back to the old ways. Marriages had disintegrated, swelling the numbers of women who now lived by their own fates, whether by choice or through widowhood.

It was at Mrs. Stanton's that Sophie met Margie Stock, a rosy-faced Yorkshire girl, some years younger than her, fresh out of secretarial school. Margie taught Sophie the basic rudiments of Pitman's shorthand and insisted that she really must take evening classes and obtain the required certificate, otherwise the best that she could hope for would be to end up in a windowless typing pool bashing away at a machine all day. It was a week before Sophie plucked up the courage to admit that that was exactly what she was doing. After a month or two, seeing as they got on so well, it was only natural that they should move on from Mrs. Stanton's together, pooling their meager resources and splitting the rent on a little place to share.

At weekends, Sophie and Margie would rummage around the bustling street market that sprung up on a Saturday, stallholders shouting *Rock-hard salad tomatoes!*, weighing goods in the flash of an eye, hurling brown paper bags, swung into knotted corners. Sophie liked to stroll through the market, wandering past the traders and sifting through displays of cheap homewares that would have been considered the very last word in sophistication in the country she had left behind. But the greengrocers' stalls seemed bland. She would buy fruit: bananas, apples, perhaps a few oranges. That was roughly the extent of the choice, and there were days when she longed for ripe mango or fresh papaya.

"I don't dislike Lucien at all," Margie said. "But are you sure he's the right man for you? I mean, he's a bit…" She struggled to find a suitable adjective. "Stiff, I suppose. He always leaves me with the impression that what he says isn't necessarily what he's thinking. There's a part of me wants to say supercilious, but that's not what I mean really, although you have to admit he can be a little, well…" She lifted her head slightly and swept the underside of her nose with her finger. "Like that."

"Is that such a bad thing?"

"Well, I suppose not, given his job."

"Not everyone is as liberal as you."

Margie pursed her lips briefly, inspecting the peeled potato in her hand before dropping it into the pan. "I'm assuming you've been to bed together."

"Margie!"

"What?"

"That's none of your business, and even if it was, the answer would be no."

"How Victorian," Margie said. "I wouldn't dream of marrying a man without going to bed with him first, otherwise how could you know whether you're compatible? If you wait until after the wedding, you might find out that he's not up to it at all. Can you imagine how miserable that would be? All this nonsense about saving yourself. Didn't you read *Married Love* when you were a girl?"

"No, I did not, thank you."

"Now there's a woman who knows what she's talking about. Most men haven't the first clue about what they're doing, and the pity of it is that their women are none the wiser. Everybody should read that book, men and women alike, and we'd all get along a lot better."

"*Must* you talk about sex all the time?" Sophie caught herself, feeling a small shudder run through her, as though her mother's voice had just spilled from her own lips. She had left her mark, the woman who had refused to acknowledge the facts of reproduction. When Sophie's periods first started, her mother had acted as though her daughter had committed some kind of mortal sin. She kept a note of Sophie's days, and every month, for that week, Sophie would be made to feel like a leper, her mother saying it was unclean, the whole house smelling of carbolic soap.

"I don't," Margie said. "I'm merely pointing out the importance of the physical side of things, and if you're as innocent as you try to make out, which I don't believe for one minute, you might just be in for a very big disappointment."

"I didn't say I was completely innocent," Sophie said. "And I didn't say that I was going to accept him either."

"Ah." Margie checked over her potato. "Now we're getting to it."

"My parents' marriage was a disaster. I've come this far on my own. Maybe it wouldn't be such a bad thing to keep things that way." Sophie's thoughts wandered to her mother's voice. "Marriage isn't for everyone, you know."

"We're not talking about everyone. We're talking about you."

"Well, why should I? I'm happy enough. I've learned to stand on my own two feet and I'm free to please myself."

"Until you turn into a dried-up old prune like the ones in Mrs. Stanton's attic."

"I'd rather that than end up like my parents." Sophie's head dipped. She felt her cheeks flush.

"Hey." Margie dropped her knife, reached over the peelings, and took Sophie's hand. "What's brought this on?"

"I don't know," Sophie said. "I always wanted to marry, to have a family, but…" She squeezed Margie's hand, closing her eyes tightly for a second. "I went to see my mother today," she said. "It was awful." She paused, as though unable to believe it herself.

"Ten years," she said. "Ten years since we have seen or spoken to each other. I don't know what I expected to find." She looked up into Margie's pale blue eyes. "I thought I could heal the rift, that she might even be pleased to see me. God knows, it's been long enough. I thought I would tell her about Lucien and his proposal, and that we would at last be able to put the past behind us and make a fresh start. I thought…" Sophie let out a terrible sigh. "Oh, I don't know what I thought. I should have left it all well alone."

"How was she?" Margie asked softly.

"It was all a bit of a shock," Sophie said. "I knew she would be older, of course, but I hadn't expected her to look quite so different. I hardly recognized her."

"Did you talk?"

"That's the odd thing." Sophie frowned to herself. "I don't really remember what we talked about. All I know is that the moment I arrived, I felt like I shouldn't be there, like I was picking at something that should be left alone. It was as though I was a child again, just like that." She snapped her fingers. "Standing there quaking in my boots. Isn't that ridiculous?"

"I'm so sorry," Margie said. "That must have been tough on you."

Sophie shook her head sharply in self-reproach. "I shouldn't have gone. It's no good getting all churned up over things that are in the past. Time to think about the future."

"I should think so too." Margie wiped her hands clean on the floury tea towel and delivered her most cheerful smile, setting her elbows on the table. "Does Lucien know you can't cook?"

Sophie slid Margie a wry smile. "If I marry him, I'm hoping I won't have to."

❧

Outside on the wet pavement, big red double-decker buses rumbled by, engines belching smoke, pungent aromas wafting out of the fish and chip shop. Margie pushed open the door of the

Marlborough Arms, releasing a thick blanket of cigarette smoke into the street, and marched toward the bar, announcing loudly: two whisky sodas, large. She and Sophie took their drinks to a dingy corner table, sliding into sticky seats.

"Here's to you." Margie raised her glass.

"Thank you," Sophie said.

"I wish Fred would ask me to marry him." Margie took a long sip from her drink. "I just don't think he's that interested."

Sophie smiled at her sympathetically. Margie had fallen in love with the cellist with the dark hair and doe eyes last autumn. He liked to play Elgar for her through the open door as she lay in the bath, and he cooked omelettes sometimes on a Saturday morning after staying over, though he always slept on the couch, never once trying to get into her bed.

"If I were to leave, what would you do about the flat?" Sophie asked.

"Oh, I don't know. I'd probably keep it on. I couldn't be doing with the bother of moving. You never know, Fred might decide to come and live with me. I don't want to be with anyone else, but sometimes I think he'll never make up his mind."

"Have you talked to him about it?"

"What's to talk about?" said Margie. "Either he wants to be with me or he doesn't."

"Of course he does."

"Then why is he taking so long about it? I'm beginning to wonder if it's not just because he feels bad about letting me down."

"He's just shy. You know how he loves you."

"I do," Margie said. "And that's the tragedy of it. He loves me but he doesn't want to sleep with me. We should be lovers by now. He should have got me into bed months ago, or at least tried to."

"He has more respect for you than that."

"I don't want respect. I want him to stop dithering and act like a man. And now you're getting married after just five months and here am I, dancing around the mulberry bush, waiting for something I know is never going to happen." Margie picked up her drink again and nursed it. "It feels so unfair."

"Unfair." Sophie laughed to herself. "Somebody else said that to me today."

Margie looked at Sophie curiously, noticing the sudden note of sadness in her. "You are in love with him, aren't you?"

Sophie felt her insides tighten.

"Yes," she said.

The word fell from her automatically. Of course she was in love with him. She had no reason not to be. In love. In sensible, adult love. This sort of love she could manage. This sort of love would not tear the flesh from her bones and eat her alive from the inside out. This sort of love would not leave her wishing she were dead, knowing that she had nothing to live for. She would be safe in this love, safe from the abyss that had once threatened to swallow her whole.

7

L ucien Grainger stubbed out his cigarette and tried not to smile, glancing over at the pianist playing thin, watery tunes from the far corner of the restaurant, an elegant candlelit affair just a stone's throw from the blackened Royal Opera House in Covent Garden. Sophie had been like a cat on a hot tin roof all evening, and he could see that the wine had gone to her head. Unsurprising after the enormous martinis they had sharpened their appetites with at seven. Let her take her time, he thought. It was perfectly obvious that she was going to say yes.

Lucien knew very well that women could be strange creatures, contrary in nature, often just for the sake of it, yet she had clearly given the matter a great deal of thought, hence her avoidance tactics over the last week, and this had served to elevate his opinion of her further. He had expected Sophie to jump at his proposal with an immediate yes, but credit to her, and somewhat to his surprise, she had seemed nothing short of shocked. It wasn't quite what he had had in mind. Later that same day, he had mulled it over while swimming lengths in the pool at his club and had arrived at the uncomfortable conclusion that he had seriously miscalculated the manner of his broaching of the subject.

He had assumed, quite wrongly it seemed, that Sophie was beyond the tender age when a girl expected to be swept off her feet with a grand gesture on bended knee. Instead, he had brought the idea to her as one might float a business proposal, confidently setting out his stall, expecting her to melt into his arms. How wrong he had been. At first she had seemed both panicked and crestfallen, as though the bottom had fallen out of her world, and at that very moment he had realized his monumental error. It was no wonder she had been so upset. She had probably dreamed of this day for years, since girlhood, the perfect marriage proposal, and he couldn't have made more of a hash of it had he tried. Poor Sophie, it wasn't her fault that he had come to the idea slightly hard-boiled, nor was it surprising that she had taken off like that. He'd been a bit of an idiot and would have to make it up to her. After all, any man about to take a wife would be well advised to learn her foibles as quickly as possible and to remember that women were just girls in grown-up clothes. A lifetime partnership required a great deal of diplomacy, and a little romance went a long way in keeping a woman happy. He wouldn't make that mistake again, and he hoped that the ring in his pocket would be more than adequate when it came to redeeming himself. It had cost a small fortune, but as the man in Garrard's had said, an engagement ring is just as much a reflection of the gentleman who gives it as of the lady who wears it, and this one would reflect on them both very well indeed.

Lucien leaned comfortably into his chair while the white-coated waiter swept a few loose crumbs from the table. Picking a stray thread of tobacco from his lip, he opened the subject she had so diligently skirted through the soup. "You realize I'm in hell, don't you?" Sophie smiled at him. He pretended to look injured. "I never thought I'd see the day when I'd be left hanging by the woman I want to marry. Why don't you just put me out of my misery and be done with it?"

"It's such a big step."

"Of course it is, but we're ready for it, aren't we?"

Sophie's head began to throb again. She had thought about it all so much that it had turned into one big, confused mess. Why was she hesitating? She had already made up her mind. If she didn't get married now, she might never have another offer, and she did want to get married, she had decided. She wanted to have a family and to build a life with a good man by her side and have a nice home and, she admitted to herself, a sense of security for her future. What else was there? It wasn't as though she had a profession, or a vocation, or anything at all that she could speak of for that matter. She should marry and have a family before it was too late, or she would probably regret it for the rest of her life, and there was not one single good reason she could think of for not marrying Lucien.

It was no accident that Sophie had ended up working at the Foreign Office. England was such a small place, so claustrophobic in its outlook. Perhaps she was one of those people who would never feel settled. She never had, not for as long as she could remember, always looking over her shoulder, waiting for something bad to happen.

She had spotted the vacancy advertised in *The Times* while eating a ham sandwich in the café beside South Kensington tube station after visiting the Natural History Museum. The museum was one of her Sunday destinations, where she could revisit, frozen in glass cases, the birds and animals that had populated the grounds of the grand palace she had once lived in, in a place far from here. The hidden cobras, the mongooses kept for the purpose of keeping their numbers down, the monkeys that gamboled across the rooftops, arms laden with stolen fruit. She would watch as the museum visitors pointed and stared, laughing sometimes, exchanging uneducated opinions about what they were like in real life. After visiting the stuffed tigers and pinned butterflies, she had headed for the café, ordering a sandwich and a cup of stewed tea from the steaming pot, and had sat at a table with only the newspaper for company. And there it was, advertised in the secretarial positions, the posting crested with the emblem of Her Majesty's Foreign Office. It had hit her, just like that. Here lay an open gateway to the whole world. It was a menial position and the salary was low, but she didn't care. Two weeks later, she found herself being interviewed by a no-nonsense matriarch who tested her secretarial skills and asked her outright whether she was on the verge of getting married or anything like that, given her age. Sophie seemed rather mature for the position, and they didn't want to hire somebody who had their mind on other matters. To work for the government was a serious undertaking, the woman had said, and she would be expected to concentrate on her job, with no chattering. This was not a venue for husband-hunting, and anyone thinking otherwise would soon find themselves dismissed. The woman's finger bore no wedding ring, and Sophie had the presence of mind to assure her that she was a confirmed spinster with very little time for the opposite sex. The letter of appointment arrived within a week, and the following Monday morning, Sophie had presented herself at the Foreign Office in Carlton House Terrace.

She had started in the typing pool, churning out endless tedious reports and minutes, and quickly garnered a reputation for her knack of deciphering other people's shorthand and the worst of the men's longhand, which she attributed to the fact that her father was a doctor, saying that his scrawl was unintelligible to anyone other than himself and her. One morning, quite out of the blue, she was told to go to the top boardroom to replace the director's secretary, who was off with a bad dose of the flu. Had she known that she was to be presented at such a senior level, she would have worn something different that day. The weather had been unseasonably warm, the vault of the upper rooms ripening to a sweltering heat, and she was wearing a cotton dress that she had thought she might just get away with, sleeveless, nipped in at the waist, with a full skirt that gratefully received every small breeze beneath its layers. Her usual light wool skirts had stuck to her and prickled at her skin, and she had noticed that some of the other girls had submitted to the humidity in less substantial garments. So long as their skirt fell below the knee and they had something with which to cover up, a light cardigan perhaps, nobody had minded.

The gravitas of the boardroom had made Sophie self-conscious the moment she walked in. A dozen men, simmering beneath their shirtsleeves, had turned their eyes to her as she scurried in with her notepad. In that instant, she had been paralyzed by nerves, realizing that she had no idea where she was supposed to sit before being directed to a chair in the corner, set back from the men, as though to remind her that she was not really there, her ears not her own. As the meeting began, she had recorded their words, their ideas, their idiotic suggestions, leaning into her pad, concentrating hard, determined to prove herself every ounce as skilled as the absent secretary, so that she might be moved up soon and spared the misery of the windowless dungeon where typewriters rattled a constant stream of meaningless transcripts that nobody would ever bother to read. When the meeting came to a close, Sophie realized with horror that the skirts of her dress had ruched up beneath her pad, exposing the beginnings of her stocking top. It was no wonder that that awful man Christopher Soames had turned up at the pool not two hours later, asking her if she had any plans for lunch while perching himself suggestively on the corner of her desk. The way he had looked at her, she had felt as though her dress had disintegrated and fallen to the floor, and she had endured the rest of the short heat wave in a stifling twinset.

Lucien saw that Sophie's thoughts had drifted. He reached across the table and placed his hand over hers.

"How long does it take to know you've met the right woman?"

"But you don't know me at all." She thought for a moment and corrected herself. "We barely know each other."

"And isn't that wonderful?" he said. "What two people really know each other when they marry? It takes years, my darling. Years and years before we'll know one another inside out. That's part of what marriage is all about. Didn't you know that?" Sophie nodded a little. He was right, of course, as usual. The waiter arrived with their entrées, a fillet of sole for her, a piece of steak for him. "You see this?" He cut into the beef, juices running red. "I like my steak bloody, very bloody. And you?"

"Not so much," Sophie said, her smile opening up a little.

"English mustard or French?"

"French."

"There, you see?" he said. "There's nothing to it."

Lucien filled his mouth, nodding his satisfaction. Sophie watched him for a little while and wondered what it would be like to sit across a dinner table from him for the rest of her life, to wake up every morning under the same roof, to go to sleep at night in the same bed. She tried to picture him old, with gray hair, wearing striped pajamas, but the image escaped her. All she could see was the man before her, solid and straight-backed, entirely comfortable in the space he occupied. It must be nice to be a man, she thought, a man full of confidence and self-assurance. She would happily bet five pounds that he had never felt vulnerable for a moment in his life. He had probably won all sorts of trophies at school and had been in the first eleven. Men like that don't like to lose. In all probability, he always knew exactly what he was going to do at any given moment. If only she could be him for a while, to know what it was like, to think what he was thinking. Sophie ate a little of her fish, but found that she wasn't particularly hungry.

"I don't want to make a mistake," she said.

"We won't."

"But how do you know?"

"How does anybody know?" Lucien said patiently. "All any of us can do is to say yes and hope for the best, and I think we're pretty much a perfect match. Don't you?"

"I'm sorry to have been such a wet blanket last Sunday. It's just that you took me completely by surprise, that's all. I really wasn't expecting it. A part of me thought you were still in love with…" Sophie stopped short, glancing awkwardly away and feeling foolish.

"Oh." Lucien shifted uncomfortably. "I see."

"I'm sorry," Sophie said quickly. "You know how people talk."

"Catherine and I were a bad habit that went on for far too long.

I wasn't in love with her, and she wasn't in love with me either. She's the last woman on earth I would have wanted to marry." Lucien discarded his fork and lit a cigarette. "I pity the poor devil who ends up with her as his wife."

"She's very beautiful," Sophie said.

"Well, good for her," Lucien replied without looking up. He didn't want to talk about Catherine Isherwood, the fine-looking daughter of a retired ambassador to the United Nations. There was a time when he had seriously considered her as wife material, but she had unnerved him with her unshakable confidence and consummate charm. It wouldn't do for him to find himself outshone by a spouse who clearly had greater experience in the service than he did. Besides, her specialty area was the Arab states, and he was hoping that his trajectory would not take him down that path. He didn't get on with them particularly well, as he had discovered to his cost when he inadvertently caused an uproar with the Emir of Oman by admiring a cigarette box crafted in the shape of a turtle, encrusted with precious and semi-precious stones. The Emir had promptly presented it to him, throwing the embassy into turmoil as they hunted to find a gift of similar grandeur to return to the prince. A cable had to be sent to the Foreign Office to explain the faux pas made by the junior member of the mission and lists had to be scoured to locate a suitable offering from the catalogue of diplomatic baubles. Some of these treasures had been doing the rounds for years, making it a tricky business to see that they never ended up in the same hands twice. Catherine Isherwood had dined out on the story for weeks, Lucien's smile wearing ever thinner as she entertained her entourage at his expense, as she was prone to do.

"I don't want to rush into a decision that one of us might regret," Sophie said.

"Who's rushing? Aren't you in love with me? Not even a little bit?"

Sophie blushed under his huge smile. How could she have doubted it? There was something about him that was irresistible,

something beyond his broad-shouldered good looks and charming manner. He had a knack of making you feel like you were the
only person in the world that mattered, a way of looking at you
just so, his attentiveness noticing every little thing. She couldn't
have asked for more, yet she couldn't help but wonder why he had
chosen her, particularly when he and Catherine had been such an
item, a woman from whom she couldn't have been more different.

They had all seen her, wafting through the Foreign Office
every now and then as though she owned the place, dressed from
head to toe in the latest Parisian fashions. Whenever she was in the
building, the secretaries would whisper to each other about what
she was wearing and how her hair was styled, speaking with envy
or admiration, wishing they could be her, the very last word in
sophistication. Lucien and Catherine had seemed like the model
couple, and that they would end up getting married was practically
a foregone conclusion. Everybody said so. Then suddenly it was all
off, the news ripping through the secretarial offices like wildfire.
They all assumed that he must have made her an offer and been
turned down, but that was nothing more than idle speculation.
Nobody in their department was senior enough to know what had
really gone on.

"Of course I am," she smiled.

"Then what's to think about, hmm? You can make an honest
man of me at last."

"One more thing." Her smile wavered. She forced herself to
look him straight in the eye. "Why me?"

Lucien felt the intensity of her gaze and was for a moment
taken aback. He hesitated, giving himself time to think. It was
the same question he had asked himself as he had walked through
Kensington Gardens last Sunday morning, cutting across the park
on his way to Kendal Street rather than hailing a taxi from his flat
on Queen's Gate as he usually did. The episode with Catherine
had taught him a salutary lesson, but there was no use in dwelling on the painful details. If anything, she had done him a favor.

Beneath his sense of humiliation, he had known all along that it would have been a disastrous coupling, but God, she was beautiful, and passionate too. He would have been prepared to go a long way for the sake of keeping a woman like that, and had hinted to her plenty of times that he would never let her go.

It would always elicit a smile from her, lying back on the pillow, smoking a cigarette, watching him with vague amusement as he gazed at her, naked against the sheets. She would joke with him that she had every intention of settling on an aristocrat, an earl at the very least, or an American tycoon with vulgar piles of new money. Lucien never got around to the proposal. It was as though she had sensed it coming before dropping him like a hot brick. He had felt like a fool and had sworn to himself that he would never again find himself in that position. But marry he must, and at least he had been spared the folly of making an imprudent choice.

Yet marriage had been the very last thing on Lucien's mind when Sophie Schofield caught his eye while he was still licking his wounds from the breakup. She had been called in to record the minutes of a meeting to do with cotton exports and had sat in the corner of the room, unaware that her dress had ridden up, exposing a pale glimpse of thigh. He had not been the only one to remark upon her, and by the time he located her desk in the typing pool shortly before lunchtime, Christopher Soames was already there, trying his luck. She had turned him down, having no doubt been forewarned by the other girls, and Lucien had kept her in his sights and had taken his time in making his approach. She might turn out to be a welcome distraction after Catherine, and he rather enjoyed the sport of seduction, particularly with the kind of woman who might take a little persuasion to get into bed.

To his surprise, Sophie had turned out to be a great deal more interesting than he had bargained for. Not only did she point-blank refuse to sleep with him, but she also had the kind of background that might well be exactly what he should have been looking for all along. India, no less, and in a royal palace at that. He had had his eye on Delhi for a while. They were plum postings, bringing with them a great deal of luxury and very little in the way of real work.

Lucien had applied for Delhi six months ago and had been given the general impression from the Foreign Secretary that he might stand a better chance were he not still playing the bachelor, particularly after that business in Paris, although the rumor had never been proven. That sort of thing was rife, of course, but it didn't do to stretch one's luck too far. There was no doubt that he was made of the right stuff. He was a skilled tactician with the charm of the devil. With the right woman by his side, he could expect to go far, perhaps rising to the highest echelons of the service, if he played his cards right.

A wife drew a neat line under various questions and uncertainties about a man's character, and Lucien had bided his time for long enough. Unmarried men begged certain uncomfortable questions in the high offices, like whether they could be trusted in the society of the other company wives, or daughters for that matter. All the senior India postings were held by married men. The job required a rock-solid reputation, an air of propriety, to keep up the side even though the British were long gone. India's problems were no longer of British concern. They could run the place into the ground if they so chose and kill each other to their heart's content without any interference, and if the last ten years were anything to go by, they had had a pretty good run at it.

"Why you?" He laughed a little. "Well, why not?"

"I'm serious," she said. "I have to know why you want to marry me."

Lucien's smile faded. She had every right to ask, and this was no time to make light of it. "Your parents' divorce affected you very badly, didn't it?" he said.

"Yes."

"Do you want to talk about it?"

"Not particularly." She looked down into her lap. "I just don't ever want to find myself that miserable."

"Did you go and see your mother?"

"No." She shook her head quickly. "I changed my mind." She had decided not to tell him about the awful visit. It would serve no purpose other than to drag things up. She should never have mentioned it in the first place. There was nothing to be had there except misery. "It's best left as it is. I don't suppose she and I would have terribly much to say to each other after all this time."

"How long has it been?"

"Ten years almost."

"That must have been some argument."

"It was."

"Did she ever remarry?"

"I have no idea," Sophie said. "Even if she had, I don't think I would have wanted to know about it. It wasn't the easiest of relationships at the best of times."

"What about your father?"

"What about him?"

"Did he…"

"Remarry? Not on your life." Sophie pulled a face. "If anything, I think it must have put him off the idea of marriage for ever, and you can see for yourself how it has affected me." She flicked her eyes to the ceiling in acknowledgement of her own skittishness. "Who would have thought I'd get into such a state over a proposal? Poor Dad. He never talked about any of it. It was as though it never happened. I think he preferred to allow people to draw their own conclusions. We must have made a very odd pair."

"You were a good daughter to have stayed with him for so long."

"How could I not? I felt terribly responsible for him, and he so needed looking after. There were times when I thought I'd never see him smile again; that's how bad it was. I have no doubt that I would still be there had he not insisted I stop mollycoddling him."

"Quite right too, otherwise we never would have met, would we? And then where would I be?" He picked up her hand. "You are everything a man could possibly want in a wife, Sophie. You're pretty and funny and clever, and we could have such a wonderful life together."

"I don't want to let you down," she said.

"How could you possibly let me down? All you have to do is make a home, wherever we are, and stay by my side." A thought passed across his mind, the same thought that had nagged at him since his walk home alone through the park last Sunday. "Sophie?"

"Yes?"

"Is it the India posting that's putting you off? I mean, I notice you never really talk about it."

"It feels like a long time ago," she said. "A different life, a different place. India is a whole other country now, warts and all. When I was first there, it was just one big melting pot, not that I ever really saw that much of it. That was the beauty of the place, I think. It was all the wonderful differences that made India what it was."

"Did you ever go to Delhi?"

"No," she said. "Well, that's not strictly true. We did pass though it, when we first went out, but I was still in my teens then and I hadn't known what to expect and it was all rather overwhelming. I remember it being huge and utterly chaotic. I'd never seen anything like it."

"You were there before Partition?"

"Yes, and during. My, what a terrible business that whole thing was. And now look what's left. They're still fighting, ten years later."

"Things have changed a lot since then," Lucien said. "There's no trouble in Delhi. All that's way up in the north. Delhi is completely civilized now." He cut into his steak again, dipping his knife in the mustard and buttering it yellow. "And the houses in the diplomatic districts are quite something."

Sophie smiled to herself. *Delhi is civilized now.* She wondered what he thought civilized meant, whether he thought it something simple like hot and cold running water and a well-cut suit, or whether he meant something deeper than that, like fairness and democracy and everybody having enough food to eat. Lucien noticed her looking at him.

"Aren't you tempted to go back and see how it has changed?"

"I don't know. I hadn't really thought about it."

Sophie toyed with her wine glass, twisting its stem, watching the candlelight reflected in the rich red Burgundy he had chosen. Something special, he had said. Of course she had thought about it. She had thought of little else. Could she go back to India? Could she really cope with it? With all the feelings and memories that would be bound to come back to her? She didn't know.

"That's a very serious expression you're wearing all of a sudden," Lucien said.

"I'm sorry. My mind had wandered."

"To India?"

"Yes."

"Was it so bad?"

"No." She took up her fork, picking at the vegetables on her plate. "It was wonderful actually, in every sense of the word. I have never seen such beauty, nor such squalor. Sometimes it feels like it was just a dream I once had."

"You know how important this posting would be to me. I won't lie to you about it."

"I know."

"But if that is what's putting you off, I'll turn it down."

"No. You mustn't do that. I know you've been keen to go, and if that's the way you feel, then that is what you must do."

"You know what they say about India," Lucien said. "Once it's got its hooks into you, you never want to leave."

"Oh." Sophie reached for a sip of water. "Is that what they say?"

"You of all people should know. It certainly seduced your father into staying, didn't it? Aren't you looking forward to going back?" He watched her face, the small shift in the line of her mouth.

How quickly the years slip by. How strange it was to think of the person she had once been, like leafing through a photograph album of faded sepia memories conjuring names long since unheard. She had thought about it every day, upon first waking and before she fell asleep at night. There was nothing she could do about it. It was part of her landscape, like waking up to find the same person sitting expectantly in a chair beside her, waiting for her to open her eyes, to remind her of what once was. It followed her, wherever she went, the constant specter waiting for her to turn and see it, its gaze never leaving her. She had learned to live with it, and as the years passed by, the specter moved further away, finally revealing days when she would wake up and it would not be there, the chair empty.

Sophie adjusted the napkin in her lap. "I don't know. It's funny the way things turn out sometimes, isn't it? The places we end up?"

"I'll say." Lucien paused his fork. "But I want you to know that the only thing that matters to me is you. So long as you're beside me, I wouldn't care if they posted me to the North Pole."

"I jolly well would! I can't bear being cold." Sophie took a sip of wine and shivered.

"Then what could be more perfect? We'll be living in the lap of luxury, and you already know the country."

"You're very persuasive."

"Of course I am. It's what I'm paid for."

"You realize it's not easy, to adjust to a new place and live in a foreign country?"

"Sophie, darling, I think you forget that I have been doing this for some time now."

"Not as a married man, you haven't. It's easy to live in bachelor quarters and have everything done for you while you swan around pleasing yourself. Having a wife in tow is a different matter entirely."

"Only if she's a harridan."

"Lucien!" Sophie feigned offense.

"Oh, come on, Sophie! We'll work it out together, won't we?

And one day, when we're old and gray, we'll look back on this day and laugh about it."

"I want to have a good marriage."

"And so do I."

"Promise me that you'll always tell me if I do anything to make you unhappy?" Lucien found himself unexpectedly moved by her sudden distress. "Promise me that you won't keep things to yourself or let resentments build up, no matter what they are or how silly they might sound?"

"Of course," he said.

"Lucien, if we marry, you have to help me to make a success of it, because I couldn't bear the thought of you regretting your decision years down the line when it's too late, and to have us hate each other for it. We must never make each other unhappy."

"Never."

Sophie fell silent, gathering herself for a moment. "And I wouldn't want a big fuss made about it either. No big arrangements or silly dresses. And no church service. After putting up with my mother all those years, I've had quite enough of God to last me a lifetime."

"You'll want your father to give you away, though?"

"Why? He abhors England. He's perfectly well settled where he is and I wouldn't dream of dragging him all the way here."

"Not even for a wedding?"

"Especially not for a wedding. I wouldn't be able to say those vows and look him in the face after what we lived through, and I certainly wouldn't want him to start getting all old-fashioned about marrying his daughter off in style. It would cripple him. We could go and visit him together afterward." She looked at him. "When we get to India."

1947

The Maharaja's Palace

8

The whole palace seemed to have woken up in a bad mood. This was generally the way things had been going lately; such were the mounting politics of the household. Without the Maharaja's indomitable presence, the palace lost something of its discipline, the various departments picking fights with each other and giving vent to old rivalries. Passions were quickly inflamed and tempers frayed at the slightest tug. It was unsurprising, given the general sense of uncertainty that seeped like a thin mist through the corridors of treasures.

The entire estate had become something of a tinderbox, what with all the trouble going on the length and breadth of the country. Knives were out and there was always some whispering going on in corners, short, staccato arguments igniting out of nowhere. Everyone was at it, from the Maharaja himself right down to the sweepers who attended to the cleaning of the latrines.

Two months after Partition, the monsoon had finally petered out, replaced by long hot days that irritated even the mildest of temperaments. That the Maharaja had gone away again only made things worse. For one thing, they were all supposed to be staying put until things had settled down, if only to keep an eye on their little patch of the new dominion and assert some semblance of authority now that the British had pulled out. After all, a king was still a king, even if only in title, and everyone preferred to turn a blind eye to the small matter of a republic having no need of sovereign rule. This was no time to dwell on such small details, the brief flash of jubilation in August quickly overshadowed by the abominations of violent disorder.

Perched on the ledge of one of the latticed porticoes that ran the length of the palace's grand facade, Sophie looked out across the immaculate gardens, watching the *malis* tending to the shrubs in the morning sunshine before the heat became too much. Counting how many had been sent out today, she tried as best she could to occupy her mind rather than searching for Jag's familiar figure. Her heart couldn't muster a smile, and everybody seemed so grumpy. Some trouble or other must be going on in the palace, the stress of it being passed down the ranks like a bad penny until it had ended up at their breakfast table this morning. One moment, all was well, as her father tucked into his soft-boiled egg; the next, in came their bearer, insisting that the doctor must abandon his plate and come to the *zenana* at once. Her mother had shot him a hostile glance as he threw his napkin to the table and took up his bag before following the bearer out to the waiting bicycle rickshaw. An entire fleet of them, all painted the Maharaja's particular shade of cornflower blue, pedaled constantly about the palace grounds, delivering people and packages around the estate. The ensuing slam of her mother's teacup was the precise moment that Sophie realized that today was going to be a difficult day. Veronica had emitted a crashing sigh and started up with a string of complaints before pushing her toast aside and marching away from the table under a cloud of indignation, shutting herself in her rooms.

Sophie found herself scouring the distance, trying to decipher every figure, hoping that one of them would walk her way, smiling a familiar greeting. But nobody did, so she sat and waited, her eyes tiring. It had become hard for Jag to slip away; there was so much work to be done. Sometimes he managed only a few minutes when she had waited for over an hour, and she would be left feeling bereft after one fleeting kiss. She longed to see him, to talk to him, to feel his arms around her, unable to tear her mind's eye from that night in the water garden when they had made love under the jeweled sky. It was as though the scales had been lifted from her eyes, the world renewed, and she could think of nothing else.

Fiona Ripperton's dressing room overlooked the blue courtyard, so called because of the three-tiered fountain that sat at its center, the clover-leaf pool lined with blue tiles, fired in the palace's signature color and decorated with white glazed images of fish and birds. The shallow covering of water in the upper two tiers carried an unhealthy green tinge. The fountain had stopped working a month ago, an invisible crack having opened up somewhere beneath the tiles. The only way to fix it would be to dismantle the whole thing, but it seemed that nobody wanted to take responsibility for doing it, and now the water had become stagnant, attracting clouds of mosquitoes, which meant that Mrs. Ripperton could no longer sit with the window open, much to her irritation. She had asked Mr. Ripperton if he might have a word with whoever it was who was in charge of such things—the Maharaja would be bound to have someone on his staff whose job it was to solely maintain the palace's numerous ponds and fountains—but nothing had been done about it. Mr. Ripperton had told his wife that there were far more pressing issues to attend to, and the division of duties was still unclear after the departure of the Moslem staff who had chosen to leave. Perhaps she should suggest that the fountain be used as a planter instead and filled with flowers, marigolds probably, which seemed to keep the mosquitoes at bay.

Mrs. Ripperton inspected her appearance, puffing on a little extra rouge, dabbing a spot of perfume behind each ear, while Sophie sat quietly on the silk chaise, leafing absently through an out-of-date magazine, lost in her own thoughts. Mrs. Ripperton watched her in the mirror. The poor girl had seemed so miserable lately, wandering around looking quite forlorn. Her face appeared drawn, her complexion dulled. Even Dr. Reeves' wife Kay had said that Sophie hadn't been her usual sunny self recently. Mrs. Ripperton had almost exhausted her repertoire of tried and tested ways to cheer the girl up: deliberately making silly mistakes when they played checkers, seeing to it that Sophie could sweep the board with a dramatically triumphant move; flagging down a pair of the blue bicycle rickshaws and bribing the drivers to race the two women through the grounds with the promise of a prize for the winner. Yet it seemed that nothing could shift the cloud that followed her around. Perhaps she was homesick, yearning for this last month or so to be over with quickly so that she could get out of this place and return to England, to a normal life.

Mrs. Ripperton wondered if Sophie knew that her father had been in their apartments yesterday evening, talking to her husband about the possibility of staying on at the palace. Mr. Ripperton had told her to keep it under her hat. Poor Sophie. She would no doubt greet the news very badly indeed. In the meantime, Mrs. Ripperton would do all that she could to see that the time passed as painlessly as possible. She clipped on a pair of earrings and spoke to Sophie's reflection in the mirror.

"Do you want to put on a little lipstick and rouge, dear?"

Sophie shook her head. "No, thank you."

"Are you sure?"

"Really," Sophie said.

"Good for you," Fiona Ripperton agreed cheerfully. "Why bother gilding the lily?" Sophie smiled at her. Of course she would like to wear a little lipstick now and then, to experiment with powder and rouge and a dark pencil for her eyes, but her mother had forbidden it. She had caught Sophie trying on her lipstick one afternoon when she thought her mother was asleep and had told her that she looked like a tart, then had stood over her while she scrubbed her face with soap and water.

"There." Mrs. Ripperton stood up. "How do I look?"

Sophie closed the magazine and ran her eyes over Mrs. Ripperton's sturdy figure, draped in the sort of dress that her father referred to as a frock. It wasn't quite her usual attire for an unremarkable Tuesday afternoon. She normally wore something much simpler, without the fussy floral pattern or the unnecessary extra length. She looked a bit odd, Sophie thought, but then again she was getting on a little and had perhaps arrived at that time in life when one dressed to please oneself. Old ladies had a habit of doing that, cobbling together outlandish outfits as though they had rummaged through a child's dressing-up box.

"You look lovely," Sophie said. "That's a very nice dress."

"Do you think so?" Fiona Ripperton glanced back at the mirror and reappraised it. "Rip says it gives him quite the headache. Are you ready, my dear?"

"Ready?" Sophie's heart sank. Oh, what now? What did she have to do before everybody realized she just wanted to be left alone? Mrs. Ripperton was starting to drive her around the bend with her incessant shows of well-meaning. It seemed that wherever she turned, there she was, waiting to drag her off to the mission or to challenge her to another interminable game of gin rummy. Admittedly, the rickshaw race had been fun, but she had been deliberately sullen with Mrs. Ripperton afterward and had felt bad when she saw the pained expression on Fiona's face as she got out of the rickshaw and said that she felt sick. She didn't mind sitting in her apartments, though, particularly Mrs. Ripperton's dressing room, where she was allowed to poke through all the lovely things on the dressing table: the jars of perfumed creams, the silver-topped scent bottles. She had magazines too, lots of them, sent from America, filled with pictures of the latest styles and advertisements for all manner of things for the modern woman. Sophie enjoyed browsing through them, deciding what would suit her, making mental lists of the things she would order, if she were able to. She put the magazine down. "Ready for what?"

"I have a most interesting little diversion lined up for us this afternoon." Mrs. Ripperton lowered her voice conspiratorially. If this outing didn't get a smile out of Sophie once and for all, she would jolly well eat her own hat. Veronica Schofield would no doubt have a blue fit if she found out what they were up to, which made it all the more exciting. "But I was thinking—perhaps it would be best not to mention it to your mother. I don't think she would approve. Let's tell her we spent the afternoon in the library learning about the history of British India and the colonies, shall we? That should do the trick."

Sophie knew that Mrs. Ripperton was right. Her mother was notoriously disparaging of anything that did not involve the church or the mission. She had never set foot in any part of the palace unconnected with the necessities of her daily life and clearly had no intention of ever doing so, as though the very air within its walls would pollute her upheld beliefs.

"Where are we going?" Sophie asked.

Mrs. Ripperton winked at her. "The prison block."

Sophie's eyes widened and she wasn't sure if she felt excited or aghast. The prison block, as she had heard some of the wives call it, was considered a heathen place, a place of slavery and shameless goings-on where women were kept behind locked doors for the sole purpose of satisfying the Maharaja's lust. No man, other than immediate family, was permitted to enter, and even then only by special dispensation unless it was the Maharaja himself. Fiona Ripperton never referred to the women's palace as the prison block, and this was the first time Sophie had heard her use the term, although it was clearly delivered with a good pinch of humor and an air of subterfuge. Sophie's mother referred to it as the *harem*, barely able to form the word on her offended lips.

"I sent a note to the First Her Highness," said Mrs. Ripperton, "asking if she would like to meet you, and of course she said yes. Who wouldn't? So pinch a little color into those pretty cheeks of yours and I'll lend you my string of pearls. You can't possibly turn up completely unadorned. They'll think you a pauper!" She took the pearls from a drawer and fastened them around Sophie's neck. "There. Nothing too fancy. One can't possibly compete with the Maharani and her ladies anyway."

❦❧❨

Guided along by a silent lady-in-waiting, it was all Sophie could do not to stare open-mouthed at the opulence of the *zenana*. They had passed through a series of antechambers, marking the end of the outside world, separating the women's palace, the architecture changing to a careful construction of windowless spaces with mirrored walls, delicate fretwork panels and shielded openings placed way up high beyond the reach of prying eyes. There were no secret doors here, no hidden panels or telltale lines in the marble. Sophie wondered if the dark passages extended this far into the palace, if she and Jag had passed behind any of these rooms, her hand held tightly in his. Perhaps he was there now, following her silently, listening for her footsteps.

Slow-moving *punkahs* waved regally from the high ceilings and enormous latticed arches, cooling the thin air as it moved through the women's palace, taming the rising heat of the season. Rich perfume filled the rooms, deep notes of sandalwood and tuberose, thin trails of incense lifting from pierced brass ornaments placed intermittently on the floor. Freshly plucked flowers floated in wide stone dishes filled with crystal-clear water, punctuating the way to the First Maharani's apartments, walls of pink marble inlaid with delicate designs of blue lapis lazuli and green agate, paintings hung upon them. Sophie kept her eyes averted, thinking of the painted faces of the men and women entwined together in the pictures gracing the walls of the Maharaja's personal study. She had seen them only once, peering into the panels until she realized the nature of the depictions before turning quickly away, cheeks burning.

Two silk-upholstered seats, balloon-backed mahogany in Victorian style, had been provided for Sophie and Mrs. Ripperton, while the First Maharani lounged on a raised dais covered in fine rugs, propped up on enormous cushions of bright jade green and saffron yellow, surrounded by her colorful retinue of ladies-in-waiting, who sat around her, two of them massaging her hands with perfumed oil, her wrists heavy with golden bangles.

Much to Sophie's surprise, the Maharani's command of English was unshakable. On occasion, there would be a sudden break in the conversation and she would speak to her ladies in dialect, translating any salient or amusing points that had passed. Sometimes they would begin to converse among themselves, pausing to stare at Sophie or at Mrs. Ripperton before chattering on or breaking into gales of laughter.

There was no need to be delicate here. The First Maharani loved to talk, asking question after question to satisfy her endless curiosity, and no subject was off limits. Sophie learned that Her Highness had been betrothed to the Maharaja since her infancy, but never met him to talk to until they were married. She thought nothing of asking how much money one's husband had, or about a woman's personal relations, or what undergarments one was wearing. Mrs. Ripperton was well used to this, and revealed to Sophie later that she had even lifted her skirt once to display her enormous petticoat, much to the ladies' delight. The Maharani had promptly instructed her *darzee* to make a dozen of them for Mrs. Ripperton in every shade, from scarlet to primrose, using her very best silks.

Today's conversation had begun with some polite enquiries about the nearby mission, the Maharani aware that Mrs. Ripperton was a keen volunteer there, and had then meandered to the general subject of religion, the women debating the pointlessness of the early missionaries who had attempted to convert India's masses to Christianity. It was, after all, a relatively new religion in comparison to their many more thousands of years of idolatry. Mrs.

Ripperton joined in with gusto, debating the finer points of various Christian church rituals and listening with interest when the Maharani knocked her down.

"Hindu wisdom says that we are but dreams of dreaming, which no real person dreams," explained the Maharani. "We are nothing, and the sooner we cease to have the horrible feeling of being something, the better. Everything is an illusion, and the sooner an illusion fades and we sink back into Brahma, the eternal place of nothingness, the sooner we shall escape this tormenting deceit called Life."

"Then why not just commit suicide and be done with it?" Mrs. Ripperton said, cheerfully accepting a sweet from the silver salver offered by one of the ladies and taking a confident bite.

"Because then I would invite bad karma, and my life of good deeds would be entirely undone! Karma is very important. Live a good life. Be good. You never know when your time will come. I am not afraid of death. By living a good life, I am always ready, for one does not know when death will come, as it does, like a thief."

"Calmer? Whatever do you mean, Your Highness?"

The Maharani said something to her ladies, inciting a fit of giggles, then returned to Mrs. Ripperton patiently. "To poison my imaginary body would only prolong the illusory agony, for I will be reborn in the form of my illusion, perhaps as a poisonous snake."

"How very peculiar."

"The deeds I do in this life will determine the destiny and the future incarnation of my soul. A man who steals honey may come back as a stinging insect. One who steals meat will appear as a vulture. The soul may crawl like a snake, bloom as a flower, or reign as a god, like the Maharaja himself." One of the Maharani's ladies leaned into her ear and said something. The Maharani listened and smiled. "Yes," she said. "A woman who dies in the lifetime of her husband goes at once to bliss, where she enjoys much blessedness and receives a crown."

"What if His Highness…" Fiona searched for an appropriate

expression for a dead king. "What if he *expires* before you do, Your Highness?"

"I will tell you," she said. "Many years ago, my husband and I made an offering to the gods by fire, and that fire has been kept alive ever since. The first of us to die will have our funeral pyre lit with its sacred flame. It has the power to save the soul from rebirths." She leaned back on her cushion and smiled. "You may call it an insurance policy, if you like."

"I rather like the sound of all that," Mrs. Ripperton said. "What about you, Sophie? What would you like to come back as?"

Sophie thought for a while and could conjure only one thing. "A bird," she said tentatively. "A bird, so I could fly anywhere."

"Ah!" said the Maharani. She spoke to her ladies again, and they all disappeared into deep conversation with no regard to their guests. Sophie sat and waited awkwardly, fiddling with her cup and saucer. The sweets did look awfully good, but she was afraid that if she accepted one, she might put it in her mouth and find it horrible, and that would be a problem indeed. She'd either have to spit it out, which was unthinkable, or eat it, which might turn out to be a great deal worse. Mrs. Ripperton finished the last morsel of her confection, mumbling of its deliciousness, then noticed where Sophie's eyes had fallen.

"Help yourself, dear! I have no idea what they are, but they're absolutely wonderful!" Sophie smiled nervously. "Oh, don't take any notice of them." Mrs. Ripperton nodded toward the ladies, immersed in debate with the First Maharani. "They could go on for hours. Time is of no consequence here. As the Maharani says, 'leave time for dogs and apes.' Rather good that, don't you think? We'll just sit here and listen or have a little natter between ourselves. It's perfectly all right. If you express an interest in her baubles, the Maharani might even show you some of her jewels. She has a box of pearls the size of ping-pong balls!"

Noticing Mrs. Ripperton's mouth empty, one of the ladies

offered her the dish again. This time, Sophie reached forward too, but before she could make her choice…

"Try one of those, dear." Mrs. Ripperton pointed at a tiny pastry affair with delicate layers, soaked in honeyed syrup, the top sprinkled with tiny pale green flecks. "They're a bit sticky, but quite scrumptious!"

Sophie picked one up, half inspected it and popped it into her mouth. In a flash of panic, she realized immediately that she should have bitten it in half, the sweet just a little too big, but it had looked as though it would disintegrate at the merest wisp of breeze, so in it had gone, whole. She sat for a moment, unsure of what to do, then raised her hand delicately to her mouth to conceal the unavoidable ugliness of her first chew. One of the ladies watched on and nudged her smiling companion. Sophie shrugged a small apology and nodded her approval at them, her mouth plunged into utter bliss, the pastry melting into a rich sensation of heavenly sweetness, layer upon layer of delicate taste explosions dancing on her tongue. She accepted another smaller one from the quickly outstretched dish and made a bungling attempt to express her appreciation in Hindi, much to the ladies' amusement. Then, unable to help herself, she half closed her eyes, a murmur of satisfaction on her lips as she ate the sweet and enjoyed the ladies' cheerful curiosity. One of them slid toward her, curling herself comfortably beside Sophie's chair. Without asking, she took Sophie's hand and opened it, examining her palm. Mrs. Ripperton smiled at Sophie.

"Isn't this fun?"

Sophie nodded, widening her eyes, her free hand at her mouth again as she cleared the last remnants. The lady-in-waiting traced Sophie's lines with her fingertip, turning now and then to whisper to her companions before smiling up at Sophie, finally patting her hand and returning it to her before sliding away. Sophie watched all this with intense fascination, the way they sat together, almost entwined, one hand resting on another's thigh, their saris spilling colorful silken folds that spread out about them. She turned to

Mrs. Ripperton and smiled in a way that she hoped would make up for the bicycle rickshaw incident. Fiona had excelled herself. Not only was this the most fun Sophie had had in ages, but it was piqued by an extra frisson of excitement simply by knowing just how enraged her mother would be if she had any idea where she was at this precise moment, deep in the very seat of heathen evil. It felt like a kind of paradise, this secret place of women, fragranced with flowers, heady jasmine oil, and burning incense. She and Mrs. Ripperton would never tell a soul that they had been here, and Sophie hoped more than anything that she would be asked to come back and that she might be permitted to dispense with the chair and to lounge on fine rugs and silk cushions and lean in and hear the whispers that passed between them.

The First Maharani quieted her entourage with a wave of her perfumed hand and sat upright. All eyes turned to Sophie.

"You must be in love," she said. One of her ladies leaned in and whispered something in her ear. The Maharani smiled. "A girl who wishes to become a bird must surely want to find her way to her lover, so that she may watch over him wherever he goes." She leaned back on her cushion, her jewelry tinkling. "So tell us, little bird, are we correct?"

Sophie flushed scarlet. She felt her blood racing, the fine hairs at the back of her neck rising and standing on end as though Jag had reached out invisibly from a hidden shadow and touched her, a small shudder passing through her flesh.

"Sophie!" Mrs. Ripperton stared at her. "Have you been keeping secrets from your Aunt Fifi?"

"Of course not." Sophie tried to compose herself while the First Maharani's ladies laughed like hyenas, congratulating each other on the accuracy of their prediction. "Don't be silly. It's just a bit embarrassing to be laughed at, that's all."

"I'm afraid your ladies are incorrect," Mrs. Ripperton said to the Maharani, patting Sophie's hand reassuringly. "Miss Schofield has yet to meet the love of her life. She was whisked away from

England before she'd had a chance to set her cap at anybody, but I have no doubt that she'll be swept off her feet soon enough when she gets back. You never know, she might even meet somebody while she's out here! Perhaps we should ask Dr. Reeves to invite his two sons for Christmas. I've seen a photograph of the older one. He's a lawyer, and he's really quite a dish!"

"Dish?" the Maharani said. "What is this dish?"

Mrs. Ripperton explained the expression, the Maharani translating to her ladies. While the women of the *zenana* laughed along with Mrs. Ripperton, the First Maharani set her eyes upon Sophie and smiled a knowing smile.

9

"I have a good mind to tell the Maharaja that I am neither a nurse-maid nor a veterinary," said Dr. Schofield, irritably forking his curried mutton. "If it were up to me, I'd shoot the damn horse and her too while I'm at it. There's nothing wrong with her, you know, but here we all go again with her *waah! woo!*" He threw his hands up and jangled his fingers, mimicking the Second Maharani, who was now claiming to have a dicky heart and making sure that everybody knew about it. His wife ignored him, concentrating on her plate.

Dr. Schofield could barely remember when the joy had gone out of his wife. She had been pleasant company once, before Sophie was born. At least that was the way he preferred to remember it, although it all seemed such a long time ago now that he found himself suspicious of his own memories. They were not to be relied upon. He had purged the worst of them as the years slid by to disguise this stagnant marriage, while Veronica disappeared into her endless abyss of misery. It was nothing to do with them coming out to India, as she had claimed. Of that he was certain. She could be equally miserable anywhere, and he had found it exhausting. At least here, he had reasoned, she would be forced to put her head above the parapet and face the fact that she was not the only one. There were other people in this world too, people who should matter to her, but she gave neither him nor Sophie any companionship or succor.

Dr. Schofield had already decided that they would stay on in

India. The trouble would be bound to die down in another month or two. Everybody had known that the business of partition would not be without its teething problems, but nobody had anticipated the scale of it. At first, people thought it would quickly blow over. They had all heard the news reports, but the Indians were fond of exaggeration, and the claims that hundreds of thousands of people had been slaughtered had undoubtedly been blown up out of all proportion. At least that had been the general opinion of the conversation between the palace officials, although as the weeks wore on, they seemed less convinced. Reports started to get through about whole trains arriving at their stations filled with nothing but dead bodies. There was fighting everywhere. Millions of people were on the move, searching for new borders that nobody could find, the partition lines making no sense, zigzagging through farms and open fields, ignoring the natural boundaries of the landscape.

Whatever was going on, the situation would be bound to settle eventually, and George Schofield had no intention of going back to the dreary grayness of their life in London.

❧

Wartime India had been the happiest time of George Schofield's life. He had been posted to Kohima shortly before the Japanese invaded, attending to the sick and injured, bandaging wounds, hacking off gangrenous limbs with half-blunt instruments that had seen too many bones. The supplies had run out quickly and there was no way to get anything, or anyone, in or out, the city surrounded. He had wanted to run away from it all, such was his sense of helplessness, to just up in the middle of the night and desert the horrors, taking his chances through the lines. But those thoughts were quickly dismissed. They had all had them at one time or another. Yet there was something about the place that had got under his skin, just the way it did with some people.

When the war ended, the demobbing process had started while

British servicemen were still on Indian soil, and a great many of the men failed to return home. The Ministry of Defense soon found itself on the receiving end of too many complaints from abandoned wives and quickly put an end to demobbing overseas, shipping the rest of the men home first so that if they wanted to abscond to the tropics and take up with an exotic lover, they would have to do so at their own expense. Had it not been for Sophie, George Schofield might have been sorely tempted to do just that. There were far worse places a man could live.

Perhaps, once they were done with the palace, he would open up a small practice somewhere scenic and popular with the British diehards. Plenty of people had elected to stay on. There were any number of enclaves dotted here and there around the country, places that were referred to as Little England or India's Sussex. If one were to look at a photograph, one could be forgiven for assuming it had been taken in the Lake District, or even in an Alpine village with cuckoo-clock chalets perched on evergreen hillsides, and the climate in some of these locations was said to be near perfect. Dr. Schofield had a few places loosely in mind, Simla perhaps, although it would be far too cold during the winter months, and they would be wise to stay away from the northern states, which seemed to be bearing the brunt of the discord. Somewhere in the south then, in the Nilgiris maybe. For certain, their funds would go a great deal further here than they would back in England. They could live very comfortably for the rest of their days if they so wished. Back home, servants would be out of the question, and they had quickly become used to the convenience of being waited upon.

India had been good for Sophie too. He had seen the change in her soon after they arrived. Perhaps it was from the sun that shone tirelessly upon one's face, or the feeling of space from the wide plains that opened up beyond the palace walls, the view stretching all the way down to the delta demarking the neighboring state. Sophie had begun to blossom in a way he had feared she never would when they were in England, the ready smile she wore lately filling him with joy and relief. He would watch her sometimes, purposefully walking through the grounds, always on her way somewhere. She had taken the palace to her heart, and it had brought her out of herself, out of the shell that she had retreated into. It had broken his heart to see her so young yet so unhappy, but how can you explain to your child that their time will come? That life will find them one way or another and that they too will make a place for themselves? There is no use in telling the young that they must be patient, for they have not yet lived long enough to know what patience means and that there is no escaping the ellipse of one's destiny. They had made poor parents, he and Veronica, with Sophie caught in the middle of their many faults and shortcomings. It was not the kind of family setting he would have wished for her, nor for himself for that matter. They would be better off staying here until she was ready to spread her wings. As far as he was concerned, the decision was already made, although he had yet to speak to his wife.

10

J ag worked through the day's heat with a heavy heart. He had seen so little of Sophie since the night in the water garden over two months ago: a few snatched minutes here and there, a rare hour when he could sneak away for long enough. He could think of nothing else, yearning for just one brief glimpse of her.

The staff who remained were faced with tasks enough for ten men each day. His father had put him to work from sunrise to sunset, leaving him little opportunity to slip away. There was always someone calling for him to do this or do that, and he had choked back angry tears when he had been discovered, time after time, and foiled in his attempt to escape. He had wanted to send word to her, to let her know that he was thinking of her, to tell her how he longed to be with her, but to send a message would be impossible. He would just have to wait, and he already knew that he would wait for the rest of his life if that was what it took. In the meantime, he was grateful for the exhausting work, his disquieted body tired and aching at the end of each long day. Without the hard labor, he doubted he would have been able to sleep at all. As it was, when he did fall asleep, his dreams were filled with her, and when he woke with the dawn, she would be his first thought and he would pray that she was thinking of him too.

His heart was spent. He had known it from the very moment he felt her soft lips upon his. It had felt like he was sinking into the ground, like a setting sun releasing all its color into the sky, his body no longer his own, but a part of the wide-open universe that surrounded them on that dark night under a shower of falling stars. He could not live without her. That much he knew. But what was he to do when he could not find a moment's peace? It plagued his every waking hour. The world was a different place now, this country a new dominion of endless possibilities where anything could happen. A free country that would never again allow the subjugation of its people. They were equals, all of them. She would be his, and he hers, if only he could find a way.

Jag washed the fatigue from his limbs, leaning over the stone trough set into the wall of the *pilkhana*, throwing water over his head, feeling his skin breathing in relief as the thick scent of elephants and straw dust came away. He dried himself with a cotton rag, put on clean clothes, and walked home, concentrating on the ground, deep in thought. Turning into the courtyard before the quarters in which they lived, he saw his father sitting cross-legged on the floor, his face set with a look of such distress that Jag found himself running to him, asking what the matter was. The way his father looked at him brought his heart to a standstill.

"Father?"

"My son." His father remained seated and glared up at him gravely. "What have you done?"

"Father?"

"I will ask you again, my son, and you will think very carefully before you give me your answer. Do you understand?" Jag nodded. His father spoke more slowly, stressing each syllable, drawing each word out like a sword. "What have you done to shame your parents?" Jag looked at him in confusion, his mind at once a blank, yet filled with the deafening sound of his own blood. "Do you know how many years I have been in service to His Highness?"

"Twenty-six years, my father."

His father nodded emptily at the ground. "Twenty-six years."

"Yes, Father."

"All so that you could have a good life, with food in your mouth, an education under your belt, and a fine employer to provide for us and protect us. And this is how you repay me?" Jag felt his insides turn over.

His father shook his head silently, breathing deeply for a while, as though it would do no good. He got up and went to the doorway of their home, pausing at the entrance, taking in the room before him: the spartan furniture, the small shelf that served as a shrine to his dead wife's memory, on which he placed fresh flowers every day and lit a small clay oil lamp at night. "You were born in this very room," he said. "Your mother died on this very spot in order to give you life. She could have been saved if you had been sacrificed, but she refused." His father looked to the floor. "She knew from the very beginning that you would be a son, and she foretold that you would grow up to be a great man. I wanted her to live. I wanted her by my side for the rest of our lives as we had promised each other. But she would not listen. It was the greatest gift she could bestow upon me, and the sole purpose of her life. A son. A son for whom she died. And *this* is how you repay her?"

Jag stared at his father, unable to speak. From somewhere deep inside of his father rose an unfamiliar voice, filled with rage. The veins in his neck swelled. His lips tightened. "Is it true, what I have heard? About you and the girl?" Jag felt the blood drain from his face. "Answer me before I shake the life out of you!" His father raised a hand in threat.

Jag hung his head in shame. "Yes, Father."

He waited for the blow to land, but nothing came. Instead, when he lifted his head, he saw that his father's face had crumpled. His father wandered into the corner and looked silently around the small room, as though taking it all in.

"Then there is nothing to be done. There is talk around the palace. I refused to believe it. My son would never do such a thing. Who would do such a thing?" Jag's father turned to him in disbelief. "You have brought shame upon us. And now we will have to pay the price."

"But Father…"

"I will request an audience with the head of household tomorrow." He picked up a wilting bloom from his dead wife's shrine and held it in his hand. "I will tell him that we have done the Maharaja a great wrong and beg his forgiveness. Then we shall gather up our things and leave the palace with our heads hung in shame."

"No!"

"We cannot live here, not now that you have brought this disgrace upon us. I shall pray that the gods forgive you. As for me, I am not sure that I ever will."

"No! It is not like that!"

"Enough!" his father said. "I have spoken."

"Listen to me!" Jag stood his ground. "There has been no wrongdoing. I love her as deeply as you loved my mother. How can that be wrong?"

"Love?" His father's anger exploded upon him. "How dare you speak of love! You know nothing! Love is meant only for those who are betrothed and married by the will of their parents and the blessing of the gods. That is what love is. It is about a lifetime of devotion to each other, to the sacrifice of your own life if that is what is demanded of you. Only when you have known the suffering I have known can you look a man in the eye and tell him you know what love is."

"But I do know."

"Enough!" Jag could not remember a time when he had seen his father enraged like this, his hands shaking. "You will never speak another word of this! Do you understand? And you will stay right here until it is settled. You are not to leave this room for one minute, or I swear I will bring the wrath of the gods down upon you. My own son!"

Mrs. Schofield slid a spoonful of sugar into the coffee she didn't want and feigned polite interest in the conversation that circled Mrs.

Ripperton's sitting room. Any talk of politics was considered vulgar, as was the mention of the terrible massacres that had taken place up and down the country. With the newspapers and palace whispers filled with little else, this had the effect of obliterating any real sense of authentic exchange. Few topics remained on safe ground, so all conversation had to be carefully orchestrated and skillfully conducted away from anything that might cause one of the women to breach etiquette and fall from her perch. An unspoken discomfort filled the room now that they had all been relegated from ruling class to mere guests in this country, as though a collective sense of guilt was being pushed under the carpet, the lumps disguised with rigid smiles and wistful conversation about the old days.

The prison block remained a popular topic behind the dainty teacups. That women should be incarcerated like that for the rest of their lives was proof indeed of how much this country had yet to learn and how backward its people were. The subject was a welcome source of endless tattling, filled with high-minded opinions and much shaking of heads, yet there were some among the wives who privately could think of far worse things than to live in luxury in the exclusive domain of female company with nothing much to do all day but please oneself and order servants around while trying on fabulous jewels.

Mrs. Ripperton pressed a piece of shortbread upon Mrs. Schofield and steered the conversation toward the story she had picked up, sharing the report that the Maharaja's intended new bride suffered from a rare congenital disorder that had left her covered in hair from head to toe. Nobody had any idea where Mrs. Ripperton got her information from, but she was always the bearer of the latest interesting snippet of news. Anyone would have thought that she had the First Maharani's ear, although that couldn't possibly be the case. None of the wives would lower themselves to visiting the *zenana*. For one thing, they would be expected to stoop to a low curtsey and to call the Maharanis *Your Highness*, and that would never do.

Mrs. Schofield stifled an inward sigh. Among the many rumors doing the rounds of the palace and its six hundred staff, a whisper had circulated as far as the ADC's room that her daughter had been holding secret liaisons with a boy, the son of one of the Maharaja's personal bearers. Mrs. Ripperton had taken Mrs. Schofield aside to tell her what she had heard and to assure her that she had quashed it as nonsense. There was always some tongue-wagging going on in corners, disgruntled servants making trouble and spreading malicious lies, and Mrs. Ripperton had said that one of the maids had probably been behind it. Mrs. Schofield had received the report stiffly, holding her face in check while her blood boiled.

Dr. Schofield paced his study, the low afternoon sun slicing through the shutters, casting bright slats across the room, catching the sparkling airborne dust. Sophie sat miserably in the chair while he hauled her over the coals as his wife had demanded.

"How many times must we tell you not to fraternize with the staff?" Dr. Schofield pulled his tie from his collar in exasperation. "It really won't do, Sophie. You know that we have nothing against these people, but you must learn to keep yourself to yourself. What on earth were you doing there?"

"Nothing." Sophie stared down at her hands clasped nervously in her lap. She felt sick, down to the pit of her stomach.

"There's no such thing as nothing, my girl, and you know what the servants are like. They're never happier than when they're going around spying on everyone and spreading poison about the *sahibs*. We're not the most popular people after all the trouble that's gone on, and now you've given them enough ammunition to make us look ridiculous." Her father sighed heavily. "It really was a very irresponsible thing to do, darling. A girl of your age? You should know better."

Mrs. Schofield took up the baton, this time shouting, cheeks flushed with fury. "Do you have any idea what would happen to any girl caught alone with a boy in this country?" This humiliation was simply the last straw. She had died a thousand deaths when Mrs. Ripperton told her, her skin still shrinking with the disgrace of it. She could have sworn that she detected a note of *schadenfreude* in the woman's voice. It seemed to her that Mrs. Ripperton had waited a long time for this, to make a mockery of her and her family, just as she always knew she would. They were all the same, the British women out here, spouting their high ideals while forgetting their own morals. Not only was Mrs. Ripperton a shameless glutton, she was a busybody too, and a ruthless gossip. Mrs. Schofield had no doubt that Mrs. Ripperton had probably been the source of the rumor in the first place. What she hadn't banked on was that the rumor might actually be true.

"We were only talking," said Sophie.

"Talking?" her mother demanded. "What could you possibly have to say to a boy like that? You stupid, *stupid* girl! You are not to speak to him anymore, do you hear me? I will not have people ridiculing us or questioning my daughter's conduct. These people may be heathen, but no Indian girl would dare be caught alone in the company of a boy. Her whole family would be ruined."

"I'm not Indian," Sophie mumbled.

"More's the pity," her father said, attempting to deflect his wife's anger. "Otherwise you might have exercised better judgment. Really, Sophie." His tone softened. "What on earth are we to do with you?"

"You should have thought about that before you dragged us out here!" Mrs. Schofield snapped at him, venting her frustration. It was all very well for him. He was thoroughly occupied most days, being taken hither and thither, enjoying the high regard that doctors do, whereas her days stretched out interminably. She simply couldn't understand all this India business. It was a ghastly, disease-ridden place, its people either crawling through squalor or living like Croesus. As for the Maharaja, he was the most ridiculous

figure she had ever seen, preening like a fat peacock, keeping a
harem of sluts for his pleasure. She had glimpsed him on one occasion, during one of their barbarian festivals, looking like a spoiled,
overfed tribesman in his gilded finery, riding atop a caparisoned
elephant in his giant silver howdah. The pomposity of it all was
grotesque, from the way he threw coins into the gutter for children
to scrabble over in the filth, to the manner in which he transported
his heathen wives in sheeted palanquins. It disgusted her. Some
took to the place like a duck to water, of course, but they were the
kind of people who didn't really belong anywhere else, lame or
eccentric types who would have a hard time fitting in with polite
society at home. Quite a few of them were clearly soft in the head,
that blasted Ripperton woman included. And as for the ones who
had *gone native*, well, the less said about them the better.

"You should have left us behind instead of dragging us out
here," said Mrs. Schofield, her shrill voice piercing right through
her husband. "You have no idea just how out of place one feels
here. It's exhausting. And as for you." She started on her daughter
again. "You are not to speak to that boy ever again. Do I make
myself clear?"

"Yes, Mother."

"If we knew who he was, we would have him dismissed
immediately."

Sophie had remained tight-lipped on the matter of Jag's iden-
tity, saying that she did not know what his name was or his role
in the household. She flatly denied that he was the son of the
Maharaja's bearer, her face so highly colored anyway that she felt
sure that the lie would pass unnoticed. The Maharaja had lots of
bearers. All she would say was that he was a boy who she had
bumped into on occasion and that that was all she knew.

"You are never again to see him, do you hear me?"

"Yes." Sophie stared at the rug, unable to look at her mother.
She had seen so little of Jag lately that it felt like less of a lie. And
when she had seen him, it had been unbearable, the two of them

burning up inside. She would feel herself trembling as they whispered to each other, hidden in the shadows of their secret passages, his arms around her as they made promises they couldn't possibly hope to keep.

"I think that's quite enough for one evening," Dr. Schofield said, bringing the subject to a close. He had been planning to speak to Veronica tonight about the matter of their staying on. She wouldn't be happy about it, but he had no doubt that he could make it sound palatable, attractive even, given reasonable conditions and a fair wind. Yet the moment had gone. That had been evident the second he stepped in through the door to find his wife in a state of high anxiety, screaming like a banshee, and his daughter aflood with tears. The brooch would just have to stay in his pocket for the time being, a gift he had picked up to soften his increasingly brittle wife. One of these days, he would stop bothering.

ↄ⁄◎Ↄ

Lying in her bed waiting for sleep to come, Sophie finally felt herself drifting off, the faint night breeze seeping deliciously through the open window, playing with the thin suggestion of the mosquito net that shrouded her bed. A small sound crept into her half-sleep, like a pin dropping to a marble floor. She sank deeply into her pillows, yearning for her dreams to take hold.

Tap. Her eyes opened. Again came the noise, a little harsher, *tap-tap*, and the skittering of a tiny stone as it rolled across her bedroom floor. She looked to the window and blinked herself awake. In the dark, moonless night, the leaf-thin curtain twitched and in came another pebble, bouncing sharply and rattling away.

Sophie flew out of bed, wrenching the mosquito net aside, snatching up her dressing gown and throwing it about her shoulders. She lit a candle, cupping the flame with her hand, illuminating the room in a soft glow, her bare feet crossing silently to the window in quick strides. Pulling back the curtain, she peered out, looking for movement below. Jag stared up at her from the shadows.

"Jag!" Overjoyed as she was to see him, she found herself immediately overwrought and covered her mouth, aware that her parents were just a few rooms away, the terrible dressing-down and subsequent row between them still ringing fresh in her ears three days later. He had never dared to come near their quarters before, and if they were to be found like this, there would be untold trouble. "What are you doing here?" she whispered.

"Come down!" he said. "I have to talk to you."

"I can't! My parents are still up." Sophie glanced anxiously over her shoulder to the closed door of her bedroom. "Where have you been? I've been searching everywhere for you!"

"Yes, you can! You must! It's important!"

"Somebody told my mother about us. Now they've said I'm not allowed to see you or speak to you and they won't let me out of their sight."

"I know," he said, his hands clenching into tight fists. "That is why I have not seen you. We have to talk. We must hurry before I am missed."

For a moment, Sophie thought she heard a movement at her door. She raised a hand of warning to Jag and rushed inside, listening intently, waiting until she was sure that the danger had passed before returning to the window.

"There is no way for me to get out," she said. "We will have to meet tomorrow. Somewhere that nobody will see us. Just tell me when and where and I will wait for you. But right now, you have to go. If you are caught, my mother will have you dismissed. Hurry! You must go."

Jag put his head in his hands and let out a small cry of anguish. He turned this way and that, as if looking for some secret passage that might take him to her, but there were none in this part of the palace. "Please!" he implored her. "You must come down."

"What is it? What's the matter?"

"We are leaving," he said.

"What?" Sophie felt her chest turn over. "When?"

"Tomorrow, first thing. My father asked the Maharaja to release him so that he can return to our family."

"No!" Sophie cried softly, hands flying to her face. "You can't leave me here on my own!"

"I have no choice," he said grimly. "I cannot leave my father. It would kill him."

"Jag! Please, no! What will I do without you?" Again she threw a glance behind her, in the hope that there might be some escape. But there was none.

"We can write to each other," he said.

"But how? We will be leaving soon too, and I have no address to give you, and nobody will allow me a letter from you anyway."

"Then you must write to me," Jag said.

"How will I know where you are?"

"I have an aunt who lives in Amritsar. That is where we are going. My uncle is a shoemaker." Jag took a scrap of paper from his pocket. "I have written the address." He bent to the ground and picked up a stone, wrapped the paper around it, and threw it up to the window, where it sailed past Sophie's shoulder, landing with a dull thud on the rug behind her. "This is as much as I can give you."

"No!" Sophie said. "Please! I don't want you to go. What if I cannot find you? What if you cannot find me?" She felt sick, so sick that her skin became clammy. "We might never see each other again."

Jag knew this to be true, but in that moment there was nothing else he could think of to say. "Don't worry," he said, yearning to hold her as her face betrayed its despair. "We will travel quickly and safely, and as soon as we arrive I will get a message to you. I will get a message to you before you leave here." Sophie began to cry. "Don't cry, Sophie! Please don't cry!" She pressed her face into her hands, unable to speak.

In the distance, voices came through the darkness. Jag looked over his shoulder, his face twisted with desperation. "I have to go," he said. Sophie reached behind her neck and undid the clasp of her necklace, a small gold locket that held a picture of her parents.

"Here." She held her hand out of the window, dropping the locket down to him. "This is all I have to give to you." He caught it easily and held it tight.

"I will find you, Sophie. I promise. You'll see."

And with that, he turned and disappeared into the darkness, Sophie watching after him long after his shadow faded from view.

Through the open window, night moths flew in, heading toward the candle's flame.

11

"What's the matter with you?" Mrs. Schofield glared at her daughter. "I hope we're not going to be subjected to another one of your enormous sulks today. That won't get you anywhere, young lady. I have a good mind to pack us up and leave him to it. Of all the selfish—"

"Mother, please." Sophie continued to try to reason with her mother, tiring as it was, when all she really wanted was to go to her room and lie down. Whether it was due to the heat or the grief of her loss, she didn't care. Wrung out and tearful, she didn't have the energy for this today, her mother sapping every last shred from her. "He only wants what's best for us."

"No, he doesn't. He wants only to please himself. He couldn't give two figs about anyone else. It's this godless country. Put a man here for ten minutes and all of a sudden, his wife's opinion counts for nothing. It's a disgrace. He knows very well how we hate it here."

"I don't hate it here."

"Of course you do. I've seen your sniveling. I'm not blind. You're just taking his side, as usual. I've told him, one year. That's all. Just one year and we will be going straight back to England whether he likes it or not. And if he doesn't like it, then we'll damn well go without him. I've put up with far more than I should have done, and now I'm expected to stay here indefinitely on his whim? He's the most selfish man I've ever met. I knew very well that it was a mistake to marry him, and I wasn't wrong." Mrs. Schofield counted her blouses and made an angry note on her list.

She didn't trust the *dhobi wallah* and kept a detailed inventory of every last little thing that was taken for laundering. "And I do wish you'd stop moping around." She picked up the blouses and shoved them angrily into a drawer. "You should be at the mission, putting your time to good use."

Sophie sat on the edge of the bed and felt her head spin. Her father had proposed they stay on at the palace for another six months, after which they would travel down to Ooty for a holiday, to see how well they liked it, *to test the waters*, he said. The Rippertons had rented a summer house there for some years running, and Mrs. Ripperton couldn't speak highly enough of the place, saying that she and Rip had always planned to retire there, if only he could be persuaded to give up work. She had shown them some photographs in an album over tea in her apartments one afternoon, and it did look beautiful, set in the cool blue hills of the south, the climate more in keeping with an English garden than a desert plain. Despite her father's enthusiasm, her mother had not greeted his decision kindly.

Dr. Schofield had assured Sophie that her mother would be sure to fall in love with Ooty, given a little time. The brooch had helped a little. Veronica's face had been a picture when she opened it, the tight smile she offered him a good deal more than he had had from her these last few months. His only regret was that he had not thought to bring anything for his daughter, who bore the news brightly enough, given her general unwellness. She had fallen prey to the sort of sickness that occasionally troubled one of them, caused invariably by a lapse in concentration with regard to the water supply. He had suffered a devilish bout of it himself not so long ago as a result of a careless wet shave. Dr. Schofield kept an eye on his daughter and made a mental note to have Dr. Reeves take a look at her if things didn't improve. One could never be too careful, and it had crossed his mind that she might have picked up a parasite. Dr. Reeves had been here for years and might be better qualified to spot the signs.

"How was your day today, my dear?" Dr. Schofield smiled patiently at his wife over the supper table, the one time of day when his family sat together lately since Veronica had started taking breakfast in her room.

"As well as can be expected, given the upheaval you've decided to subject us all to," she replied. "I wrote to Mother this morning, asking her to send out more clothing."

"Why don't you order some things from one of the big stores in Delhi? Fi Ripperton can tell you where to go. She's always ordering something or other."

"No, thank you," Mrs. Schofield said. "I'd rather send home for them."

"But this is home." Dr. Schofield reached his hand across the table to cover hers. "At least for a little while. So why not do as the Romans do, hmm?"

Veronica's hand shrank away. She picked up her cutlery and attended to her plate of plain grilled chicken with boiled potatoes. She couldn't tolerate Indian food, the very thought of it making her stomach turn, and their cook had daily instructions to serve her meals plain, with salt and pepper provided in a cruet set from which she would help herself if she deemed it necessary. She abhorred the thought of his black hands touching her food and had to put it firmly out of her mind.

"I'm sure we can manage with what we have." Dr. Schofield spoke to his daughter. "We'll just have to work it out, won't we, Sophie?"

Sophie stared down at her supper, a simple plate of dhal and rice given to her in the hope that she could be tempted into eating more than the few small mouthfuls she had managed recently.

"Sophie?" Dr. Schofield peered at her. She didn't answer. "Sophie?" He stood from his chair. "Veronica!" he shouted to his wife. "Quickly!"

Sophie buckled in her seat, clutching at the table to steady herself as her face turned gray, pulling the cloth and everything laid upon it to the floor with an almighty crash.

Dr. Reeves emerged from Sophie's bedroom, his face set with grim determination as he closed the door quietly and came away.

"She's sleeping now," he said to her waiting parents in the sitting room. "I've given her an anti-emetic to stop the sickness and a mild sedative to help her rest."

"What's the matter with her?" Mrs. Schofield demanded, wringing her handkerchief. "Will she be all right?"

"Yes," Dr. Reeves assured her. "She'll be fine. She just needs to rest. See to it that she stays in bed for a few days, and no rich food. Some beef tea and toast. Perhaps a light vegetable broth, a few slices of banana. Coconut water would be good." He noted Mrs. Schofield's eyebrow, raised in disapproval. "It's very nourishing, no matter what it looks like. Just make sure she eats little and often and stays off her feet for a while. I'll pop back and check in on her tomorrow."

"This place is full of disease," Mrs. Schofield said. "It's a wonder we haven't all gone down with the cholera, the state of the water."

Dr. Reeves gathered up his bag and made ready to leave.

"Not staying for a peg?" Dr. Schofield said hopefully.

"No thanks, George." He gave him a brief smile. "I'll catch up with you in the morning. I think we've all had enough stimulation for one evening." He patted his friend on the back. "Try to get some rest, the pair of you. And don't worry about Sophie. She'll be fine."

The palace's clinic was housed in a wide bungalow set in the grounds behind the game lodge, where an open surgery was held five mornings a week for the household. The small waiting room was full, as was the norm on a Monday, with the usual collection of commonplace ailments ranging from bumps and bruises to amoebic dysentery. Most patients were usually dispatched within a matter of minutes with the necessary medicines to aid their recovery, some clutching a note excusing them from duties, trying to disguise their delight. The Maharaja made a point of preserving the health and well-being of his household—a most generous gesture considering the high level of pilferage that went on. The palace's supply rooms were said to resemble Fortnum & Mason, stacked from floor to ceiling with every conceivable delicacy. The wine cellar too was the envy of many a royal visitor, the vaults stocked with rare vintages and fine champagnes alongside crates of Johnny Walker whisky and Bombay Sapphire gin. The issue of temperature control was a constant headache and was attended to with great diligence, particularly in the dry season when the heat soared.

Everybody knew that the staff had been helping themselves for years, creating a localized black market that ran through the ranks, exchanging one favor for another, pockets lined along the way. It was believed that there was so much of everything that nobody would ever notice if something went missing, and nothing was allowed to run out anyway, so replacement stocks would arrive well before the store master ever got wind of a shortfall. Yet a problem had arisen. Word had gotten about that the new Third Maharani had decided to involve herself where she had no business and that she had demanded an inventory of the palace's supplies, intent on introducing a rationing system to stem the alarming outward flow of the Maharaja's reduced coffers. Such a move was unheard of. Everybody knew that no woman could possibly get to grips with something as complex as the palace accounts, yet that was exactly what she had set out to do, and according to the reports, she could even speak French, a language most of the staff had never even heard of. It was no wonder the waiting room was so full, thought

Dr. Schofield as he arrived ten minutes late. Half the palace must have been sick with worry that their tidy little arrangements were soon to be uncovered, with the inevitable punishment that would follow. A sacking at the very least. At worst, jail.

"Good morning, namaste, salaam!" Dr. Schofield said cheerily as he picked his way through the patients sitting on the floor, partially blocking the way to his chaotic consulting room. "Good morning, Miss Blanche," he added, passing the secretary. "A cup of tea whenever you're ready, please."

"Dr. Schofield..." she started, but he had already walked past her little window and entered his room, where Dr. Reeves sat waiting for him.

"Robert!" Dr. Schofield closed the door. He placed his sun hat on the stand and reached for his white coat, slipping off his jacket and replacing it with his daily uniform. "I was just about to come and find you to thank you for coming to our rescue last night. Veronica was almost hysterical." He dropped himself into his chair. "I've asked Briony to bring in some tea. We'll grab a few minutes before opening the floodgates, shall we?" Dr. Reeves shifted uncomfortably in his seat. "Poor Sophie. White as a sheet she was. I popped my head around her door this morning. Fast asleep, but it looked like some of the color had returned to her cheeks at least. Thank God it's nothing serious. I was beginning to wonder if she hadn't gone and picked up some kind of nasty—"

"George," Dr. Reeves interrupted him. Dr. Schofield looked up from his list of messages.

"What?"

"About Sophie."

It was the way Dr. Reeves said it. The way he fixed his colleague with the same benign expression they all used when delivering bad news. George Schofield had seen that look before many times and been the bearer of it often himself. The paper became still in his hand. "What?" he repeated. "What's the matter?"

Dr. Reeves drew a heavy breath and sat back a little, as though withered by the heat. "Before I tell you this, George, I want you to know that I am absolutely certain about it. God knows this is not the kind of news that I would deliver unless I was completely sure. I also want to say that if there is anything I can do, anything at all, you have only to say the word."

Dr. Schofield felt his blood run cold, and in that moment, he was reminded of all the textbooks, all the papers, all the cramming he had done on tropical diseases and the litany of early deaths visited upon so many of those who came out to live in these far-flung places.

"All right, Robert," he said quietly. "Just spit it out."

Dr. Reeves removed his spectacles and rubbed the bridge of his nose where they had pinched his skin. He let out a dismal sigh, took a handkerchief from his pocket, and began to clean the lenses. "I'm sorry, George." He paused a while, placing the spectacles back on his nose. "There's no easy way to tell you this." Robert Reeves looked his friend straight in the eye. "Sophie's pregnant."

12

D r. Schofield had no idea how long he sat there, staring blankly at Dr. Reeves while the enormity of his diagnosis sank in. The door opened, Miss Blanche steadying a small tray as she cleared a space on the desk. Neither of the men looked at her. She set the tray down quickly, uncomfortable in her apparent intrusion, and left the room. The tea remained untouched for a while, the thin curls of steam rising from the cups the only animation between them. At last, Dr. Reeves spoke.

"I know," he said, nodding slightly. "It's a shock, isn't it?"

"Christ." Dr. Schofield sat back in his chair, his arms resting limply against his sides. "Jesus Christ."

Dr. Reeves put some sugar in one of the cups, stirred it and placed it in front of his colleague. "Here," he said. "Drink this. We won a war on hot tea."

"How long?"

Dr. Reeves picked up the other cup and took a sip. "Three months, maybe four. I can't be entirely sure."

"And she knows, does she?"

"Oh, come on, George. She must do. I expect she was probably hoping it would all just go away if she ignored it long enough."

"Christ." Dr. Schofield took up his cup, feeling overwhelmed, as though he'd been knocked sideways by a truck. Almost to himself he said, "What the hell am I going to tell Veronica?"

"I can't help you there, my friend." Dr. Reeves thought for

a while. "But you won't be able to hold it off for long. She'll be starting to show soon."

Dr. Schofield could see no sliver of light between the two evils: the thought of his daughter ripening a bastard child and the prospect of breaking the news to his wife.

"Who else knows about this?"

"Nobody."

"And I can be assured of your strictest confidence?"

"Now, George. You know me better than that."

"You haven't told Kay?"

"No." Dr. Reeves shook his head. "And I won't do either. This is between you and me and these four walls."

"Jesus." Dr. Schofield put his cup down, took a deep breath, and got up. "Do you think you can handle that lot in the waiting room on your own?"

"Of course." Dr. Reeves stood too.

"I'd better go and tackle this now."

"And George?" Dr. Reeves stopped him as he headed toward the door, his hand resting on the handle, blocking his exit for a moment.

"What?"

"Go easy on her, huh?" He opened the door for him, resting a hand on his shoulder as he passed. "She's scared out of her wits. I think she's probably suffered enough already."

Dr. Schofield nodded briefly, his insides hollowing out. Oh, how he wished that that were true, yet he knew that his daughter's suffering had barely begun. His wife. It was all he could think of. His wife's reaction to the news that would blow them all to kingdom come. His heart clenched in his chest, the thought of it filling him with dread, and even as he walked through the compound, his pace brisk, his gut tightened at the sense of foreboding. All he knew was that he must get back quickly and do whatever he could to contain the damage.

Sophie heard her father's fast footsteps approaching, and in that moment, she knew that he knew. She stood paralyzed by fear, waiting for him to come crashing into her bedroom, expecting him to be furious beyond anything she could imagine. The footsteps slowed and stopped. Sophie held her breath as the door opened.

Her father's face was almost white. He barely glanced at her, his hand still resting on the handle as he spoke.

"Sophie. I want you to stay here, please, and lock this door."

"Dad..."

"Just do as I say."

He turned and walked away without waiting for an answer. Sophie did as she was told, then sat on the bed, her heart pounding, squeezing the key in her hands, watching the door. Hearing voices from outside, she got up and crossed to the window, from where she saw their maid, the bearer, and the cook, the three of them looking perplexed as they took to the pathway, the maid glancing back over her shoulder uncertainly. Her father would have sent them away. He didn't want anyone hearing what was about to take place. Sophie went back to her bed, lay upon it, and started to cry, pulling a pair of pillows into her chest and hugging them hard, rocking herself gently, waiting, waiting.

The distant howl of her mother's screams turned Sophie's insides to liquid.

Veronica Schofield paced back and forth unsteadily, worrying at the glass she clutched in her hands, her face stricken, ugly from the hysterical tears that had thundered for a full hour behind the locked door that George had physically pulled her away from. A trio of angry red welts ran down his left cheek where her nails had caught him and dug in before he had managed to restrain her. It was as well that he had come prepared, and he had given her the shot that she had refused, not caring whether it hurt her as she lashed out blow after blow while he pinned her tightly to the wall and sank the needle into her flesh. The drug had hit home soon enough, blunting her movements as she circled the room, stopping now and then to glare at him with a look of sheer hatred.

"I'll understand if you want us to return home immediately," he said.

"Home?" she screamed at him. "We can't go home!" She collapsed into a chair. "Dear God in heaven! What have I done to deserve this? This is all your fault. You made us come out here. You never cared about what would happen to us. We have both been thoroughly miserable, can't you see that?" She wrenched herself from her seat and began pacing the room again. "Oh dear God! Dear God! What are we going to do?" She pressed her sodden handkerchief to her mouth. "It must have been that boy! That one she was sneaking about with. How could you have let this happen? Why didn't you do your duty as a father and see to it that she didn't fall into the clutches of one of these damned savages? He must have forced her!" She gripped the arm of a seat for support. "And that, *that…*"

"Please, Veronica." Dr. Schofield ran his hand across his hair. "I'm trying to think, for God's sake."

"Think? *Think?* And what good will your thinking do us now? We're ruined! Are you satisfied?" She turned her back on him, gripping the chair, her breathing labored. "That boy." She spat the word like dirt. "He must be found." She spun around. "He'll hang for this."

"Veronica!"

She broke off, thinking hard, her face darkening. "You knew about this, didn't you? You knew all along what she was getting up to." Her mouth fell into a sneer. "Your precious daughter, debasing herself like those prostitutes in the harem."

Dr. Schofield's fist came down on the table with such force that it sent a vase of flowers crashing to the floor. "Will you shut up and sit down!" he bellowed at her. "Be quiet, woman! For heaven's sake! Do you want the whole palace to hear?"

Sophie stood in the hallway, leaning against the wall, her feet cold on the marble floor. She pressed her forehead into the paneling, listening to the deadened shouts coming from inside the drawing room. For a while, she had thought it had stopped. An hour she had waited, locked in her room. It was her they should be shouting at, not each other, so she had gathered what courage she could and ventured out, knowing that she would have to show herself and take whatever punishment was coming to her.

"I hate this place!" Veronica threw her drink at her husband, the glass sailing through the air, smashing against the paneled door, shards flying. At that moment, the door opened, Sophie standing there in her nightgown, tears streaming down reddened cheeks.

In one swift move, her mother crossed the floor and struck her hard across the face, knocking her to the ground.

❧❧❧

Veronica Schofield locked herself in the bathroom and cried like a broken woman. She cried until she could no longer see, eyes swollen shut. Then, steadying herself against the washbasin, she threw cold water over her face and stared at her reflection in the mirror, a puffy red-eyed mess, cursing the day she had met George Schofield. The humiliation of it still clawed at her insides whenever she thought of it, the way her mother had pushed her at him, going out of her way to see to it that they ended up together, and Veronica had gone along with it because that was what she had been told to do. She had learned while young always to do as her mother said. Hers was the kind of mother who knew how to instill discipline, and there was only one kind of discipline handed out at Ranmore.

Veronica's mother had told her to marry the doctor, so that was what Veronica had done. But nobody had told her what marriage would be like, that she would be expected to submit to him without complaint. It had filled her with bile, his nakedness repulsive to her, and not once had she removed her nightgown in the few years they had shared a bed. She found every reason she could to avoid his overtures, making excuses or skillfully igniting an argument late in the evening before insisting he sleep in another room. On those occasions when he would not be put off, she would lie there passively, her head turned away as he did what he needed to do before rolling aside and turning his back on her. And then she had found herself expecting Sophie, and she was forced to parade her shame in public, women smiling at her in the street when she passed by, her swollen figure testament to her husband's actions. She had wanted the ground to swallow her up. But that was nothing compared to the shame she was put through as she lay back, knees open, while the doctor put his hands on her and looked at her there. Each time it happened, she had gone home and wept furious tears. How dare anyone make her expose herself like that, like it was nothing? It had made her sick to the pit of her stomach, and when the baby was born, she had told her husband outright that she would never again subject herself to such degradation. He had looked pained when she told him, but she didn't care. He didn't know the meaning of the word pain. No man did. Not even the ones who had lost limbs on the battlefields. Only a woman who had given birth knew what pain was, and Veronica Schofield would never subject herself to it again.

Amid her anger, she knew that her husband was right. They must send Sophie away from here as quickly as possible, somewhere nobody would know her and no one would care. Everybody knew that there were places where disgraced girls could be sent for their confinement, where they would be put to work to teach them a lesson for their easy ways. Sophie would be punished for the sin she had committed. She would finally be forced to suffer the way her mother had, and then she would know what it was to be a woman. And why shouldn't she? She might as well learn now that a woman's lot was filled with pain and humiliation; then at least she would know what to expect from her life. Veronica had tried her best with her daughter, to bring her up in the fear of God, seeing to it that she was not spoiled, unlike those insufferable mothers who went around hugging their children and boasting about how damned marvelous they were.

If anyone had failed Sophie as a parent, it was her father. He had no idea how to raise a child, and once he knew that Sophie was the only one he was going to get, he had fawned over her like a simpleton, allowing her to twist him around her little finger. Well, they were welcome to each other, as far as Veronica was concerned. Had he adopted her own parenting methods rather than undoing her good work at every turn, this would never have happened. It was his fault, and his fault only, and now it would be his responsibility, for she would have nothing to do with it. He could damn well make the arrangements himself and get Sophie out of her sight right now. It was too late to do anything else about it. That had been her first thought, her first demand from her husband despite the horror of his response: to get it out of her, that disgusting black thing. But that was out of the question now. It was beyond removal. The only thing that mattered now was that nobody should ever know.

But the palace already knew. The whisper had traveled through every wall, across every corridor, into every chamber, passed along from lip to lip, the laughter from the *zenana* audible for miles.

13

J ag picked his way to the top of the ruined ramparts and surveyed the devastation that stretched out before him as far as the eye could see. Why he insisted on coming here each morning, as though expecting to be greeted by something else, he didn't know. It was as though he could never quite take it in. Across the ragged, scarred landscape lay a scene of biblical catastrophe, an ocean of human misery in all its degradation and filth, punctuated by the flames of the funeral pyres that never ceased, ash and smoke blowing through every distant corner of the camp, a smoldering battleground awash with the wreckage of mankind, a sea of wandering souls. An eerie stillness seemed to hang over it, the countless thousands with little left of their once peaceful lives. People amassed around the few crowded wells. Elsewhere, long queues snaked into the distance from the distribution points, waiting patiently to be given handouts from ever-diminishing rations. There was no arguing among them, no fighting, the only sounds being those necessary for survival, to live from one hour to the next.

This was not the way it was supposed to have been, the rebirth of their ancient and honorable country, the longed-for freedom that so many had sacrificed their lives to secure and welcomed with such joy. There was no joy here. Nothing but misery and death. Where were the songs of celebration? The fireworks? Instead, now the nights were lit up by the fires of destruction that scorched the far horizon, setting the sky ablaze. And his father, struck mute by the horror as they leaped from the train when the mob attacked.

They had scrambled beneath it, clinging to the underside of the
wagon as the screams of terror rang out around them, pressing
their faces into the filthy ironwork, flattening themselves against
the foul-smelling oil-caked structure, blood dripping through the
floor of the carriage above.

Over a hundred and fifty miles they had walked, joining one of
the human caravans that stretched endlessly ahead of and behind
them, most of their belongings stolen or discarded, their clothes
soaked in grime. Jag's father had not uttered a single word after
their escape from the train. Gone were the stories he used to tell of
his beautiful home city, describing for his son the life that awaited
them there, the people that he had not seen for years, and the ones
he had yet to meet.

Jag wished that his father would talk to him again, so that he
might feel less alone. When they had first set out, his father had
shared the old tales with him, his anger toward his son softening
a little. As he spoke, he had smiled and remembered his childhood, the way the sun came up over the lake and how his mother
would sing as she ground rice in the stone quern he liked to clean
for her in the evenings. They would look to the future now with
open hearts, and his son would come to know the family that had
longed to greet him. They would choose for him a beautiful girl
who would become his wife, and she would bear him a son to
carry his name.

Jag and his father had walked in silence, and when the silence
became too much, Jag had taken up the story, this time his own.
He told his father of how he had been raised in a palace by a brave
man who had left his home many years ago after taking a wife, and
of how that brave man came to be the personal bearer of a maharaja. He described how he had learned to steal around the palace
as a child, hidden in the walls, after discovering a long-forgotten
door. He said that his father was a great man, and that he had
encouraged his son to learn everything he could, and to grow up to
be good, like him, in honor of the memory of the mother he had

not known. Although he had never seen a picture of her, Jag knew her just as he knew his father. He described his mother's delicate face, her sweet voice, her devotion to her husband. He said that she had been rebirthed as a bird and that she watched over them always, circling high up above them where she could not be seen, filling the air they breathed with her love. She was watching over them now, he said, protecting them, guiding them homeward.

On they walked, day after day, week after week, until one evening the exhausted caravan reached the crest of a hill and looked down upon this unimaginable scene of human tragedy. A vast refugee camp, with barely a patch of land visible between the inadequate, haphazard tented dwellings. They could walk no further, their exhaustion all-consuming. His father had just stood there, then dropped to his bony haunches and put his head in his hands.

Jag returned to where he had left his father in the shade of their shelter, a thin piece of worn sacking propped up on sticks, offering little protection from the daily sun and nightly cold. He found him sitting there, unmoving, exactly as he had left him.

"Father," he said, crouching beside him. "Lie down and rest. The well is less busy now. I will go and fetch water." Gently he took his father's shoulders and lowered him to the ground.

It had taken Jag hours to remove all the stones from their patch, scraping at the dry earth until his fingers bled, determined to fashion at least one small place upon which his father could lie without rocks digging into his diminishing flesh. He had become so thin that there was precious little of it left to protect his aching bones.

"Come," Jag said, rolling his blanket into a pillow. "First I will bring water, then I will go and queue for food. There are a lot of people waiting, so I may be gone a while. Best for you to sleep now." His father's eyes remained open as he allowed his son to lay him down. "Here," said Jag, and began massaging his father's limbs. "Your joints will get stiff. We have to keep them moving a little bit. We don't want them getting sore." The old man accepted his son's therapy passively, his foot limp in Jag's hand as he supported his leg and gently rotated his ankle. "When we enter your city, you will want to stand tall and walk right in! It is your home, after all. And now it will be my home too. We will find a nice cozy house to live in, in the same district as Mother's family. Can you imagine how happy they will be to see you?" Jag switched to the other foot, shuffling along the ground beneath the thin canopy. "They have probably already decided where we are going to live," he thought aloud. "I expect they're waiting for us now, but we shouldn't worry. They will know that we are here, waiting our turn like everyone else."

News in the camp was virtually nonexistent, merely stories passed from mouth to mouth so that people might have something to talk about. The dispatches that did the rounds were nothing more than speculative whispers drifting through on the wind.

A flash of color caught the corner of Jag's eye. Foot still in his lap, he turned from his father to see a man squatting at the edge of their tiny patch, his head wrapped in a red turban, peering at them from beneath the canopy.

"How is your father today?" he asked. Jag looked away.

"He will be fine. He just needs to rest."

"Here." The man offered him a small bundle. "He must eat. And so must you."

Jag looked at the bundle, a corner of dry roti peeping through the cloth.

"No," he said. "You have your own family to look after." He recognized the man, a Sikh, whose family occupied the small patch of ground behind them.

"Please," the man implored him. "My wife and I will not eat unless you do. We will feed our children, but not a grain of rice shall pass our lips unless our neighbor is eating too."

Jag continued rubbing his father's legs.

"No," he said. "We cannot take your food."

A small sound escaped from his father, like a gasp for air. Quickly Jag leaned forward, his ear close to his father's mouth. The old man tried to speak, but no sound came, just thin flecks of movement as he moved his dry lips. Jag felt something on his side, and looked down to see his father's hand clutching for his loose clothing.

"What is it?" Jag asked softly, urgently. His father's eyes pleaded with him silently. His mouth opened and closed. Then his head fell to one side, exhausted. Jag turned to his neighbor. "I don't know what to do," he said, and for a moment he thought he might weep. The man crawled in beside him.

"Eat." He pressed the bundle on him. "Eat something. You have to keep your strength up, otherwise what good will you be to your father?"

Jag opened the bundle and broke off a piece of bread. He pushed it into his mouth, so guilty at his hunger that his tongue refused to move. Forcing himself to chew, he felt the skin tightening across his jaw, his eyes stinging with tears.

"That's good," the man said. He reached out and placed a hand of concern on Jag's shoulder. "You must do whatever you have to to survive this. We all must." He took up Jag's father's foot and placed it in his own lap, and began massaging his calf as Jag had done.

"My wife thinks that we will be going home soon." Jag's neighbor shook his head sadly. "She keeps asking me every day, when are we going back? I tell her that we shall never go back, but she refuses to believe it. All she sees is that we have left everything. Our home, our livelihood."

"Where did you come from?"

"A village near Lahore. My wife asked our neighbor to look after the house for us. I expect it has been burned to the ground by now, or that another family has moved in and taken it over."

"Our train was attacked," Jag said quietly. "My father has not spoken since."

They fell silent for a while before the man spoke again. "I don't think any of us believed it could happen, but gradually things started to get worse all around us, and then the radio reported that Pakistan was to be formed. It began to dawn on us that we would have to leave, all of us, the whole village." He stopped massaging and laid Jag's father's foot down gently. "Then the mobs started attacking." He paused to drink a little water. 'We thought that we would be able to get to the border in fifteen days, so we took enough rations. Flour, ghee, and other eatables. There was no time to be choosy. They were watching us, and as we packed up and moved out, we saw them flooding into our village to ransack our properties and take the cattle."

From the man's dark expression, it seemed as though he had been waiting a long time to unburden himself. "Fifteen days," he whispered to himself. "It took us almost two months. There was no road to speak of; most of the way it was just mud. Our convoy moved at a snail's pace. Other villages joined us along the way. I think we stretched for more than fifty miles. The rations ran down quickly and the cattle needed green fodder, but all along the path, thugs were looking to loot us and would not allow us to get anything from the farms. Then we heard that Balloki Bridge was broken. That was a terrible moment for all of us."

"I'm sorry," Jag said, ashamed of the way he had dismissed his neighbor's offers of help, refusing his aid day after day.

"Water was a big problem," the man went on. "At first we would drink from a small stream that ran alongside the muddy route, but when we saw what was in it, my wife refused to touch it. If there was a Persian well on the way, we would take water from that, but people were so thirsty that they would use it all up too quickly and the water would run dry and dirty within half an hour. Nobody was prepared to wait for it to fill up again. Many continued to drink from the stream." He looked at Jag grimly. "There would be dead people floating in it, one bloated body passing by after another. There was nothing else to do except to wait for the bodies to pass before filling the water vessels."

Jag watched the man quietly, the heaviness upon him seeming to drag him into the dry ground.

"You were lucky to get out alive," he said. The man nodded.

"Finally we heard that the bridge had been repaired and our convoy moved on again. We were met at Khem Karan by the Gurkha army, who escorted us over the border. They did as much as they could, feeding our remaining animals, but everyone was so exhausted."

"I hate the Moslems," Jag said.

"Do not ever say that." The man looked at him sharply. "Most of the harm is being done by looters and bad elements, and they are godless, no matter what they claim. Godless people without heart or conscience. We had Moslem friends once. They were good people. On Eid, they would invite us into their homes and share food with us, although we only ever took dry fruits because we were not allowed anything else. As children, we were always coming in and out of each other's houses. All people are made by the same God, so we are sons of the same God, no matter what we call ourselves. The new border is an artificial boundary. It does not exist in the eyes of God, only in the eyes of men who have been blinded by the pride of controlling politicians."

"Do you not seek revenge?"

"No," he said. "There will be no peace until the vengeance stops. First come the attacks, then the reprisals, and the circle feeds upon itself like a hungry bird until there is no one left." He shook his head sadly. "There is nothing in my religion that says that a non-Sikh is my enemy. My faith teaches universal brotherhood, and the respect of all religions as equal. My father was one of the village elders, a wise man who would not allow any Moslem to be molested if he could prevent it."

"Where is your father?"

The man looked at Jag. "They killed him. Cut off his head. I didn't see it happen, but some of the villagers did. They said that he tried to put his head back on, that his body sat up and his hands searched in the dirt for it before he fell down dead, but I don't believe it." A terrible silence hung over them for a while. "Now eat," he said to Jag. "Then you can go and fetch food. The queues are long. I will stay here and look after your father."

14

Christmas lunch was one of the few occasions when servants were excused from the ADC's formal dining room, a spacious marble affair with a long teak table, set aside for high days and holidays and now festooned with colorful paper chains and Chinese lanterns. The carving of the goose was an honor awarded to the longest-serving Britisher, who for the last two years had been Dr. Reeves. The table groaned with dish after delicious dish, the classic trimmings of Christmas lunch given an exotic twist here and there with the addition of cloves to the red cabbage, black mustard seeds in the potatoes, a hint of cardamom lacing the gravy. The plum pudding, provided this year by Mrs. Ripperton, had been made to her mother's recipe, a complicated rigmarole of fruit, spices, and suet handed down through generations, tinkered with on occasion to take into account wartime shortages and the odd ingredient missing altogether, in this case the vital suet. There was none to be had anywhere, so nobody was quite sure how this season's effort would turn out. Nevertheless, Mrs. Ripperton had taken the bowl around the offices so that everyone could have a good stir of the mixture to bring them luck for the following year.

Dr. Reeves tapped a spoon against his glass, silencing the table.

"Dear friends," he began. "Before we unleash our appetites upon this splendid feast, I feel that now would be an appropriate moment to say a few words in honor of those of us who, in all likelihood, will probably never grace this table again." A dull murmur rose from those gathered. "This great tradition of Christmas lunch has followed us Brits to every far-flung corner of the globe. The world over, families will be settling down to a roast goose, just like this, so let us think of them for a few moments and raise our glasses to their health and happiness." He picked up his glass. "To absent friends," he said. Everyone followed suit, repeating the toast and taking a sip. "And next year, among those absent friends will be quite a few of us too. The Schofields, the Rippertons, the Bridgeports, Kay and I, of course, and dear Miss Blanche. Perhaps this table shall become a thing of the past, and this palace shall never again see the likes of these gatherings."

It seemed a fair assessment. The Maharaja was away again, having attended the grand silver jubilee celebrations of the Maharaja of Jaipur earlier in the month before moving on to the celebrations in Baroda. Most of those at the table would be leaving soon, and word had it that they would not be replaced. They had clung on to the last vestiges of the life that once was, huddling around the dying embers of the Empire, leeching what warmth they could from the fading flames of this, the jewel in His Majesty's crown. Soon trunks would be packed amid drawn-out good-byes and promises of everlasting friendship.

Dr. and Mrs. Reeves had decided to go back to England and retire, taking one or two servants with them to ease the transition from luxury to the plain living of the common man. The Bridgeports were off to try their luck elsewhere, to make a new fortune in the remaining colonies. This had been the preferred choice for many of the leavers, setting off for places like Bermuda, Rhodesia, and Hong Kong. Although British in their citizenship, some had barely set foot on home soil: a few years at public school perhaps or sobering holidays spent with relatives. Indeed, even their mode of language seemed strangely antiquated, a peculiar form of English that had sprung up long ago and remained largely untouched by the progress of time. In many ways, they were the odd ones out now, and the whole occasion felt like the end of an era, a great one at that, one they would all remember for the rest of their lives. Everybody felt it, even the cooks, who had been unusually solemn while preparing the many dishes for the sahibs' Christmas festival. The goose had been basted with quiet ceremony, the potatoes roasted with extra care. At one point, the pastry chef had taken a moment to wipe his eyes on his sleeve and blow his nose on his cloth before returning to his quietly simmering sugar syrup. How softly some things ended. How violently some begin, like the bursting forth of a new star.

Veronica Schofield sipped from her water glass, strictly teetotal in the presence of company. The brandy she drank in the confines of her own room she considered to be no one's business but hers. George stole a brief glance at his wife. The water would be no hardship for her. She was probably half cut by the time she came down to lunch anyway. He didn't care. She became morose under the influence of alcohol, and he would rather that than have her shrieking at him. He had even gone so far as to encourage it recently, seeing that decanters were quietly replenished in the hope that Veronica would take herself off and rest more often, aided by the tinctures he administered to her, old remedies ground from powerful natural herbs. They had helped to calm her, to some degree, each dose suspended in a good measure of brandy, which she pretended to suffer.

It had become intolerable, the atmosphere between them, although perhaps it was nearer to the truth that he had finally come to the end of his patience. He had done everything he could think of to salvage his family, to make something good come of it, but there was no helping Veronica. She did not want to be helped. She wanted to wallow in that twisted world of hers, wrought from bibles and beatings and cold baths. There was nothing he could do for his wife, and it had taken him half a lifetime to see it. What a fool he had been, and now here he was, marking off another Christmas Day, another year gone by.

"The final scene of the British in India has been played out," Dr. Reeves continued, "and in years to come, we will all be able to say that we had some small role to play in that great point in history." He looked at his wife, seated to his right, and placed an affectionate hand on her shoulder. "As for Kay and I, we would like to think that you will all come and visit us in Dorset. There will always be room for you, although we won't be able to promise a *khitmutgar* at dinner and a boy to polish your shoes." An appreciative patter of laughter passed down the line. "In the meantime, there is always the option of taking a little of the fine hill air with the Schofields in Ooty. Some of us may even make it to Simla at the invitation of the lovely Miss Blanche, whose impending marriage we shall add to the celebrations today." A loud call of *hear, hear* came from the end of the table, where Miss Blanche blushed prettily beside Mr. Ripperton.

"I'm crushed," Rip called to the table. "If only Fi had agreed to the divorce, Briony and I would have been able to skip off into the sunset together!"

Everybody laughed except Mrs. Schofield, who remained detached from the proceedings, twisting the stem of her water glass, her gaze fixed on the flickering candles.

"Not on your life!" Mrs. Ripperton said, knocking Sophie with her elbow. "Until death do us part, my dear, whether I like it or not!" A roar of laughter went up. "And what would the fair Miss Blanche want from a silly old goat like you anyway?" She turned to her side and winked at Sophie good-naturedly. Momentary distraction over, everyone returned to Dr. Reeves' speech.

"So today, let us eat, drink, and be merry," he said, his voice wavering a little. "Speaking for my wife and I, it has been the most wonderful adventure, and I hope that we shall all have many more." He picked up his glass. "To King and country!" he declared.

⤎⦿⤏

By the time it was served, the goose was almost cold. Nobody minded. If anything, it seemed that everybody would have been happy for the lunch to go on forever, suspending the moment when they finally bowed to the last curtain and allowed the lights to dim.

"You've been awfully quiet, my dear," Mrs. Ripperton whispered to Sophie when the pudding finally came around.

"Sorry," she said, their exchange masked by the gay hubbub of chatter.

"Don't worry." Mrs. Ripperton eyed Sophie's untouched pudding. "Just shove it all around your plate a little and hide it under a bit of custard. Nobody will notice." Sophie smiled briefly. "We shall all miss you when you are gone, my dear, but I have to say that I think it is a marvelous idea for you to strike out on your own. There's nothing worse than being marshaled around by one's parents. It's about time you took yourself off and had a little adventure."

"Yes," Sophie said, the pattern of conversation now so well-rehearsed that it fell from her lips automatically. She would be leaving two weeks hence to spend a few months at a teaching mission in Orissa, leading a group of children through the rudiments of the English language, a legacy left by the Empire that India had no intention of relinquishing. That was what they had told everyone anyway. While she was away, her father would complete his service to the Maharaja, while her mother traveled down to Ooty and looked for a suitable house to rent. Her father had it all worked out. By the time Sophie's time was over, her parents would be ensconced in the delicate climes of the hill station perched over the Nilgiris, waiting for her. A place where they could all start over. A place where they could forget.

Sophie had been admired and congratulated as the news of her imminent departure spread, and had been reassured by everyone that she would be a gifted tutor due to her cheery nature and endless patience. She had felt such a fraud, accepting their good wishes with a false smile and a heavy heart. Her mother had wanted her to go away sooner, but her father had refused, unable to bear the thought of his daughter incarcerated in some far-off place while he choked on his conscience. The idea of spending Christmas without her was unthinkable, and the aggressive silence his wife meted out as punishment for his decision was a small price to pay in order for him to be able to kiss his daughter on this exalted morning. He had given her a pair of ruby earrings as she lay in bed and told her not to mention them to her mother.

"By the time you get to Ooty, all this will feel like a distant memory." Mrs. Ripperton tucked into her pudding. "It's quite lovely. Rip and I have spent many wonderful times there and I'm longing to see it again. You know, I have found that memories have a habit of storing themselves up, like shoving things into the back of a closet. They'll live there for as long as you care to leave them, and then, many years from now, you might find yourself clearing out that closet one day and out they will tumble, all your memories of yesteryear."

Sophie hoped that that would not be so. Right now, she could hardly bear the burden of moving from one day to the next. It was like a living death, the only escape coming in the form of her dreams at night, when she would spend hours with Jag, talking to him about her worries, feeling his arms around her as he comforted her and told her that everything would be all right. She would bury her face deep into his chest, inhaling his scent, his perfume still clinging to her when she woke in the morning, yearning for him. As the baby grew, so did her thoughts of him, running riot as she slept, leaving her tossing and turning, restless for hours.

"When you're done at the teaching mission, you must come and stay with us for a while," Mrs. Ripperton said to her quietly. "Your father will have his practice set up by then, but you don't want to go moving back in with your parents. You'll probably find it far too claustrophobic. No doubt you'll be feeling much too grown up for all that."

"No," Sophie said blankly.

She hadn't thought about any of it, unable to picture a future for herself at all, only the next few months. What happened after then was not something she could contemplate. It did not exist. Spring would come, and then the rainy season, and somewhere in between she would bear a child, a child that slumbered quietly within her now, hidden beneath the folds of the awful dress that she had altered last night, unpicking the seams, resewing it with a little more forgiveness. It had taken hours, but she had been glad of the task, to be able to sit and concentrate on something in the quiet of her room, taking her mind from its troubles.

Her mother refused to speak to her at all since the shocking news had been uncovered, barely looking at her except to issue her with the occasional furious glare, as though scheming some terrible revenge. Sophie had nothing to say to her anyway. She had had enough of her mother's rages. When she was younger, much younger, she hadn't understood why her mother acted the way she did, convincing herself that it must be her own fault, that she somehow invited the wrath upon herself. She had tried so hard to please her, taking up and diligently completing any chore she could think of, in order to lighten her mother's load and brighten her mood. Yet the punishment would come regardless, sometimes in a shower of criticism, sometimes in the form of a garden cane passed smartly across the backs of her legs, leaving thick red welts that burned like fire. Her room had not been tidied properly. The dishes had not been stacked straight. Her piano practice had been hesitant and full of mistakes. No matter what she did, the outcome was the same.

Her mother no longer ate with them, and Sophie was grateful for her absence, leaving her to sit with her father, who would adopt a pained air of cheerful normality, greeting her with a kiss on the head and offering snippets of interest from the newspaper to fill the silence. Together they had tiptoed through the ghastly daily routine as though stepping through a minefield, the constant effort of it wearying for them both, the air rigid the moment Mrs. Schofield emerged from her two rooms where she remained in solitude. Sophie had heard her parents arguing this morning, something to do with Christmas lunch, judging by the way her mother had finally shown herself half an hour late with an angry slash of lipstick across her tightly clenched mouth. Sophie was glad that she could not see her mother's face from where she sat beside Mrs. Ripperton. She couldn't bear to look at her.

"I have a little gift for you, my dear," Mrs. Ripperton whispered. Sophie felt something pass into her lap under cover of the tablecloth. "I noticed you no longer wear that pretty little locket of yours and I thought perhaps you felt you had outgrown it. It's not much. Just a little trinket to keep as a reminder of the wonderful time we have had together."

Sophie's hand went to the small package, a silk pouch drawn closed with a slender cord. She looked into her lap and opened it. Mrs. Ripperton's pearls gleamed quietly back at her.

"To remind you of our secret afternoons," Mrs. Ripperton said. "I want you to know that I think you're a marvelous young woman. You've brought a very welcome ray of sunshine into this rather staid life of mine, and I hope we shall remain friends forever."

Sophie knew that she was going to cry. There was nothing she could do about it. She could manage almost anything except kindness. Mrs. Ripperton's tender words unraveled her completely. She wanted to pass the gift back to her, to say that she didn't deserve it and that oh, if only she knew, what would she think of her then? Dear Mrs. Ripperton, who she had been so very rude to, deliberately avoiding her when she knew her to be looking for her, ducking into doorways, hiding in the shadows as the call of her name faded. She had found her ebullience embarrassing, the way Fiona linked her arm through hers and rattled on endlessly about the things she used to get up to when she was her age. She would insist on them doing idiotic things together, like playing old parlor games that were no fun at all with just two mismatched people. But today all that fell away. Today there was no one else Sophie would have rather been sitting next to, safe in her enormous shadow, the size of her obliterating any suggestion that Sophie's own waist had thickened so. Oh, if only she knew.

Sophie slipped the package into her purse, feeling nothing but shame and guilt. She wished so very much that she had brought something for Mrs. Ripperton in return, a small token of her thanks now that their time together was almost over. Had she known she would feel like this, she would have hurried to finish the sampler that she had stitched reluctantly so that her hands might have something to do while in her mother's dark presence. It was a mess. Needlework had never been her strong point, but Mrs. Ripperton wouldn't have minded. In fact, Sophie expected that she might have liked it all the more for its dreadful incompetence. She could have wrapped it up in colored paper and tied it with a ribbon and used a festive tag, written on it: *To Aunt Fifi with love, Sophie.* That was what she could have done, had she thought of it.

Mrs. Ripperton's hand came into Sophie's lap again, this time with a lace-edged handkerchief. She leaned her bulk into the table slightly, hiding Sophie from view, calling, "Robert darling! Is there any more of that delicious pudding?"

Later, in the still of the night, Sophie dreamed of Jag. They were in the water garden, sitting by the lotus pool, the ornamental fish shimmering golden beneath the surface, sliding through the lotus stems. Jag held her hand and whispered to her. Sophie found herself awakened, a strange sensation low in her belly, like the flick of a fish's tail. She lay there and waited, her eyes now wide open. And there it was again, tiny, almost indiscernible, like a butterfly fluttering deep inside her. She held her breath and lay still, and knew it was her baby.

⁕• 1958

The Diplomatic Enclave,

New Delhi

15

A rush of warm air flew into the Dakota's cabin the moment the door opened, bringing with it the thick smell of aviation fuel and clouds of dry dust. Sophie unclipped her seat belt and smoothed her hands over her hopelessly wrinkled dress. She had so wanted to look just right today and had changed several times before settling on her outfit for the last leg of their journey. She should have worn something more tailored, she thought with irritation, a light two-piece with a silk blouse perhaps, rather than the softly cut dress she had opted for. Now she would descend the steps looking like she had slept in her clothes. She felt her heart pounding, her palms clammy with nerves.

"Ready to face the firing squad?" Lucien touched her hand lightly. She had been unusually quiet during the flight, and he had noticed her chewing at the corner of her lip. She turned to him, having not heard a word. "You'll be fine," he said. "I'll have the driver drop you off at the house so you can have a good look around and get yourself settled."

"Must you go straight off?"

"I'm afraid so, darling. Best foot forward and all that. I'll be with you before you know it. Don't forget about the reception this evening, will you?"

Out of the window, Sophie saw a black car slide silently alongside the Dakota, the small flag fixed to its bonnet hanging limply in the heavy stillness of the air as it drew to a halt. Sophie felt sick, her face set rigid as she willed herself not to tremble. In that moment, she wanted to stay on the plane and ask the pilot to turn around and go back, to take off and detach her from this land, fearing that the moment she descended the steps and set one foot on the ground, it would swallow her up and claim her. It was as though a part of her had taken root there long ago, a part of her that she had left behind that would be forever missing. She had cut it out of her heart, trying to sever it, but never quite succeeding. It would grow back like a rose every year, refusing to die, and she would hack at it again until it bled. She couldn't go there. She must put it out of her mind and never think of it again, because whenever she did, in those moments when her thoughts refused to be censored, it would leave her ailing and hopeless and unable to breathe. She feared that everyone would know, that anyone with even half an ounce of sense would be able to tell the moment they looked at her. She had never planned to come back, not consciously anyway, but now that she was here, about to disembark, she wondered if she hadn't known all along that her return was inevitable.

There was nothing else that she could have done. It had been the right decision, and she had reconciled with her conscience long ago, before it crucified her. So long she had spent in that dark, grim place. It had taken years to emerge from the depths, one year before she could pass a whole day without crying, two before she could bear to hear the sound of music, three before she could hold her concentration sufficiently to read a book, and so it had gone on, her slow recovery, inching painfully along under her father's watchful eye. Indeed, there had even been times when she had managed to kid herself that she had erased the specter of the past, that she had finally succeeded in getting on with the business of making a life for herself. But then the aircraft door had opened, bringing with it the rush of hot air, thick dust, and memories.

As she stepped out of the plane, the temperature hit her like a blast furnace, bolstered by the heat rising from the baked concrete below, the sweltering engines of the aircraft. Her lungs lurched with the first breath, the noise of the airstrip drowning out her

gasp. As she stepped onto the tarmac, she felt her soul pulled inex-
orably into the earth beneath her feet. India. My India. My love.

Sophie sat politely in the drawing room of her neighbor's house,
sipping from a second cup of tea, the creases in her dress forgotten.

"So this is your first posting?"

"Yes," said Sophie.

"Poor you. Nothing like being thrown in at the deep end, is
there? Mind you, it could be a lot worse. My first was Damascus.
God, what an awful place that was. The heat was like a bread oven
and the house was practically falling down around our ears. It's all
right for the men, of course. They're not the ones who have to
conjure home comforts out of nothing and entertain endless lines
of spitting Arabs. Couldn't wait to get out of there. Nairobi was
a disaster too, although the wives were a nice bunch, unlike this
lot." Tessa picked up her teacup. "Whatever you do, try not to get
stuck with Rosamund Appleton. She's terminally dull."

She took a sip and returned her cup to its dainty saucer.
"Melanie Hinchbrook is quite good fun. Beast of a husband, mind
you." She smiled slyly. "Not that Melanie cares much. She's perfectly capable of making her own entertainment, although the
last time she got caught out, he threatened to shoot her and him
too. Nothing worse than a jealous husband, don't you think?
He's madly in love with her, of course, and who wouldn't be?
But it's all terribly unhealthy if you ask me. He likes her to wear
revealing dresses when they're out just so that he can the watch
other men ogling her. Strange that, isn't it?" Sophie wasn't quite
sure what to say. "But what else would you expect after marrying
someone who's practically old enough to be your father? Perhaps
he's not able to…well, you know. Shall we have something a
little more interesting?"

She got up and went to the drinks tray on the cabinet in the corner of the pleasant drawing room and set out two glasses without waiting for an answer. "Gin and it?"

Sophie stole a glance at her wristwatch. Not quite eleven-thirty.

"She had a thing going on with Charles Smythson for a while, your husband's predecessor. Everybody knew about it, except his wife of course. She was quite the raving beauty in her day." Tessa brought the drinks to the table and handed one to Sophie. "Cruel that, isn't it? How some men get more handsome with age while their wives turn into gargoyles?" Sophie took a sip and shuddered at its strength. "I don't know how she could have let herself go like that. She wasn't even forty and she knew very well that her husband was an incorrigible philanderer. You can usually tell who's doing what with whom because they go to such lengths to avoid each other at all the parties. It's Lucinda Bevan I feel sorry for. I swear her husband is the most attractive creature I have ever met in my life. I'm sure there's something going on there."

Sophie had liked everything about Tessa Wilde instantly. Her chic beige polka-dot dress, her honey-blonde hair pinned into an elegant chignon, her perfect red lipstick, her disarming candor. It was not what she had expected at all, and certainly not on her first day. Lucien had been quite specific about the rigors of wifely etiquette and had warned her that she would in all likelihood have to get used to a charitable coven of stuffy do-gooders while he went about his business.

"How did you and your husband meet?"

"I worked at the Foreign Office for a while."

"Oh!" Tessa raised an eyebrow in surprise. "So you're one of those dangerous independent types, are you?"

"Well." Sophie took a thoughtful sip. "Yes. I suppose I am."

"The DWs won't like that. They like their new members meek and eager to please."

"DWs?"

"The diplomatic wives' association. They like to think it keeps us out of trouble, running our own little trades union to squabble over the ins and outs of minor dramas like who's going to organize the Christmas raffle. Rosamund Appleton is our chairman, and oh, doesn't she let us know it. Her husband is head of mission. To say she has a thick skin would be something of an understatement. It's not skin. It's hide."

"How long have you been here?"

"Two years. It's turned out quite well actually. Once you work, out the lay of the land, there's very little to complain about. There's quite a big expat community, as you can imagine. It's quite surprising how many people stayed on, but why leave when you can live like this? I hardly have to lift a finger, except when the children come out for the holidays, and even then they're quite happy ordering the staff around and lounging around the club all day."

"How many do you have?"

"Two. A boy and a girl."

"You must miss them."

"Not as much as I pretend to. One feels obligated to miss one's children, I suppose, but I have to say that ten years of parenting was quite enough for me. I couldn't wait to pack them off and put my feet up." She gave out a small, tinkling laugh. "Oh, I don't mean it really. You'll understand what I'm talking about when your own children come along. You are planning to have a family, aren't you?"

"Well," Sophie flustered, the question unexpected. "Yes, once we're settled in."

It was the simplest answer, she decided. Of course they would have children. They might take a little time to arrive, that's all. Not everybody fell straight away, and perhaps she wasn't quite as young as was generally considered ideal childbearing age, but yes, they would be bound to come along eventually. After all, it had only been five months.

"In that case, best to hurry up about it and get it over with."

"Yes, well…" Sophie hesitated a little. "I'm hopeful that it won't be too long."

"Oh, listen to me! Now I've gone and made you feel uncomfortable." Tessa tutted to herself. "Here I am rattling on when you've barely had time to unpack."

"It's all right." Sophie smiled. "There's just so much to take in, and my feet have hardly touched the ground lately. The last week has been chaos, what with all the packing and redirecting of post and trying to tie up a hundred loose ends."

"And your husband expects it all to happen by magic, of course?"

"Naturally."

"Welcome to the diplomatic wives' club. The first thing you'll need to do is to sort out your staff."

"Is the house not fully staffed already?"

"In theory," Tessa said. "But the fact of the matter is that all the good ones will have been poached the moment the Smythsons moved out. Rosamund took your cook. I'm not sure where your maid got to or your gardener, but the chap who's been trimming the hedge lately is definitely new. I'll have to ask Vicky if he knows anything about it."

"Vicky?"

"Our bearer. He's an absolute dear." Tessa went to the wall and pressed a small electric button. A few moments later, a tall, slender Indian man of indiscernible age appeared and stood in the doorway, dressed in manila pajamas, awaiting instructions.

"Memsahib?"

"Vicky, this is the new memsahib next door, Mrs. Grainger. She wants to know about the staff." Vicky moved his head slightly and offered Sophie a small respectful bow. "Can you tell us anything about what's going on?"

"Memsahib, there have been many changes in your servants. I recommend that you test them first," he said. "You must not let them trick you or cheat you. If you need any replacements, I will be able to help you find suitable workers."

"Hmm," Tessa said. "Thank you, Vicky. That is good advice."

"Is there anything else, memsahib?"

"No. That's all. Oh…" She picked up her empty glass and rattled the naked ice a little. "Would you be a dear?"

"Certainly, memsahib." He smiled and took both glasses away. It was a moment before Sophie realized that he was merely refreshing them, his measure even more generous than the one Tessa had poured.

"Vicky's right," Tessa said. "For all you know, your cook might not even be able to boil an egg. The outgoing staff have a habit of selling their positions to the highest bidder, saying that nobody will notice the change because they all look the same to us. It causes all sorts of bother, especially if they turn out to be hopeless. You have no choice other than to get rid of them, otherwise the whole household falls apart. Reputations have been made and lost on the competence of one's staff. Entertaining is a very big thing here. You might as well start off the way you mean to go on." Vicky placed the drinks on the low table set between them and left the room. "Don't let things slide, not for a moment, otherwise they'll assume you're a soft touch who doesn't mind being taken advantage of. It's all about discipline here. Once everyone knows where your standards are set, you shouldn't have too many problems. You'll be staying for lunch, won't you?"

༄༅༅

"Sophie! What on earth do you think you're doing?" Sophie felt herself shaken roughly awake. "Just look at the time!"

Her state of disorientation was overwhelming; for a moment, she was unsure of where she was before it all came flooding back. She had only meant to lie down for a moment, to close her eyes for a few minutes, but then she had felt queasy, the room seeming to sway around her. A little travel sickness, she had thought. It would soon pass. She just needed to rest a while.

"Sophie!" Lucien pulled at her. She sat up on the bed, head pounding, trying to adjust her eyes to the darkness, the room a haze of unfamiliar shadows.

Lucien marched to the door, calling, "*Koi hai?*" There was no answer. "*Koi hai?*" he shouted again. "Will somebody please explain to me why the house is in complete darkness? For heaven's sake," he muttered under his breath, switching on a table lamp. "Really, darling! Whatever were you thinking? We're supposed to be at the reception in half an hour." He continued around the room, turning on lights.

"Oh Lord." Sophie brought her hands to her face, rubbing her eyes. She felt wrung out, her mouth parched. "I'm so sorry," she said. "I must have fallen asleep."

"Well don't just sit there! Shake a leg!" Lucien disappeared into his dressing room.

Sophie pulled herself to her feet, steadying herself for a moment. "I need to call for some tea."

"Tea?" he shouted through the door. "We don't have time for tea! Just throw a dress on and hurry up about it."

"Just give me a minute, would you?" She picked up her wrist-watch from the bedside table. It took a moment for her eyes to register the time. "Oh *Lord!*"

Sophie was on her feet in seconds. She went quickly to the dressing table, sat at the stool and reached for her hairbrush before catching her reflection in the mirror. She could scarcely remember a time when she had looked such a fright, and cursed herself for having made such a schoolgirl error, accepting gin at eleven in the morning followed by wine with lunch, their glasses being topped up constantly by Vicky until she had absolutely no idea how much she had drunk. Tessa was obviously a hardened lush. Sophie would have to watch herself from now on. Lucien had every right to be furious with her. They had been here for less than a day, and already she had fallen at the first hurdle. Sophie grasped her brush and set about her hair determinedly with one hand while reaching for a lipstick with the other.

CSGO

Lucien glanced anxiously out of the window as the car rushed
rudely along the wide boulevards of New Delhi, the grand buildings floodlit beyond high walls and railings, the new city quite at
odds with the chaos of the ancient parts and more reminiscent of
a modern capital like Washington, DC. The driver thumped impatiently on the horn, clearing a path through the rickshaw *wallahs*
and the wandering cows, who took little notice, before taking the
final turn on to Rajpath. Rashtrapati Bhavan, the grand construction once known as Viceroy House, rose majestically out of the
distance to greet them, set impressively on the crest of the hill, its
vast dome dominating the vista, painting the very picture of impe-
rial greatness.

They traveled in silence. Lucien hoped to God that this wasn't
a sign of things to come. All Sophie had had to do was to supervise
the unpacking and organize the servants. It was hardly a taxing
task, and she would have had plenty of opportunity to rest and
be ready in time. She knew damn well how important this kind
of thing was, that they should make the very best impression on
first presentation to the most senior members. Oh well. There was
nothing to be gained in making a big thing out of it. It would only
sour the evening. He turned to look at her. She was still upset. He
could tell by the line of her mouth, pinched slightly at the corner
as she concentrated her gaze out of the window. He shouldn't
have shouted at her like that. It wasn't her fault that she had been
pounced on the moment the car dropped her off. In fact, he should
have predicted that something like that might happen. But where
the hell had the servants been? Heads would have to roll. Lucien
reached for Sophie's hand. He should have stayed with her rather
than going straight to the embassy. Nobody would have minded,
but he had been keen to make his presence felt as quickly as possible and to assert himself as a man who could travel all night and
work all day without missing a beat.

"Sorry I was cross," he whispered. Sophie turned to him, her
face creased with disappointment. "Forgive me?"

"No," she said. "It's me who's sorry. I can't believe I was so stupid."

"You're not stupid. It was a perfectly natural situation to get yourself into, and you did absolutely the right thing in accepting her hospitality."

"Now we're horribly late and it's all my fault."

"Don't give it a second thought." He brought her hand to his lips and kissed it. "Nobody will have missed us, and even if they have, I'm sure we'll think of something to tell them. It's hardly a major international incident, is it, Mrs. Grainger?"

"No." Sophie slid along the seat, pressing herself close to him. "But still, I should have known better. It was irresponsible of me."

"Nonsense." He winked at her mischievously. "You go ahead and be as irresponsible as you jolly well like."

By the time they alighted and made their way up the enormous flight of steps, they were almost an hour late.

"Grainger!" A stout man with a sparse covering of white hair and a ruddy complexion made his way through the crowd to greet them. "We were all wondering where on earth you'd got to! You've missed the welcome speeches, which is no hardship. Same old, same old."

"Do forgive us." Lucien shook his hand warmly. "The driver took a wrong turn, and before we knew it, we were halfway to Timbuktu. Allow me to present my wife. Sophie?" He turned to her, all smiles. "Tony Hinchbrook, one of the seniors."

"How do you do," Sophie extended her hand.

"My dear Mrs. Grainger." He placed a small suggestion of a kiss above her dress ring. "What an absolute vision you are."

"Thank you." She gave him her most charming smile, although he was clearly drunk and disguising it rather badly.

"I'd introduce you to my wife, but she seems to have disappeared into thin air." He looked around halfheartedly. "She's probably with the rest of the DWs, huddled in a corner somewhere, plotting away. There's nothing quite like the scent of fresh blood to set tongues wagging."

"I hope we won't be too bitter a disappointment," Lucien said.

"I doubt that very much, Grainger." Hinchbrook tapped his nose. "Let's just say your reputation precedes you."

"And is that a good thing or a bad thing?"

"Who knows?" He smiled an impenetrable smile. "We shall just have to wait and see, won't we?"

A bearer arrived silently, offering flutes of champagne from a silver tray.

"Oh." Sophie looked at it, then to her husband. "Do you think I might have a plain tonic water instead?" Lucien acted as though he had not heard her. Taking two glasses from the tray, he handed one to her.

"Is Appleton here yet?" he asked.

"Somewhere," Tony Hinchbrook replied. "Although he's probably tied up with Gresham, one of our American colleagues. Everyone's a bit twitchy about the Kerala situation, especially the Yanks."

At that moment a gong sounded, sending a deep, sonorous vibration through the reception hall.

"Too late," Tony said. "Dinner is served. I hope you know where you're sitting." He turned to Sophie, a twinkle in his eye. "People have been taken outside and shot for messing around with the seating plan."

৩/৩৬

The banqueting hall opened up before them like a gilded cavern, the long table set with a hundred or more places, each laid with ruled precision, cutlery gleaming, glassware sparkling, vast candelabras shimmering dimly, setting the room aglow. Sophie held on to Lucien's arm and tried to ignore the way everyone seemed to be staring at them, whispers passing from lips to lips, heads turning, some openly looking her up and down. She remembered to smile and hoped it might give her an air of confidence. It was probably just as well that they had been late. If this was the DW's idea of making a newcomer feel welcome, heaven only knows what they would have done had they been able to give them a proper once-over at the reception. Probably asked her to open her mouth and checked her teeth.

"Grainger!" Lucien scanned the room at the sound of his name. "Over here!"

A tall, fair-haired man smiled broadly at them from the far end of the table, hand raised in recognition.

"Ah," said Lucien. "That's Bevan. The man I was telling you about."

"Of course," said Sophie, hoping to gloss over the fact that she had absolutely no idea who Lucien was talking of. She had been bombarded with so many names that they had all blurred into one huge tangle. She didn't know who anybody was, or what they did, or who they were married to. She couldn't even remember the name of the man they had been speaking to just before the dinner gong sounded. Knowing her luck, she would probably end up seated next to him and would have to somehow avoid addressing him directly all evening.

"Bevan." Lucien shook his hand. "My wife, Sophie."

"How do you do," Sophie said, trying to embed the name.

"James Bevan," he said. "Jim." Sophie nodded and shook his hand. "You must have had a long day."

"Yes," Sophie replied. "It has been rather."

"Well don't let all this nonsense overwhelm you. It's just a bunch of friends having a spot of dinner, only much bigger and a lot less interesting." He smiled at her and she couldn't help but notice how extraordinarily attractive he was. The name dropped into place. The man Tessa Wilde had mentioned to her that morning. "Grainger, you're over there." He pointed to a particular seat. "Pole position, right next to the old man. He's obviously planning to bend your ear tonight."

"Mrs. Grainger?" Sophie turned to find a heavyset woman loitering beside her. "Ros Appleton." The woman extended a

gloved hand. "David Appleton's wife. I've been looking out for
you all evening."

"How do you do," Sophie said. "I'm afraid we got caught up
in the traffic. Our driver took a wrong turn and—"

"You're along here with us."

"Oh," said Sophie, sliding her arm reluctantly from Lucien's.

"You really don't want to be stuck with the bigwigs when they
start talking shop."

Sophie glanced at Lucien, hoping for a swift rescue, but he was
already occupied elsewhere, shaking hands with another man while
the impossibly handsome Jim Bevan spoke earnestly in his ear.

"Come along!" She felt Rosamund Appleton's hand on her
elbow, and before she knew it, she was being guided firmly away.
"I've seated us with the Hinchbrooks and put you opposite General
Hurst. British Army. He's visiting with his wife for a few days. Nice
enough fellow, but rather frightful to look at, I'm afraid. Glass eye."

Beneath the low drone of conversation from a hundred voices,
Lucien took a moment to breathe in his surroundings: the fabu-
lously ornate interior, the finery of the satin-gowned women and
decorated men. This was what he had wanted all along, the reason
he had joined the service. It could be a charmed existence for those
talented enough to scale the heights, and now there was nothing to
stop him from progressing just the way he had always intended. He
smiled contentedly to himself and returned his undivided attention
to David Appleton.

"You'll notice a few tight smiles hiding ruffled feathers,"
Appleton said. "The general election didn't go quite to plan, but
that's the Congress party for you. The Kerala situation has been a
real boot in the backside. Nobody saw it coming. Perhaps if the
Indians weren't so keen to get embroiled in silly personal squab-
bles, they might make better politicians."

"What about Nehru?" Lucien asked. He had read everything he could get his hands on, of course, the piles of dispatches and classified documents, but it was always better to get a personal opinion directly from the horse's mouth.

"Nehru? Well, what would you expect? Tired, overworked, depressed. Who wouldn't be? He's a good man, no doubt about that, very charming too, but he's getting on now and I doubt he has the energy to assert himself as vigorously as he used to. Losing Kerala to the communists has been quite a blow, and it hasn't gone down at all well with the Americans." Appleton puffed on his cigar. "But that's what happens when officials start feathering their own nests. The Indians, I mean, of course. They're all at it here. Corruption is rife, and not all voters are completely stupid, regardless of widely held attitudes to the contrary. At least Nehru had the good sense to publicly denounce the Congress party's faults, but what good is that without offering a viable alternative? The ordinary citizen of India doesn't care tuppence about politics. What he wants is food in his belly and a reliable water supply."

"And how does all this affect us?"

"It doesn't," David Appleton said with a relaxed smile. "It's none of our bloody business anymore, I'm very happy to say. There's no clear-cut long-term policy on anything, as far as most of us can make out. It would be downright laughable were it not such a delicate situation. Independence was different. Everybody wanted the same thing, but that was ten years ago. Now they're left with just one major political party who can't even agree on what to have for lunch." He rolled the ash from his cigar thoughtfully. "Some of them are determined to see India built into a modern state with all the scientific and social benefits that come along with it, while the rest of them want it to remain a simple-minded nation of self-sufficient villages. And if central government can't sing the same tune, what hope for the rest of the country?"

"What about the socialists?"

"Oh, nobody's worried about them." He sucked on his cigar.

"They're a pretty feeble bunch. Nehru stole their political clothes long ago with his socialistic ideas for Indian society, so they haven't much to argue for, and not one of them has any flair for the practical side of politics. No, it's the communists who have everyone sitting up and taking notice. They're well organized and efficient, and they have plenty of money for campaigning, and we all know where that's coming from."

"Russia?"

"Undoubtedly. And China. They're only too happy to fund the expansion of the communist agenda, although none of that's been officially verified, of course. That's what happens when you start shaking hands with the likes of Khrushchev and Bulganin. There are those among the Congress leaders who realize now that this was a very serious mistake. You would have thought that somebody might have had the good sense to think that one through, eh?"

"So what now?"

"Nothing." Appleton shrugged. "The Congress leaders in Kerala can't even pull together a cohesive opposition. The communists are well and truly in, and I wouldn't like to hazard a guess as to how long it will take to get them out. You'll find a lot of that out here. Far too much hot air and not enough firm action. That's what this country needs. Strong, decisive leadership."

"And that's not Nehru?"

"As a national statesman? I can't fault him. The man's a genius. He has won the hearts of the people, no doubt about that at all, but as a leader?" Appleton gave a small puff. "He's weak as a kitten." Lucien nodded quietly. "But who can blame him? There is only so much one man can do. There are four hundred million people in this country, and most of them are ignorant peasants. Think about that if you will. Four hundred million. Governing them is nigh on impossible while there is so much dissent in the ranks."

"Dissent from whom?"

"You'll pick it up as you go along." David Appleton chewed on his cigar for a while and regarded this new member, wondering if he really was as good as everyone said. Things were about to get complicated, particularly with the tour scheduled for the new year. He could have done with Smythson sticking around for another six months, with all his experience, but perhaps this one would work out well enough. "You'll like Nehru. And there are some good men around him too, but it's early days still. We just watch from the sidelines and lend friendly support without getting our hands dirty."

"Anything else I should know?"

"Kashmir remains a bone of contention." David Appleton adjusted his seat, finding a point of greater comfort in the gilded chair. "The usual noises are being made, but there's no way we would agree to make any sort of military commitment if things continue to escalate, which they probably will, judging by the looks of things. They'll just have to sort it out for themselves, like everything else. After all, you can't ask a sovereign state to leave the party, then call them back to clear up the mess, can you? But do mind what you say if you find yourself cornered, Grainger. It's all rather precarious and needs delicate handling."

"I see."

"Apart from that, I think you'll enjoy it here. There's a lot of grand-scale socializing, and nobody seems to care much about doing any real work. The Indians are quite capable of messing things up on their own without any assistance from us."

⚭

Sophie watched Rosamund Appleton's mouth moving and wished it would stop. It was unbearable, but bear it she must, together with the overwhelming urge to yawn. She felt the muscles in the back of her throat contracting, her nostrils beginning to flare. Take a deep breath, she thought sternly, and for heaven's sake try to keep up with what the woman is saying.

"...home for the incurables. In some ways it seems rather

pointless, doesn't it? What good are a hundred beds when there are a thousand invalids? But one doesn't like to say anything. They're so terribly fond of their institutions. You'll find there's plenty to get involved in. The difficulty is trying to fit it all in!" She paused to take a sip of water. Perhaps she had finished, Sophie thought. Perhaps this purgatory had finally come to an end. "You'll need to get your bearings first. See all the usual things. I could take you off for the full tour, if you like. Our driver's done it about a thousand times and I could practically tell you everything about everything, I've seen it all so often. You must see the Qutb Minar, the famous thirteenth-century tower. One of the Maharaja of Kapurthala's wives threw herself off the top of it and committed suicide! It's a wonderful city by Indian standards, the new part anyway. The whole thing was designed by Edwin Lutyens, although I doubt the British would have bothered had they known they'd be giving it all away a few years later. And don't take any notice of the beggars. They're everywhere, and if you give one so much as a penny, you'll be swamped by a thousand more. You must learn to turn a blind eye to it. And there's no point in attempting to help people who aren't prepared to help themselves, don't you think?"

Sophie stared at her, her eyes so tired that she could feel them watering, stinging sorely at the corners. It was a few moments before she noticed that the woman's mouth had stopped. Rosamund Appleton looked at her curiously, and Sophie realized with horror that she was clearly waiting for an answer. What had she said? Her mind had wandered so far away that she might as well have been asleep. She dug her fingernails into her palms, blinking her eyes to attention.

"That's very interesting," she said. It was all she could think of, except that she had to find a way to make the woman talk to somebody else. "I wonder what the General thinks?" she said quickly, turning to him. The glass eye stared back at her coldly, the other half-closed. "General Hurst?" Her voice carried rather further than she had intended, halting the conversation amid her immediate neighbors, who turned to look at her.

"What?" the General said, as though he'd been interrupted from something important.

"Nothing," Sophie tried to apologize. "I was just—"

"You'll have to speak up," he boomed at her. "Deaf in this ear." He raised his finger slightly to his left. "Burst an eardrum in the South Pacific."

"Oh," she said. Then, a little louder, "Must be awful."

"That's very kind of you, dear, but you need not concern yourself unduly. Deafness has its benefits." The good eye roamed to an oblivious Rosamund Appleton, who had now started on the General's wife seated lucklessly to her left.

❧❀☙

"I thought the evening would never end," Sophie said, slipping out of her dress, weary through to her bones. "Tessa Wilde was right about that Appleton woman. I've never heard anyone talk so much."

"Here." Lucien offered up his cuffs. "Take these out for me, would you, darling?" Sophie turned to him and released the gold links from his shirtsleeves.

"She's asked me to call on her in the morning around eleven. I don't think I can bear the thought of it."

"Comes with the territory, my dear, I'm afraid. I deal with the tacticians, you deal with the women and children. Just smile and think of England."

Sophie pulled off her earrings. "I have an awful feeling she's planning on presenting me to the DWA, and we're not even properly unpacked."

"You'll be fine."

"So long as she doesn't try to press half a pint of gin on me before lunchtime." She turned her back for him.

"Which reminds me," Lucien said, unzipping her dress. "It was rather bad form for you to ask for tonic water at the reception this evening, darling. I don't think anyone noticed, thank goodness. To refuse a drink is tantamount to issuing the host a personal slight. It smacks of taking the moral high ground."

"Oh!" Sophie said. "I didn't even think."

"Of course you didn't." He kissed the nape of her neck. "But nothing stirs suspicions in the service quite like a teetotaler. I don't want everyone thinking I've married a prude." He smiled at her and went to the bathroom, closing the door.

16

S ophie felt like an exhibit in a goldfish bowl, all eyes upon her as she answered question after question. "It was all a bit of a whirlwind," she said. "It came as a complete surprise when he asked me. I even said to him, are you quite sure?" The other women laughed.

"It's not like an ordinary marriage, of course," said Melanie Hinchbrook. "We ought to be paid a king's ransom for the work that is expected of us."

"I've adored all our Indian postings," said Lucinda Bevan. "Calcutta was tremendous fun. There was no end of parties."

"Oh, the parties." Tessa effected a huge, bored sigh. "That's something you'll have to get used to."

"Listening to the same old dreary conversations from the same old dreary people."

"Watch out for Lance Corporal Fellowes. We call him the octopus."

"And you're exactly his type."

"How long did you work at the Foreign Office?"

"Two years," Sophie said.

"Oh, to be in London," said Melanie Hinchbrook. "Right now I'd give anything for a decent department store."

"Any woman thinking of marrying into the service should be permitted to take her husband on a trial basis for the first year, and if it doesn't work out, she should be allowed to tear up the marriage certificate and have it annulled!"

"Delhi is a piece of cake in comparison to some postings. China is generally regarded as the shortest of straws, and I'd stay well clear of some of the African positions if you can. I couldn't wait to get out of Nairobi."

"If your predecessor is anything to go by, you'll be very happy here."

"June Smythson was quite beside herself when Charles was called back to Whitehall. I think she was hoping they'd stay on, even though he'd clearly had quite enough of the place. Anyone would have thought that she had taken leave of her senses, the way she behaved!"

"It doesn't do to stay on indefinitely," said Tessa. "People have a habit of going native when all vestiges of home are erased. Poor June was in pieces when they left. How are you finding the house?"

"It's perfect," Sophie said.

"No problems with the staff?" Melanie slid a sideways glance toward Ros Appleton.

"Well." Sophie hesitated a moment. The bearer would definitely have to go, particularly after that business yesterday when Lucien had come home to find the house in darkness and her fast asleep. She had even wondered if he hadn't gone and done it on purpose, just to make her look bad. It was clear that he didn't like her, and she didn't like him either. There was something about his brooding manner that made her feel very uncomfortable. "A few wrinkles to be ironed out, perhaps. I'm not at all sure about our bearer, Santash."

"I told you." Tessa nodded sharply toward the other women before turning to Sophie. "June Smythson thought the man a saint, but I have to say I never warmed to him. Some of these people have a bad attitude. It's June's fault. She was far too familiar with her staff. Especially with him. I think it gave him ideas. You know, once…" She hesitated, and lowered her voice. "Once, I saw him out where the dhobi was hanging the washing, and you know what I saw him doing?" She leaned forward into the circle of women. "He was *touching* her undergarments. Can you imagine that? Yes," Tessa said, returning her attention to Sophie. "There was even talk that she was—"

"Tessa." Ros Appleton glared at her. "We'll have no more of that vicious gossip, if you please, particularly as the poor woman is no longer here to defend herself."

"Like that business with Edwina Mountbatten," Melanie Hinchbrook said, raising a thinly plucked eyebrow. "She was very fond of Nehru, you know. A little *too* fond, if you ask me. The man was quite smitten."

"That's quite enough of that, Melanie," said Ros Appleton.

"What? It was the worst-kept secret in Delhi!" Melanie gave a small sigh of amusement.

"But imagine the scandal if it turned out to be true," said Lucinda. "Lady Mountbatten with a *Hindoo*."

Sophie felt as though she had swallowed a stone, the smile on her face sitting rigid, her stomach churning at the undercurrent that had entered the room so easily. "Oh, Lucinda! Do stop!" Melanie said. "And it's hardly in the same league as June having a soft spot for her husband's bearer, now is it?"

"You have to get rid of him, Sophie," Tessa said. "Pay him off if it makes you feel better. Just get him out of there. He's a bad apple."

"But what about finding a replacement?" Sophie asked.

"I'll have a word with Vicky. Let me send him to you tomorrow morning once he's done with Stephen. He'll know what to do."

"Thank heavens for Vicky," Lucinda said. "One has only to say the word and he'll move heaven and earth! The maid he found for me last year is a treasure."

"Thank you," Sophie said. "I've been so looking forward to coming here."

"You won't be saying that next summer when the temperature hits a hundred and ten."

"Those of us in the know haul out for the difficult months and leave the men to it. May and June are utterly unbearable."

"You're not to feel bored for one moment," said Rosamund.

"There are a hundred things needing our attention. There won't be a single gap in your diary by the end of the week, and you mustn't hesitate to call upon any of us if there is anything you need."

"That's very kind of you," Sophie said, heart sinking a little.

❧❀☙

True to Tessa's word, Vicky appeared at Sophie's door on the stroke of ten the following morning. Sophie had attempted to get Lucien to do the dirty work for her, saying over supper the previous evening that it would be so much better coming from a man, but he had dismissed her concerns, saying that anything to do with the household staff was well and truly her domain. Not more than five minutes after Vicky's arrival, the entire household staff—cook, sweeper, maid, dhobi, gardener, bearer, and driver—were gathered on the back veranda looking very nervous indeed. All with the exception of Santash, who bore an expression so severe that Sophie found herself unable to look at him. She steeled herself before addressing them all, Vicky translating as she spoke so there could be no room for misunderstanding. They would come into the study, turn by turn, where she would set out their duties and tell them what she would expect from each of them. Sophie then retired indoors and waited for Vicky to bring in the first of them.

"Santash," she began. "The sahib would prefer to bring his own bearer to attend him. He appreciates that you have been in service to the household under the Smythsons, but it is time for you to move on." She picked up the envelope she had readied for him. "In here you will find a reference and severance pay. You may finish now. We'll manage the rest of your duties." Santash stared at her for a moment, then took the envelope without uttering a word.

"That is all," Vicky said, indicating the door with a sharp nod of his head. Santash glared at him with a look so vicious that it sent a shiver through Sophie's bones. "Out," Vicky said. Santash turned abruptly and left the house, slamming the door as he went.

Sophie waited a brief minute before dropping into the seat behind the desk.

"Thank heavens," she said. "I don't mind telling you that I found that rather awkward."

"Do not worry, memsahib," Vicky said. "I have made enquiries and there is a very good bearer who is looking for placement in the private house. His name is John. He is a Christian, but he is a very good man with excellent references. I will try to secure him for you." He dropped his eyes in a show of discomfort. "It may take a little money, to release him from…"

"Of course," Sophie said. She opened the drawer of Lucien's desk, took out a few notes of modest denomination and gave them to Vicky, who slid them into his pocket, not even glancing in his hand. "I'm most grateful for your help, Vicky. Santash did seem awfully cross. It's a wonder Mrs. Smythson didn't get rid of him herself with an attitude like that."

Vicky looked at her for a moment, as though he were about to say something, then changed his mind.

"Your cook is not a problem, memsahib," he said. "He has very excellent qualifications, but he is not speaking very good English. He is keen to please the memsahib's house. You must tell him what you expect of him and give him clear instructions that he can understand, then he will be happy. A happy cook is a good cook, memsahib. I will bring him now."

With Vicky gone from the room, Sophie composed herself with a few deep breaths, smoothed her dress, and stood up. Vicky came back with the cook, who slipped the cap from his head and held it nervously in his hands, eyes fixed on the floor. Vicky told him to stand up and mind himself.

"Memsahib," the cook mumbled.

"Dilip," Sophie said. "Is everything in the kitchen to your satisfaction?"

"Yes, memsahib."

"Good." Sophie smiled at him.

"Do you have a problem cooking beef?"

"No, memsahib."

"Good," Sophie said. "Mr. Grainger likes his steak bloody. Very bloody."

17

Around the table, classified documents were passed around and opened. David Appleton looked up. "Now, I realize how much thought has gone into planning for this already, but the Prime Minister has accepted an invitation to visit Australia within the same tour, which means that our watch has been reduced to only four days."

"Four days?"

"I'm afraid so. Four days in India, four in Pakistan, and less than two in Ceylon."

Jim Bevan pulled his spectacles off and let out a gasp of irritation. "Well that's nothing short of ridiculous."

"Downing Street had very little choice in the matter, although you would have thought that somebody might have anticipated it earlier."

"Marvelous," muttered Tony Hinchbrook.

"Nevertheless, it is up to us to see to it that this visit feels particularly special, and there's to be no wandering from the agenda."

"Four days," Jim Bevan repeated. "It'll be impossible to extend the tour outside of Delhi in such a short time."

"They're already aware of that." Lucien flicked through the pages. "Looks like we'll be hosting the whole thing here, then the PM will fly straight on to Karachi."

"I suppose it could simplify things quite nicely," nodded Hinchbrook. "Get in and out as quickly as possible and there's less time for trouble."

"What about Lady Macmillan's arrangements?"

"We'll have to work out a separate program. Get the DWs to organize a couple of tea parties or something."

"Is there anything about the press arrangements?"

"There'll be three British correspondents with the party, but the home press is pretty much out of our hands."

"How friendly are we anticipating this trip to be?"

"Very," David Appleton said. "I don't want to detect so much as a whiff of protest, particularly when there are journalists around."

"What about security?"

"I don't think we'll have too much to worry about there. Downing Street will be making the usual arrangements and our Indian colleagues will no doubt be pulling out all the stops. Our own security will be stepped up accordingly, so do mind your movements, gentlemen. It might prove embarrassing to turn up at a lady friend's with a bodyguard in tow." A few smiles passed around the table. "We'll up the security in the residential compounds too, just to keep an eye on things." He closed his dossier. "That's all for now. We'll reconvene at three."

෴

Vicky held court from his corner table in Apna Stop, a small hole-in-the-wall chai shop set along Janpath, hidden behind the chaotic stalls of the noisy bazaar that lined the commercial end of the street, selling everything from cotton sheets to baskets of raw spices and paan. It was rare that he ever put his hand in his pocket to pay for his own Coca-Cola, for everybody knew that he was a powerful man who could be persuaded to use his influence to magic a reliable job out of nowhere. He had placed scores of people, and come Sunday, there would always be a steady trickle of hopefuls stopping by at his table, faces filled with despair or gratitude, depending on his favors. Vicky took pleasure in their attention, reveling in the respect that they showered upon him, the clamor to pay for his food.

On Sundays, Vicky was no longer a servant. He was a business-man, commanding a certain high regard from those he passed on the street on his way to Apna Stop where he would spend most of the day, talking business with the regulars, taking his time whenever he noticed someone hovering nearby, hoping for an audience with the man who was said to control all the jobs in one of the residential enclaves in the diplomatic district. Sometimes Vicky would make up his mind before the applicant had stepped one foot beyond the door. Too ugly. Bad teeth. Dirty clothes. Too old. In the early days, he had soon found himself unable to manage the deluge. Word had spread and he would arrive to be greeted by a queue. It had quickly become a serious headache, not just for Vicky, but for the poor besieged café owner, so Vicky had paid a man to get rid of the hordes of no-hopers who showed no sign of being able to make the initial down payment. He wasn't a charity. He was putting his own reputation on the line every time he agreed to take on an applicant. They would need reliable, cast-iron written references in order to be considered for any of the private households, and if they didn't have the required documentation, then that would of course cost a lot more. If they were successful in their application, which he could by no means guarantee, they would then be bound to show their grati-tude by way of a small commission paid to him out of their wage packet. He would not ask for much, just a very reasonable thirty per cent, and only for the first year, after which he would make a small reduction in his fee. He was not like those greedy, exploitative sorts who tricked workers into making agreements that they had no hope of ever repaying.

"It's a little cold today." The café owner wiped Vicky's table over and replaced the tin ashtray with a clean one. "Winter is creeping around the corner."

"It is October," Vicky said, as though the man were stupid.

"How is business?"

"I cannot complain," Vicky replied loftily.

"My cousin has a son who needs a good job," the café owner

mentioned casually, rubbing at an imaginary mark on the table's cracked surface.

"Then why don't you give him a job here?" Vicky said.

"He wants to be a driver."

"And where did he learn to drive a car?"

"Anyone can drive a car," the café owner said.

"And anyone can make your *makai na bharta*." Vicky stubbed out his cigarette and lit another. The café owner nodded a little, letting out a small huff of exasperation.

"He's a useless fellow. His mother thinks he's some sort of guru, always lazing around and thinking he's better than everyone else." Vicky dropped the spent match in the ashtray and appeared not to be listening. "And they expect me to make a man out of him? To pull a job for him out of thin air because they are too afraid to tell him the way it is?" He flicked his cloth in disgust. "You and I are successful, hard-working men, but you cannot teach that to these young people. Their heads are full of rubbish." He tutted to himself and went off to serve his customers.

"Mr. Vivekanand?" Vicky startled slightly at the sight of the figure who had appeared silently before him. He glanced quickly over his shoulder to the man seated on the single chair outside the café door, the one he paid to stop people coming in and bothering him. The man outside raised an eyebrow at Vicky and offered him a small gesture of innocence. Vicky looked back at the stranger.

"Yes?" he said.

"I understand that you are looking for security guards for one of the residential enclaves near Connaught Place."

"Where did you hear that?"

"The guard on the gate told me."

Vicky looked the man over. Tall and lean, strongly set, with broad shoulders and a fearless expression; a man like that would have no need of a broker to find work. Perhaps he was a migrant, Vicky thought. Delhi was full of them, able-bodied, eager men who had drifted in from the rural areas looking to make their fortunes in the city. He was probably penniless, yet his clothes were clean and well-pressed, his face freshly shaven, hair combed and oiled. "And who are you?"

"My name is Ramakrishnan. Jagaan Ramakrishnan."

"Well, Jagaan Ramakrishnan, you heard wrong, and I don't see people without an appointment. Can't you see that I am busy?" Vicky looked away with an air of boredom. The man stood his ground. "Hey!" Vicky snapped his fingers at the café owner. "Bring me a Coke, and make sure that it's cold." The café owner brought the drink to the table, opening it in front of his customer. Vicky put the bottle to his lips, took a long swallow, then looked back at the stranger. "Are you still standing there?"

"I want a job at the enclave, as a night guard."

"Oh do you now?" Vicky smiled his amusement. "And what makes you think that I have any interest in what you want?"

"I know what you are interested in," said the man. He tossed a thick envelope on to the table. Vicky's eyes sliced toward it for a split second. His smile began to waver, feeling stiff under the stranger's cool glare.

"You seem very full of yourself," Vicky said. "Particularly for a man in need of a job."

"I want to be posted at the second guardhouse, the one on the corner between the two—"

"I know where the second guardhouse is," Vicky snapped, setting down the Coke bottle in agitation. "Who do you think you are?"

"Check the envelope."

Vicky slid it from the table and into his lap, opening it and thumbing through the money, his face reddening. Whoever this man was, he was clearly a fool for the taking. "Have you done this kind of work before?"

"I have done all kinds of work before," he said.

"And where are your references?"

Jagaan reached into his pocket and pulled out two pieces of paper.

"I see," Vicky said, looking them over carefully, pretending to

examine each one in detail, camouflaging his poor literacy. "And
how long have you been in Delhi?"

"A while."

"You're a long way from home," Vicky said. He judged that it
would be a fair guess, the man's distinctive eyes a reliable indicator
for those descended from the far northern tracts. The man gave
him no answer. "Still, I suppose you look like you can handle
yourself." He pushed the envelope inside his shirt. "I'll see what
I can do.

Almost two thousand miles Jagaan had traveled, from Amritsar
in the north to Ootacamund in the far south, crossing six states,
passing through cities and towns and villages in a succession of
crowded trains and cramped, overloaded buses, sleeping on the
move, breaking his journey in the bigger stations where he could
wash properly and clean his clothes and eat a hot meal. He tried to
recall the moment when he had found the doctor's house, the sign
on the gate, *Iona* carved into the softwood, the way he had gone
straight to the door and knocked on it without hesitating. He had
gone to fulfill one purpose, to announce himself to Dr. Schofield,
to tell him who he was and why he was there. The newspaper
announcement had said that she had been married in London, the
notice placed by Dr. G. J. M. Schofield of Iona, Ootacamund, and
it was Dr. Schofield Jagaan had come to see, knowing that he had
nothing to lose.

A middle-aged woman had come to the door, plump and distracted with a duster in her hand, and had looked him up and down
with an air of superiority. When he asked if this was the house of
Dr. Schofield, the woman had demanded to know who he was and
what business he had being there. Jagaan had said that he had come
to speak to Dr. Schofield on the matter of his daughter's wedding.
It was the first time he had said her name aloud for as long as he

could remember, and it had echoed right through him, but the woman must have misheard or misunderstood, because she had given him a bemused frown and said that Miss Sophie didn't live here. She was Mrs. Lucien Grainger now, and she lived in New Delhi, in a very expensive house. Her husband was a diplomat, practically an ambassador, Mrs. Nayar had said proudly, as though it were her own daughter she was boasting of. She had kept on talking, oblivious to his shock while he stood there, his whole world upended at the mention of her name and the news that she was here in India.

He had to see her. Only then would he know what to do. So he had gone north again, a thousand miles, at times feeling her presence so surely that he could almost reach out and touch her. He never once doubted that he would find her; he just hadn't expected it to cost quite so much. His uncle's money was now gone, all of it, and Amritsar seemed a long way away.

18

Sophie shook an aspirin from the bottle and swallowed it with a mouthful of water before returning to her wan reflection in the dressing table mirror. Taking up her lipstick, she leaned forward and dabbed the ruby red top and bottom before slicking it into place with the tip of her finger and pressing her lips together. She sat back and sighed at herself, opened a small drawer and chose a pair of earrings, then fastened them before reaching for the single string of pearls that had been given to her one Christmas long ago, when she had been in a dark and lonely place. She held them in her hand for a moment, turning them over, thinking of dear, sweet Fiona Ripperton. She would be an old lady now. Sophie slipped the pearls around her throat and closed the small diamond clasp.

There would be no getting out of dinner tonight, even though she had sworn just last Friday that she would rather throw herself off a cliff than sit through another interminable evening with her husband's cronies. Perhaps she might feel differently if Lucien didn't insist on getting quite so drunk at these things. Not that everyone else was the picture of sobriety. Everything seemed to revolve around drinks, at any given time of day. In the morning it would be sherry, or bloody Marys if there had been a party the night before. As the clock neared lunchtime, gin and tonic would be offered, then wine with lunch, perhaps a liqueur afterward with coffee. The sherry would reappear should a caller drop by in the afternoon, then cocktails at six before facing a dinner served with the usual selection of vintages. It was a wonder anyone remained standing.

This was not the India she had fallen in love with, this colorless comedy of manners, each morning heralding the same long, boring routine stretching dully ahead. She went through the motions, smiled when she was expected to smile, shook hands with people she neither knew nor cared about, and stood by her husband's side when she was required to do so, running the same routines, having the same wretched conversations, eating the same food from the same table over and over again. There were times when she would sit and brush her hair in the mirror and yearn for the clatter of the typing pool and the bitter smell of burnt toast in a cramped, steamy kitchen. She shouldn't complain. It wasn't Lucien's fault. She should count herself lucky that a man like him would choose her for his wife.

She wanted a child so desperately, and she knew this now more deeply than ever. That first day, when Tessa had asked her outright if they were planning to have children, she had felt her heart burst open with the shock of her yearning. All those years locked in her own denial, unable to allow herself to even think of it, a baby, soft and warm, tiny in her arms, slumbering against her skin. How the void inside her ached.

They had had another argument last night. Lucien had not come home until one in the morning, and instead of going to bed at eleven as she usually did, Sophie had stayed up, picking over her frustration until she was so cross that she barely knew what to do with herself. By the time Lucien came through the door, she had been so exhausted that the wind had gone from her sails. She had intended to ask him where he had been all evening, and if he was planning on making a habit of leaving her on her own like this several nights a week, but something prevented her from uttering the words. It would make her sound like a shrew, and she had sworn to herself that she would never become that woman. Instead, she had told him that he might have let her know that he was going to be so late, to which he replied that he was tired and in no mood to deal with her petulance.

"Aren't you ready yet?" Lucien appeared in the doorway.

Sophie stood up from the dressing table, the train of her black evening gown spilling to the floor, and picked up the shawl draped over the corner of the bed. Delhi was cold at this time of year, and it was damp and foggy outside. Lucien flicked his eyes over her slender form for a moment, then turned and walked away. It seemed that only yesterday he would have sat with her while she dressed, helping her fasten her zipper, placing jewelry around her neck, patting her bottom affectionately. Sophie took up her small evening bag, a black velvet pouch with a pearl clip, and dropped her lipstick inside with a gold compact and a lace handkerchief.

Outside, Lucien was waiting for her on the porch, smoking a cigarette. "At last," he muttered as she stepped out to join him, sliding her hand into the crook of his elbow as they headed toward the waiting car.

"Do try not to get too drunk this evening, darling," she said gently. "It'll only make you feel ghastly in the—"

"Oh for God's sake." He lifted his arm clear of her hand. "You're not going to start all that again, are you? Because if you are, then you can bloody well stay here with your damned headache."

"No!" Sophie forced a smile and caught up with him. "I'm sorry, darling. It's just that I—"

"What? Just that you can't stop yourself from being a nag? Because that's what you're turning into. Nobody likes a nag. It's a bloody bore."

Sophie quieted and slid into the back seat behind the driver, Lucien walking around to the other side and wrenching the door open irritably before climbing in beside her.

"I'm sorry," she said.

Lucien glanced down at his wife's hand over his and ran his thumb over her wedding ring, circling its looseness around her finger. There had been more of her when they married in the early summer, and he remembered a time when she had filled her evening dress with soft curves and promising glimpses of smooth alabaster flesh. That first night after the simple ceremony in the somber surroundings of Marylebone register office, as he admired her in the moonlight, he could barely believe his good fortune. She was like a Canova, her skin almost translucent in its delicate paleness, her breasts soft and rounded like perfect fruit. With his eyes closed, she could almost have been Catherine.

⟢⟢⟢

"There you are!" Tessa Wilde negotiated her way through the crowd and took hold of Sophie's arm. "For a horrible moment, I thought you weren't coming!"

"So did I," said Lucien, placing a kiss on Tessa's cheek. "Where's that husband of yours?"

"In the billiard room, talking shop with David Appleton and his entourage. Oh! Will you look at that!" She lifted her hand to his face and wiped away the tiny flash of lipstick she had left there with her thumb. "There! Much better! We can't have you wandering into battle wearing half my make-up, now can we?" Lucien took his handkerchief from his pocket and rubbed the spot of skin briskly.

"See you later," he said, disappearing into the throng.

"Well!" Tessa huffed. "Thank God you're here. My face is positively aching from all that smiling. Don't those men ever stop talking?" She took two glasses of champagne from a passing orderly and handed one to Sophie. "I wouldn't mind so much if it stopped at the door, but of course Stephen will want to give me a blow-by-blow account of every little thing that was said when we get home." She shook her head and took a sip from her glass. "I don't know why he thinks I'm interested."

Sophie tipped her eyes in agreement, encouraging a sense of camaraderie between them, as though she too had to endure hours of tedious detail from her husband rather than the long silences that had ceased to be uncomfortable. She had given up any pretense of real conversation, preferring to stick to the safe ground of what was in the newspapers or who was coming to dinner. Lucien had not the slightest interest in her views and had displayed a penchant for making her feel stupid when she aired them anyway. "What do you know about it?" he would say, flexing an air of superiority. "That's the trouble with you women," he would remark. "A little knowledge is a dangerous thing."

Tessa let her eyes wander the room. "Good heavens," she hissed under her breath. "Whatever is Ros Appleton wearing?" Sophie waited a moment before stealing a glance, only to be caught red-handed. Tessa clasped hold of her arm, cursing her behind gritted teeth as they moved toward the offender. There was no other way out of it. "Ros!" Tessa said brightly. "What a *heavenly* dress!"

That night Sophie lay in bed nursing a hot-water bottle. Her period had come again.

1948

Cuttack, Orissa

19

The palace seemed very far away. For two days, Sophie and her father had traveled, crossing the vast expanse of India's central regions, heading east, over the heartlands of Madhya Pradesh, then into Orissa, almost as far as the Bay of Bengal. Under the hours of darkness, as the sleeper train crawled through the landscape, Sophie would watch the moon from her bunk, listening to her father's steady breathing, the carriage clattering slow and heavy from track to track, rocking her gently as the moon shone down on her, full and white, heavy in the night sky, the film of dirt on the window smudging a dewy halo around its glow. While watching the moon, Sophie thought of Jag, under this same moon somewhere, bathed by the same blue light that rendered everything beneath it so fragile.

The journey passed in a haze. Trains and rickshaws and waiting rooms and functional meals eaten without either of them noticing what was served or which town they were passing through as they neared their destination; the place at which she would be left to bring her child into the world. Last night, they had reached Cuttack and had stayed in the *dak* bungalow, where Sophie had lain sleepless again through the darkness hours, listening to her father's breathing, wondering if he too were awake, dreading the prospect of tomorrow.

At noon the next day, they arrived at the mission, its door set firmly into the windowless rust-red wall that ran half the length of the narrow street. There could be no mistaking it, the landmarks all as described: the stonemason's workshop on the previous corner, the flame tree with the missing limb. The street was quiet, one small tributary in a maze of winding passages that ran like a catacomb off the beaten track. The door to the mission was much larger than all the others, with an ornate frame, a square viewing hatch set within it. The aged wood, wrung out by the arid land-scape, bore tendrils of cracks where the sun had baked it dry. The masonry around it had decayed here and there, but that was to be expected for a wall of such age, and its general fabric seemed in a far superior state of repair to most of the other buildings that crammed the street. A tangle of electricity cables, threaded pre-cariously from house to house, fed the erratic power supply. Dr. Schofield checked the piece of paper on which he had written the address. He found that his hand was shaking, and he struggled to decipher his own handwriting, then examined the door again.

"This must be the place," he said. He recognized it from the description, the carved flowers cut deep into its timbers, but apart from that, there were no outward signs to announce its existence, no plaque on the wall, not even a name. It was all exactly as the shopkeeper had said, pointing them in the right direction while eyeing the suitcase he carried and the young woman who stood nervously at his side, knowing why they were there. Everybody here knew what that house was.

Dr. Schofield knocked on the dry wood with the head of his cane and concentrated hard on the door, willing it to open quickly, unable to look at his daughter, to see the fear and uncertainty on her face.

Sophie leaned a hand briefly against the wall to steady herself on the uneven ground. It had been a wearying morning, the last leg of their long journey a jolting, sickening ride in a hopelessly inad-equate cart drawn by a ripe-smelling camel. She felt wrung out and so tired that she would happily have lain down in the street if she thought it would bring her some respite. Sleep eluded her at every turn. She would lie awake night after night, tossing and turning, listening to her baby, unable to imagine the fate that awaited them. She had heard about these places, where fallen women were made to scrub floors and work in steaming laundries and were forced to suffer every humiliating waking hour in penance for having conceived, regardless of how and by whom. She had considered ending it all. She could kill herself, but that would have meant killing the child too. His child. *Their* child.

Perhaps she had known all along what she was doing, that night in the water garden, but in that moment nothing could have stopped her. She had wanted to, and she had wanted him. She had yearned for him with every bone in her body, and although she had known that she would surely pay for it for the rest of her life, she didn't care. But the baby, the baby she had not thought of, not for a moment. It had never crossed her mind, and now she would have to bear the consequences. The baby felt it too, unsettled inside her, sensing her fear. And now they were here, at the place her parents had refused to discuss, the place that had been referred to only as *going away*, her father staring at an imposing door in a sprawling town set within a barren landscape, unable to look at her.

From somewhere deep down, Sophie's panic began to rise. She could burst into tears and throw herself upon his mercy and beg her father to take her home. He would be unable to refuse her. He had been nothing but kind to her from the outset, and he would surely not let her down now. But she couldn't ask it of him. He had been crushed by the news, his face contorted as though he had been punched in the stomach. She had broken her father's heart, and the shame of it had eaten her alive. She couldn't even look at him, because every time she did her eyes would fill with tears, and she too would feel her heart breaking.

She had thought about her father every day during those years he was away, watching out for him constantly in the hope that she might see his figure appear in the street, tall and handsome in his uniform, dropping his kit bag and scooping her up, swinging her around as she smothered him in kisses. And then it seemed almost as if she grew up overnight, and that she had become the woman at the door, waiting for the man to return from war, her mother staying in the house as she always did. In their misshapen normality, father and daughter would embrace on the garden path, and she would lead him into the kitchen where her mother would stand from the table and look at him as though he were a stranger. Then her mother would turn her back on him and prepare something for supper, and a cloud would descend upon them all. It was the same black cloud that had descended the morning Dr. Reeves had told her father that she was in trouble, when Sophie's mother had flown at her in the drawing room, first with a stinging slap that had knocked her to the floor, then with a rain of blows that seemed to go on for ever until her father finally dragged her off, kicking and screaming. Sophie's bruises had been terrible, and her father had had to make something up about how she had tripped on the hem of her dressing gown and fallen down the marble steps outside their apartments.

At least he had been there to intervene. Sophie thought of the child growing inside her and found herself thinking of all the occasions when there had been no one to protect her from her mother's fits of rage, like the time she had picked up a tortoiseshell brush and broken it over her head. Sophie had dared to flinch while her mother tore through the knots in her hair, so she brought the brush cracking down and said, there, that'll give you something to cry about. It didn't happen when her father was around. Sophie could breathe easily then, his presence alone enough to ensure her safety. Not that she had ever said a word about it to anyone, but sometimes her father would go quiet, frowning over the top of his newspaper, then ask her to come closer so that he could take a look at the back of her legs, or the top of her arms, or a bump on her head. Sometimes he would bring out his doctor's bag and let her play with his stethoscope while he dabbed with cotton wool or applied a little ointment and gave her a special bandage tied with a bow. And then her parents would not talk, sometimes for days. Not that Sophie minded. It heralded better times when they did not speak. Her father would keep her close to him, taking her for outings, perhaps to have a glass of lemonade in the local pub while he enjoyed a pint of beer, or to visit a friend of his, to see a man about a dog as he liked to say, although rarely was a dog ever involved. She would be with him all the time, barely seeing her mother at all, but then the war came and he was sent away, and the cloud descended once more. Now the cloud had returned, and this time Sophie knew it would never lift.

Out in the noonday sun, Sophie realized just how parched she felt and wished that she had accepted the cup of sweet chai from the shopkeeper. She could have sworn that she had put a small flask of drinking water in her bag before they set out that morning, but where it had got to was anyone's guess. She concluded that she must have either forgotten to pack it in the first place or left it behind at the *dak* bungalow with the kind lady who had sung to her softly and helped her to dress while she cried her eyes out.

The January sun seemed much fiercer out here in the narrow street, the close proximity of its high walls trapping and baking the air. Dr. Schofield knocked on the door again, a little harder this time, and looked around self-consciously as the rap from his stick amplified around the ancient houses that lined the other side of the street.

"Come on," he muttered to himself. He jolted as a bucket of water was thrown from a nearby window, splashing to the ground a few yards from their feet. Even as it moved toward the gulley it began to evaporate, the dark marks of the furthest droplets disappearing almost instantly. Sophie squinted up at the faceless window and felt herself dissolving. She looked back at the door anxiously, knowing that she would not be able to stand for much longer. The baby was asleep inside her, unmoving. She stole a glance at her father's reddening face. He sighed at the door in exasperation. Perhaps no one would come, she thought, and they would have to turn back. She closed her eyes and prayed.

Light footsteps approached. The sound of a bolt being thrown. The viewing hatch opened and a woman's face appeared behind the fretworked screen.

"Yes?" she said, peering out to see who had dared to knock on her door. It took a moment for her eyes to adjust to the glare sufficiently to take in the two figures standing before her. She seemed too busy to smile and looked at them with suspicion.

"Is this St. Bride's mission?" Dr. Schofield asked, holding up the slip of paper.

"Who are you?" The woman came closer to the screen, checking the street in both directions. From behind the door they could hear evidence of occupation, that constant, dull cacophony when there are too many people in one place.

"There's no sign on the door," Dr. Schofield explained. "I wasn't sure if we had the right address."

"What do you want?" the woman asked.

"My name is Dr. George Schofield, and this is my daughter, Sophie." He paused a moment. "I think you're expecting us. It's very hot out here," he added, removing his hat to display his fatigue. "Might we come inside?"

The woman assessed him for a little longer, then slammed the hatch closed. In a few moments, the heavy timbers were heaved open on a hidden hinge that seemed to split the door in two, as though one entrance had been secreted within another. The woman stretched out her arm to aid Sophie's negotiation of the step, bringing her into the cool of the shade beyond the thick stone wall. Dr. Schofield climbed in behind her.

"You must excuse me," said the woman, bolting the door shut and finally offering them a smile. "We get some unwelcome visitors here. There are still a lot of people who don't approve of our activities and try to make trouble for us. Here," she noticed Sophie's fatigue with concern and urged her to sit on the cool stone block that ran the length of the wall, "let me bring you some water."

Sophie sat gratefully and pulled the sari from her head, using her hand to fan herself a little. The air was less unforgiving here, and she took a few moments to rest and take in her surroundings, sitting beneath the shade of the deep archway that passed under the building. A few yards ahead, it appeared to open out into a small square courtyard that dropped down through the center of the house like a hidden cloister, where a squabbling group of sparrows bathed in the overspill from a stone water trough fed by an old hand pump. Sophie breathed deeply, taking in the thick scent of dry dust and rich spices that clung to the inner walls.

The woman returned carrying a clay jug and two cups. Tall and lean, with jet-black hair and pale, translucent skin peppered with freckles, she sat down beside them and poured some water before handing a cup to each of them. Dr. Schofield guessed that she was not quite Indian, a woman of mixed blood. Sophie took her cup and began to drink, gulping down all of it, and nodding gratefully as the woman refilled it for her. Dr. Schofield sipped at his cautiously.

"Don't worry. I haven't given you the water from our well," she said with a smile. "It doesn't seem to agree with everyone. This has been boiled."

"Thank you," Sophie said, returning the cup to her. "Gosh. That's so much better."

The woman gave her an approving nod. "Dehydration is a very real danger. You must remember to drink plenty."

"This place certainly took some finding," Dr. Schofield said.

"We don't exactly advertise ourselves." The woman poured some water into the cup Sophie had used and quenched her own thirst. "Where have you traveled from?"

"East," Dr. Schofield said evasively, frowning briefly to himself. "Although we are from England."

"I can see that." The woman laughed, a big, generous laugh filled with white teeth. "But isn't this rather out of the way for a..." She paused, suddenly embarrassed. "Never mind. It just seems that you've traveled a very long way only to find an overcrowded, tumbledown house. We do our best," she said. "It's not too bad at the moment, but there are times when we've been quite overrun. Forgive me for the way I answered the door. We have to be careful of reprisals. Nobody ever wants to admit that a girl doesn't get into that condition on her own. Some are raped, sometimes by members of their own family." She spoke matter-of-factly, unruffled by Dr. Schofield's evident discomfort. "Others have been led up the garden path and left in the lurch. You know how these things are." She smiled at Sophie. "We don't ask questions here. We've seen it all before."

"Your English is very good," Sophie complimented her.

"I went to school in England," the woman said.

"Really?" Dr. Schofield straightened himself, determined to appear suitably impressed, despite his exhaustion. Thank God, he thought. Thank God this place was as he was told. He couldn't have borne to put Sophie into one of those terrible places people talked about. He would have refused, and he had told his wife as much, vowing that he would not leave her anywhere if he thought it unsuitable. Veronica had screamed at him and had thrown a vase and told him that if he dared to come back with Sophie, she would leave. She would not suffer the humiliation of it.

Dr. Schofield felt a wave of tiredness as some of the tension seeped from him. With all his remaining strength, he somehow managed a smile for the woman who had shown them kindness today. "So, if you went to school in England, may I ask how on earth you ended up in a remote place like this?"

"My mother founded the mission years ago."

"Your mother?" Dr. Schofield sat to attention slightly. "Miss Pinto is your mother?"

"Yes." The woman smiled. "She had a love affair which she foolishly assumed would end in marriage, then discovered that she was expecting me. The man couldn't get away fast enough. He was British, of course, and already married to someone else. They always were in those days." Sophie stared at her incredulously, taken aback by her openness. "Don't worry. It could have been a lot worse. At least he had the decency to give her a generous payout before deserting her, enough for her to buy herself a house and not to have to worry about putting food in my mouth. She found this place and bought it for next to nothing, then placed the rest of the money in trust. My mother turned out to be quite a whiz with her investments, and sometimes we receive donations." She looked at Dr. Schofield with a sudden air of deference. "And your generosity was a gift from God."

Dr. Schofield nodded in small acknowledgement. All this talk of saving for a rainy day, after the war and all; he had thought it a stupid expression. But he had saved anyway, regardless of the vagaries of life and death, and now had come the downpour. God knows he would have given it all, and more, to have made this go away, to have saved his daughter from this cruelty. But there was nothing more that he could do, and the money might at least go some way to salving his conscience.

Noticing Dr. Schofield's drifting expression, the woman brightened with a small clap of her hands. "Well!" she said. "We've never wanted for anything. Right now we have twelve women here, but that could change tomorrow. Some don't stay very long, others have been here for years, too afraid to leave."

"Well, well." Dr. Schofield looked up and admired the decaying old house, its battered state lending its faded pink grandeur a suitably feminine charm. "Who would have thought it?"

"Would you like to come and meet the family?"

Recovered from the heat, Sophie and Dr. Schofield followed the woman across the courtyard, through a door in the far corner that opened into a small, untidy office. She called hello, switching effortlessly to Hindi as she announced the arrivals, showing the pair of them into the cramped room where an elderly woman, plump and soft-figured, looked up from a pile of paperwork.

"Maa? This is Dr. Schofield and his daughter, Sophie."

"Ah." Miss Pinto stood up. "We meet at last." She shook hands firmly with Dr. Schofield and offered Sophie a sympathetic smile. "Do take a seat." She gave them a moment to settle themselves. "I see you have met my daughter, Pearl."

"Yes," they said.

"Can I offer you some tea?"

"Yes please," said Dr. Schofield, and they entered into a ritual of small talk about the heat and dust. When the tea came, he could feel his hand shaking, the cup clattering lightly against its saucer.

"You mustn't worry," Miss Pinto said. "Your daughter will be safe here with us, and when her time comes, we will take good care of her."

Miss Pinto had never had to suffer the act of separation from her daughter. She was all she had left, this perfect child she had birthed into her own hands. The fear and pain had been unbearable, but to lose her child would have been beyond any suffering she could imagine. Alas, this was not the way it could be for the women who came here. Their babies would be taken from them, never to be seen again. For some of the girls, this was the way they wished it to be. Yet others would plead and cajole to no avail. The lucky babies would be adopted. The rest would be taken in by the many orphanages that mopped up the remnants of those who were either unwilling or unable to take responsibility for the lives they had created. But, above all, none would be killed, left outside to die of exposure or poisoned by their own mother's hand. It was the best Miss Pinto could offer, each child having to make what they could of the unfortunate life that had been bestowed upon them.

Dr. Schofield put his cup down on her desk. "And what about the infant?"

The words were out of his mouth before he could stop himself. Why he asked, he didn't know, but it had suddenly seemed so important. He knew it was too little and far too late. None of them had ever mentioned the word. Not his wife, not him, and not his daughter. She was to have a child, and all he could think of in that cramped office with the noisy, sluggish ceiling fan, all he could think of was the way he had been awash with love for her when she was born, this young woman who now sat beside him, a child growing inside her, a child she would never come to know. It tore him up, that she would have to bear this terrible thing, this thing that would leave an indelible mark on her for the rest of her years. He wondered if she would ever be able to put it behind her, to forget all this and get on with her life. He couldn't bear it. It was his worst nightmare, not that he had ever known it until it presented itself to him. She was supposed to have a happy future, this girl of his. He had pictured it so many times, imagining her grown up, finding her stride, discovering the joys of life, walking up the aisle on his arm one day. He had seen it all, dreaming of her in a place where all those wrongs that had been done to her had been put right, a place where she was safe and happy. But he had never seen this.

"The infant will be taken care of and placed with a good family." Miss Pinto smiled at Sophie. "It is hard, I know, my dear, but it is for the best. In time, you will see that. You are young. You have your whole life ahead of you, and there will be other children." Sophie nodded bravely, her lips held tightly together. "I promise." Miss Pinto got up from her seat and came to comfort her. "You will recover from this, and your baby will have a good life."

Dr. Schofield couldn't bring himself to look up from his cup. He didn't need to witness his daughter's expression to know that she was already in pieces. He could feel it as surely as he could feel the thin wafts of air from the rusting fan. He finished his tea in silence, not noticing that the suitcase had been taken.

"Now, Dr. Schofield, it is time for you to say good-bye to your daughter."

Sophie felt her heart lurch. They had only just arrived. She had expected him to stay with her until she had prepared herself, at least for a few hours, so that she could come to the point of departure ready for the moment of separation. She looked at her father in desperation, wanting to shout, *Don't leave me here!*

"I will give you some privacy for a moment, but don't take too long. It only makes it worse." Miss Pinto left them in peace, closing the door quietly.

Dr. Schofield, a sad figure in his crumpled suit, stood from his seat and seemed to sag. He dipped his face toward the floor, raised his hand, and pinched the bridge of his nose hard.

"It's all right, Daddy," Sophie said. She felt unable to reach out and touch him, to squeeze his hand or press upon him one of their warm embraces. Instead she just stood there, ashamed. "I'll be all right. You mustn't worry about me."

"Oh, Sophie." He stepped forward and hugged her. "I'm so sorry, my darling."

Sophie had never seen her father cry before.

20

The train pulled in almost six hours late. Dr. Schofield, weary from the journey, put his hat on and climbed down from the carriage. A boy rushed to his side, pulling at his bag. "Me carry! Me carry!" he shouted.

"*Chale jao!*" Dr. Schofield brushed him off, clutching the bag to his chest. He had learned his lesson about street rascals long ago, brazen little louts who would run off and disappear into the crowds with anything they could carry. Pushing his way through the swarm of people, he exited the station to see Mr. Ripperton waiting beside one of the blue palace cars, driver at the wheel. The Maharaja must be back and expecting someone important to send the first ADC to greet them. Dr. Schofield turned and made his way to the area where the rickshaw *wallahs* gathered.

"George!" He halted at the call of his name. "George!" Mr. Ripperton raised a hand in greeting, threw his cigarette to the ground, and stamped it out before marching over. "I thought you'd never get here." They shook hands.

"Rip," Dr. Schofield said. "What brings you here? Waiting on an esteemed guest?"

"Only you. Thought you might need a lift back to HQ. Can't be too careful at the moment. There's still a lot of saber-rattling going on. We had a stabbing on the estate on Monday. Nobody will say who did it, of course. Poor chap damn near lost a kidney." The driver jumped out from behind the wheel and took Dr.

Schofield's bag, placing it on the front seat before opening the back doors for the men. "How was your trip?"

"All right," he said. "Dusty."

"It's a fine thing young Sophie is doing there, going off to do her bit like that, particularly at a time like this. She'll have them all whipped into shape in no time. Did you get to look the place over?" The car pulled away, honking its way through the crowds.

"Yes, a bit."

"I suppose they're all the same," Rip said, adopting some of his passenger's fatigued manner. "Still, good for her to get out of the old mausoleum, I suppose. It can't be easy to be the only young bones in a place like that, although I have to say that poor Fiona is bereft, missing her like mad already."

George stared out of the window, unable to concentrate on the patter of small talk that fell from Mr. Ripperton's mouth. It was part of his job, to impart polite conversation, keeping the Maharaja's guests entertained and attended to, and he was very good at it. All the way to the palace, his steady, melodious voice imparted useless snippets of information about matters in which Dr. Schofield had no interest. He would reply with a nod or a small yes or no, and that was all it took to maintain the flow. George wished that Rip hadn't bothered to collect him. He would have been just fine traveling solo and felt the need to be alone with his thoughts.

The prospect of dealing with his wife hung around his neck like a dead weight. All he wanted was something decent to eat, and his bed, yet before that he would no doubt have to go through the performance of allowing Veronica to remind him of just how useless a husband and father he had been. There would be no sidestepping it. She had had too much time to sit there scheming, building up a fine head of steam that she would unleash upon him the moment he got back, sparing him nothing, hurling every error she could trawl from her memory. He would utter no word of protest today. It would serve only to extend the misery of the encounter and he was too damn tired. There was only one way to deal with it: walk straight into it and get it over with quickly. A glass of whisky and a sleeping pill would probably help, either before or afterward. Perhaps he would have them before, to soften the assault.

After what seemed an eternity, they arrived at the palace, passing through the high gates, up the long showy driveway. The car pulled to a halt.

"Take the doctor's bag to his apartments, will you?" The driver saluted, Mr. Ripperton waiting until he had gone. "George, before you dash off, there's something you'd better know. Come and have a peg for a minute, would you?" Too tired to argue, George followed him through the blue courtyard.

Mrs. Ripperton stood at the open window in her parlor, looking out on to the fountain, newly planted with bright marigolds, a gin and tonic in her hand.

"George!" She had the door open for them before they had ascended the steps. She kissed his cheek and led them inside. "Oh George, do come in and sit down. You must be completely exhausted, you poor dear. Was there any trouble on the trains?"

"No," he said. "Just running hours late and a whole lot of chaos as usual."

A look passed between Mr. Ripperton and his wife. Mrs. Ripperton waited until both men had a whisky in hand before sitting with them.

"Oh George, I'm afraid we have some rather awful news," she said. Dr. Schofield looked up, his face expressionless, as though there could be no news to touch him after what he had been through these last few days. "It's Veronica. Her mother has been taken ill. She was very upset about it."

Bearing in mind his wife's foul mood when he had left her, Dr. Schofield understood the reason for the early warning. The last thing he needed right now was to walk into a situation even worse than the one he was already anticipating.

"I see," he said. "Well, thanks for the advance notice. I'd better finish this on the double and go and see how she is."

"Well," said Mrs. Ripperton, glancing briefly at her husband. They had talked about it over supper last night, discussing how best to break the news. The business about the sick mother was a downright lie. No telegram had been delivered for Mrs. Schofield that day, nor any letter. If it had, it would have arrived at the ADC's office first, to be noted as received and sorted before being passed along with the rest of the day's post and wires. Veronica Schofield had barely waited a day before packing her bags and leaving.

Heaven only knew what had gone on in their apartments behind closed doors, and Fiona had ventured to her husband that she wouldn't be surprised if they hadn't had some kind of terrible row and she had upped and left for good. Everybody in that part of the palace had heard the commotion, the crashing and banging and shouting. It was none of their business, Rip had reminded her, and she was not to go interfering. They would give George the plain facts of her departure, then leave the poor man alone. "That's the thing, you see, George." Fiona Ripperton girded herself with a good sip of her drink. "She's gone." The glass in Dr. Schofield's hand halted midway to his mouth. Mrs. Ripperton gave him a rather pathetic smile. "Oh George, I'm so sorry."

George Schofield sat in silence as though cast in bronze, a lifetime running through his head. The war had left a gaping chasm between him and his wife. Sophie had been just twelve years old when he left, a sweet girl, awkward and thin, uncomfortable in her own presence. He'd grown runner beans in his garden, and they'd had a cat named Pumpkin who liked to sleep in the vegetable patch. But then the war came, and by the time he got back, Sophie was seventeen. He had hardly recognized her, this lovely young woman who had come running through the door the moment she glimpsed him from behind the curtain where she had been waiting all day. She had greeted him with tears of joy. Sophie carried no resemblance to her mother at all, the wife who had become a burden to him, the years having worn him down to this pathetic shadow of a man, hell bent on keeping his family together, no matter the cost.

He sat and thought about his wife. There were times when he had wished her away, hoping that she might just pack up and leave one day, or, in darker moments, imagining her dead, seeing his figure mourning at her graveside, his daughter by his side. At least it would have been over then, this hell, the sinking feelings that filled him with dread as he neared the threshold of his own home, wherever that may be, like entering a vacuum where nothing could breathe. He would try to anticipate her mood, picking his way carefully through her neuroses. He didn't mind so much for himself. It was his daughter he worried about. That was why they had come here, to force open his wife's isolated existence into which she was pulling Sophie, sucking her down like a calf caught in quicksand. At least the beatings had stopped. Or that was what he had thought. It was the first time he had witnessed it first hand, the day he had broken the news about Sophie. Perhaps, had he not been so shocked, he would have acted more quickly to shield his daughter before his wife picked up the ashtray and hit her with it.

As a youngster, Sophie had never said a word about her mother's behavior, not once, and even when he had questioned her about her bumps and bruises, she had said that she had fallen over or banged her head by accident and he had chosen to believe her and told her to be more careful, because he couldn't bring himself to think that his wife was responsible for her injuries. All mothers disciplined their children. It was a necessary part of raising them. Whether he agreed with her methods seemed almost by the by, as he was not the one who was there to do it. Veronica should never have had children. She had never been able to cope with it. Even when Sophie was a baby, he had seen his wife staring down into the cot, looking on impassively while she cried, walking out of the room and closing the door on the wailing infant.

He had expected it to pass, the indifference, the complete absence of interest. It wasn't unknown for a new mother to feel overwhelmed at first, yet nothing had lifted her blackened mood, and she made it clear to him that there would be no more children. It was just as well, he had thought, as the years wore on and his wife hardened further. Even then, he hadn't realized the full extent of it, until one evening he came home to find his daughter hiding in the coat cupboard under the stairs. The sight of her had brought his heart to a stop, one side of her face coated with a thin veil of dried blood. Veronica had refused to speak to him. She wouldn't even tell him what the hell had happened. Sophie was just seven years old at the time.

He had told Veronica that if he ever found their child in that state again, he would have her committed. He would have her locked up with the rest of the wailing harpies who filled the asylums, and if she thought it an idle threat, she was very much mistaken. It would take just one other doctor, he had told her, and he'd be able to get a second signature in a flash. Veronica had heeded the warning, or so George had thought, for he never saw Sophie's blood on the floor again.

Fiona sipped from her gin and tonic and gave her husband a feeble smile. Dr. Schofield seemed to have drifted, his eyes fixed on the view across the courtyard, the pale stone wall split in two by shadow. All at once he put his glass to his lips and swallowed the whisky in one long, steady motion. He put it down on the table and tapped the side for a refill, his eyes set upon it. Mr. Ripperton fetched the bottle without a word and filled his friend's glass generously, pouring another for himself to keep him company.

Nobody spoke. There was nothing to say.

• 1958

Ootacamund,
"Queen of Hill Stations"

21

Mrs. Nayar's hands flew to her face, an outward rush of joy spilling from her as she threw her arms around the unexpected visitor. "Miss Sophie!" She squeezed her hard before shouting into the house: "Salil! Miss Sophie is here! Salil!" Sophie felt the bag pulled from her hands, Mrs. Nayar grasping her arm and heaving her in through the door. "The doctor not here. He at the clinic. Come, we go now!" She tugged at Sophie's sleeve. "He will be so pleased to see you. Where is husband?"

"It's just me, I'm afraid," Sophie said.

"Why you not call before?"

"I wanted to it to be a surprise."

"Oh!" Mrs. Nayar laughed. "He will have *big* surprise!"

"How is Dad?"

"The doctor is very fine, miss. He is always talking about you and telling us that you marry burra sahib with big job in important matters. We are all so happy for you and wishing you would come soon. The doctor was very proud. He put big notice in all the newspapers, even in the *Times of India*! Dr. G. J. M. Schofield of Iona, Ootacamund, announces proudly the marriage of his daughter Miss Sophie to important mister so-and-so in London! He was making sure everyone will know that his daughter is doing so well in making the excellent marriage! We have visitor coming from far away to give you congratulations, but I tell him you no live here, you live Delhi!"

"Miss Sophie!" The cook thundered into the hallway, crashing in like a buffalo from the back of the house, his face split into a beaming smile.

"Salil!" Sophie reached out to squeeze his hand fondly. "It's so nice to be back. Please," she turned to Mrs. Nayar, "let's not disturb the doctor. I'll stay here and get settled and we shall surprise him when he gets back from the clinic."

Mrs. Nayar looked disappointed for a moment, then exchanged words with Salil, a rapid fire of harsh dialect that Sophie had never quite managed to get to grips with. "OK," she conceded. "I shall bring you some tea and Salil will make special supper for celebration."

"You want me to make gunpowder chicken?"

"Oh goodness, no. I'm not sure my constitution is up to one of your famous baptisms of fire tonight," Sophie said tactfully. Salil had an iron-plated palate and, if left to his own devices, would happily throw in enough chilies to kill an elephant.

"Gunpowder chicken?" Mrs. Nayar tore into him, wagging her finger in his face. "You want to give Miss Sophie nightmares? You will not be making gunpowder anything. Make tea. Not masala chai. Proper English tea with boiled milk."

"Thank you, Mrs. Nayar. I'll take it in the doctor's study."

Pulling off her gloves, Sophie wandered into her father's private room, dominated by the big mahogany desk set into the bay window overlooking the garden, its surface scattered with untidy papers beneath the usual clutter of medical odds and ends, a bone-handled patella hammer, the top half of a steel otoscope, a blue-rimmed enamel kidney bowl filled with rubber bands. The wedding photograph she had sent by airmail six months ago as summer broke over England sat among it all in a silver frame, the same frame that had once held a picture of her parents on their own wedding day, standing stiffly side by side outside a church vestibule.

Sophie perched herself comfortably on the edge of the desk and looked out of the window, loosening the silk scarf tied around her neck, her free hand wandering to the old black and white cat that lay snoozing in her father's chair. "Hello, Poocha," she whispered. The cat half opened one lazy eye and curled into her fingers, purring.

Outside, the garden lay shrouded in the permanent mist that veiled the hilltops of the Nilgiris during the winter months, lending it a dreamlike quality, trees appearing and disappearing through the milky-white haze. Sophie had spent a great deal of time in that garden, recovering slowly under the protective bough of the jacaranda tree, heavy with lilac-blue blossoms, watching from the silvered teak planter's chair as Salil tended to his kitchen garden while Mr. Nayar huffed and puffed up and down with the old rotary lawn mower. Salil had a gift for nurturing tender seedlings, and liked nothing better than to harvest a fine dish of freshly plucked vegetables for the supper table, setting it down amid grand claims of how it had all been growing quite happily while they had breakfasted that morning.

Poocha rolled on to his side and pushed his head into his paws, the pillow of the seat radiating warmth where his body had lain. Sophie left him in peace and went to the window, pulling back the lace curtain. The essence of her father filled the room, the musky scent of teak oil, the rich beeswax soaked thirstily into the wood-paneled walls, the sweet tang of the cigarettes he liked to smoke while fiddling with broken instruments he had no hope of ever repairing. It was as though Iona had absorbed some part of him, the part that he had needed to put down, to discard as no longer useful or necessary, and it weighed heavy in the fabric of the walls. The house had been built at the turn of the century by a one-time Scotsman who had gone on to a more permanent residence in St. Stephen's cemetery some twenty years ago. A pretty two-story building of dove-gray stone and smooth timbers set amid a silver-blue grove of fragrant evergreens and eucalyptus trees, it had taken them in kindly, and had seemed gladdened to have its fires lit once more by a family in need of shelter. The moment she first set eyes upon it, Sophie had let out an unexpected sigh. All at once grand yet quaint, it was everything she might have wished for herself had she been looking for a house of her own. From beneath a green shingled roof, the four bedrooms faced east, Swiss gables overlooking the deep ravine of the sharply falling valley, its dense forests filled with chittering wildlife. To the west of the house, where fewer windows looked out, the forest rose again, revealing clearings in the hillside here and there to make way for the picturesque houses that clung prettily to the steep landscape amid the woods, taking in the best of the views. Her father had chosen well, and it had felt like a sanctuary. A place to heal.

A small knock came from the open door. Salil, bearing a wooden tray, entered quietly and set it down on the table beside the fireplace where a single thick log crackled softly in the grate.

"I make you nice vegetable and butter sandwich," he said, taking the poker and pushing the glowing wood back in the grate before throwing in another log from the basket. "It is so very nice for us in seeing you." He straightened himself and grinned at her. "We are saying always, 'When is Miss Sophie coming?' And now?" His head wobbled in satisfaction. "Now you are here."

"Thank you, Salil. It is good to be back."

"Please." He indicated the tray, a small spray of pale primroses placed beside the teacup. "You tell me if you want something else."

"This is lovely." She sat beside the fire. "Really. I couldn't wish for anything more."

⅋⊘⅊

The warmth from the hearth curled irresistibly around Sophie's travel-weary legs, wrapping her blissfully in its glow. She slipped off her shoes, giving in to temptation, and tucked her feet into the soft armchair, resting her head against the worn green leather, unable to resist the urge to close her eyes for a little while. It had been a long day.

The book slipped quietly from her fingers and fell silently into the pile of embroidered pillows scattered loosely around her, her face softened into sleep. For the first time in a long while, her rest was deep and untroubled, taking her far from the world in which she now lived, lifting her into the subtle realms of endlessness where all was well, all things revived. They were dancing, him whirling her around, her head thrown back and laughing. She had never felt so happy, so warm in his arms, lifted by the music, being swept along, the durbar hall empty but for them and the orchestra. She was weightless, her heart filled with love, gazing into his smiling face, his pale green eyes. She sighed in her sleep, wrapped in a warmth so delicious that it felt like heaven. Her father's voice came into her dream. They were out walking, trekking the gladed pathways through the forest, sunlight dappling through the shivering leaves, spots of bright light carpeting the forest floor beneath their feet. Her legs were complaining, tired from the dancing, her muscles aching. "Why didn't you call me?" he was saying. Her eyes opened.

"That's what I said!" Mrs. Nayar clucked from the hallway. "I said come, let us go to the clinic now, but she said not to worry the doctor!"

Dr. Schofield rushed in, coat half on, half off, one sleeve hanging untidily behind his back as he shrugged out of the tangle while Mrs. Nayar tugged at it. Sophie unfurled herself from the chair and pulled herself into a long stretch, smiling as she tried to stifle a satisfied yawn. She had been fast asleep and dreaming. She didn't remember what about.

"Hello, Dad," she said, wandering carelessly into his hug, closing her eyes as they squeezed together.

"When did you get here?" he asked, chin resting on the top of her head.

"Couple of hours ago, I think. Fell asleep."

"You wash for dinner." Mrs. Nayar bumped past them, breaking their embrace, and threw another log into the grate.

The pitch black of the night outside threw reflections of the fire on to the dining room windows, where the shutters had been left open, moths and night insects bouncing off the glass, desperately making for the light. The ceiling had been painted, Sophie noticed, the awful oppressive nicotine brown now an airy off-white color that brightened the room up no end. There was something else different too, although it took a moment for her to pinpoint what it was.

"Where's the piano?"

"Chopped it up and used it for firewood."

"No!" Sophie said.

"Yes, I did. And very satisfying it was too. Dreadful old thing. I got rid of all sorts after you'd gone. Not intentionally, of course. Just started doing a little sorting out one day, and the next thing I knew, half the house was standing out on the lawn."

"Dad!"

"What? It's just a lot of old junk when you think about it, all this stuff we drag about with us. I don't even know where half of it comes from. It just wears you down after a while. There's a lot to be said for having as little as possible. You can just up and away without giving it a second thought."

"Suffering from wanderlust?"

"No fear," he said. "Whatever for? I always wanted a little rural practice somewhere quaint; I just never imagined it would be in India. I'm quite happy to stay put, although I don't mind getting on a train now and then when the fancy takes me. You really should have let me come up to Delhi to welcome you."

"We wanted to get settled first. You know how it is."

"I wouldn't have minded a bit. It's been a long time, and I've missed you."

"I've missed you too," she said. Oh, how she had missed him and longed to see him, but she was a wife now, and her first duty was to her husband, and there had always been something to get in the way whenever she had tried to make the arrangement. Lucien had finally declared that if it was that important to her, she should go on her own, for he was far too busy. She would not say anything to her father or tell him of her doubts.

Perhaps she and Lucien were not so well suited after all. She had come to realize that they had nothing in common, apart from the India connection. Or perhaps it was because they had come here that she was having such trouble with her adjustment to married life. It was not what she had hoped for. It felt artificial, as though she were spending most of each day pretending to be something or somebody that she was not. The persona she presented was an invention, and she wore it like a heavy overcoat drenched with guilt. Sophie looked at her father, and wondered how long it had been before he knew his marriage was a mistake.

"Must have taken you ages to get down from Delhi," he said.

"Don't be silly. I flew in." Sophie helped herself to a little more of Salil's home-made pickle. She hadn't realized how hungry she was until the lid came off the rice dish, releasing a delicious vapor of saffron and fried onions. "One of the perks," she said, adopting a self-mocking air as she tapped the teaspoon sharply against the side of her plate. How nice it was to dine so casually, her shoes kicked off, her father resting an elbow on the table whenever he felt like it. "I got a lift on one of the regular runs from Delhi to Bombay, then picked up a flight into Coimbatore, which was a little hair-raising, to say the least. Pickle?"

"Thank God I didn't know about that in advance," Dr. Schofield said, taking the dish from her and setting it carelessly aside. "Do you know, a plane went down in February on that same route, killing everyone on board? One of the Air Force's. A de Havilland, I think. It took off from Coimbatore heading for Mangalore and never arrived. The weather was so bad they couldn't even send out a search party. It was four days before they found the wreckage. Swimming in leeches, apparently."

"How gruesome."

"It's certainly not the way I would choose to go." He topped up their wine glasses.

"Any news of anyone?"

"Not much you don't already know about, I expect. The Rippertons went to Canada to be nearer to their son. I don't think it's worked out particularly well. Rip started to lose his faculties soon after they arrived. From what I can gather, I think he's become pretty senile. They always send a card at Christmas, so we shall have to see what Fiona has to say about it this time. I hope they're all right. Fiona blamed it squarely on the move. She sounded quite cut up about the whole situation."

"Poor Fi." Sophie shook her head. "I wish I had been kinder to her when I was young. She so went out of her way to be nice to me. I used to hide from her."

"I know." Her father smiled. "So did I."

"What about Kay and Dr. Reeves?"

"Back in England, last time I heard from them. I ran into him a little while after you left, when I was doing a stint in one of the refugee camps." Dr. Schofield paused for a moment. He picked up his glass and took a thoughtful sip. "You wouldn't believe these places, Sophie; still, after all these years, thousands of people, and I mean countless thousands living in camps and colonies without a hope of much help. I don't see how it can ever be resolved. There are just too many people and not enough resources. I think the government was hoping they'd all just disappear." He tutted to himself, reflecting on it. "You can't displace millions of people and expect it to be tidy, can you? I don't know what on earth they were thinking of."

He stopped for a moment, having forgotten where he'd started. "Rawalpindi was the worst. What a hellhole that place was. I'd never witnessed so many people in my life, like a carpet of bodies with virtually nothing to call their own." He shook his head gently in disbelief at his own recollection of the carnage and destruction he had witnessed first hand. He had done five voluntary tours in the camps, and the memory of it would never leave him.

"How are things at the clinic?" Sophie asked.

"Fine. We're up to twenty beds now. The extension made all the difference, and it turned out to be a much simpler job than we first thought. Dr. Pretti looks after the women and we have half a dozen nurses on rotation and a ready supply of junior doctors keen to join us for a busman's holiday. They come in from the big cities and lend a hand in return for a nice little sojourn here at Iona or in one of the guest houses in the town."

"You don't mind people staying in the house?"

"Never in your room, of course," he assured her. "But yes, why not? I'd rather that than let the cobwebs set in. Besides, it's nice to have a bit of young blood around to talk to. It doesn't do for an old codger like me to be sitting around on his own for too long."

"You're not old."

"Tell that to my knees."

"I do miss it here," Sophie said. "Delhi feels like a madhouse by comparison."

"Rather you than me," her father said. "I can't remember the last time I set foot in that kind of bedlam. Calcutta probably, on my way back down from one of the camps. I could barely hear myself think."

"It's not so bad, once you get used to it."

"And how is married life treating my girl? I won't say it's about time or anything like that, but I was beginning to wonder if you'd ever take the plunge." He set down his glass. "Then again, I don't suppose your mother and I set the best of examples in that department." Dr. Schofield sighed to himself inwardly and shook his head. What's done is done, he thought, and there was nothing else to be said about it. Sophie was a grown woman now, and she was certainly smart enough not to repeat the errors of her parents. Given the circumstances, it was a blessed wonder she had turned out so well.

"Better late than never," said Sophie.

"So what's he like, this chap of yours?"

"He's very clever."

"Is that all?"

"And hugely ambitious." Dr. Schofield looked at her over his spectacles. "What I mean is that he has excellent prospects, so you needn't worry that I've gone and married a no-hoper."

"I'm not worried about that in the slightest. You're more than capable of looking after yourself and you've never been one to suffer fools. My only concern is that you're happy." He peered at her. She had lost a great deal of weight since he last saw her. Perhaps it was the fashion. "Are you?"

"Yes," she said. "Very."

"Good. But I won't pretend I'm not disappointed that he couldn't come along with you. He's already denied me the honor of giving my daughter away."

"We didn't want any fuss."

"You mean *he* didn't want any fuss."

"Not at all," Sophie said. "It was my decision entirely. Best get it over and done with and get on with it. I couldn't have been doing with all the airy-fairyness of a big do."

"Did you…" Her father stopped himself, his sudden halt awkwardly obvious. Sophie felt it, the unsaid. "Your mother, did you ever…"

"No. I didn't see the point," Sophie said. For months she had agonized over whether to say anything to him about the brief visit that had churned everything up and left her feeling ill, and she had remained undecided until this moment. "Best let the past alone, I think."

"Yes," her father said quietly. "Yes. I think you're probably right."

"Gosh." Sophie sighed uncomfortably. "I don't think I can manage another thing." She pushed her plate away. "It's this fresh air. Gives me the appetite of a horse."

"How are you finding Delhi?" her father asked.

"Much colder than I expected, especially at night, but the house is lovely. It's set in one of those little residential enclaves.

You know the sort of thing. A private gated road of about a dozen houses, so it's all very safe and we don't have to worry about being broken into or having beggars pitch camp on our doorstep." Sophie heard the vacuous words coming out of her mouth and felt herself cringe. This was not the way she spoke with her father; it was the way she spoke in Delhi, in the company of her husband and the people she now mixed with. She had forgotten where she was, and for a moment had slipped into the other Sophie, the one who tried to fit in and talked like a stuffed shirt. She felt herself blush.

"Sounds to me like you're nicely cosseted with the real world held at arm's length," her father said.

"Yes. I suppose we are."

"Well, don't let it go to your head."

Sophie smiled at him and tried to remember who she was. "We're in the new colonies area, not far from Lodhi Gardens," she said. "The people next door have been in their posting for two years, so I've had plenty of help getting to grips with everything, but it still feels a little strange."

"What does?"

"Being somebody's wife," she answered, although she wasn't entirely sure if that was what she had meant.

"He's a very lucky man." Dr. Schofield cleared the last of the rice from his plate. "And if he's half as clever as you say he is, he'll already know that."

"Thanks, Dad."

"You realize I'm going to have to meet him one of these days, don't you? So far all I know is that he's a fine-looking fellow and you make a very handsome couple. I put your photograph on my desk."

"I saw."

"So why didn't he come with you?"

"He's terribly busy," Sophie said. "I've hardly seen anything of him myself recently. There's a big tour coming up which I'm not supposed to say anything about. Harold Macmillan is coming to visit and it's got everyone jumping up and down and rushing about."

"Oh, really? When?"

"Beginning of January."

"Do you think you'll get to meet him?"

"The Prime Minister? I don't know, but I'll definitely get to meet Lady Macmillan."

"That'll be exciting."

"I'm not getting my hopes up," Sophie said. "It'll probably turn into a lot of squabbling and backbiting over who should sit next to whom. Everybody will want to have their photograph taken with the Prime Minister so that they can hang it on the wall at home where everyone can see it. It seems that Lucien and I are the only ones who don't have a whole gallery of us posing like mad alongside a string of dignitaries, although he assures me that there is one of him with Nehru somewhere, not on his own of course, but one of those group pictures."

"Well, you be sure to push to the front when your time comes," Dr. Schofield said. "And send me a copy so that I can display it prominently in my office in the clinic and tell everybody that that's my daughter."

Sophie laughed. "You're as bad as the rest of them."

"Worse," her father said. "I'm far prouder."

Mrs. Nayar appeared. "Finished?" she asked.

"Yes, thank you." Dr. Schofield leaned back in his chair, touching his stomach briefly and groaning his appreciation. "That was delicious."

"Good." Mrs. Nayar started clearing the plates. "I'll bring you some sweets."

"Oh, heavens no!" Sophie lifted a hand in protest. "I really couldn't eat another thing."

"Yes," Mrs. Nayar said sharply. "You will have sweets."

Sophie's father raised half an eyebrow at her. "You should know better than to argue with Mrs. Nayar."

"I'm not allowed to argue with anyone at all these days," Sophie said. "One has to watch one's Ps and Qs all the time. It's like living in a military camp. There's always someone watching and listening." She sighed and passed the rice dish to Mrs. Nayar. "I do miss London. I had a letter from Margie recently. It was so nice to hear her voice in it. She's getting married to Fred, her doe-eyed cellist. She's been in love with him for years."

"And is he in love with her?"

"I think so. He certainly seemed to be, although Margie complained that he was far too gentlemanly about it." Her father smiled into his wine. "Heaven only knows how Fred will cope with her. Margie likes nothing better than a good old argument after supper, although she prefers to call it a lively discussion."

"So no arguing with Lucien, then?"

"No. We don't have anything to argue about."

"Give it time," her father said with a playful wink. "I'm sure you'll both think of something."

"I hope not," Sophie said, feeling suddenly grown up. It was good that they could talk like this, make an everyday joke out of something that just a few moments ago had seemed unspeakable. All married couples argued. Some a little, others a lot. Everybody knew that, and the exchanges that she had had with Lucien could hardly be called arguments. Nothing had been broken. Nobody had been hurt. And the silences were soon over. He would go out, saying that she should have a rest and that he didn't care to be around her when she was being like this, and then come back later, in the dead of night, and slide into bed, the scent of whisky on his breath as he reached a cool hand to find her warmth under the covers. Sometimes he would make love to her silently before falling into a deep slumber, and in the morning he would hum to himself while he shaved and would give her a kiss before leaving the house.

As a girl, Sophie had dreamed of the handsome princes and castles and happily-ever-afters that didn't exist except in fairy tales and fables, as all girls one day discovered. Those stories of childhood lay far away now. This was the backdrop to the way she lived, and she was beginning to become accustomed to it: the marriage that she had entered into, the husband to whom she was bonded. She had not expected it to be easy, but nor had she expected it to be quite so hard, the idle hours that filled her with emptiness, the awful sense that she was somehow wasting her life, watching it seep through her fingers as though it were out of her hands. If her marriage to Lucien was somehow lacking, then she must accept her part in that and make it stronger, a firm foundation upon which to build the family she yearned for.

"And how does it feel to be back in India?" Dr. Schofield ventured the question tentatively, having considered it carefully before its delivery. He had always feared that she might return one day and that it would do her no good. It had been hard enough to get her to leave in the first place.

"It feels strange," Sophie said quietly. "When I was away, I missed India so much, but in the same breath I was afraid to come back. I hadn't realized quite how mixed up I felt about it all until Lucien started talking about Delhi. I can't help it." She shrugged at her father. "I belong here."

Her father looked into his wine and nodded silently in a small way. "Did you hear about the Maharaja?"

"Yes. Such a shame, although I'm surprised he lasted as long as he did, the size of him. The maharanis would have been heartbroken."

"I doubt it," her father said. "I expect the First Maharani will have been rubbing her hands together with glee. With the old man dead, her son would have stepped into his shoes and she'd be sitting pretty. He's a pretty useless sort, I understand. It's probably just as well that there's nothing left for him to rule. He'd only drink it or lose it on the tables. His mother was an impossible character, from what I heard, although I never actually got to meet the woman."

"You couldn't be more wrong," Sophie said. "She adored the Maharaja." Her father glanced at her in surprise. "Fiona Ripperton and I used to go and visit her for tea sometimes in the *zenana*. It was unbelievably grand, and she was the most wonderful company."

"Well, I never." Dr. Schofield sat back in surprise. It was the first time they had spoken of their life at the palace, that wonderful fool's paradise of his that had come crashing down around their ears. Perhaps she had come to that age now, that age when one began to take stock of one's life, the mind wandering the shadows of the path that had led them to this time and place. He watched his child as she remembered, his heart clenching for a moment before being released by the small smile that settled on her face. It was a good memory visiting her. He shared in her smile.

"She had her jewelry caskets brought out one afternoon so that I could feel for myself just how difficult it was to wear. You simply wouldn't believe the things she had in there. It was like a pirate's treasure chest. Her ladies must have spent an hour or more sifting through it all while the Maharani told them to find this or find that. They covered me from head to toe and I could barely get up from my seat. It was like trying to walk with two huge lead weights clamped to your ankles and a yoke around your neck. She told me how painful it had been when they were first married and said that her skin had been so bruised and grazed that she had cried and howled when the jewelry was finally taken off her at the end of the day." Sophie glanced down at her own engagement ring, the expensive diamond glinting insignificantly, a mere speck in comparison to the myriad gems that had spilled like icicles from the Maharani's gilded caskets. "You know, she used to smoke an enormous hookah pipe. I had a try of it once. Almost choked me to death. Fi Ripperton was a dab hand at it." Her father laughed. "Do you ever think about the palace?"

"Sometimes," he said, skirting quickly over his memories. "It's being turned into a hotel."

22

Night fell across Delhi, the lampblack sky holding the freezing mists that drifted coldly down from the distant Himalayas. Throughout the city, chilled figures squatted around bonfires, huddled in groups, swathed in blankets and shawls, ghostly streams of warmed white breath pouring from their mouths into the bleak December air. When morning came, it would do so reluctantly, moving slowly through the thick fog that hung around with the stubborn persistence of an unwelcome guest. It would be hours before the sun showed itself, if at all, barely able to pierce through the winter blanket that held over the city before evening fell again, drawing in another long cold night.

Lucien lit a cigarette, pulling deeply into his lungs, his mind wandering as his eyes fixed on the reflection thrown back at him from the shuttered window. He must tread carefully and steer the cart without disturbing the natural order of things. Patience had never been his strongest suit, and he mulled this over now for a little while smoking his cigarette. It didn't do to push too hard. He would be well advised to take a leaf out of his wife's book. Sophie never pushed. There was something powerfully stoic about the way she handled herself that he couldn't quite pinpoint. It was disarming, and even on those occasions when he had wanted to vent his frustrations upon her, he would find himself sidestepped, left standing with nowhere to place his argument. He hadn't really noticed at first. It was only since living with her, sleeping under the same roof night after night, that it had begun to dawn on him that perhaps she was not quite as guileless as he had thought. She had a way with people, a way that left them with the impression that she was whiter than white, without agenda, and he wasn't entirely sure how she did it. He would have to study her more closely, to see if he couldn't pick up a little of her subtle temperance and learn how to use it to his advantage. It might prove valuable in matters of persuasion. He puffed again on his cigarette, deliberately softening his manner before inquiring, "Has Tony mentioned anything about the final pecking order for the PM's visit?"

Melanie Hinchbrook frowned at him. "Why on earth are you asking me?"

"You're his wife. If anybody's in the know about the workings of the inner circle, it's you."

"Well I'm afraid I don't have the faintest idea. Tony knows I'm not interested in those sorts of things. I stopped listening years ago. Not that he minds, I suspect. So long as I toe the party line and smile charmingly at the right people."

"But you must have heard something? The PM's itinerary is all pinned into place. Surely you've seen it?"

"Whatever for?"

"Lady Macmillan. You're supposed to be—"

"Oh, don't be a bore." She helped herself to a cigarette, leaning toward the flame he offered her. "Tea parties and tittle-tattle." She let out a plume of smoke. "That's all I ever hear, because it's always the same. Cutting ribbons here, patting the heads of vile little invalid children there, while adopting a look of great sympathy for the cameras."

"Oh," Lucien said.

"You sound disappointed."

"I am, I suppose."

"Then why don't you speak to him about it yourself?"

"I was rather hoping you'd be able to give me the inside track."

"Afraid not." She took another puff. "He'll be back on

Thursday, although I wouldn't bother trying to tackle him until the journey's worn off. He's a terrible traveler, you know. Puts him in a foul mood. I always thought it was very strange that he should have joined the Foreign Office at all." She paused for a moment, noticing Lucien's uncharacteristically quieted manner. "We're having the Appletons over for dinner on Saturday. It was supposed to be just the four of us, which really means the two of them cozied up over cigars while I have to endure Rosamund all evening. Perhaps you'd like to come along?"

"Won't Tony mind?"

"I don't see why he should. And even if he does, I'll just tell him that it was my mistake and it's too late to undo the invitation."

"I wouldn't want you to get yourself into an awkward situation on my account."

"Nonsense. Come at six-thirty for cocktails and I'll make sure the two of you get a little time alone together."

"Well, if you're absolutely sure," Lucien said. "Although I'll have to check with the little woman, of course. See that there's nothing else in the diary."

There wouldn't be anything else in the diary. Of that Lucien was sure. Aside from their official engagements, there was never anything in his wife's diary.

"Wasn't she supposed to be back by now?" Melanie asked.

"Four days ago, but the weather's been bad, so she decided to stay on for a bit, then take the train up to Madras and pick up a flight from there."

"I told her she shouldn't have gone," Melanie said. "Ros Appleton is mightily unimpressed with her absence. The run-up to Christmas is such a headache, especially now that everyone's children have descended. The club is a complete madhouse, youngsters hanging around and making a terrible racket. At least there'll be no shilly-shallying about sending them all back this year. Appleton wants the whole lot gone by January third so we can get everything shipshape by the time Macmillan flies in."

"To be frank, I've rather enjoyed her absence," Lucien said, dragging hard on his cigarette.

"Oh, *tush!* Now look what you've gone and done!" Melanie Hinchbrook flicked the satin coverlet aside and brushed the spilled ash from the bed.

23

D r. Schofield broke stride and waited for Sophie to catch up with him. "Do you want to stop for a minute?"

"No. I'm fine." Sophie puffed on, snatching hard gasps from the brisk air.

"That's the trouble with you young people," her father said. "No stamina."

"No exercise, you mean." She gave in and stopped, hands on hips, panting a little. "I swear I've hardly walked two hundred yards since we left London." She took a moment to recover herself, pressing a hand against her hammering chest. "It's all very nice having a driver at one's disposal, but it never even occurred to me what it might be doing to my muscles. Goodness me." She pulled in another deep breath and let it out with gusto. "I doubt I could get from one side of Hyde Park to the other nowadays." She rested herself for a little.

"Better?"

"Yes," Sophie said. "Much." Her father took off again at his regular pace.

"Then let this be a lesson to you. A good bracing walk every day keeps the doctor at bay."

"Lucien won't hear of it. I went off to Lodhi Gardens on my own a few days after we arrived and anyone would have thought that I had run through the streets in my underwear, the way he went on about it." To Sophie's relief, the pathway began to level off beneath their feet, opening on to the narrow roadway. "He was right, of course," she admitted. "It doesn't do to be out on one's own. It only invites trouble and endless pestering."

"Then get your husband to go with you."

"He's a swimmer, not a walker. He likes to get up early and do laps in the pool at the club. Nighttime too, sometimes. Says it helps him think."

"I wish you didn't have to go back so soon."

Sophie stopped and thought for a moment. She had already stayed far longer than she had cleared with Lucien, so she would be in trouble anyway, and she might as well be hanged for a sheep as a lamb. She had meant to speak to Lucien about it before she left, but she could never seem to catch him at the right time. He would always say, *later, we'll discuss it later,* but of course they never did. When later came, he would be too tired, or too busy, or *for heaven's sake, can't it wait?*

"Come to us for Christmas?" Sophie asked.

"Christmas?" Her father mulled it over for a moment. "Why not?"

Veneet Gupta wandered into the guardhouse and pulled up a stool at the rickety table set with a single kerosene lamp, the small brazier on the floor radiating a welcome pool of heat around his legs. "It's quiet tonight," he said, picking up a blanket and wrapping it around his shoulders.

"Have you walked the perimeter?" asked Bhavat Singh.

"There's nobody around," he said. "I'm not freezing my balls off for nothing."

"Waiting for your fancy woman to get back, are you?" said Bhavat Singh. He turned to the newcomer. "The woman at number six leaves her bathroom shutters open. She thinks nobody can see her." He grinned widely and put his hands to his chest. "Ripe white mangoes with pink teats. Isn't that right, Veneet? You would like to try some of that fruit for yourself one day, huh?"

"Her husband is a fat pig. I could show her a thing or two."
Veneet grabbed his crotch, laughing.

"You should be walking the perimeter," said the newcomer.

"And who are you talking to?" said Veneet. "You've only been
here five minutes and you think you can tell us what to do?" The
newcomer got up.

"Then I'll go," he said, stepping out into the night.

Jagaan Ramakrishnan set off at a slow pace, his footsteps deadened by the cold, damp air, his breath spilling out in thick white
streams. The houses were quiet, a few lights left on here and there
to keep the ghosts at bay while soft-footed servants turned down
beds and hung up discarded clothes. A porch light came on at
number five, the door opening. The housekeeper emerged and
lit the storm lamps, their warm yellow glow softened by the mist.
"Namaste." Jagaan called a softly voiced greeting and raised a hand,
showing his presence as he continued along his route. Through
the window of number eight, he saw the man from the café, the
one the women called Vicky. He was asleep in an armchair in
the memsahib's drawing room, his head tilted back, mouth hanging slackly open. Jagaan smiled to himself. He hoped that he was
so deeply asleep that he would not wake up when his household
came back. With any luck, the sahib would walk in and find his
servant snoring in his favorite armchair, empty whisky glass by his
side, and he would be dragged from it and thrown out of the door
with the sack. That would be a fine result, Jagaan thought to himself, a fine result for the scavenger who would be reborn as a rat.

He walked on, surveying the shadows, listening to the steady backdrop of frogs and night insects. The cold air hung still, punctuated
only by the warmth of his breath. He stopped outside number six
and looked up at the building. The porch light was on, one upstairs
room illuminated, the rest of the house in darkness. Jagaan took the
flashlight from his pocket and turned it on, aiming its beam across
the white rendering, backing up a little to peer around the wall. He
flicked off the flashlight and leaned over the wrought-iron fence,

stretching his frame, taking his weight easily on his hands. He thought as much. That crude devil must be creeping into the garden to spy on the woman in the bathroom. He would know if the light was on because it would cast its reflection against the windowless wall of the house next door. Jagaan tucked the flashlight back in his belt and continued toward the last house in the enclave. As he approached, he caught voices arguing, a pair of servants by the sounds of it, the louder of the two complaining that he did more work than the other.

Jagaan reached the end of his round and stood for a while, hand on his night stick, looking up at the faint stars held back by the mist. He used to know about the stars, stories that had been passed down to him, but he had forgotten them now. He must remind himself of them some time. Ask someone who knew about such things. An old person, probably. It was important to remember the stories and to hand them down, especially now that so many people had left their history behind and started again somewhere else. Delhi was a strange place. Or perhaps it was a place of strangers. He couldn't decide. It seemed to him that it was a lost city, that it had been tipped upside down and emptied out and refilled with people from elsewhere. A lost city with no memories and no one able to recount its past. How unforeseen, that he should end up here in this place where all the yesterdays had been erased.

He turned and began to retrace his steps, patrolling slowly on his way back to the guardhouse. More lights had been turned on since he had set out on his rounds, storm lanterns lining pathways, illuminating hazardous steps. The armchair in number eight was empty now, the glass beside it gone. A sliver of disappointment passed through him. Not that it mattered. People had a habit of getting what was coming to them, whether in this life or the next, and Jagaan did not care to concern himself with the mere issue of timing. He stopped outside number four, looking up at the darkened window of the bedroom where she slept. She was not there now, of course. She was away somewhere, according to the log in the guardhouse, and her bed would be empty, the sheets cold.

His first glimpse of Sophie had shaken him to the core. He had seen her, coming out of her house with her husband, and it was as though no time had passed, as if they had seen each other just yesterday, sitting by the fountain in the orange garden. She seemed unchanged to him, the only differences too small to notice: her hair tamed and pinned, the smart clothes and high-heeled shoes. And then, within a few days, he had seen through the veil of darkness what life had done to her, and it had cleaved his heart open. He wished he could spirit himself through the walls and lie upon her bed, warming it for her, praying for her. He would leave it appearing untouched so that when she lay down to her rest, she would wonder how the sheets had come to feel so perfect against her skin, and she would fall into a deep slumber wrapped in the protection of his prayers and dream of him. Jagaan's hand wandered instinctively to his breast pocket, resting briefly against the letter that lay there always, held in the small protective sheath of blue silk that he had sewn so carefully with his own strong hands. He took his eyes from the window and walked on.

"Here he comes," Bhavat Singh said. "The lone ranger."

"Everything's quiet," Jagaan said.

"Ha!" said Veneet. "I told you, so now you've been out and freezed your balls off for nothing!" He turned back to Bhavat. "You should see the size of her brassieres! They are like hammocks! You could take one down to the river and catch fish all day long."

Bhavat Singh looked at Jagaan. "What's the matter with you?"

"I don't care to hear about the woman in number six."

"Number six? Who said anything about number six!" Veneet laughed. "We're talking about her in number ten. The old woman with the fat bottom. Her brassieres are like—"

"Hammocks," Jagaan said. "I heard you."

"And how about you? I bet you would like to have a white woman. Mrs. White Mangoes from number six, huh?"

"No," said Bhavat Singh. "He likes the fat missus from number ten, don't you, newcomer?" Jagaan ignored them, pouring himself a small cup of chai from the pot stewing on the brazier. "He wants her to squash him with her big fat breasts."

The beam from a car's headlights passed across the guardhouse window, bathing them momentarily in a shaft of harsh light.

"Car!" Bhavat Singh leaped up from his seat and rushed out of the door.

"Huh." Veneet bucked his head and followed after the other guard. "Now we all have to go back outside and freeze *all* our balls off. Are you coming?"

"In a minute," Jagaan said, his back to the window. "Let me drink this."

24

The streets lining the periphery where the old city met the new heaved with the colorful business of daily life. Horse-drawn carts, some overloaded with passengers, struggled along, past the tightly packed shop fronts crammed with all manner of goods. Busy women flowed along, saris and shawls pulled closely against the cold. Men gathered by open chai stalls, squatted on haunches, smoking beedies. Shrines clutched to the old walls here and there, strung with bright golden marigolds, thin trails of incense rising through them, the larger ones adorned with more complicated arrangements of pale carnations and fragrant pinks, set into concentric patterns. Groups of policemen stood idly on corners with long black batons, blanketed against the chill, shorts covered over with long shirts belted tightly at the waist, khaki headdresses flashed through with bands of red. They talked among themselves, taking little notice of the chaos passing by. All around, the old city swarmed with people and animals, cows roaming through the bazaars, dogs scavenging in gutters, thieving monkeys watching for opportunity from the rooftops. For thousands, the streets were home, a place for buying, selling, eating, sleeping, performing their ablutions. Fakirs with matted hair, oblivious to all around them, inflicted punishment on themselves, piercing their skin with metal skewers, lying on beds of nails. On a corner, a sadhu rocked and chanted to the ground, smoking hard from a clay chillim, his face white with the ash of the dead. Thin notes rose from a snake charmer's pipe, hooded cobra swaying hypnotically before him, a shallow reed basket laid out, hoping for coins.

"Must be quite a change from Ooty," Lucien said.

"I don't know how anyone can stand it." Dr. Schofield looked out of the car window on to the passing scene. "I think that a man has a certain amount of time for cities before the charm wears off. Less in a place like this. One gets to the point when one can no longer keep up with the pace."

"I can understand that."

"I must say, I have always preferred the countryside. I'd be quite happy to live in the middle of nowhere with nothing to do except count sheep."

"I'm a city man myself. Although I wouldn't mind having a little place in the country one day. Something with a decent bit of fishing."

Lucien thought Dr. Schofield looked like the sort of man who probably liked fishing, and heaven knew they needed to find something to talk about over the next two hours. Sophie had deliberately maneuvered him into this outing, orchestrating the conversation over supper last night until she had him well and truly cornered. Had he realized what she was up to, he would have been more careful and said that he was tied up all day. And now he was stuck with Dr. Schofield on his wife's cheerful insistence. Had the old man not been sitting right there at the table, he would have told her it was out of the question. All this getting-to-know-each-other rubbish that she had spouted at him as he got into bed. She had tricked him and he told her so, but she was so pleased with herself that she didn't even notice how intensely irritated he was. There was no point in him feeling peeved about it. They were here now, so they might as well make the most of it, even though their conversation had dried up before they had gone much further than the compound gates.

"Fishing, eh? Trout or carp?"

"I don't mind," Lucien said. "So long as it puts up a decent fight."

Dr. Schofield seemed cheered. "You should come and try your luck in Ooty. The lakes are gorged with fish. It's impossible not to catch something."

"I might just do that. Perhaps in the summer, although it can be difficult to get away when things are busy."

"What about your annual leave?"

"Yes. But one is expected to go back to England to see family and deal with the usual matters. It's better to get out of the country one is serving in, I find."

Dr. Schofield watched Lucien as he spoke, the words so carefully crafted, falling so easily from this man now married to his daughter. He listened to the well-presented disclosure wrapped up in euphemisms and pleasantries and was left with the clear impression that his son-in-law had absolutely no intention of visiting him in Ooty. It did not figure in his plans and would no doubt be nothing more than a grave inconvenience. Lucien bore the most earnest of expressions, his face carefully arranged as he spoke of his commitments and feigned disappointment.

The once congested road began to clear around them, turning into a wide avenue, leaving behind the burgeoning throng of street life, the car windows now looking out on to the open parkland that surrounded a grand white hotel built in the old colonial style.

"Here we are," Lucien said. "They have a jolly decent bar and rather nice gardens. With any luck the sun will be out soon. Looks quite promising. What do you think?" He peered out of the window, skyward.

*

It was usually only on a Sunday that Dr. Schofield might partake of a little whisky before lunch, sitting at his desk, fiddling with bits of instruments that he was sure he could fix, if only he could work out how. He had trouble getting to grips with the mechanics of things. It was not that he wasn't interested. He was. He had always been fascinated by how things worked, but the science of it eluded him. Still, he stuck at it, particularly on a Sunday morning, while delicious spicy aromas wafted in from the kitchen, Salil busy with his pans while Mrs. Nayar chattered away to no one in particular and her husband slept in a chair on the back porch, pretending to keep watch. There were even times when he thought the pieces were all about to fall into place nicely, but then he would lose hold of his train of thought and put them down again with a sigh of defeat. He held up his glass and admired the pale straw-colored single malt.

"It's a Speyhawk," Lucien said. "I think you'll like it. Cigarette?"

Dr. Schofield thought about it for a while. "Yes. Why not?" He put one to his lips and accepted Lucien's light, then relaxed into his deep leather chair. "Single malt and cigarettes at lunchtime. I don't think a man could ask for much more, do you?"

"Don't get the wrong idea." Lucien smiled. "This is a far cry from my usual daily routine. But yes, I could get used to it very easily."

"How are you enjoying India?"

"Delhi's an excellent posting," Lucien said. "Had my eye on it for a while. I would have tried for it sooner, but there were…" He stalled briefly. "The timing wasn't right."

"Ah," Dr. Schofield said, taking a sip of his whisky, savoring it, nodding quietly. "A man in need of a wife, eh?"

"Well." Lucien let out a small laugh. "Not that I planned it like that at all. But as luck would have it…"

"You just happened to fall in love with a girl who knows her way around the place and speaks a bit of the lingo. Are you learning?"

"Not specifically." Lucien opened his menu and glanced over it casually. "Picking up a few phrases as I go along, but nobody really needs it these days. Everybody speaks English. Everybody we need to deal with anyway."

"How long are you planning on staying?"

"The full term, if we can." Lucien scanned the descriptions of the lunch dishes perfunctorily. "Four years, although those kinds of decisions are pretty much out of one's hands if the powers that be decide to move one elsewhere."

"Has Sophie settled in all right?"

"Yes, I think so. The DWs are a pretty good bunch. Always busy with something. She'll soon find her feet." He took a puff of his cigarette. Maybe if Sophie would just learn to relax, she might stop making such hard work of it. She was uptight, and he didn't know what was wrong with her. Of course it was all a big change, but what else had she expected? His was a very serious career, requiring a great deal of his time, and she had known that from the outset. If she had wanted the kind of husband who hung around the house smoking a pipe and wearing slippers, then she had married the wrong man. No doubt she was broody, he thought, although he wished she would be less obvious about it. Her availability dampened him, her air of hopefulness. It was unexciting. Sometimes he could almost hear her thinking: *maybe this time…*

Lucien closed his menu with a decisive clap. "I think I'll chance the roast beef."

"Good idea," Dr. Schofield said, his menu unopened. Lucien relayed their order to the waiter and relaxed into his chair. Dr. Schofield looked at him thoughtfully. "They do say that the first year of marriage is the hardest. Getting used to each other and all that. You mustn't think me prying. I'm very glad that Sophie has found a good man to settle down with. She's my only child, you know, which makes me overly protective, I suppose, although heaven knows she's grown up enough to make up her own mind and take care of herself. I was rather hoping that…" He cut himself short.

"What?"

"That she would meet a good solid sort." He smiled briefly. "I don't suppose I might trouble you for another cigarette?"

"Of course."

"Thanks." Lucien offered his lighter. "I must say," Dr. Schofield sat back, puffing, "it's rather nice to have some male company. It had quite slipped my mind that I might actually have a son-in-law one day. I hope we shall become good friends."

"I'll drink to that." Lucien motioned to the waiter with his empty glass. "How about another?"

"Why not?" Dr. Schofield said. "Can't fly on one wing."

"Don't worry. We'll walk it off after lunch."

"Walking? Now there's an offer, although I hear you're something of a swimmer."

"Yes. When the mood takes me."

"I don't suppose you'd mind if I joined you? It's been a long time since I've had a pool at my disposal. I could do with loosening up the old limbs a bit."

"Good Lord, no," Lucien said. "It's much too cold to swim in this weather."

❧❀☙

Ros Appleton tapped her teaspoon against her saucer and called her drawing room to order, every seat occupied, the chatter high-pitched and a little unruly. Taking position before the fireplace, she held before her the sheet of paper detailing the itinerary everyone had been speculating upon. "Let's get down to business, shall we? Lady Macmillan will be visiting the new Cheshire Home for Incurables. And before anyone says anything," she raised a hand against the looks of horror, "the place will be cleared of anyone who's even remotely contagious, and Lady Macmillan will be kept at a safe distance from unfortunates."

"And who will be escorting her?"

"Lady Macmillan will have her own staff with her."

"Surely we will all have an opportunity to meet her?"

"Well, of course the more senior of us will, but it's going to be a very brief visit."

"So we won't be hosting a special luncheon or tea in her honor?"

"Not this time."

"Oh, that *is* disappointing."

"This isn't some kind of Kensington tea party, Tessa." Ros glared at her. "If you want to put on a grand display to impress your friends, then I suggest you invite Cary Grant to supper and call all the newspapers." Sophie bit the smile forming on her lips. "We are naturally all very excited, and I am sure that everyone can be fitted in somewhere."

Sophie stole a glance at her wristwatch, the hands nearing two o'clock. She wondered if they had eaten lunch yet, and whether they were getting on well. Lucien had seemed quite put out when she had told him of the invitation she had extended to her father, with it being their first Christmas together and all. It was almost as though he was deliberately trying to avoid meeting her father altogether, and it had led to another one of those awkward spells when she had tried to mask her upset while he huffed and puffed before announcing he was going out to work off his tension in the pool. Her father had warned her of this, the opening movement of any marriage being a trial of fire in the ways of forging a life with another human being. She had left it late, he had told her, which would make it all the more difficult, as she had no doubt become a little set in her ways. Men preferred to be at the center of things, to believe that they are the ones wearing the trousers, as it were. He had said so with a pleasant smile, and had lit a cigarette as Mrs. Nayar cleared the remnants of their supper away after pressing upon them another plate of Salil's sweets.

"Are you all right?" Tessa nudged her lightly.

"Yes," Sophie said, returning her attention to Ros Appleton and her interminable list.

"That was some dinner," Dr. Schofield said, dropping himself into an armchair with a sigh of exhaustion. "I shan't need to eat for a week. Tony Hinchbrook is quite a character, isn't he? Not many of his sort left these days. A colonial old-timer if ever I saw one. Charming wife, mind. Shame she had to duck out like that, although I expect I would have done the same in her shoes."

"He's an absolute beast when he's drunk." Sophie threw her shawl aside. "It won't be the first time she's stormed off and locked him out. She's probably hoping he'll pass out on their doorstep. He won't remember a thing about it when he wakes up in the morning. Never does, apparently. Why some people have to get so utterly plastered every time they step out of the house is completely beyond me."

"Dear, oh dear. I pity the man's poor liver."

"Care for a nightcap?" Lucien went to the tantalus on the sideboard.

"I'm going up." Sophie placed a weary kiss on her father's head.

"Good night, darling," Lucien said. "I won't be long."

"Not for me." Dr. Schofield waved a polite refusal. "I think I'll turn in for the night as well. Oh," he placed a hand on his chest, "I don't suppose you have any indigestion salts handy? That rich supper is playing havoc with my constitution."

"There should be some in the bathroom cabinet. Would you like me to fetch them for you?"

"No." Dr. Schofield stifled a small belch. "I'm sure I can find them." He stood up. "Would you mind if I stepped out for a few minutes?"

"Not at all." Lucien poured himself a drink.

"I think I might catch a few breaths of fresh air and stretch my legs. Just for a moment or two. See if I can shift this stitch."

"By all means. Take your time, but don't leave the compound."

Dr. Schofield stood out on the porch and lit a cigarette before pulling his collar up against the chill and descending the few steps to the pathway. His gullet was burning. He should have been more careful, or steered away from the champagne, which clearly wasn't as good as its label purported. Damned stuff. Enjoyable enough at the time, but a wicked mistress when it came to paying the bill for her company. He passed through the gate and on to the road, strolling a few paces, enjoying his cigarette. There was a light on in the guardhouse. He wandered toward it and looked through the sliding window, but there was no one home, the hut empty. A few yards ahead, a thin shaft of brightness fell from a flashlight. The guard walked toward him.

"Sahib?" Veneet quickened his pace. "Are you needing something?"

"Sorry," Dr. Schofield said, feeling suddenly awkward at having been caught poking his nose into the guardhouse. "I was just stretching my legs for a while."

"It's cold tonight," Veneet said.

"Yes, it is rather." Dr. Schofield looked around uncertainly.

"Everything is well, sahib. We are here all night when everyone is sleeping."

"Lucky for us."

"Did you have an enjoyable party this evening, sahib?"

"Yes. Yes, we did."

"It is a very good Christian festival, along with your Easter. A very good festival."

"Yes. Well. We like it."

"But I think it would be better if you had more fireworks, sahib." Veneet nodded to himself in firm agreement. "All festivals are much better with fireworks, but I think perhaps you are not having sufficient fireworks in United Kingdom in matters of the Christmas and the so forth."

"No." Dr. Schofield nodded politely. "I think you are probably right about that."

"You are smoking an American cigarette?"

"Er," Dr. Schofield looked down at his hand, "American? I'm not sure. Player's. Are they American?"

"Player's cigarettes very fine. I like Player's cigarettes." Veneet hovered expectantly.

"Oh. Yes. Of course." George took the packet from his pocket. "Would you care to..." Veneet helped himself to three and put them in his pocket.

"You want some chai?" Veneet gestured toward the open doorway of the guardhouse, a pot stewing on the stove. Dr. Schofield thought about it for a moment.

"Yes. Why not?" He stepped inside. "I'm not disturbing you from your work, am I?"

"No, sahib. We are taking turns walking up and down and seeing that everything is fine and there is no trouble or undesirable persons hanging around."

Veneet took two clay cups from the table and poured some chai into each one. Dr. Schofield hesitated for a moment, seeing that the cup had been used before and not washed. Ah well, he thought. When in Rome. He sipped at it, hot, sweet, and milky, cinnamon tanging on his tongue.

"You are staying at number four?"

"Yes. My daughter lives there."

"You are father of Mrs. Grainger?"

"Yes."

"That is very good." Veneet drank some of his tea and felt pleased with himself. Perhaps they were not all so bad, these Britishers. This one at least seemed to know that he was no better than him and had given him American cigarettes. The ones in the houses were a different matter. It wasn't that they looked down their noses. They didn't look at all, passing the gatehouse day in, day out without so much as a good morning or a good evening or a thank you for being outside all night freezing your balls off. He would like to live in a house like that and to come home drunk from parties at two o'clock in the morning and not care about who kept it clean or made it safe. And if he did have a house like that and came home in the middle of the night drunk, he too might go for a little walk and smoke an American cigarette and have a little chat with the *chowkidar*, just to show that he was not snobbish. He might even give him a tip, a little something to show his appreciation for the fellow freezing his balls off. Perhaps this man was going to give him a tip; after all, it was his Christian festival, and everybody knew that the English *wallahs* gave tips at Christmas festival. "Are you enjoying your chai, sahib?"

"Very good," said Dr. Schofield, finishing, careful not to drain the dregs that had loosened whatever it was that had stuck to the bottom of the cup. Footsteps approached the hut. Dr. Schofield put the cup on the table. "Well, I shall wish you good night and leave you to your post."

Veneet clicked his heels together and nodded, standing straight, his eyes following the hands that failed to offer him a tip as Dr. Schofield walked out of the door.

Dr. Schofield collided with the man before he had even seen him, feeling himself knocked sideways as solidly as if he had marched into a tree. Strong arms steadied him at the shoulder.

"Sahib!" Jagaan stepped back to check the man over. Thank the gods he hadn't been walking any faster; otherwise he might have knocked him clean over.

"I'm so sorry." Dr. Schofield fumbled around, righting his spectacles. "My fault entirely. I didn't even think to look where I was going."

"You are fine, sahib?" The moment the man lifted his face, Jagaan felt the wind ripped from his chest. He turned quickly away, his voice thick as he said to Veneet, "Please escort the sahib to his door and make sure that he is all right."

Veneet looked at him indignantly. "Me? Why don't you..." but Jagaan had already disappeared into the darkness. Veneet tutted to himself, then readied a smile for Dr. Schofield. If he took him home, he would definitely and certainly be bound to get a tip. "Come, sahib. If you feel unsteady along the way, take my arm. In fact, take my arm anyway, then we can be doubly sure."

"Really, I'm quite all right," Dr. Schofield said, realizing that his heartburn seemed to have gone off miraculously, wondering if it might be something to do with the tea he had just had. Ginger, perhaps. It had tasted like it had ginger root in it, and something else, something that was nagging at the back of his mind, something that he couldn't quite put his finger on, like a distant memory. A few yards further, Dr. Schofield slowed. A fractured image came into his mind's eye, a face he had once known, but he couldn't think from where. He stopped and turned around abruptly, looking back toward the guardhouse, a faint glimmer of recollection tugging at him deep down somewhere.

"Sahib? You are all right?"

"Yes," Dr. Schofield said with a frown. "That man at the gatehouse, the other guard…"

"Yes, sahib. He will be in very big trouble for banging into you like that. I will see to it that he is given a talking-to. In fact," Veneet puffed himself up, "I will speak to him myself, as his superior."

"No. Don't do that. It really wasn't his fault. I just thought for a moment…" He brought his hand to his chin, unable to piece together whatever it was that had flashed through his thoughts for a second. That guard he had glimpsed for a fleeting instant. Something about that face. Those *eyes*… Unable to place it, he frowned to himself, shrugged it off, and continued back to the house.

25

D r. Schofield came to the breakfast table suited in his traveling clothes, a comfortable ensemble of linens that had softened over the years and a cotton shirt of a similar ochre hue, open at the collar, with a red kerchief tied at his neck. Sophie looked at him for a moment, as though seeing him differently, before realizing.

"What happened to your mustache?"

"Better?" He smiled self-consciously, his hand coming to his denuded face. "John offered to shave me this morning, so I thought I'd have it off. I'd forgotten what I looked like without it."

"I rather liked it." Sophie, entirely wrong-footed at the sight of him, poured him a coffee as he sat down. She glanced at him again. It was as though the clock had been turned back to a different time and a different breakfast table, where nobody spoke and you could cut the atmosphere with a knife.

"Good morning, George." Lucien strode in. "Darling, have you seen my wallet?" He glanced briefly at Dr. Schofield. "I've gone and put it down somewhere." Sophie was already out of her seat.

"I'll go and find it for you."

"Coffee?" Dr. Schofield picked up the pot.

"I don't really have time, George."

"Of course you do." Dr. Schofield poured anyway. "Sit down for a moment while Sophie fetches your wallet." Lucien accepted the cup reluctantly. "Busy day ahead?"

"Yes."

Dr. Schofield took a sip of his coffee. "I hope the visit goes well. You must ask Sophie to let me know."

"Thanks. It'll be all over the newspapers."

"I'll look out for you in the photographs."

Sophie came in holding Lucien's wallet. "Here you are." She smiled at him. "It was in your other jacket."

"Thanks, darling." He kissed her cheek. "Right. Well, I'd better be off then." Dr. Schofield stood up. "George?" Lucien shook his hand. "It's been an absolute pleasure. Thank you so much for taking the trouble to come and see us. I hope your journey back isn't too arduous, and you must call and let us know that you've arrived safely. Do you have everything you need for your trip?"

"Yes, thank you." He felt the firm grip of Lucien's hand. "It's been a wonderful visit, although I have to say that you have ruined me with your fine whiskies. Now I shall have to go home and reduce myself to the ordinariness of my Black Label."

"Until next time," Lucien said, tucking his wallet into his pocket and heading for the door. A silence hung over the room for a while. Sophie returned to her seat.

"Did you see that?" she said. "He didn't notice a thing." Her father looked at her. "Your mustache. Perhaps if you had dyed it pink... Oh well. Will you have some breakfast?"

"I've already beaten you to it. I was up at six while you two were still fast asleep. Dilip made me some eggs. He's a good lad. I think I gave him the fright of his life, wandering into the kitchen to help myself like that. I didn't see him. He was dozing in the corner. Almost jumped out of his skin." He sat back down. "I'm happy to see you settled, my dear. Lucien seems like a decent chap. I'm sure you've chosen well."

"Thanks, Dad." Sophie reached across the table and put her hand on his. "I'm so glad you were able to come. It meant a lot to us."

Dilip came into the dining room, slipped the cap from his head and put a small package on the table, tied neatly in greaseproof paper.

"Your picnic, Dr. George," he said.

"Ah, Dilip! Thank you. That should sustain me nicely through the inevitable delays." He stood up and shook Dilip's hand, Dilip smiling with embarrassment. "Now you mind you take good care of Mrs. Grainger while I'm gone, and see to it that she eats a decent breakfast once in a while."

"Yes, Dr. George." Dilip slid a bashful smile to Sophie and went back to his kitchen.

"A decent roast chicken sandwich." Dr. Schofield waved the package aloft. "A picnic fit for a king."

"Are you sure you don't want me to come to the airport with you?"

"Gracious, no. You know how hopeless I am at good-byes. All that hanging around and not knowing what to say. No. You stay here and get on with your day, while I forge ahead into the great unwashed."

"Memsahib?" John came in, the new bearer, who had worked out very well. "The car is ready. I have put the doctor's bag inside."

"Thank you, John." Dr. Schofield smiled brightly. "So! I'm guessing that's my cue to be on my way." He hugged his daughter, closing his eyes briefly, wishing that he could say something to her to reassure her that everything would be all right. He had seen that all was not well with her. There had been a moment when the awful thought had crossed his mind that perhaps she had inherited a predisposition toward nerves from her mother. It had shocked him, that he should even consider such a terrible thing, and he had quickly brushed it aside. Yet not once had he heard her laugh like she used to when she found something terribly funny, like the time in Ooty when Poocha wasn't much more than a kitten. He had lost his footing and fallen into the pond while going after one of the house martin chicks. He had struggled furiously to clamber out, a wide-eyed look of horrified indignation on his face as the house martin parents dive-bombed him mercilessly, a bedraggled feline wretch, drenched to the skin. Sophie had been beside herself, laughing so hard that she had tears streaming down her face. The noise of it had brought them all running from the house, and they had laughed madly at the sight of her bent double, holding her sides. It was the first time any of them had heard her laugh for months.

"You may walk me to the car." Dr. Schofield offered Sophie his arm. "But no nonsense, all right?" He smiled at her bravely. "You'll only go and set me off."

Sophie hadn't meant to cry, especially not in front of a neighbor, but Tessa had taken one look at her and asked her immediately whatever the matter was. Sophie had only called in to say a brief hello, perhaps to stay and have a cup of coffee and talk herself back into normality. She would have been all right had Tessa not been so nice to her. Kindness is the hardest thing to bear when one is feeling low.

26

Jagaan arrived at the guardhouse shortly after sundown. He had had trouble sleeping that morning, the family next to his cramped lodging room making all kinds of racket while he pulled a pillow over his head and tried to shut out the noise. Then, in the afternoon, he had queued for an age at the post office while the man behind the counter took his merry time with each exasperated customer. The night shifts had taken their toll, turning everything upside down until daytime took on the unnatural curve of an unworldly dimension. Nights had become Jagaan's realm, beginning as the sun sank and dusk filled the city, the moon climbing slowly from east to west then sliding out of sight, leaving only the stars whose stories he had long forgotten. And then the blackness would begin to give way to the deepest sapphire blue before fading to lilac, then pink, then orange as the sun stretched wearily over the fog-bound rooftops of the old city.

Bhavat Singh opened the door of the brazier and pushed in a knot of wood.

"It's going to be another cold one," he said, straightening up and rubbing the small of his back. "But I shall be in bed with my wife, enjoying her heat." He flashed Jagaan a manly smile.

"How was the day shift?" Jagaan asked.

"The guest from number four left this morning. He came to the guardhouse and gave us a tip. Here's your share." He took ten rupees from his pocket and gave it to him. "Don't tell Veneet. I'm not giving him any. He never lets on when anyone gives something to him." Jagaan thanked him and pocketed the note. "Now I'm going home to my family." He slapped Jagaan on the shoulder. "To spend some time with my wife and children. That son of mine is quite a handful and runs his mother ragged. My wife complains that she works ten times as hard as me just chasing around after him. I told her she has nothing to complain about, although between you and me, I'm glad I'm not the one who has to deal with him all day long." Bhavat Singh looked at Jagaan's drifting expression and laughed to himself. "You don't even know what I'm talking about, do you? Maybe one day you will be married and have a son and then you'll know what it's like to get home and walk into a lion's den."

"I too have a son," Jagaan said quietly. "He is nine years old and has the energy of fifty men."

Bhavat Singh stared at him, his breath snagging, unable to conceal his immediate embarrassment. "Why didn't you say something?" He put a hand to his head. "Why didn't you tell us you had a wife and child? How could you let Veneet speak to you like that? I would have knocked him out cold rather than hear such insults as a family man."

"I didn't say I had a wife." Jagaan went to the brazier and poured himself a cup of chai. Bhavat turned away in discomfort.

"Oh," he said. "I'm very sorry."

Jagaan studied Bhavat Singh's face in the reflection of the window. It carried the same expression he had seen so many times before, jumping to the same conclusion. A dead wife, for there could be no other explanation. Not that he had ever explained himself to anyone. Why should he? It was nobody's business but his, and his business was not yet concluded. He had thought that he would never see her again. To his shame, he had given up all hope. He cast his mind back to the day his infant son had first been put into his arms, a well-fed bundle with soft round cheeks and a silken cap of jet-black hair. It had taken his breath away, and he had seen Sophie so clearly in his son's golden face. There was no news of the mother, they had told him. Over the following months, Jagaan had exhausted every avenue he could think of, pestering Mr. Shirodkar, the neighborhood advocate, to send letters to the Red Cross or to the shipping companies requesting passenger lists, all of which yielded nothing. "There is no finding someone who does not want to be found," his uncle had said to him on the day his son had taken his first steps. Those early years in Amritsar had been the hardest, Jagaan asking himself the same questions over and over. He had had a long time to think about it, and two things carried no doubt in his mind. He loved her with every grain of his being, and she loved him too. He was sure of it. There would be a reason why things had turned out the way they had; it was the will of the gods, so he would wait, just as he had promised to wait for her his whole life if that was what it took. He would wait, and keep faith, and never give up hope.

It was the last Saturday of June this year, another summer beyond hope, and Jagaan had tried hard to think of Sophie less. The sun had been merciless, beating down over the city, the Golden Temple shimmering in the searing heat, molten in the glare. His uncle's workshop had felt like a tandoor, sweat pouring from them as they worked through the morning before abandoning all physical exertion as the sun burned higher and staked its claim on the day. Mr. Shirodkar had seen the notice in the *Times of India*. The name he had never once forgotten in eight years, and suddenly there it was, right in front of him, in the newspaper announcements. Mr. Shirodkar had left his house without finishing his breakfast, walking more quickly than any man should in such heat, heading toward number seven Kim Street. He had shown the newspaper first to Jagaan's uncle, Parvesh Gupta the shoemaker, even though Parvesh Gupta could neither read nor understand English, then they had taken it to Jagaan. After kissing his son good-bye, Jagaan had left Amritsar with his family's blessing and half his uncle's life savings.

"Your son is at school?" Bhavat Singh's manner had altered in an instant, his voice now respectful.

"Of course."

"And…" Bhavat Singh hesitated, unsure of whether he should continue the conversation with this poor bereaved man. "He lives with your family?"

"Yes. In Amritsar."

"Amritsar?" Bhavat Singh tipped his head in surprise. "You don't look like a Punjabi."

"And what is a Punjabi supposed to look like?" After a moment, Jagaan smiled. So did Bhavan. They both knew exactly what a Punjabi looked like. A Punjabi looked like Bhavat Singh, and Delhi had filled up with them long ago, after their homeland was ripped in half.

"It's your eyes," Bhavat Singh said. "I thought you might be of Afghani descent or something like that."

"No," Jagaan said. "Although you are not the first person to say so. My father's family came from way up in the north. He always used to say that everyone there could see in the dark."

"Please accept my apologies." Bhavat Singh stood before him and put his hand on his heart. "I am deeply sorry for the way we have teased you. I will speak to the others and—"

"No," Jagaan said. "I would prefer that you do not say anything to anyone. My family is nobody's concern except mine."

"But…"

"But nothing, Bhavat Singh."

"Then why tell me?" Bhavat Singh frowned hard, confused by the sudden disclosure and the man's preference to endure the ignorant torment of the other guards, who liked to make him the butt of their jokes. Jagaan smiled softly to himself.

"I have a friend back home," he said. "A Sikh like you. He is a good man. I suppose you remind me of him a little."

Jagaan watched from the guardhouse window as Bhavat Singh left for home and thought about the wife he was returning to. She would be busy preparing their supper. He wondered if she had washed her hair today while thinking of him. If she had picked out a colorful sari and dabbed kohl on her eyes. He thought of Bhavat Singh's two children, a girl and a boy, and imagined them together in their home, warmed by a fire, climbing on their father and laughing while their mother cleared away their supper and told them to leave him alone.

A car came through the main gate. It was the man from number four. The man who lived with her and slept in her bed. The man who was rarely home and came back sometimes in the dead of night looking disheveled, skin dampened with whisky. Jagaan turned down the storm lamp, his features shadowing into darkness, and watched as the car slid by and slowed outside her gate.

Sophie stood by the fireplace, the plain tonic water in her hand jazzed up with ice and lemon, another glass waiting for her husband, laced stiffly with gin. She hadn't worn this dress since their honeymoon, thinking it far too good for everyday use. Earlier that afternoon, after a long lunch with a little too much wine, Tessa had returned home with her, and they had spent almost two hours sorting through Sophie's closet. Finding the dress packed away in layers of tissue, Tessa had gone mad over it and had asked if she might borrow it sometime to give to her *darzee* to copy. The moment Sophie put it on, she had felt cheered, and they had rummaged through her things and had a thoroughly enjoyable sorting-out.

"Darling!" She greeted Lucien with a kiss.

"What's all this?" He looked at her. "Are we entertaining?"

"Yes." She took his hand and led him to the settee, placing his drink on the table. "I have decided that I am entertaining you this evening. Just the two of us. I've given the staff the night off and told them to go to the pictures or something. Dilip's prepared cold supper for us, so we can eat whenever we like and please ourselves."

"Thank God for that." Lucien reached for his newspaper and took a large swig of his drink. "For one awful moment, I thought we were going to be stuck with him over New Year."

"What?"

"Your father. Now perhaps we'll be able to live in our own house without standing on ceremony and laboring through hours of conversation about flora and fauna."

"Lucien!" Sophie stared at him. "What a mean thing to say!"

"Oh, do give it a rest, dear." He opened his newspaper. "You've had your little Christmas theatre, showing us off and giving him a fine display of our life. Now he knows that you're not on your uppers or married to a ne'er-do-well, perhaps he'll leave us to get on with it."

"That's incredibly rude of you." Sophie felt heat rising to her rouged cheeks. "He's my father and I want him to feel welcome in our home, because he is."

"Of course he is, dear, just not too often, please."

Sophie stood there. He wasn't even looking at her, after all the trouble she had gone to, fixing her hair, spending half an hour on her make-up, placing a perfectly arranged vase of freshly cut flowers by the bed. And here he was, just sitting there, browsing his newspaper, ignoring her in the manner he had honed so well.

"Will you please do me the courtesy of looking at me when I am speaking to you?" she said, her voice low and even. Lucien folded his newspaper, his movements slow and deliberate, before putting it aside. Only then did he look at her, a look that made her want to cry. What had she done to make him behave like this? Had she been so wrong in her assessment of him? It wore her down, day after day, and still she could never see it coming.

"Happy, Sophie?" he asked. "Now that you have my full attention for whatever it is you are about to complain about?"

Sophie allowed herself a moment to compose herself, her heart hammering in her chest. "I am not about to complain about anything." She spoke quietly, willing herself to stand straight and have it out with him once and for all without the evening descending into another fight. "Although the temptation to do so is sometimes very strong. My father is very important to me and I will not have you speaking about him like that. He is a good man, which is more than I can say for you at this precise moment, and I have every intention of seeing to it that he is properly included in our family."

"What family?" Lucien picked up his newspaper again. "In case it has escaped your notice, my dear, that is one thing that we appear not to have." He turned a page, casting his eye over it casually. "I would have thought that you might have been well on the way to producing a child by now." Sophie stared at him, open-mouthed. "No? Well, I can't say that I haven't given it some degree of effort on my part. Perhaps you should go and see a doctor and find out what's stopping you, because either there's something wrong with you, or you're, well... Let's not get involved in conjecture, shall we?"

"I can't believe you said that." Sophie felt her insides shrivel. "Of all the awful, terrible, dreadful things to say to me. I am your wife, and you will show me the respect that I deserve." She felt herself shaking. "Look at me, damn you!"

"Oh, for Christ's sake." Lucien stood up and threw his newspaper to the floor. "I won't have this. Do you hear me? I won't put up with it."

"Put up with what?" Sophie followed him out of the drawing room, pursuing him across the hallway as he went for his coat. "I do everything that's expected of me. I run your house and entertain your friends and tell your colleagues how marvelous you are. I trot alongside the DWs like an obedient dog while being dragooned into their pointless do-gooding and petty politics. And I sit here alone for hours on end while you swan around and do whatever it is that you do while I am left here to rot. It's like a nightmare."

Sophie felt sickened, as though glimpsing an awful moment of clarity, a small patch rubbed into a dirty window through which she could pick out the truth of what went on in the room that lay beyond. She was losing herself, drifting out to sea where no one could hear her cries, longing to feel the safety of dry land, something solid beneath her feet. Her heart was like a wasteland filled with yearning. For years, she had thought that she'd forgotten what love felt like, but she had not. It had embedded itself in her, the feeling of an emotion so overwhelming that it left her unable to breathe. How could this be love, this mournful existence of charades? It was like floating on the surface of life when she wanted to swim in it, to drown in it, to have its water fill her lungs and overwhelm her.

She stood and stared at Lucien. "Sometimes I think to myself that this cannot be happening, that it simply isn't possible that my life has become this, this *thing*." She threw her hands in the air.

A terrible silence filled the hallway. Lucien pulled his coat on and glared at her, cold as a winter wind, biting into her like she had lost her mind. Perhaps she had, she thought. She couldn't even remember what they were arguing about. Her head emptied and she stood there, heat running through her veins.

Lucien threw his scarf around his neck, not once taking his eyes from her.

"I'm going out," he said. "And I suggest you go to bed and sleep off whatever it is that you've been drinking today."

❦

The shouting had stopped. Jagaan stood rigid, his blood rising as he watched the silhouettes behind the vented shutters. If only he had got to her earlier. If only he had not lost sight of the doctor, he might have found her sooner.

The door to number four opened. Jagaan stepped back into the shadows and watched the man as he walked around the side of the house, calling for his driver. A light went on upstairs and he saw her at the window, wearing a yellow dress with white flowers and a blue sash that went up from her waist around her shoulder. She was pulling a pin from her hair. Her head was bowed, her hands coming to her face, and she stood there like that for a moment before turning away, the lights going on in the room beyond.

An engine started, the car sliding slowly to the front of number four, where the husband got in and rode away, leaving Jagaan standing there, looking up at the light spilling softly from the bedroom window. Be strong, he said to her, for I am close by and I will find a way to make this right. Through the cold evening mist, he saw her come back to the window and close the shutters.

1948

Northern India

27

I t was the nighttime that Sophie found hard to bear, the sorrow that crept through the cool walls as the moon rose. Some wailed unashamedly, others shed silent tears beneath their covers when no one was looking. Sophie's own eyes remained dry, like the dust that circled the upper rooms, blowing in through the open windows with each hot gust thrown in from the desert plains. With March had come the change in season, the heat beginning to climb. Sometimes she would wander through the house, running her fingers across the walls, tracing the outline of the shelves, every surface yielding the same fine patina, leaving her fingertips tinged rust red. She would lift her hands to her nose, taking in the aroma of ancient winds that moved the soil from one parched land to another. It grounded her, the scent of the earth, and she told herself that this too would pass.

It was as though she had become someone else, someone different. She didn't feel like herself at all, even when she lay down to rest and the thoughts came flooding in: thoughts of her childhood, her years at school, the war, the palace, the water garden. She thought of Jag too, missing him so badly that it caused her heart to contract painfully. But the memories did not belong to her, they belonged to someone else, someone she had once known before she went away. That girl had gone now and would never return. Sophie had only to look in the mirror to know.

The saris had proved a godsend from the moment Mrs. Chowduray in the dak bungalow offered up one of her own that morning two months ago when Sophie had struggled hopelessly to fasten her dress, crying her frustration. She had spent her last few weeks at the palace held together with threads and pins, her mother refusing to acknowledge the issue of her growing figure, leaving her to weep over her daily wardrobe agonies alone. Sophie had been reduced to conjuring whatever outfit she could squeeze into, regardless of its ugliness, her mother as good as gloating when she appeared looking like a heap of rags. On that morning in the dak bungalow when nothing could be cajoled into submission, Sophie had finally broken down, throwing her useless dress aside before shutting herself in the washroom.

Mrs. Chowduray had been swift in her rescue. Wife of the local postmaster, she knew about the mission. Everybody around here did. Sophie was not the first of her boarding guests to have passed through hiding a secret child. After coaxing Sophie out of the washroom, Mrs. Chowduray had gathered her into comforting arms, hushing her not to worry, and had dressed her with gentle hands, speaking softly, smiling as she pulled her into a short white *choli*, settling the sky-blue cotton of the sari around her middle and over her shoulder. The fabric had held the faint perfume of cloves, enveloping Sophie in its scent as the woman lifted the final fold over her head.

At first Sophie had felt naked, unused to the absence of tailoring, the air touching her skin where it should not. She felt the unfamiliar garment around her uncertainly, a piece of cloth wrapped about her with nothing beneath it but a brief cotton blouse and a loosely tied slip. It had felt wrong, giving her the sensation that the whole arrangement could slide from her body and settle at the floor around her feet at any moment. When she finally dared to step out of the washroom and saw her reflection in the window by the door, covered from head to toe in folds of white and blue, nothing visible of her remained.

Sophie had become used to her new clothes. They forced a certain serenity in her movement as she walked barefooted through the house, venturing into the courtyard now and then to scatter crumbs to the squabbling sparrows. She kept her head veiled always. It gave her a sense of protection. Beneath its canopy, nothing could touch her. Nobody could hear her thoughts.

If only she had known that she loved him. If only. But she hadn't understood what it was, not then. She had been young and confused and unaware of what she was feeling and what it meant, and now it was too late. It had come out of nowhere and she hadn't expected it. Nobody had told her. Nobody. Not even in the great love stories of the books she had read. You were supposed to know when you were in love. You were supposed to recognize the signs and feel the unmistakable feelings she had heard about. But she hadn't known. She hadn't known anything. For God's sake, why did nobody tell her that love creeps in when you are not looking? Perhaps it could have been so different, if only she had known.

The baby moved inside her, content in her womb, her swollen belly uncomfortable for a brief moment. Sophie straightened herself, leaning one hand to the wall, arching the ache from her back. She was hungry, with a yen for mashed banana and coconut milk. She would eat now, then rest through the heat of the afternoon and wake as the sun sank away to the west, releasing the pressure cooker.

"Sophie!" The girl called Lotus waved a coconut from the kitchen door. Lotus wasn't her real name. It was a courtesy extended to all the girls who came there, to preserve their anonymity if they so wished; they were encouraged to choose a new name to go by before entering the household. They didn't have to, but the advice was always dispensed with a sense of gravitas in protection of their futures. For those who couldn't think of a name to call themselves, Miss Pinto would suggest they pick their favorite flower, hence all the Roses and Irises and Violets who had passed through these walls. Sophie had refused the offer. She felt so unlike herself anyway, so alien, that she feared she would disappear entirely if she relinquished her name. One girl had decided to call herself Rumpelstiltskin. Rumpel, as she became known, wasn't one of the criers. She was hard, like stone. Lotus, on the other hand, was soft as butter. It was as though she had more love inside her than she knew what to do with.

They were not supposed to ask each other what had brought them there, but everybody did, so word got around just the same. It was as though this place did not exist, their time here a temporary suspension of the ordinary world, a layer between heaven and earth that nobody else could ever know or understand. Once the heavy door of St. Bride's had closed behind them, everything beyond its sunburnt cracks simply evaporated in the heat. There was no world other than this. Within these walls they remained, babies growing, wanted or unwanted. There was nothing else, just the unborn, making their way into this world. And while they waited to be birthed and given away, their mothers talked.

Rumpel was due any day now. She was huge, the distortion of her belly frightening the other girls who still had some way to go. She didn't say much, but when Lotus asked her if she too would get that big, Rumpel had smiled kindly. "No," she had said. "You won't get this big, petal. It's just me, you see. I've got two of them in here."

No one was regarded as staff, not even the ones who lived there only to serve. Jinty, the cook, had been at the mission for nearly fifteen years, having had nowhere else to go after her baby came. She had consoled herself in the kitchen ever since, nurturing every dish with a mother's love.

Ruth, a sturdy widow now well into her sixties, had arrived out of nowhere just before the war broke out. She had heard about the mission from a friend of hers in Calcutta. Ruth had been dreading the prospect of a long, lonely retirement without her husband and had spontaneously packed her things one day and got on a boat before her children could get wind of what she was up to. She had heard them talking about her like some kind of unwanted parcel, too old to be of any use except to watch over her three beastly grandsons. There were plans afoot to ship her back to England and move her into a granny flat beside her son's house in Hove, and she had absolutely no intention of ever subjecting herself to an English winter again.

To run away had seemed like the perfect solution. Ruth had only intended to stay for a while, just to teach her children a lesson and to make herself useful while she decided what to do about her future, but one thing had led to another, and she kept forgetting to leave. There was always somebody wanting for something, and it was nice to feel needed.

The housemaid, Roopa, a quiet girl who was not entirely sure of her age, had not been there for long. Her baby had been born the previous spring and promised to a childless couple from Talcher. They had been overjoyed to receive news of such a gift, a perfect baby boy with ten fingers and ten toes and a soft cry, and had pledged a generous gift of money to the infant's mother to help her to make a new beginning somewhere. They had arrived the night before the handover, staying at the dak bungalow with Mrs. Chowduray, and had given a solemn promise to love the child and raise him well. Roopa had heard none of this first hand. The mother was never permitted to meet outsiders or to be present when a baby was given away. Not only was it too painful for her, it was also uncomfortable for the adopters, their minds usually set on the convenient provision of a child to call their own. The mother did not exist, as far as they were concerned. She did not want the child, therefore she had no right of claim over it.

There was a special room in the house on the first floor with a door that opened out on to a small balcony overlooking the courtyard, flanked by windows on either side. The mother and baby room was painted powder blue. It had a carved wooden bed with a large, comfortable mattress dressed with crisp white sheets and plenty of big soft cushions. Pictures of gods and goddesses and mythical animals adorned the pastel walls; pieces of colored

glass were threaded through and hung from the ceiling, catching the sunlight as it passed through them, throwing brightly colored reflections around the room. There was a side table against
one wall with an enamel basin for bathing the infant and a small
chest for clean linens. It was in this room that each baby spent its
short time with its mother, a place to whisper secrets and promises.
Nobody was allowed to enter the room except Miss Pinto and her
daughter. They cleaned it every day, opening the door to the balcony to invite the day's air, allowing the girls in the courtyard to
look up and catch a glimpse of the colored glass baubles glinting,
knowing the time would come when they too could lie for a few
days, perhaps daring to dream. It was the only room in the house
where they would be acknowledged as mother and child and given
as much privacy or comfort as they wanted. Behind its door, they
would have to make their peace with their baby's destiny.

Sophie had found a rare companionship in the unlikely mixture of
girls in the mission. One way or another, they were all in the same
boat, and it was a relief to shake off the overcoat of shame she had
worn so heavily. They had nothing to be ashamed of, because they
all were God's children, even the unborn. Miss Pinto reminded
them of this every day and took care to point out that Adam and
Eve had not been married. She had a habit of dipping in and out of
the teachings of various religions, occasionally choosing to amend
or reinterpret the ancient scriptures to better suit the purpose of
her lessons.

The mission ran to a loosely held daily routine. Breakfast at eight,
consisting of porridge or *dosas*, thin rice pancakes filled with whatever was left of the previous night's supper. Before then, anyone
who got up in time would be expected to join Miss Pinto in the
courtyard for yoga. At first, Sophie had felt too self-conscious to
join in, watching instead from the window of the shared bedroom

on the first floor. Miss Pinto could fold herself into any position at will, exerting no effort at all as she bent to the ground or stood on one leg with her eyes closed, hands raised to the sky while her charges laughed and wobbled before giving up. Miss Pinto would open one eye and smile a little before releasing her pose.

Sophie had never known a household like this, where everyone rubbed along together just fine. There were no eggshells to walk over, no angry silences. She had held the same feeling in the pit of her stomach ever since she could remember, like a gutful of sand churning constantly down a cold riverbed. It followed her every day, every night, the shadow of a sinister malevolence, knowing that the blade could fall at any moment. She had become used to it, living in a permanent state of readiness to bear whatever onslaught might be about to come. It was as though she had been carrying a sword and shield her whole life, dragging them around with her, heavy in her hands. She ached to put them down. Perhaps here, in this strange place, she could finally feel safe. She had expected there to be hardship and punishment, angry words and stern, unsmiling faces. Instead, she had found tenderness in a way she had never known. It unnerved her.

☙❧

"How are you feeling?" Ruth took Sophie's pulse, checking the silver fob watch she kept pinned to her pocket.

"Fine."

"Let's have a little feel of that baby, shall we?" Sophie lay back on the couch and allowed Ruth to palpate her swollen abdomen.

"Ruth?"

"Yes, dear?"

"Will it hurt an awful lot?"

"I'm afraid it will rather." Ruth smiled at her. "But it'll soon be forgotten. Women have babies every day. It's what we're designed to do."

"I'm scared."

"Of course you are, dear, but there really is nothing to worry about. I've delivered more babies than I care to count and, dare I say it, you youngsters are better equipped for it than some of the older ladies I have attended. Your body is fit and healthy, with nice young bones. It'll be a breeze. Just you wait and see. There." She rearranged Sophie's sari, having finished her examination. "Everything feels perfectly normal. There's no need for you to fret about anything."

"Will it be obvious, afterward I mean?"

"In what way?"

Sophie blushed. "Will I look the same as I did before?"

"Of course you will, dear. Just do your exercises and no one will be any the wiser."

Sophie lay in her bed, pretending to sleep, listening to the other girls talking. She had not spoken to any of them about her child. They had tried to wheedle it out of her at first, but she had avoided their questions until they stopped asking.

"Do you ever wonder what's going to happen to your baby?"

"It's easier to find homes for the boys. Everybody wants boys. It's the girls that get left behind. The orphanages are full of them."

"That's so unfair."

"It's the way it is. It's bad enough if you have a girl when you're married, then you're stuck with it, but nobody's going to want to take one on unless they have to."

"Why not?"

"Something to do with dowries."

"I thought they'd done away with all that."

"Who? The government? And since when did anybody here take any notice of anything the government says?"

"I suppose so."

"I'm not going back to my parents after this," said Rumpel. "And there's nothing they can do to make me."

"You can't do that," Lotus said.

"Yes, I can. I'm old enough to look after myself."

"But where will you go?"

"My sister is coming to get me." The other girls looked at each other. "She's five years older than me. She ran away from home when she was seventeen. My parents never heard from her again." Rumpel gave a satisfied smile. "I know where she is. She's working as an import clerk in a big shipping firm in Cochin. We're going to get on a boat and go away together." The girls became quiet. Everybody knew that her father did it.

Sophie closed her eyes and began to dream, blackness closing in around her. Quiet, so quiet. Quiet as a mouse hidden deep in the cupboard under the stairs in the house in Islington, cozy within the coats that hung there, wrapped in the heavy oilskin of her father's waxed cape, the one he wore whenever he was called out in the middle of a harsh night, rushing out into the downpour. She could smell him, sleep drifting in. Then, hours later, the door slowly opening, a shaft of light sliding in to find her.

She blinked against the brightness to see her father kneeling down and reaching out to her. He didn't say anything, just offered small soothing sounds as he coaxed her out. Then being lifted and held strongly against a shoulder as he carried her into the kitchen, sitting her on the edge of the table as he took a washcloth and rinsed it in a basin of warm water. He began to clean her up, her face first, gently wiping away the dried blood, the cloth gradually becoming red in his hands. With his back turned to her as he rinsed it out, the water pink, she stole a glance at her reflection in the mirror of the old dresser that stood by the wall. But the face that looked back at her couldn't be hers, just a strangely disfigured child, its hair darkened and matted with blood.

People like to think that children forget, that they make

unreliable witnesses in matters of history. But they don't forget. They remember everything. Instinctively Sophie's hands went to her belly, resting protectively over the soft mound.

28

Leaving the palace had been one of the easiest decisions of Dr. Schofield's life. The newspapers were full of it, the rioting and mindless violence, the attacks and reprisals, the rapes and slaughter. He didn't even think about it once he knew Veronica was gone. She wouldn't be back, and he was glad of it. In that moment, everything had changed, and the last thing he had needed was to stay at the palace, pandering to a spoiled maharani who knew nothing of real suffering. That was not why he had become a doctor. He had failed his own principles by taking the easy option, as though he had earned the right to a leisurely life simply by doing his duty for a few years. He had forgotten who he was and why he had been put here. He wouldn't stay. It would be unconscionable. They needed every doctor they could get.

Dr. Pretti was attached to the women's clinic, serving under India's commission for recovered persons. Her role was to attend to the missing girls who had been rescued and brought back to the camp, many of whom had been savagely attacked. It was difficult work, to bear witness every day to the brutalities they had suffered, knowing that she was gradually becoming desensitized to the distressing nature of the sights that had initially caused her heart to freeze. Why must men do these things? What hope was there of nurturing a civilized nation when a woman's life and honor counted for so little? She sat with Dr. Schofield in the mess tent set up beside the clinic enclosure. It was the only place they could get away for a while, the doctors and nurses, the orderlies and volunteers, to take a desperately needed cup of tea and a biscuit, hidden from view so that they might be able to eat and drink or rest awhile without feeling wretchedly guilty.

"There was a girl in the next village who ran away," Dr. Pretti said. "She was a very good girl, but she was in love with a Moslem. They had been in love since childhood. Of course, the families would never have agreed to it, so she ran away from the convoy to join him, claiming to be his wife. Later she was captured and taken to the border camp to join her family, but she ran away again. It is very difficult to deal with girls like that. Eventually I told her that we would not hold her name on our records. I told her, 'Just go and don't tell anyone about it.' What else was to be done? Otherwise she would have been kept here against her will. Some parents will not come to collect these girls; they simply deny having a daughter of that name. We end up sending most of them to the girls' home in Ludhiana. It's an awful place. Many of the girls there are exploited. Their parents should be ashamed of themselves, leaving their daughters like that to be molested by *goondas*." She noticed Dr. Schofield's lost expression. "Professional looters. *Badmash*, bad people."

"What is being done about reuniting lost children with their families?"

"It's hopeless," she said. "You ask them what their name is and they say Qasib or Sanjay. So you try asking what is their mother's name, and they will say Amma, Amma, because of course they don't know what their parents' names are. There are so many children, crying Amma or Abba, with no names for us to go on and no one coming to claim them. Who is to know who they are or where they have come from? And how can we possibly trace their parents? They could be anywhere. Or dead. Most will be adopted, we hope, or otherwise sent to an orphanage, or left to fend for themselves." Dr. Schofield drank from his tin mug and felt useless. "There is a lot of bad feeling. The Sikhs and Hindus left a great deal of property over the border which has now been taken over.

They feel cheated. When they do finally get out of the camp to be resettled, they will only be given a modest piece of land, or allocated a small house, and perhaps given a government loan to help them get back on their feet. Some have arrived here with absolutely nothing, their valuables looted along the way, their possessions dragged from their hands." She tutted her defeat. "There is nothing we can do to help them except to give them shelter, food, and blankets while they wait. I think it will take years to clear the camps. Progress is so slow and most of the helpers are volunteers. They have set up community kitchens along the main routes to feed the refugees, and people have been very generous, donating food and clothes and bedding. Whatever they can give, they give, but sometimes I think that it is an impossible task."

Dr. Schofield could not disagree, and nodded his head sagely. "I should have come sooner," he said.

"Housing is gradually being allocated in Amritsar and the surrounding villages from the properties left behind," said Dr. Pretti. "But the *badmash* are at work, of course. Some greedy people already living on this side are claiming empty houses and moving family members into them. Refugees lucky enough to have been met at the border by their relatives have been taken in and will probably be allocated housing much more quickly than the ones left here."

"What will become of them all?"

"There are endless lists being compiled, and as we process the people, they will be allotted properties or given land settlements. No doubt money will change hands. It always does. Some have their jewelry still." She looked at him. "Anyone who managed to arrive with money or valuables will have a better chance of securing a decent property deal. Houses, land, business premises, and shops. The lists go on and on. Have you finished your tea?"

"Yes." Dr. Schofield drained his mug quickly and set it down.

"Ready to go back in?"

"Ready when you are," he said and stood up.

As he walked back into the medical tent, he made sure not to look around, focusing instead on the next person in the queue, thinking only of what he could do for that patient in the here and now. To lift his head and look up would only fill him with a sense of defeat before he had even started. It was a miracle that anyone ever got seen.

The field hospitals he had worked in during the war had been a different matter. They were much better organized, everyone knowing what to expect and what was expected of them. The whole thing had operated like a well-oiled machine, whether stuck in the middle of nowhere or caught in the midst of heavy shelling, the lights flickering on and off or knocked out completely. The adrenalin had kept them going, pumping through their veins. Work fast, work well, remember that this man has a family somewhere. He'd had letters from some of his patients after the war, soldiers and airmen who had taken the trouble to track him down and send word of their fates, sometimes with a photograph enclosed, a picture of them standing with a smiling bride or a newborn baby.

He had treasured those letters. They had reminded him of what it felt like to be needed, maybe even cared about a little by somebody far away. They always said that they hoped he was doing well and enjoying life on Civvy Street. He would smile to himself, taking pleasure at the sight of their happiness, the joy of life having been restored to them when death had been so close by. He remembered the field hospitals, where they had found moments here and there to open a bottle of whisky and sing drunken songs, arms slung around each other's shoulders while the sapper with the big smile coaxed a few tunes from the broken-down piano they'd dragged in from the abandoned school on the hill. He had felt differently then. He had felt like a man.

His first glimpse of the refugee camp had knocked the wind from him. He had been told what to expect, certainly, but he would never have believed it had he not seen it with his own eyes. A full seven months had passed since the night of Partition, yet still they came in droves, people in their thousands, exhausted, half dead on their feet. He had thought that he had fortified himself, mentally at least, having read the newspaper reports and seen the newsreels, but nothing could have prepared him for this. Why had nobody planned for it? What kind of leaders would have plunged so many into utter destitution? It was incomprehensible to him, that anyone could have thought that this was a workable idea. The dead were uncountable, to say nothing of the sick and injured. Had the new dominions descended into out-and-out civil war, he doubted the results could have been any worse.

He had already seen Amritsar. It looked like a bombarded city, battered by riots and arson. Bodies lay strewn in the streets, stiff and bloodied, grotesquely posed in states of rigor mortis, blood everywhere, houses burning, women and children crying. The larger camps, some sprawling for miles, seemed futile, the logistical problems colossal. The inmates of the ones he had passed through on the way narrated innumerable tales of woe, all of them subdued by the same sense of grimness and despair.

Thousands had been murdered, injured, or maimed for life. Masses of non-Moslems streamed out of the towns and villages in one-time India that had now become hostile country. The stamp of terror on their faces was always the same as they clamored to cross the border from Pakistan to the safety of India. Frenzied acts of destruction were commonplace, and those who escaped the mob fury arrived in the refugee camps filled with tales of looting, murder, and rape. Villages had been surrounded by enraged hordes who killed all the men, burned their homes, and took away the women and livestock. Every day, another line of desperate people would come to the military office in the Indian cantonment, imploring the major general to locate their kidnapped womenfolk.

The few British officers who remained under his command were sent to carry out the duty, as no non-Moslem Indian would be permitted to cross the border, uniformed or not, just as those of the Baluch regiment were not allowed to come back to India.

The detail would travel far into Pakistan, some as far as Dera Ismail Khan, Bannu, and Peshawar, searching out girls and bringing them back hundreds of miles to their families. The British would liberate all they could find, whether they were named on their list or not, sometimes having to tear them away from their captors. The British officers found their violent reluctance perplexing, until such time as the girls were brought back to the Indian camps. Those parents who had listed their daughters as missing would be overcome with joy and near hysterical at the reunion, whereas those girls who had not been sent for by name would be faced with families who refused to take them back, their purity lost, their presence bringing untold shame upon them. The major general, a proud, thickset Sikh, accused those parents of cowardice for throwing their daughters to the *goondas* while escaping themselves. Many of his *jawans* came forward and offered themselves honorably, volunteering to marry those girls who had been denied by their families.

29

D r. Schofield sat quietly with a cigarette, looking up at the stars, thinking about his daughter. He pulled the blanket closer around his shoulders. The nights were still cold here, winter not quite over, clinging on for these last remnants of March. It would be warmer where Sophie was, way over in the east and further south; summer would have broken already. She would be heavy with child by now, in her seventh month, and he tried not to think of it. Oh, how he missed her. Away from his day's toil, he found himself worrying about her again, as he did whenever his mind was idle. He worried for her constantly, for the act of childbirth and what it had done to his wife, for the aftermath, and perhaps most of all, he worried about how it would be when he saw her again. It would not be long now.

It was good that he was here, working himself hard so that he might be spared the agony of an unoccupied mind. He would stay a little longer, a few weeks perhaps, before packing up and hauling out. The distance down to Ooty was practically the whole length of the country, and he must see to it that everything was ready before fetching her back to him. There would also be the business of telling her about her mother, although he worried about this less, having reasoned that she, like him, would probably feel nothing more than a sense of relief after the initial shock of it. Dr. Schofield had had a great deal of time to think over the past few months, to reflect upon all that had come to pass, to consider his future, and his daughter's. It was just as well that he and Sophie were not permitted to correspond. Miss Pinto had been quite clear about that. It was better that the girls at St. Bride's remained closed off from the rest of the world. News from the outside invariably caused upset and tears, and the girls were not permitted to send letters. They only ever led to trouble. Dr. Schofield would just have to wait, and hope, and do his best to help her to get over this terrible thing. He would devote himself to her once they were reunited, and to hell with everyone and everything else. They would go south, as far away from this trouble as they could go, to the peace and tranquility of the Nilgiri Hills.

Fiona Ripperton had written a week ago to say that there was a lovely house available with wonderful views at a reasonable rent, and that if he was happy for her to do so, she would go ahead and make the necessary arrangements to secure it for him. She and Rip had summered in Ooty many times, and they remained on amiable terms with their seasonal neighbors, exchanging cards at Christmas time, promising to meet up at the Ooty Club next time they were there. Dr. Schofield had written back to thank her and had gratefully taken up her offer to travel down herself after Easter, to see that everything was in order and make sure they were not being hoodwinked into leasing a hound.

She had said (and Dr. Schofield suspected that it was not true) that she was planning on going anyway and that she would be quite delighted to have an excuse to get out of the mausoleum and start the season early. What a pillar of support that woman had been, never once asking a probing question nor venturing an opinion about the sudden dissection and scattering of his family. Dr. Schofield had even considered telling her the truth of it, if only to share the awful burden, before dismissing the thought. It was not his tale to tell.

He thought about Sophie all the time. He couldn't help himself, the same tangle of wishes and regrets running over and over in his mind, the things he should have done and said, the blind eye he had turned too often, wittingly or unwittingly. No family was perfect. That was what he had told himself. No marriage was what a man thought it would be, his hopes and dreams nothing more than a naïve fantasy of youth and inexperience. Until death do us part, they had promised, yet the death had come so soon, the death of all hopes and dreams. He should have left her years ago, the wife he had chosen so hastily.

The bracing December wedding had heralded the first of many disappointments. They moved into the house in Islington, where his parents lived a quiet life in too many rooms since his mother began to crumble beneath the disease that had crept in without warning and refused to leave.

A sweet-natured woman with an infectious laugh, Isadora Schofield would not be too long in this world, and his father had worn the burden of it heavily, sitting up for hours long into the night, staring into the fire, a glass of whisky in his hand as though waiting for her executioner. Not once had George heard an unkind word pass between his parents. To his mother, his father was the moon and stars. To his father, she was the source of all the good in his world. It was not right that she had been made to suffer this affliction, that pain should be her constant, unrelenting companion. No merciful God would visit this upon a woman so kind and selfless. That was what his father had said, renouncing the Church, renouncing any God who would treat his dear wife in this way. "You can keep your God," he said to those friends and neighbors who asked why he no longer went to church, looking upon them as though they were fools. "And if you want to go and worship an invisible being who dare not show himself for the misery he has caused, then go ahead. Don't you see? There *is* no God."

It was only a matter of time before Veronica's presence became intolerable to George's father. Almost from the moment they moved in, the friction had been palpable. There were even times when George wondered if she didn't do it deliberately, her incessant references to the Bible, her insistence upon praying over her food with head bowed while they waited on her, his father's fists clenched in anger. George had tried to speak to her about it, had tried to explain that his father was not himself since his mother's decline, but Veronica would not hear of it and said that he was a godless man and that that was why he was being punished through the suffering of his wife. George remembered it so clearly, the way they had been standing there in the bedroom as her words hit him like cold water, the expression on her face almost triumphant, and he had known, at that very moment, that he had made a terrible mistake.

Isadora Schofield died peacefully in her bed that summer, on a Sunday morning while the church bells were ringing. Veronica said that it was God's way of calling her to him. There was no funeral service to speak of, just a brief civil affair without ceremony before the cremation. George's father took her ashes to France, to the small town on the Riviera they had honeymooned at and dreamed of moving to one day, and scattered her remains in the rose garden of the hotel at sunset before ordering six bottles of their most expensive champagne and inviting every guest to drink a toast to his wife, the most beautiful woman in the world. His body was found the next day, washed up on the beach at Juan-les-Pins.

How rare their love had been, George thought, and how foolish of him to have thought that he might be lucky enough to find the same.

He took a last drag of his cigarette, flicking the butt to the ground. He hadn't smoked in years. Veronica had hated the smell of cigarettes, so that was another thing that he had given up, along with his penchant for taking a couple of pints at the local pub on occasion. Just one or two, never more, in the company of a few honest-to-goodness hard-working men. The conversation would always turn to the war. It was unavoidable really. There was nobody to listen at home, nobody who would appreciate what it had meant, so they kept those stories for themselves, man to man, and everyone understood. They were bereft, some of them, returning home to find the world a changed place and unsure of where they fitted in. Their lives were their own again, but many of them didn't know what to do with it. There was nobody to tell them where to sleep and what to eat and when to stand at ease. They missed the bark of orders, the shared hardship, the camaraderie.

All George Schofield had ever really wanted was a wife to love, who would love him too. With that, everything else would have fallen into place. Veronica had never loved him. He knew that now, yet it had never crossed his mind to put an end to it. They had promised themselves, for better or for worse, a vow from which there could be no return for an honorable, if misguided, man. He should have taken his daughter and walked away, no matter how impossible it might have been, but what would have become of Sophie then? And even if he had attempted such a thing, what trouble would it have unleashed? These were the things he thought of now, out in the darkness, listening to the sounds of the camp, the bitter smell of fires lacing through the still night air. He lit another cigarette and shook out the match, drawing the smoke deeply into his lungs, picking a thread of tobacco from his lower lip. His fingers wandered to the mustache he now wore, touching it absentmindedly, comforted by the way it felt, the sensation of the short bristles suddenly giving way to the softness of clean-shaven skin. He must be getting old, he thought, the whiskers having come through peppered heavily with gray. He hoped Sophie would like it. If she didn't, he would take it off, but in the intervening weeks, he would keep it and enjoy it, simply because he was free to do so, at last.

Dr. Schofield finished his cigarette. He stood from the camp chair and stretched, long and slow. Perhaps he should turn in for the night. He would write to Fiona in the morning. He was too tired to think about it now. With any luck, his sleep would be dreamless.

30

Jag washed his father's fragile body and dressed him in cotton robes, wishing they could be cleaner. There were no flowers to adorn the body, not even a single garland of marigolds. He anointed his father's head, marking him for the last time with the ritual of his prayers. Death comes to every man, like a long-awaited friend, but Jag had hoped to be much older before he performed his final duty as his father's only son. He had promised himself that when the time came, he would take his father to the holy city of Benares for the closing chapter of his life, so that he might achieve immediate liberation from *samsara*. To die in the city of light would be to pass through the gate to *moksha* and enter spiritual bliss. He would have scattered his father's ashes into the River of Heaven, the sacred Mother Ganges, washing away his past, erasing the sins of many lifetimes. There would be no need for his father to return to earth, having freed himself from all material desires. Instead he would enter the realm of immortality, the highest among the heavenly planes, the dwelling place of Brahma, where his wife would be waiting for him, wearing a crown.

"We have come to help you honor your father."

Jag looked up from his father's body. His neighbor, Navinder Singh, stood with two other men. Jag nodded as they removed the shallow canopy from the shelter, and the four of them lifted the shrouded body, the meager weight no burden. As they passed through the camp, a path opened up before them, the people parting as they approached, heads respectfully bowed. Jag felt as though he were moving through a terrible dream, the world around him slowing and silencing as the smoke of the eternal funeral pyres neared, his eyes smarting.

The pyre seemed inadequate for such a great man, Jag thought. He would have seen his father placed atop a stack as tall as he, but there was little wood to be had, the landscape around the camp bare, and that which could be found was thin and dry. Jag worried that the small allocation for his father's mound would not be sufficient to release his body. He must burn properly and be cleansed by the fire.

Accepting the burning twigs from the *dom* who tended the pyres, Jag walked around his father, counterclockwise, for everything was backward at the time of death. He leaned down and pushed the burning twigs into the belly of the stack, his father now an offering to Agni, the fire, to convey him to heaven. Thin lines of smoke appeared, curling tendrils around his father, touching his face with pale fingers that slid through the stained cotton robes. A faint crackle began as the twigs gave up their flames, passing their sacred fire into the kindling and dry grass packed beneath the kerosene-soaked wood. Head bowed, Jag circled his father's pyre, reciting the prayers for the dead, intoning a low chant, *ram nam sit hair, ram nam sit hair*. The smoke thickened and the fire took hold, flames licking, softly at first, before reaching up and engulfing his father's body.

For three hours, Jag watched on silently as his father burned, the shrouded figure blackening as it willingly released what remained of its earthly flesh, the fire leaping heavenward. As the fire began to die, Jag turned and walked away without looking back. He felt utterly alone. Moving through the camp, passing by the hospital tent, he wondered how many more would die today.

☙❦❧

"Hey! You there!" Jag kept walking, head bowed to the ground, unhearing of the voice. "Yes, you!" He stopped and looked up and saw a man approaching, an orderly with blood on his shirt. "You look like a strong chap. Could you lend us a hand? We're absolutely swamped and short of at least ten able-bodied men. There's been another outbreak of dysentery and half the medical staff have gone down with it." Mutely, Jag followed the man into the hospital tent. "Go and give your hands a good scrub." He indicated a basin and jug set up on a stand. "Have you eaten today?" Jag looked at him. "You can grab something from the mess tent if you want. No good trying to work on an empty stomach. It's through there." The orderly pointed toward a flap opening at the back of the tent. "There's no need to look so worried, lad!" He slapped Jag on the shoulder. "Somebody will tell you what to do."

Jag stood quietly and stared at the table in the mess tent. Two enormous silver urns, warmed by burners, sat side by side, one filled with coffee, the other with hot water. Plates of sandwiches, piled high, covered over with thin cotton cloths. A tin barrel packed with biscuits. A basket of apples. Another spilling over with bananas. Jag wanted to weep, to cry out and say that this table would have saved his father, his father whose remains now blew through this awful place, death carried on the breeze. A white-sleeved arm reached across him, lifting a cloth and taking a handful of sandwiches.

"Go ahead, lad," Dr. Schofield said. "Help yourself. We all have to keep our strength up." Jag looked at the man and felt his skin turn inside out. Dr. Schofield studied his face. "It's all right, lad," he said gently. "You mustn't feel bad."

George Schofield had seen this before. It was probably the first decent meal this young man had laid eyes on in God knows how long. "I know it looks like a lot, but it soon goes, let me tell you, so best have a few of these while they're still around." He took another plate from the stack, loaded it with sandwiches, and handed it to Jag. "Tea?" He filled a couple of tin mugs from an enormous pot. "There's milk in that jug if you want it."

Jag stared at him, unable to believe his eyes. It was Sophie's father, right here beside him, pouring him *tea*. His heart thundered in his chest.

"New volunteer?" Dr. Schofield said cheerily. "I haven't seen you before."

"Yes," Jag tried to say, but his throat had closed. He cleared it uncomfortably. "I mean, yes."

"You speak English?" Dr. Schofield smiled. "Splendid! Well, eat up, lad, then get in there and make yourself useful."

"Thank you," Jag said, watching him walk away to join a pair of nurses at a far table, knowing that everything was going to be all right.

Jag lay awake through the night, restless despite his fatigue. He heard her calling to him, saw her face in the stars that shone down from the night sky way above the mountains. So clearly they shone, so relentlessly. He must be strong. He must now put to the test all that he had learned over his life, for it was time for him to become a man, a good man, in honor of his mother's memory, and now of his father's too.

31

S ophie couldn't see her toes, much less touch them. She skipped the exercise and stretched her arms to the sky instead, breathing deeply, counting along in her head.

"Breathe in, two, three, four, five, six." Miss Pinto flexed herself upright. "And exhale."

Sophie loosened her shoulders, closed her eyes, and pointed her face to the morning sun, its gentle warmth upon her skin. Given another hour or two, its rays would intensify to a searing heat, sending an airborne haze rising from the uneven roof tiles. The whole place turned into a dust bowl at this time of year, bleaching the landscape, shrouding everything in a thin mist of fine red sand.

She hadn't slept much last night, unable to get comfortable, her body grumbling and overloaded, back aching, a nagging stitch catching in her abdomen each time she turned from one side to the other.

Miss Pinto ended the session in the same way she always did, rubbing her hands together, warming her palms before placing them on her face and sweeping them gently down, finishing in a silent moment of prayer. Sophie knew the routine like a poem by heart, the rhythm of each movement bringing a comforting sense of familiarity as her body opened itself to the day. She had felt awkward at first, huffing and puffing through the breathing exercises and struggling to follow the most rudimentary of instructions. Miss Pinto had manhandled her into position on more than one occasion, pulling at her arms, adjusting her footing until she posed,

just so. It had taken Sophie two weeks to master her own center
of gravity, and the difference it had made to her had been remark-
able, affecting her every move, her balance more pronounced, a
heightened consciousness of her body and the space it occupied in
this life. It seemed to settle her mind too, even on those mornings
when she woke filled with all the worries of the world.

Sophie pressed her palms to her face, passed them down over
her body and brought them to rest at her sides. As she opened her
eyes, she became aware of a warm sensation below her sacrum.
Instinctively she stepped back, a thin trickle of water seeping to
the parched ground from her bare foot. She stared down at it, confused, clutched the sari between her legs and said *oh*, before looking up and noticing that the other girls had fallen silent, watching
her. Miss Pinto clapped her hands briskly.

"Breakfast," she said, shooing her class away. As they dispersed,
she took Sophie by the arm, holding her hand. "Come," she said
softly. "Let us go and make you comfortable."

In the night, Sophie had known that her baby was coming. It had
been so still, filling her completely, her body tight like a drum.
She had held her breath, waiting for the stitch to pass, hoping that
it would stop, wishing she could make time stand still. She could
not give birth. She did not want to feel the terrible things that she
had heard through the thick walls. It would be too much for her.
She would never be able to tolerate the pain. It would not be like
the beatings. They had been easy to bear, coming suddenly out of
nowhere and over with quickly, each blow a short, sharp shock
against which she would grit her teeth. She would count them
off in her head, rarely passing ten, and would then be left alone
as the pain gave way to a dull ache. Something had always ached,
and she had become used to the sensation of bruised tenderness in
unexpected places. It had been her constant, lonely companion,

aching bones, darkened patches on her skin that moved from lilac and mauve to green then pale yellow. The beatings she could take. The birth of this baby she could not. She was afraid of the pain, not wanting to go to that place where she knew she must. It was unthinkable that such a thing could pass through her body without ripping her apart. She had cried in the night, such was her fear.

If she stayed quiet, perhaps the baby would remain there. She was too young, too unprepared. And then she knew. She knew that this was the seat of her mother's fury, the reason why she looked at her the way she did, anger unchecked, hands flying. How could you feel anything but resentment after being put through this agony? What punishment was this to endure for giving the gift of life? It should not be this way, a baby causing its mother so much suffering before they had laid eyes upon each other. It was too great a sacrifice, too much to ask just for the privilege of being born.

And she had made her mother suffer indeed, Sophie knew; she had been told often enough that she was not worth the pain she had caused. It was something that she would never be able to make up to her, and she could never expect her mother's forgiveness. Nobody could be absolved for such a wrongdoing, the ruination of one woman's life for the sake of another. Her mother had told her that she too would have to go through what she had, that the day would come when she would know what it was like to have her innards torn out. It would be her comeuppance and would wipe that smile off her face and give her something to think about. Her life would be over and she would have to submit to an existence of servitude and drudgery, for nobody would ever care about her again, because nobody cared about mothers. Then she would learn what it was to be a woman, and she need not expect any help from her mother, because she had already raised a child and she would not do it again.

The hours drew out until they felt like days. How much longer? She heard her own voice as if from a distant room. How much longer will this go on? I can't. I can't.

If only he were here with her now, he would know what to do. He would hold her hands and look into her eyes and she would find all the strength she needed in that infinite gaze of tourmaline green and she would feel no pain. He would hold her close and whisper words of comfort to her, and while he held her, their child would come into the world without pain or fear, emerging from them both, appearing in their arms as though they were one.

Sophie felt herself detach from the world, set adrift. Her eyes remained closed, her body not hers any more, emitting sounds she did not recognize. She breathed deeply, two, three, four, five, six, and exhale. Thoughts rushed in and out of her head. Water, air, the sky inside her, the fields of poppies in June. And fire, oh the fire, burning like a furnace. Her body was aflame. She tried to block it out, holding herself in a faraway place as the fire raged. Sounds circled around her, a deep cracking, like ice giving way on a frozen lake, a deep-throated glacial groan opening out like a crevasse.

"Good girl!" Ruth shouted, holding her hands as Sophie leaned forward, hair soaked with perspiration, and pushed with all her might.

"It will help if you feed him," Ruth said gently. "But you don't have to. We can take him and feed him for you if that is what you want, but it would be better for you and the baby if you feed him yourself." Sophie didn't reply, lost in awe at the infant in her arms. She opened the front of her nightdress and slid him inside. "That's it," Ruth said. "Just relax. He'll know what to do." Sophie smarted for a moment as the baby latched on to her breast. Her eyes darted to Ruth. "It's all right." Ruth smiled and put a hand on her arm. "Strong little things, aren't they?" Sophie nodded. "He will be well nourished and content if you let him feed whenever he wants to."

Sophie lay back on the pillows, feeling a warmth spreading through her, a soporific sensation enveloping her as she watched him at her breast. His tiny hand came to her flesh, and he murmured softly.

"His father's name is Jagaan Ramakrishnan," she said. Ruth turned away, as though she had not heard, and tidied the few things on the small linen chest. "We wanted to be together, but my parents would never have allowed it. They found out about us, and it was terrible." Sophie's finger wandered to her baby's hand and he clasped it tightly. "If he hadn't been Indian, we would have been married by now, because that's what would have happened, isn't it? Everyone would have insisted that we marry straight away, if he had been white." Ruth sighed a little and nodded. Sophie swallowed hard. "It's not fair."

"No, dear, it isn't."

"He doesn't know about the baby."

Ruth came back to the bed and took her Sophie's hand. "It's for the best, dear."

Sophie felt the heat in her face, the ache behind her eyes. "How can it be for the best?" She looked at Ruth. "They won't let me keep him, but what about his father? What if he were to come and take him? What then?"

"Now, now, dear." Ruth stroked her hair. "Don't upset yourself. This is a very difficult time for you. You have just given birth and everything is still topsy-turvy. You mustn't go and make things harder on yourself."

"How can this be any harder?" The baby squirmed at her breast and she quieted herself, hushing him closely to her. "He didn't ask to be born," she whispered. "I can't just give him away."

"I'm sorry, child," Ruth said. "It's the only way, and the quicker it's over with, the better. Your father will be here soon to take you home. It will get easier, that much I promise you, but once you have left this place, you must put it out of your mind. You have your whole life ahead of you, a life that will be filled with other joys. Just you wait and see." She reached out a gentle hand, tucking a stray lock of hair behind Sophie's ear. Sophie felt her baby detach. She looked down at him, slumbering now, his open lips resting at her skin. "One day, all this will be far behind you and it will seem like a distant memory. Look at you. Such a pretty girl. Such a kind heart. He will be taken good care of, and you will have other children to love."

Sophie swallowed hard. "Have you already made the arrangement?"

"Not quite," Ruth said. "Things are all a bit up in the air still." She went to the window and rearranged the curtain. They hadn't realized the child would be a half-caste, which complicated matters rather, and there was still so much trouble going on that most prospective families had far more pressing matters on their minds than homing an unwanted baby, particularly one of mixed blood. The orphanages were overflowing, swelled by the thousands of refugee children who had been lost or abandoned through Partition.

"Will he stay here with you?"

"Yes," Ruth said. For the time being, at least, the child would remain with them. They would give it three months, after which, if no family had been found for him, he would be taken to the orphanage, just like all the others, their fates placed in the lap of the gods.

A gentle knock came at the door. Pearl appeared, holding a tray, one plate covered over with another, a glass of fresh mango juice placed at the side. She set it down on the table.

"Here." Pearl reached for the infant. "Let me take him for a while. You need to eat and rest." Sophie's arms tightened around him instinctively. "Just for a little while," Pearl said, taking the baby from her. "You'll feel better when you've had a sleep."

Ruth brought the tray to Sophie's lap. "Eat, then rest," she said, and followed Pearl out of the door.

Sophie waited for the footsteps to fade, then slid the tray aside. She got up and went to the window, watching Pearl and Ruth as they crossed the courtyard to Miss Pinto's quarters, carrying her son. She could feel him still, attached to her by the invisible cord that bound them together, a cord that could not be cut by the sharpest dagger. She brought her hands to her breasts, hard and heavy, to the dampness creeping into the cotton of her nightdress. She turned away, snatched up her dressing gown, and pulled it on. Going quickly to the small chest of drawers, she began to pull them open, her hands searching furiously, feeling between the neat stacks of cotton squares and towels for the bible she had seen Ruth reading while she had thought her asleep. A moment later, it was in her hands. She opened it, and took a sharp breath for what she was about to do. Steeling herself a moment, Sophie tore out the flyleaf.

❦

Lotus felt herself being awoken, a gentle shove against her shoulder. Her bleary eyes opened a little.

"Sophie!" She pulled herself up to her elbows. "What are you doing here? Are you all right? I've been thinking about you constantly."

"I'm fine," Sophie said quickly. "I have to ask you to do something for me." She reached into her dressing gown pocket and took out a fold of paper, gilt-edged, torn from a book, its thinness indented where a pencil had passed over it. "Take this. It's important."

Lotus rubbed her eyes and blinked herself awake. "What is it?"

"It's a letter. You have to find a way to send it for me. I've written the name and address on the back but I didn't have anything to put it in. Find an envelope, make one if you have to, and send it as quickly as you can."

"But…" Lotus began to protest.

"Please!" Sophie implored her. "You have to do this for me. Give it to Jinty. Give it to anyone who can be trusted to get it to the dak house. I don't have any money. Here." She pressed a pair of ruby earrings into Lotus's hand. Lotus looked at them uncertainly. "Please," Sophie said. "Nobody will suspect you."

Lotus hesitated. "All right," she said. "I'll try."

"Thank you," Sophie said. She felt her face flush and swallowed hard against the knot forming in her throat. "Thank you."

Lotus rested her hand on Sophie's arm. She had never seen anyone look so sad. "Was it really bad? The birth?"

"No, it wasn't all that bad." It would be Lotus's time soon, in another few weeks, and she would experience for herself what it was like to bring a new life into the world. There was no getting out of it. Every baby must be born, so what was the point of talking about it and telling the frightening stories she had heard so often since coming here? "It's soon over, and Ruth will be with you. You'll be fine."

"What's the baby like?" Lotus asked. At this, Sophie smiled easily, just for a moment, then pressed her face into her hands and began to weep.

"I can't do it." She rocked herself gently. "I can't."

"Sophie!" Lotus put her arms around her and hugged her hard. "Please don't cry. Everything will be all right. I promise." She felt Sophie nod and pull herself upright, wiping her sleeve across her face, breathing deeply and composing herself.

"If only," she said.

Oh, how things fall apart.

32

I love you. I love you like nothing I could ever have imagined. I love you
like the moon and the stars and the universe that holds them. I love
you like the dawn mists that linger in the forests, like the first snowdrops in
springtime, like the sweetness of honey on my lips. I love you with every
grain of my body, my body that is now your body, my breath that is now
your breath. You are my flesh and blood, my heart and soul, my love. I
would give my life for you, my son, my child. I will love you until the day
I die. I will stand before you and protect you with my sword and shield.
No harm shall pass through me. I will be like a wall of fire. I will hold out
my hand and take yours and nothing shall ever come between me and the
love I have for you. I will think of you every day and wish you back to me.
I will pray every moment that you will hear me calling you with my heart,
for no one will ever love you like I do. No one.

ᘓᕟᘔ

Time stood still. So peaceful, a heavenly tranquility where everything fell away, leaving nothing but warmth and love, a love so
divine that there was nothing else. Nothing in the whole world.
He was sublime, his fragile beauty beyond anything that she could
have foreseen, sleeping at her breast. She gazed at him, unable to
take her eyes from him, playing with his tiny fingers, watching in
awe as they closed around the tip of her own. So small, so vulnerable, like the first bloom of apple blossom, its petals soft as air. She
leaned her face to the top of his head, her lips brushing the soft

dark hair, taking in his intoxicating scent. She held him closely, so closely that they became one, and slid down into the white sheets, pulling them over her head, the two of them held in a soft cocoon, disappearing from the world.

A small knock came at the door. Sophie held fast under the sheets, hearing the door open, the light footsteps, the creak of the bed as she felt Pearl's figure sit beside her.

"It is time," Pearl said. "Let me take him now."

Sophie closed her eyes and held her baby to her. She felt the sheet lift away, light flooding in, air upon her skin. She curled around her child.

"Come on," Pearl said softly. "Don't make it harder."

Sophie felt her face streaming, her eyes, her nose, her mouth, her breasts. She couldn't breathe, gagging on the air, unable to swallow, unable to live. Her eyes remained shut as she felt Pearl peel her arms from her son, her movements fast and firm. The baby stirred, small, awkward squalls as it detached from its mother. Sophie shrank into a tight ball, hugging herself closed. She pressed her hands to her face, to her ears, and felt herself dying, a talon reaching into her chest, ripping out her heart.

Forgive me, she wept, oh God, forgive me. I'm sorry. I'm sorry. *I'm sorry.*

33

Sophie sat in the garden, curled into a low planter's chair, breathing the clear air, staring out listlessly at the beautiful vista, the layers of hills that stretched effortlessly into the distance, the pleasant breeze shivering through the leaves of the tall trees, lawns sloping gently away. Here, high up in the blue mountains above the clouds, lay Ootacamund, Queen of Hill Stations, a Shangri-La where each day the sun rose and set, huge and red over the distant peaks, casting long shadows across hill and dale and fields where Jersey cows wandered, their mellow bells sounding distantly. It was heavenly, and strangely peculiar in its familiarity, as though a piece of Victorian England had been scooped up and rearranged in filmic perfection, with frivolous gardens and gothic archways, and tranquil boating lakes for lazy days and fishing. On the last leg of their journey, the car had strained along twisting lanes through sylvan glades, passing high wooden gates and pretty arbors with neat signs outside—*Lyndhurst, Glendale, Lushington Hall*—before slowing into the turning marked *Iona*. She had seen a chital yesterday from her bedroom window, delicate and shy as it disappeared with the lifting mist, tiny cloven hooves tripping into the silent forests that clung to the hillsides.

Sophie lay back, head against the cushions, and closed her eyes. For now, her tears were spent, her head aching from the agony of being awake for these last few hours. Amid the birdsong, she heard the rustling of skirts, the short puffs of a heavy-footed woman.

"Are you warm enough, dear?" Mrs. Ripperton deposited the

small silver tray on the table, dropping herself on the smaller seat set beside Sophie's chair. She had only been gone a few minutes, to fetch the bottle of tincture and to see to the hullabaloo coming from the kitchen. It had turned out to be nothing, of course. A mouse nibbling at a flour sack in the storeroom or some such minor drama. They had almost gotten a conversation going too. Poor girl. She still looked as though she'd had the stuffing knocked out of her, a dull pallor clouding her complexion, her eyes red-rimmed and tired. What she must have been through. She was a wicked woman, that Veronica Schofield. Cared not one jot for her family and had returned every one of Fiona's letters unopened. She shouldn't have bothered with the wretched woman. Heaven only knew what Sophie and her father had suffered. No man should have to put up with a woman like that, with her endless histrionics and her vicious tongue. She wasn't even pretty, her face thin and sour like pressed limes. He should have got shot of her long ago, before she could ruin his life and their daughter's too while she was at it. Now look at the poor girl. Wrung out like a dishcloth. It was no wonder with a mother like that. If she were here, she would jolly well give her a piece of her mind that she wouldn't forget in a hurry.

"Here." Mrs. Ripperton stirred a little tincture into a glass of water, dropping from the pipette four drops as prescribed by her father, plus two more because she thought Sophie looked like she needed it. "Drink this. Just a few sips." She pressed it into Sophie's passive hand, rearranging the blanket around her. "I've asked Salil to make us a nice fish curry for lunch. Mr. Nayar caught two lovely plump ones from the lake this morning. You'll manage a little, won't you?" Sophie seemed not to hear, lifting the glass to her lips, drinking obediently. "That's better." Mrs. Ripperton took the glass from her and placed it on the table. "The house martin chicks have made their first appearance," she said brightly. "Darling little things came shuffling out of the eaves on to the electricity wire above the bathroom window this morning. You should see them!

Tiny little wings aflutter, going *cheep cheep cheep!*" She sat back in her chair, pulling at a loose cushion. "Then off they go! Not very far, mind. There they are, clinging on to the nearest bush, bobbing around like they don't know what to do, calling for their mother!" She turned away, screwing up her face for a brief moment, silently damning herself for using the word *mother*, before soldiering on with her cheerful chatter. "It's a good thing your kitty has been shut in your father's room. It would have made a quick breakfast of the lot of them."

Sophie smiled absently to herself and remembered Pumpkin, the fat tabby who had wandered into their Islington garden one day and decided to stay. She had hidden him, making a bed for him in the shed behind the rusty old lawn roller. She thought that no one had noticed and that she had got away with her secret pet, until one day she went to feed him and found a pair of saucers, one filled with milk, the other with a few scraps of boiled ham. She knew that it was her father. Her mother never went in the shed. He was a survivor, that cat, nonchalantly tossing his nine lives around, one of them left beneath the hooves of the rag and bone man's moth-eaten horse that had caught the end of his tail. He didn't care much for people either, quite happy to live in the shed, helping himself to mice and bitter voles, which he preferred to leave on the kitchen doorstep, much to her mother's horror. Sophie had thought Pumpkin her only friend. He had let her pick him up and carry him around and put old baby clothes and bonnets on him. He'd be dead by now, she thought, hoping that it had been a peaceful end in a nice vegetable patch somewhere.

Pumpkin had eventually tired of the house on Percy Street and had moved out one day while no one was looking. Sophie had searched for him everywhere, saving morsels of meat from her supper, putting them in the garden with a saucer filled with the top of the milk, to no avail. She had cried for him for a while, before her mother put a stop to it. Her father had wanted to get her a kitten, she had heard him say so, but her mother had told

him that if he brought another living creature into this house, she
would drown it. It was all right for him. He wasn't the one who
would be expected to look after it. Voices had been raised, and her
father said that she had never looked after anything in her whole
life, and that the cat had bloody well looked after itself. And then
they hadn't spoken for days, and Sophie's father had taken her to
the pictures and they had eaten ice cream during the intermission.

Sophie sighed to herself and blinked at the distant view, her
thoughts suddenly taken again. She could still feel him, his soft
brown skin against hers, her aching breasts bound tightly with
wide bandages to stop the milk that refused to be banished. *I'm
sorry. Please forgive me. Oh God, forgive me.* She closed her eyes and
inhaled the fresh green air of the hillsides, tinged with the scent of
high alpine trees and flowing streams.

Her father's voice drifted into the garden.

"Hello, my darling," he said softly. "And how is my beautiful
girl today?"

Sophie nodded in a small way and tried to smile. He leaned
over her and kissed her head. Mrs. Ripperton stood from her chair.

"Have a seat, George," she said. "I'll ask Salil to fetch another
and hurry along with lunch."

Sophie pulled herself up, tucking her legs beneath the blanket,
and watched Mrs. Ripperton cross the garden toward the house,
calling for Salil. Fiona had been the very last person Sophie had
expected to see when they arrived in June. Even her father had
seemed taken aback to find that she had stayed on and waited for
them, uninvited, yet there she had been, solid and dependable, as
though she had known all along what was going on. Sophie had
fallen to pieces upon sight of her, and they had hugged like there
was no tomorrow. Over the days that followed, it had all come
tumbling out, and Sophie had felt as though a great weight had
been lifted from her.

Sophie looked at her father. He seemed to have aged so much
in the last year, flecks of gray touching his temples, face etched

with deep lines that cut into his brow, his cheeks redder than they
used to be. She approved of the mustache. It gave him a certain
air she rather liked, distinguished perhaps, even a little Hollywood,
if Clark Gable had been fair. It had been the oddest thing at first
when he had come to Cuttack to collect her, like seeing him anew,
the eternally unchanged features of her father suddenly different.
She looked at it again now and found herself smiling. Dr. Schofield
smiled back at her, picked up her hand and kissed it, then relaxed
into his chair.

"That's some view, isn't it?"

"Yes," she said.

"I bet I could grow more runner beans than a man could eat in
a garden like this."

Salil crossed the lawn bearing a tray and approached them with
a wide smile.

"Peg, sahib?" He set a glass down beside Dr. Schofield.

"Chota peg," Dr. Schofield said, measuring small with his fingers. Salil shook his head.

"Memsa'b say burra peg." He poured a generous inch or so
before returning the bottle to his tray and setting a glass of lemonade beside Sophie. "Is freshly made, Miss Sophie," he said.
"Freshly made just for you."

"Thank you," Sophie said.

Her father took up his glass and helped himself to a splash from
the soda siphon, then drank a little. Eyes on the heavenly view,
he said, almost to himself, "I finally heard from your mother this
morning." Sophie nodded and sat back, turning her face to take
in the same vista. She would not ask whether her mother had
inquired after her. She never did. Never had. Dr. Schofield relaxed
into his chair and took another sip. "She's agreed to give me a
divorce." He pulled a letter from his pocket. "Do you want to
read it?"

"No," Sophie said.

She looked at the envelope in his hand and thought about her own letter. It would never find its way, not among all the chaos, so many people dead, so many lost. Nobody would care about a scrap of paper, a thin flyleaf torn from an old book, scribbled upon so quickly in the face of her hopelessness. There had been photographs in the newspapers of the destruction wreaked upon Amritsar, the dead bodies lying out in the open, bloated and stiff, swarming with flies. She had had no idea, having not seen a newspaper or heard a radio for months. What hope would there be for a message sent into the midst of such desolation? She should never have written it, to end up who knows where, to bring trouble to the mission. She had not been in her right mind. Sophie knew what it was to have a mother and to lose her, to be abandoned, no matter if it were for the best as her father had said when he told her that her mother was gone. She could not do that to her child. She *must* not do that to him. May he never know that he was given up, that he was born by another woman and handed over like an unwanted gift. Let him find peace in his world and comfort in the love of whatever woman had come forward to take her place.

There was no going back now. She had given up her child, and she must reconcile herself with that and trust that he would be loved and well cared for. A good family would have taken him. Anybody would have seen that he was a rare prize, a perfect boy-child, with golden skin and dark hair, so very beautiful. He would always be a part of her, and so would Jag, her first love. Everybody had a first love, Fiona had said, and it was always the most precious, and because of what had happened, Sophie's first love would be more special than any other. She must learn to lock it away in her heart as every woman does and to treasure it.

Without taking her eyes from the view, Sophie reached out a hand. Her father took it silently and squeezed it hard. Sophie's tears rose again, spilling down her cheeks, the words flooding back to her, her heart turning over as she remembered what she had written, the last line burnt into her flesh.

We have a son. Find him.

1958

*New Year's Eve,
Delhi*

34

Rich clouds of cigar smoke billowed from the open clubhouse windows, curling upward in great streams out into the chilly night, floating high to the strains of Glenn Miller's "String of Pearls." Dancing toward midnight, everyone wore silly party hats, colorful paper streamers littering the floor, half-finished drinks discarded on messy surfaces, some with cigarette ends tossed in. Waiters scurried around, rushed off their feet, clearing up spillages, carrying away trays laden with spent glasses, cleaning and replacing overflowing ashtrays.

Tessa appeared at Sophie's side, loosened by several cocktails, toying with her straw. "I smell trouble," she said. She nodded briefly toward the Hinchbrooks, Tony's face high with color, Melanie's set with barely concealed sufferance behind a tight smile as she picked someone out in the crowd to wave to before walking off. Tony Hinchbrook threw back the rest of his drink and marched away in the opposite direction, knocking into a bearer, sending his tray crashing to the floor. "What say you?" Tessa said. "Looks to me like somebody's in for an interesting night. Where's that man of yours?"

"In the billiard room," Sophie said. "They've lifted the limit to fifty guineas for the night. I just have to hope he doesn't lose his shirt and end up in a foul mood later."

"Aw, now." Tessa pulled a sad face and linked her arm through Sophie's. "Let's go and see if we can't find ourselves somebody to torment for a while, shall we? I'm just in the mood for making a little mischief. That's the thing I love about New Year's Eve. Tomorrow is a fresh start for everybody, isn't it? But tonight," she gave Sophie's arm a little tug, "tonight we play."

They wandered toward the billiard room, Tessa fiddling coquettishly with her necklace, eyes roaming the crowd, offering counterfeit smiles here and there. A sudden roar went up from behind the wall in appreciation of a well-taken shot. In that instant, Lucien appeared with the American, Gresham, both men still deep in conversation before Lucien noticed Tessa and Sophie loitering in the doorway.

"Well, well," he said. "What have we here?" He ran his eyes over Sophie. "Look out, Gresham. My wife is spying on us."

"We were just wondering where all the interesting men had gone to," Tessa said. She slipped her hand into the crook of the American's arm. "Care to dance?"

"I sure do," said Gresham, leading her onto the crowded floor.

"Shall we?" Sophie offered her hand to Lucien. He looked at it and took a sip of his drink.

"I have a game to play," he said, turning away from her, heading back to the billiard room.

∩›››∩

The night blackness began to lift, fading out as the first suggestions of dawn crept over the cold, mist-bound rooftops. Veneet stood beside the brazier, lifting the tail of his shirt, catching the heat. "What are you looking so serious about?" he asked. He had hardly had a word out of the newcomer all night. He wouldn't even take a drink with him from the flask he had brought along to celebrate the new year. They had gone out to watch the fireworks at midnight, flying up into the sky in the distance, and he had pulled the flask from his pocket and offered it, but Jagaan had said no and had looked at him disapprovingly. "Suit yourself," Veneet had said, putting the flask to his lips and tipping his head back. He dropped himself into the chair, put his feet up on the table, and belched.

Jagaan ignored him and looked out of the window. She had come home alone hours ago, brought back in the car from number seven, where the lady had gone in while the husband escorted Sophie to her door and saw her safely inside before returning to his own house. The light had gone on briefly in her bedroom, then the house had fallen into darkness. Her husband had not come home yet, and soon it would be getting light.

Jagaan had walked the perimeter twice in the last hour, while Veneet put his feet up on the table and refused to budge. Then he had walked it a third time, when he thought he had seen something out of the corner of his eye. He had heard it too, sensed it almost, and had taken extra care as he paced the enclave slowly, aiming the beam of his flashlight into the gardens, across the sides of the houses. A cat had dashed out from the bushes at number three, its eyes shining a bright reflection as it ran across the road, slipping under a gate and disappearing into the garden of number eight.

Jagaan felt deeply unsettled tonight. Never in his life had he knowingly allowed fear to hold him back like this, and he was angry with himself for his apprehension. He must show himself to her, and then he would know. He would know the instant she saw him whether her love remained, for there could be no secrets between them. Not then, and not now. It would be easy for him to come into her path. He could step out from the guardhouse and open the gate for her car, or pass her house as she was emerging, or, and he had thought of this often, he could walk right up to her door, just as he had done that day two months ago in Ooty, expecting to find Dr. Schofield, instead discovering that she was here, in India, his whole world turning upside down.

How he wished he could know what was in her heart, but he was confounded, troubled by the sight of her unhappiness, unsure of the ground beneath his feet. This could not be the life she wanted, this existence he had witnessed with his own eyes. They had talked of it so many times when they were young, of futures filled with happiness and laughter, and children. Whatever he might have gone through over the years, the doubts and uncertainties and guilt of it all, he had not known the extent of the price Sophie had paid until he saw her. She was lost. He could see it in her as clearly as night followed day. He had found her sadness unbearable, and he had held back and watched her suffering, knowing one thing with complete certainty: she needed her son. Just one look at him and she would surely never feel heartache again. She would find bliss, and every emptiness she had ever felt would disappear. He must show himself, but the thought of it filled him with angst. What if he was wrong? She might look right through him, pretend not to know him, and if that happened he would have to bear it, even if it killed him.

Jagaan got out of his seat. He would walk the perimeter again, he decided, just to make sure.

"I'm going back out," he said.

"More fool you." Veneet settled himself in his chair and pulled a blanket around his shoulders. "I'm going to take a nap. And don't bother waking me when you get back."

Jagaan put down his cup, wound his scarf around his neck, and went outside. He had not gone more than five steps when the car appeared, driver yawning widely, the husband half asleep in the back. The car stopped outside her house, the driver jumping out and opening the passenger door, her husband getting out, brushing the driver off as he tried to assist him toward the path, pushing him rudely away. He stood there, swaying, watching as the car moved off, sliding quietly to the back of the house before the engine stopped and the headlights died. Lucien fumbled ineptly in his pocket, pulled out a cigarette, and put it to his lips, the flame of his lighter moving unsteadily as he crouched into it.

He was drunk, Jagaan thought with disgust. So drunk that he could barely stand up. He watched as Lucien staggered forward, steadying himself on the gatepost for a moment before dropping his cigarette then looking down for it, bending and scanning the ground as he swayed to and fro.

Jagaan heaved an angry sigh and shoved his flashlight into his belt before crossing the road toward the staggering man. He would have to help him, before he fell into the gutter and cracked his head open. Perhaps he would land a blow on him while he had the opportunity, just one, big enough to give him a blackened eye and a bloodied nose, before depositing him on her doorstep. Nobody would see. Veneet would be snoring beside the brazier and the lights were out across the enclave. He could hand out a short, sharp punishment to this man who did not deserve her, the man who had stolen what was his. It was still dark enough, that brief place between night and dawn. If ever he needed an opportunity to give the man a little of what he deserved, this was it. He walked toward the drunkard, thinking about how it would feel to have his fist come into bloody contact with the foul mouth he had heard shouting at her so often.

All at once, Jagaan heard a sound from somewhere behind him. He stopped, twisting toward the noise, and saw something moving, a flash of brightness in the undergrowth. A raw-throated groan, like that of an animal, filled the street. Jagaan pulled the night stick from his belt, moving carefully, peering into the dimness. Suddenly a figure lurched from the shadows, an old man, white-haired and red-faced, heavily disheveled, dress shirt open down to the waist, steam spilling dense whorls from his twisted mouth, his face shining with thick sweat as he raised a loaded hand and shouted…

"*Grainger!*"

Jagaan looked to the man, then to her husband, and broke into a run.

In the thick mist of that early dawn, a single shot rang out across the enclave. Birds screeched, flying out of the trees, and the acrid smell of gun smoke bittered the cold, damp air.

The force of Jagaan's body hit Lucien like a truck, his full weight upon him. Lucien staggered back, hands grabbing out instinctively to steady the man who had slammed into him, staring in horror at the open mouth, gasping for air, the wide, disbelieving eyes.

Jagaan clutched at Lucien's jacket, dragging him into him while Lucien fought to pull away.

"Please." Jagaan tried to speak, his right hand pulling at his breast pocket until it tore from its seam, his fingers staining red as a peony of blood bloomed darkly through his shirt. "Give it to her." His hand came free, a pale blue silk sheath crushed into it. He began to choke, blood and spittle on his lips. "Tell her…" He pressed his hand into Lucien's chest. Lucien tried to hold the man up as he took it, but the weight was too much for him.

"Who?" Lucien said, his stomach rising. "Tell me who?"

Jagaan closed his eyes and whispered her name.

"Sophie."

❧☙

They say that at the moment of death, a man's whole life flashes before his eyes. He sees the moment of his birth, the faces of all the people he has known and loved. He feels the might of the oceans and the infinity of the stars. He sees the miracle of his children and his children's children. He relives every moment that has made his life what it is, every breath of it, each piece falling perfectly into place as he reaches his single moment of clarity, the very end of his time on this earthly plain. They say that this is what happens at the moment of death, but this is not so. Jagaan Ramakrishnan felt nothing as he fell to the ground.

35

Sophie woke with a start. She had heard something. Something so violent that it had penetrated the two sleeping pills she had swallowed. A loud crack, like the earth splitting open. Outside, a terrible commotion. Her hand reached out, the space beside her empty and cold, the clock on the bedside table ticking five a.m. Quickly she got up and threw on her dressing gown, stepping into her satin slippers before switching on the light and heading downstairs, where the house staff were already roused.

"What's going on?" she called out, her head groggy. "John?"

As she reached the bottom of the stairs, Dilip rushed past her, barefooted. He opened the front door and ran outside, Sophie close behind him. John was already crossing the garden, his legs thin and bare beneath his long white sleeping salwar.

"What's happening?" Sophie tied her belt tightly around herself as she took the steps at a pace and rushed toward the people gathering in the middle of the road. Doors began to open everywhere, people coming out in varying states of undress, lights going on although the night had started to lift away, the soft dawn revealing the scene laid out before her. Tony Hinchbrook, slumped in the road, shirt filthy and open to the waist, head lolling in his hands as he wailed and sobbed. Some staff from the nearby households, all shouting and talking at once, three of them crouched to the ground, cradling a limp figure, one of the night guards, Sophie saw, collapsed in the street, the other guard standing over them, yelling hysterically at the people attending him, something in his hand. Was that a *gun?* And Lucien. Sitting on the pavement by the gate, leaning against it, shirt soaked in blood, a pool of vomit on the ground beside him. Sophie flew to his side, grazing her skin as she dropped to her knees on the roadside.

"Lucien?" She put a hand to his face. "Somebody call for an ambulance!"

"I will fetch brandy," said Dilip, his face ashen.

"No! Not brandy. Bring some water. And get some blankets. Lucien?" She tore his shirt open, looking for his wound. "Lucien!" she shouted. "Where are you hurt?"

He stared at her, a thin sneer rising on his lips.

"For God's sake!" she shouted over her shoulder. "Tell them to hurry! Lucien?" She pulled off her dressing gown, oblivious to the cold, and laid it across him. "Darling? Are you all right?"

He smiled at her, lifting an unsteady finger, and beckoned her toward his lips. She leaned into him, her arms around him.

"Lucien, darling. What happened?"

He pulled her closer and whispered in her ear.

"You *whore.*"

ᏉᏇᏉ

Sophie sat on the edge of the settee, arms clutched about herself, rocking with sickness, staring blankly at the wall. He was shouting. Screaming at her. She could hear his voice, see him careering around the room. A full whisky bottle hurled into the fireplace, exploding with a loud, dull pop, sending shards of glass splintering through the air. Crossing the room like a tornado, standing right in front of her, towering over her, spitting venom, kicking the table over.

"Deny it! Go on! Deny it if you dare! With that bloody *wog!*" He began to laugh, a terrifying high-pitched gurgling sound spewing from his mouth. "Pushed it right in my face and said, *Here! Give it to her! Tell her!*" A chair smashed against the wall. "You fucking whore! Right under my nose! I'll fucking tell her all right. I'll fucking give it to her!"

Sophie's heart stood still.

I didn't even see him. They took him away before I could see him. I didn't know you were there.

She pulled her arms more tightly around herself.

Oh, dear God, I didn't know you were there! How long were you out there watching? Why didn't you tell me? What did you think I would have done? Did you think for a moment that I wouldn't have taken your hand and run a thousand miles to the ends of the earth with you?

She clutched at her chest, at the terrible pain searing through her, the scrap of paper, torn and bloodied, balled in her hand. Lucien ripped pictures from walls, wrenched lamps from their sockets, splitting the plasterwork, shouting and hurling abuse at the staff, landing punches as he threw them out. The scrape of heavy furniture. Lucien jamming the door closed with the walnut secretaire desk, John running outside and calling for help, Dilip banging on the door, pleading with him.

Oh my love. They took you away before I could see you. Where have they taken you? I have to see you. I have to lay my eyes upon your dead body or I won't believe it. You couldn't die. You wouldn't leave me like this.

The blow came so hard that it knocked her to the floor. She heard her head hit the upturned table, her face bouncing away and spattering against the marble floor. She tasted blood, coppery on her lips, inside her nose. She saw the side of his brogue as it came into her cheek, feeling nothing, numb from the inside out, numb and cold and dead like the corpse of the uniformed man she had seen being carried away and loaded into a car. She caught a glimpse of the standard lamp, lifted high above Lucien's head.

I didn't know it was you. I didn't know it was you.

A howl rose from her belly, spilling with the blood from her open mouth, a groan so loud that it shook the walls, and then she began to scream.

36

Bathed in a thin shaft of soft white light, floating high up on a cloud, drifting listlessly, Sophie was enveloped by an irresistible warmth, voices fading in and out. *Is this death?* she wondered, feeling herself fluid as water. She was lying in a flower meadow, soaring above the mountains, resting on a wide stretch of golden sand, waves lapping gently around her.

"Sophie? Can you hear me?" A woman's voice, vaguely familiar, pulling at her when she wanted to be left alone, to sail peacefully into the warmth of the light. "Oh, my dear. You poor, poor dear." She felt herself unable to move, her body elsewhere, taken from her. A hand touched hers. She tried to open her mouth, stuck together, dry. "Here." She felt moisture on her lips, on her tongue. "Just a little." A trickle coming into her mouth, spilling down her chin, dabbed softly away. "There, there."

Her eyes flickered, lids so heavy she could barely lift them, her whole being cushioned in silk-soft eiderdown, dulling the pain, caressing her skin, tiny shivers passing over her. Another voice. A shape peering at her closely, swathed in white, a gentle hand coming to her face.

"I'll fetch the doctor."

"Yes," said the woman. "Quickly."

Sophie felt herself blink, a tiny faint movement.

"You poor, poor dear." The woman leaned over her. "He should be locked up for what he's done to you. And carrying on like that with all and sundry. And that despicable Hinchbrook woman, like butter wouldn't melt in her mouth. Oh, my poor, poor dear. Oh, just look at you." The woman was crying softly now. "You mustn't worry." She felt the hand come to hers again. "We are going to take excellent care of you."

"Mrs. Appleton?" A man spoke. "Perhaps you would be kind enough to wait outside for a moment."

"Yes. Yes, of course."

Sophie felt a gentle pull on her eyelid. A harsh light came into her and she flinched a little, expelling a low *hmm*.

"Sophie? Can you open your eyes for me? Sophie?" She tried to do as the voice asked. So tired. So very tired. "Just a little. Come on now. I know it's hard."

She felt herself moving, being lifted, a dull metallic cranking sound. "Sophie? Come on now, there's a good girl, open your eyes for me a little."

The hazy outline of a man began to appear before her, softly focused. A kind face, almost smiling but not quite, a stethoscope around his neck, but not her father.

"Well done," he said. "That's good. Just look at me?" Something passing in front of her face. "Can you follow my finger?" She felt her eyes move. "*Very* good. Excellent." Her arm being lifted, fingers painfully splayed. "Can you squeeze my hand for me? Squeeze it as hard as you can. Come on. Harder." She felt herself drifting off again, the feeble effort exhausting. "Excellent. Very good. Well done." The voices faded out, talking among themselves. "Sophie?" A hand on her arm. "You're in the hospital. You've had a small operation but you're going to be fine. We're going to keep you here for a while. All right?" She heard a distant *hmm, hmm*. "Now you rest, and there will be someone right here beside you at all times." She tried to say thank you, thank you, hearing it in her head, unable to move her lips.

The woman was there again, hand coming into hers. Sophie felt herself slipping from consciousness again, drifting into a lotus garden, the gentle sound of water trickling from pool to pool, soft white orchids clinging to the trunks of nimbu trees. *How did you find me?* Jag smiled at her. *You knew I would find you.* The night was warm, soft against her skin, and the frogs were singing, the night insects buzzing under the glow of the full moon. Sophie turned away. She did not want to speak to him. She was too upset. She had waited so long, sitting there all alone in the lip of the farthest pavilion. *Why did you take so long? Where have you been?* She turned back to him, but he was gone.

1948

The Road to Amritsar

37

J ag had arrived early at the hospital tent, the sky still red from the swollen morning sun, hanging low on the horizon, its first rays creeping over the distant ramparts. He had slept soundly, his body spent from the previous day's work, and had woken feeling strong again, ready to fetch water and carry the sick just as he had done every day for three weeks. The doctor did not know who he was. He had never laid eyes upon him, although Jag had seen Dr. Schofield many times, watching silently from hidden panels in long-forgotten passages in a palace far away. The doctor liked him, though. He gave him biscuits and told him to sit down and rest and drink some water, and Jag knew that everything was going to be all right. The father of the girl he loved had been sent to him by the gods, placed right here in the middle of his camp. He would stick close by. He would follow him to the ends of the earth, knowing that it would lead him to her.

Jag worked through the morning, washing sheets and boiling bandages, stirring and pounding the laundry in a wide vat set upon a fire, the sweat pouring from him until he was relieved by the next shift. He went back to the mess tent and slaked his thirst with seven cups of water straight down, then ate a sandwich before being called in again. There were patients to be moved, and more stretchers were needed outside. Jag did as he was asked, all the time looking out for the doctor, checking every white-coated figure that caught his eye. Hours passed, and he began to tire.

"You look like you need a break." One of the orderlies

slapped him on the shoulder. "Why don't you go out back and rest a while?"

Jag looked at him for a moment and nodded vaguely, suddenly aware of the fatigue nagging at his muscles. The orderly turned to go.

"Excuse me, sir," Jag said. "Do you know where Dr. Schofield is? I have not seen him today."

"Dr. Schofield?" The orderly seemed perplexed. "Why do you ask?"

"No reason in particular," Jag said. "I was just wondering where he was. He was very nice to me yesterday and I wanted to thank him."

"Oh, I wouldn't worry about that," the orderly said with a smile. "We're all in this together."

"But still," Jag said. "I would like to see him to say thank you."

"I'm afraid you've had your chips with that," the orderly said. "He left this morning. But I'm sure he won't mind. Now why don't you grab yourself a quick chai and forty winks, eh?"

Jag felt the blood drain from him, his stomach churning and tightening.

"Where did he go?"

"I don't know. Back to England probably."

"*England!*" The orderly's words struck him like a hammer blow.

"Steady on, lad!" Taken aback by Jag's distress, the orderly came close to him and hushed his voice a little. "There's no need to get upset about it!"

"But he can't have gone to England. It's…it's…" Jag struggled to breathe. "I have to find him."

"Now come on." The orderly tried to sound stern. He cleared his throat a little and looked around. "Hey!" He called to one of the nurses. "Does anybody know where George Schofield was headed?" The nurse shrugged vacantly before turning to her colleague and passing the inquiry on.

"I'm not sure," said one of the other nurses. "Maybe he's moving on to another camp."

"No, he's not," said someone else. "Dr. Pretti said he was going south."

"Any idea where?"

"Don't know. Kerala, I think."

"No, it definitely wasn't Kerala. My sister lives in Kerala, so I would have remembered that."

"Then I'm not sure."

"Wasn't he going to one of the hill stations?"

"Didn't he say something about Orissa?" another nurse said.

"I don't remember." The first nurse turned back to the orderly. "You'll have to ask Dr. Pretti."

"She's gone to the border post," the other nurse said. "Won't be back for weeks."

"Thanks," the orderly said. He turned to Jag. "I'm afraid you've had it." He shrugged. "That's the way it is with the doctors. They come in and do a stint then go off again. Don't feel bad about it, lad. There'll be some new doctors here soon who'll be just as nice."

Jag felt as though his whole world had caved in. It was hopeless. He might as well search for a needle in a haystack the size of a mountain. With a heavy heart, he wandered to the mess tent, filled his pockets with biscuits, and walked disconsolately back to the small patch of ground his father had died upon. He lay down and closed his eyes, hands over his head, every ounce of his strength taken from him.

The doctor had gone. There was nothing left for him here. He must leave this place right now, before he too gave out and died.

Jag crouched down quietly beside his neighbor's shelter. Navinder Singh was resting, his wife sleeping nearby, their two children curled closely into her body. Jag set down the few things he had brought with him: a small bundle with some of the biscuits, the folded sacking that he had taken down from his own shelter, and a pair of bowls that he no longer needed. He must carry as little as possible. Nothing must slow him down.

Navinder Singh opened his eyes. He saw Jag, then looked to his sleeping family before unfurling himself from the ground and crawling out.

"What are you doing?" He glanced over the things that Jag had left there.

"I am leaving," Jag said.

"Where are you going?"

"To Amritsar. To find my mother's family."

"You can't," Navinder Singh said. "The roads are full of danger."

"I don't care."

Navinder stared at him for a while, as though thinking. He sat back on his haunches.

"You are right," he said grimly. "There is nothing here for any of us." He turned and looked at his family. "But you will not go alone. We will come with you."

"No," Jag said. "I am leaving now. You have a family to look after. I have no one."

"We have no one either," Navinder said. "And I am just one man, with a wife and two children to protect. We will travel together, and I will have the comfort of knowing that there is another man walking beside me who will do whatever he has to to safeguard his family. You are part of our family now, Jagaan." He placed a hand on Jag's arm. "Help me to deliver them from this." He looked at his wife and children again. "They deserve better, and I am at a loss."

ᘓᘔᕊᘖᘙ

The officials at the guard post did all they could to dissuade the sparse groups of refugees who refused to be contained any longer. They urged them to be patient, to return to their shelters and wait to be processed. "We have already waited," people said. "And what good has it done us?" More voices joined the protest.

"I have been here for six months and still you tell me to be patient?"

"Other people have been given papers and moved on before us because they bribed some officials!"

"Yes! They took my wife's gold bangle and said we would be given a house and then we never saw them again. You are all crooks!"

As they argued with the soldiers, other groups filed past on their way into the camp, too tired and broken to notice the untidy ranks of arguing people, some reluctantly turning back toward the encampment, others breaking away from the officials and heading for the open road.

Their few belongings had fitted easily into just two tied bundles, both of which Jag bore while Navinder Singh and his wife carried their children.

❧❧❧

All along the Grand Trunk Road that ran between Amritsar and Lahore, which now lay over the border in Pakistan, stretched miles upon miles of refugees, thin lines simultaneously going eastward and westward carrying paltry possessions, forlorn and desolate.

Jag walked on steadily, concentrating on the ground, Navinder Singh's son now riding on his shoulders, Jag holding his small feet while the boy clung to his head with both hands. His stomach felt empty, his thoughts filled with images of warm chapattis and bowls of hot, thick yellow dhal. Navinder Singh glanced over at him and said, as if reading his mind, "We will stop soon and rest for a while and have something to eat."

"I am fine," Jag said. "You do not have to stop for me."

"Not for you! My wife is tired. Look at her."

Jag twisted a little and saw Mrs. Singh behind them, the little one asleep against her shoulder, her face thin and fatigued. He looked back at Navinder and nodded.

"This is not so bad," Navinder said. "On our first journey, it was a wonder we didn't all starve. As for the cattle, they had

hardly any food either. We couldn't get a quarter-bucket of milk
out of them. When our rations ran out, we bought whatever we
could from *jangli* people who would sell us flour sometimes. They
were charging five rupees for flour. Five! And anyone who needed
opium was in big trouble, as it was being traded only for gold,
weight for weight. Everyone on the Pakistan side had been told by
the Baluchi army not to sell us anything, not even a grain of rice,
so anyone who chose to break this rule could name his own price.
One of them was caught selling flour." Navinder broke off for a
moment. "They tied him behind an army truck and dragged him
along the ground until he was dead." He shook his head. "What I
cannot understand is that the government knew that people were
having to leave their homes, they knew about the trouble, yet
they would not arrange a smooth transfer or safe passage for us.
They knew people were suffering, but we were stuck there, with
nobody to help us."

"How much longer do you think it will be before we reach
Amritsar?"

"What does that matter?" Navinder Singh smiled at him. "Every
step we take brings us closer, and before we know it we shall be
standing before the Golden Temple, and I will take you into the
gurdwara and they will give us a good hot meal, and afterward we
will go and visit the holy of holies and hear them chanting the
sacred texts."

"You have been there before?"

"No. All Sikh temples chant the holy scriptures. It is very beautiful. And everyone is fed before they go to pray."

"Everyone?"

"Yes, everyone, no matter what their religion. Even if they
don't want to pray, still they can come in and eat and they will be
welcomed."

"Even a Moslem?"

"Yes." Navinder Singh fixed his eyes upon him soberly. "Even
a Moslem."

The boy was becoming heavy on Jag's shoulders, his body slumping against Jag's head, as though too tired to hold on properly any more. "Abba," the boy said. "I want to pee." Navinder stopped and put the bundles down before reaching out and taking his son from Jag's shoulders. Jag picked up the bundles and waited while the boy hitched his pajamas down and relieved himself, Navinder ruffling his hair.

"We'll stop here," Navinder said when the boy had finished, seeing another group of refugees who had halted for the day, the women sharing out sparse rations, a child being washed roughly with a handful of water. There was no trouble here, not from the looks of it. Everyone was too tired for trouble. The boy pulled up his pajamas and Navinder lifted him on to his shoulders. "Come," he said to his wife. "We will go and join those people in the field. I think we have walked far enough today."

38

Jag had never seen a city before. At first it seemed like a mirage in the distance, a shimmering spectacle coming no closer no matter how long they walked. And then the road began to thicken with people and animals, and all kinds of stalls started to appear, tables of blankets and clothing, cups of clean water and food being handed out. At last they entered the city, the family sticking closely together, Navinder at the front, Jag at the rear. A smattering of people, all wearing the same distinctive strip of red tied around their upper arms, milled through the crowds calling advice and directions. This way for food, come this way, this way, there are hot meals this way. Does anyone want to report missing persons? This way for missing persons, please. This way for missing persons register. Is anybody coming here to meet relatives? This way for information about relatives, please, this way…

Jag called out: "Navinder! Stop!" He pointed to the volunteer, who was now wandering the other way. "Navinder! We have to ask that man! He said we go that way for information about relatives." Navinder peered into the crowd, saw the volunteer, and nodded back to Jag, making his way toward him.

"Excuse me!" he shouted. "Wait! Excuse me!" He pushed his way along, through the people and confusion, catching up with the volunteer with the red armband. The man turned, a little distracted. "Which way for finding relatives?"

"Over there," said the man, pointing to a building surrounded tightly by hundreds of people, part of its outer wall missing.

Jag broke away from Navinder and rushed forward, pressing his way through. Navinder kept sight of him as best he could, following behind with his family.

Over six hours they waited, just to speak to somebody.

"Are you on our lists?" asked the man sitting behind the table, piles of papers held down under broken lumps of rock. He was one of many, a whole line of them manning the long row of information points set up in the street outside the damaged building, trying to bring order to the chaos.

"I don't know."

"Name?"

"Ramakrishnan."

"Where have you come from?"

"One of the border camps."

"Did you register your details there?"

"No," Jag said. It seemed to him like the more sensible answer, rather than telling the man that yes, he had registered six months ago and it had been a complete waste of time.

"You really should have registered there and waited to be processed." He pulled out a form. "We can do it now."

"Please, sir, I do not need to register with you. My family is here," Jag said. "They are waiting for me. I have to find my way to Kim Street, so if you could tell me where it is, please, that is all I need."

The man looked at Jag for a moment, weighing him up. They were supposed to register everyone and send them on to the most logical next point of call. Most were being directed toward temples and mandirs and camps for further assistance, and many became frustrated, particularly those who had already come from another camp. They all wanted to be allocated proper housing, just like they had been promised. It was a headache, all these people flooding in and nowhere to put them, the big family groups in particular. The man scratched his head. If this youngster said he had relatives waiting for him, then the best thing he could do was to get him out of his queue and move him along.

"You're sure you have family here?"

"Yes."

"Hm. You don't look like a Punjabi."

"My mother's side," Jag said.

"What was the address again?"

"Kim Street."

"In which area?" he said.

"Area?"

"Yes. Which part of the city?"

"I don't know."

The man sifted through some papers, before pulling out a map. "Kim Street," he said to himself. "Is it big or small?"

"I don't know."

His finger traced over the tangled diagram. He half lifted his head, raising his voice to anyone who would listen. "Does anyone know where Kim Street is?" No one seemed to take any notice. Jag stood impatiently, wanting to snatch the map from the man's hand and run off with it.

"Kim Street?" somebody shouted back. "It is on the other side of the railway, on the Gurdaspur side."

"Do you know the best way to get there?"

The owner of the voice stood up, a head appearing from another crowded table. "Tell them to follow the Bari Daab canal. Cross over the railway lines and keep going straight for a while, then ask someone else. Everyone there will know Kim Street. It has tradesmen's shops."

The man before Jag raised his hand vaguely in thanks. "Did you hear that?" he asked. Jag nodded. "If you follow this road to the end and turn left, then right, you will come to the canal. Do you want me to draw a picture for you?" Jag shook his head. "All right," said the man. "Now move along. Who is next?" he shouted into the crowd.

Navinder Singh came forward but was pushed aside by another man, who stepped into Jag's space. Jag reached into the crowd and

pulled Navinder's sleeve hard. "This man is next," he said firmly.
For a moment it looked as though an argument might break out.
The man who had barged in began shouting, his hands in the air.
Other people shouted back at him, saying that he had pushed in
front of them too.

"Good luck," Navinder said to Jag. "I hope you find your family."

"Name?" the man asked.

"Navinder Singh."

"You have family registered here?"

"No."

"No? Then you are in the wrong place."

"Please," Navinder said. His wife was beside him now, the baby
in her arms, the boy by her side, their belongings reduced to one
pathetic bundle. "We have come such a long way, and we have
been living out in the open for months. I have to find housing for
my family. The baby is not well, coughing all the time."

"You are in the wrong place," the man said. "You will have to
go and register properly. You would be best to make your way to
the station and join one of the camp convoys."

"Camp convoys? We don't want to join a camp convoy! We
have already come from a camp. We need to be housed!"

"Did you register in the camp?"

"Yes! But we were just left there."

"Then you should have waited to be allocated."

"We did wait! We waited and waited until we couldn't stand it
any longer. Please! You have to help us!"

"What do you expect me to do?" the man said, throwing his
hands up. "You see all these people? They all want the same thing,
the same thing as you. You think I am a magician? You think I can
just pull a house out of my sleeve and say here you are?" He shook
his head incredulously. These people. Even if he wanted to help,
there was no housing left to allocate, not within this part of the city
anyway. Sure, there were no doubt some properties available, but
they were valuable commodities that were being kept and sat on

by all manner of people higher up the chain. "There is nothing I can do," he said. "You really must go and register properly. Why don't you take your family to one of the gurdwaras? You can get them some food and refresh yourselves for a while, but then you will have to go and join the lines and sign up officially, otherwise you won't receive an allocation."

"But…"

"It's that way," the man said, pointing ahead, straight into the crowd. "Ask one of the volunteers with the red armbands. They will give you proper directions."

"We can't go back to another camp!" Navinder bent toward the man and leaned his hands on the table, coming close to his face. "We would rather die than go into a camp again."

The man stood up, his expression a grim picture of determination. "Then that is up to you, my friend. Now, if you will excuse me." He faced back into the crowd. "Who's next?" Navinder felt himself pushed aside, his body swaying as he gave way to the two men who shoved past him.

"I'm sorry," he said to his wife. She reached out and touched his face, and the pair of them stood for a while, looking at each other, being jostled on all sides. Navinder put his hand to his wife's cheek, his fingers resting on skin and bone where there had once been a soft mound of flesh. A few steps away, Jag watched them. Without thinking, he pushed back through the crowd. Taking hold of the boy, he lifted him quickly on to his shoulders and started off into the throng.

"Come with me," he shouted. "We have traveled this far together. I will not leave you now."

"But…" Navinder began to protest.

Jag kept on walking, the boy clinging to his head.

They crossed the city quickly, averting their eyes from the bodies in the canal, black and bloated, the air ripe with a pervasive rotting aroma like dustbins that had lain unemptied for years. Over the railway tracks they picked their way, then onward, through a maze of fly-blown alleyways, stopping only to ask directions, some useful, some not, sending them in circles before they found their way again.

The day began to dim, the sun starting to sink. They halted again, asking an old woman rummaging through a stinking pile of rubbish.

"Kim Street?" she said. "You have already passed it." She pointed them back in the direction from which they had come. "It is there, behind that blue building with no roof."

ও/ঙ৬

Kim Street lay battered and exhausted, a once busy line of shop fronts now mainly boarded up, some of them burnt out and in ruins. A few stalls punctuated the way bravely with meager displays of goods long past their best and dusty sacks of rice and gram. There were no numbers, so Jag began to ask again, calling out to no one and everyone: "Number seven Kim Street? Does anybody know number seven Kim Street?"

"Over there," a vegetable seller called out, pointing.

Jag followed the line of his outstretched hand. There, across the street, stood another shop, its boarding hastily banged into place, old, rough pieces of wood hammered up untidily. The sign above was still visible. *Gupta Shoemaker & Quality Leather Goods.* Jag bent down, sliding the boy from his shoulders, and walked over. He pulled at the door but it stuck fast, reinforced from the inside.

"There are windows open upstairs," Navinder said, bringing his family off the street on to the cracked slab pavement that fronted the brief row of buildings.

Jag banged on the door. "Hello?" he called. "Number seven Kim Street! Please open the door." Nobody came. He pounded harder, shouting louder, wrenching at the door, hearing nothing back except the rattle of the strong lock and chain that held it shut. He ran out into the street and called up to the windows: "Number seven Kim Street! Please come down! It is me! Jagaan Ramakrishnan! Please! Mr. Gupta! It is me! I am the son of Mrs. Gupta's sister!"

People began to gather in the street. The vegetable seller left his stall, wiping his hands on his shirt, his pace quickening as he came to see to the commotion. Jag continued to shout, his voice howling up to the open window. The vegetable seller set his bulk before him and caught hold of his arm. Navinder Singh moved forward protectively.

"What is all your shouting?" the vegetable seller demanded.

"My family is in that house!" Jag wailed. "My name is Jagaan Ramakrishnan. My aunt lives there. My mother's sister."

"And where is your mother?"

"She is dead! They are both dead!"

The vegetable seller looked him over. Could this be the boy? The one Parvesh Gupta had told him about? The one everyone had been speaking of? He looked like he'd walked all the way from Delhi, the state of him. Navinder held his ground, standing ready for trouble, his wife and children behind him.

"Wait here," the vegetable seller said, then went to the door, pounding on it hard. "Mrs. Gupta!" he shouted. "It is me, Deepak! Come down and open the door!" He went back out into the street and looked up at the window, hands on his hips. A woman's face appeared briefly, peering cautiously from within. The vegetable seller waved up at her. In a while, movement came from behind the door. It opened, just a slit, a heavy chain still visible across the small gap. "Someone has come," the vegetable seller said to Jag. "Wait here. I will speak to them. What did you say your name was again?"

"Jagaan Ramakrishnan. And this is my friend Navinder Singh and his family. They are the ones who brought me here safely."

"Ah," Deepak said. He offered Navinder a cautious greeting, nodding to him. "You wait here too."

The vegetable seller leaned in close to the door, speaking to whoever it was who had opened it. Every now and then, he stopped to look over his shoulder, before turning back again.

Slowly the door opened, a woman of slight build standing there, sari pulled over her head, while two other women, much younger, peered out from the shadows behind her. She lifted the sari from her face and stepped out into the street. Jag moved toward her, quickly at first, before halting as he saw the look on her face. It was as though she had seen a ghost, her whole person standing frozen, unable to move. Jag came forward, as if to present himself to the Maharaja himself. He bowed his head.

"My name is Jagaan Ramakrishnan," he said. "I am the son of Abheek Ramakrishnan. My mother's name was Naisha. She died when I was born."

The woman's hand came to her mouth. She turned quickly, one of the younger women rushing out to her. The older woman reached for her hand. "He is here," she said.

"Is he the one?" Deepak asked.

"Yes," said Mrs. Gupta. One glance at him was all it had taken. He had the beauty of his mother, his mouth exactly the same as Naisha's, the beloved sister she had missed so very much. She stepped toward him. "I am your aunt," she said. "Deepak. Close up your stall and come sit with us so that we have a man in the house."

"Where is my uncle?" Jag asked.

"Come," she said. "Let us go inside. You must be tired."

Navinder stood with his family, unsure of what to do. Mrs. Gupta spoke to his wife. "Come. Bring your family inside. We shall have to make more bread."

❧

Within an hour, dusk had fallen, the rooms above the workshop warmed by the yellow flames of half a dozen clay oil lamps, the light just enough to illuminate the plentiful supper they shared.

Together they sat and ate, Navinder and his family, Jag and his aunt, Deepak the vegetable seller, and the two young women, Geeta and Komal, introduced by his aunt as close neighbors whose husbands had gone missing. They were staying with Mrs. Gupta while they waited for news, the three women feeling safer for being together. Jagaan tried to recall the last time he had eaten supper with a family, a high stack of warm chapattis quickly diminishing, torn up and scooped into a big dish of curried vegetables before disappearing into hungry stomachs.

"You must miss your home," Mrs. Gupta said to Navinder.

"Yes," he replied. "But I believe in karma. We were preordained to leave. Our *anjal* is here, our destiny. We will trust in that and build our lives again."

Navinder's boy began to fall asleep, food still in his mouth, his head slipping forward sharply, then back, eyes opening for a moment before sliding closed again. Navinder gathered him up, one of the young women rising to take him through to the second room where the family slept on mats laid out on the old wooden floor.

When Navinder returned, they were talking again, his wife this time, speaking softly, telling of the conditions in the camp, the scenes on the roads as they had trudged endless miles.

"They said we will have to go into one of the camps again," she said, "and hope that a house can be found for us soon. But the baby…" She looked down into her lap where the infant lay sleeping, rattling short breaths. "It is not good for the baby."

Mrs. Gupta fixed her eyes on Deepak. He stopped eating, setting down the piece of chapatti in his fingers.

"I know what you are going to ask me," he said.

"Well, why not? It is what Taj Din would have wanted."

Deepak looked at Navinder, at his wife, at the infant in her lap.

"What if somebody objects?"

"By somebody, you mean your wife."

The talking stopped, everyone eating quietly for a while before Navinder broke the silence.

"Have things been very bad here?"

"Very bad," Deepak said. "You can see for yourself what it has done to our beautiful city. There was rioting in the streets. Pitched battles being fought right outside that window."

"Are things better now?"

"Yes. Thank God. At least the worst of it is over, but now we have all the refugees streaming in. We are trying to help them as best we can, but still they come in their thousands."

"We saw," Navinder said.

"They wanted to put Amritsar behind the line, to make it part of Pakistan. We were lucky to be able to stay in our homes. It is the ones who had to come over the border who we feel sorry for."

"We had to leave our home behind," Navinder said. "My wife thought we would be able to go back one day. Now she accepts that we shall never return. We have to start again and make a new home somewhere, but with so many people…" He noticed that his wife was weeping, silent tears she tried to hide behind the veil of her thin, stained sari.

"Let her cry," Mrs. Gupta said. "We saw our neighbors crying when they left. Taj Din, the Moslem tailor, came to every Hindi house and wept openly before leaving." She looked at Deepak again.

"He was my neighbor," Deepak said. "His family lived in the rooms above ours. All day long and half the night we would hear the beating of his little sewing machine. He made beautiful clothes. My wife had the best *cholis* and I the best shirts. He was a good man."

"And what did Taj Din say to you?" Mrs. Gupta asked him.

"He gave his home to me," Deepak said. "He said that he had blessed it so that it would never feel the shame of the blood that had been spilled, that its walls would never be tainted by the hatred that infected our city and its people." Deepak looked at Mrs. Gupta. "He said that we must always remember to love our neighbor as we do our own family." He turned to Navinder, face covered in shame. "We have been using the space," he admitted.

"My wife said that we needed it, for the day our son marries and brings his wife into our home."

"He is two years old!" Mrs. Gupta said. "And you have plenty of room."

"Then it is settled." Deepak drank a little water, thinking for a while, and said to Navinder, "But I will warn you now, you will not find my wife the easiest of neighbors. She snores like a water buffalo."

Jag watched from the open window as Deepak, Navinder, and his weary family crossed the dark street on their way to Deepak's home. A few minutes earlier, Jag and Navinder had embraced like brothers, Navinder's eyes red-rimmed, his throat unable to speak.

"Your aunt has put a basin of water for you downstairs in the kitchen at the back of the workshop." Jag turned to see Geeta, one of the neighbor women, standing there. She set down a small pile of clean cottons—fresh pajamas and shirt, some cloths with which to wash and dry himself.

"Thank you," he said. She turned to leave. "Geeta?"

"Yes?"

"How long has your husband been missing?"

"Three months." Her eyes held the floor. "He went out, with Komal's husband. Komal's mother-in-law had the cholera. They said they would fetch the doctor or bring some medicine at least."

Jag looked at her and wondered if she knew that her husband was dead. They both were, hers and Komal's. He thought about the bodies he had seen in the canal, the ones along the railway tracks, and wondered if any of those blackened remains were their menfolk. *What had happened?* he thought. How could this country have descended into such wretchedness? It seemed to have happened overnight, this once happy and peaceful land now an unfolding nightmare of death and destruction at every turn. Geeta's head remained bowed.

"They must have got caught up with the crowds," Jag said lamely. "I hope they return safely soon."

"Thank you," Geeta said. She lifted her eyes to him. "Komal and I both know that our husbands are gone, but for so long as we believe them alive, we shall not have to live as white shadows. No woman wants to be a widow. It is our darkest fear."

Mrs. Gupta appeared in the doorway. "Jagaan," she said. "Go and wash." She picked up the pile of fresh cottons. "Take these down with you and put on something clean. You can leave your clothes there on the floor. We will lay a bed for you here. We will sleep in the next room."

"Thank you, Aunty."

❦

Jag steeped a cloth in the basin, water dripping to the floor as he brought it to his naked body, the outline of bone and muscle illuminated by the golden glow thrown out by the lone oil lamp. His skin bore scars here and there, superficial marks on his arms that would not stay for too long, a deeper twisted river across his shin where he had gashed it open as he leaped from the train. Another scar ran for three red inches just below his right shoulder blade, but he was not aware of it. He rinsed the cloth, the water clouding, and passed it over his face again, around the back of his neck, scrubbing hard. Bending forward, he dipped his head into the basin, massaging his fingers into his scalp, his hair slicking out into the water, grown long again since one of the nurses had cut it for him in the camp. He stood up, flicking his head back, a trail of water flying through the air behind him, spattering against the wall.

Without warning, his reflection stared back at him, and he stopped, not recognizing it for a moment. It had been a long time

since he had seen his own face, thrown back at him now in the
small blackened window, the dim glass fractured across one corner.
He leaned toward it and inspected himself, tipping his head back,
lifting his chin, seeing the jut of his collarbone, the smooth, hard
round line of his shoulder. He rinsed the cloth again, pressing it
into the water, and washed his body, freeing his skin from the
long journey, consigning it to the layer of grime that settled at the
bottom of the basin.

Upstairs, his aunt was waiting for him. His bed had been laid
out. A mat and a colorful blanket sewn of myriad patches. And
cushions, three of them, to arrange however he wanted. A cushion
for his head, he thought, the one thing that he had stopped longing
for more quickly than anything else. It was nothing more than a
luxury, unnecessary for the purposes of survival. He had forgotten
about cushions. He had forgotten about many things.

"I hope you will be comfortable," his aunt said.

"It is a bed fit for a king," Jag replied.

Mrs. Gupta looked at him, so tired, so thin, sharp elbows
poking through her husband's cotton shirt. She was still reeling
from the shock of it, that he had somehow found his way here. She
knew of her sister's son, of course, but they had never expected
to see him. That was the way of it when sisters grew up and married away, moving into the households of their husbands, leaving
their own families behind, often never to be seen again. A wife
belonged to her husband and his family. It was the sons who stayed
behind, bringing wives into households, swelling the family's tribe.
All these years, she had not even heard his name.

And then the letter had arrived, and they had not known what
to make of it. They had stared at it, as though it were some strange
object just dropped out of the sky, wondering what it could be.
Her husband had made the decision. He had opened it, peeling
back the roughly made envelope, its folds stuck down with rice
glue dried powdery white into the corners. Inside, folded small,
had been a scrap of paper, so thin that he had shaken it open

carefully, exposing patterned, foreign writing, its figures looped in thin pencil lines.

"What is it?" she had asked, wringing her hands.

"A note of some kind," her husband had said. "It is written in English."

They studied it anyway, even though they were unable to read it. Mr. Gupta took it to the vegetable seller, and together they took it to the barber. He knew some English words, but the letter had made no sense to him either. The only person who would be able to get to the bottom of it would be Mr. Shirodkar, the advocate who lived on the corner. So they had taken it to him, the three of them, and he had told them what it said.

"What should we do?" Mr. Gupta had asked his wife when he returned home many hours later. The men had discussed it at length in the advocate's office, and the news was already sweeping through the street, passing quickly from door to door.

Mr. Gupta had sat before his wife, watching her thinking. His wife was a wise woman. She was not afraid to speak the truth. Nor did she fear any man. She claimed she had no need to, for her husband would protect her from any man who came into her presence, and he would never wish her to be dishonest with her own husband. There had been times when he had wished he had married a less outspoken woman, but not often. He loved her very much, and her honest manner of thinking and clear advice had saved him from his own hot temperament many a time. Mrs. Gupta had thought long and hard before she spoke.

"We know that Jagaan and his father left the palace months ago. They could be anywhere. They are probably dead."

"Yes," her husband had said.

"I believe that what the letter says is true," she said. "Why else would someone send such a thing?"

"Yes. I believe it too."

"And you ask me what should we do?"

"Yes."

"Now I will ask you the same thing, husband. What should we do?"

"I don't know! That is why I am asking you!"

Mrs. Gupta had taken his hand. "You and I, is our blood the same?"

"Of course it is!"

"Then you forget, my blood is shared with my sister too. I had hoped to see her again one day, perhaps when we were old, so that we could share the stories of our lives while sitting around getting fat on sweets." She smiled at her husband. "A grandchild," she said. "My sister has a grandchild. A boy, born through the line of her own blood. And what has happened to him? He has been thrown away like rubbish! Don't you see? He is alone somewhere, waiting for someone to claim him. Perhaps he has already been given away, a child, connected to me by blood. Connected to *us*. So now I ask you, husband, what do you think we should do?"

Mrs. Gupta thought of all this as she watched her sister's son, sitting on the floor beside her, fighting his fatigue. And now she asked the same question of herself, *what should we do?* wishing her husband were there to answer her. It was not in her nature to hold back, but now was not the time. He needed to rest, to regain his strength and replace some of the flesh that had fallen from his bones.

"I will leave you to sleep now." She got up from the floor, adjusting her sari over her shoulder. "I cannot believe that you are here. It is a miracle."

❧❦❧

Jag did not wake until noon the following day, and when he did, he was so tired that he managed only to eat a little, to drink some water, before his body waned and he fell asleep again. The women left him in peace, keeping to the other room, slipping past quietly whenever they went downstairs to wash or prepare food.

Mrs. Gupta watched Jag sleeping. He seemed so peaceful,

untroubled by his dreams, and she studied his face closely, the marked resemblance to her sister. His mouth twitched, just slightly, and for a moment it looked as though he were smiling.

Jag had heard her come into the room, the sounds of the day drifting into his half-sleep, unable to rouse himself. He had not slept like this since forever, always on his guard, ready to spring up and defend, or flee, or respond to whatever threat might creep up on him while he lay down. Sometimes he would wake with a start, realizing that he had fallen fast asleep, and he would check every-thing around him quickly, feeling angry with himself for slipping off like that, and then he would force himself awake, shifting to a less comfortable position to reduce the temptation to drift into full sleep. He and Navinder had taken turns keeping watch, but still, one of their bundles of belongings had been stolen in the night, lifted and carried away from right under their noses.

Jag knew his aunt was close by, the scent of her, cinnamon and cloves, all around. He felt himself slide into sleep again, and thought of Sophie. If only he had not lost sight of her father. He should have said something to him. He should have introduced himself and said that he knew him from the palace. But then Dr. Schofield would have known. He would have put two and two together and realized that he was the boy that his daughter had been seeing secretly. And if he had said something, what did he expect to happen? Did he think the doctor would have greeted the news well? No. It would have been a mistake. He might even have turned on him and given him a thrashing.

He thought of Sophie and wondered where she was. Back in England, no doubt. Who in their right mind would have stayed? Dr. Schofield would have sent them home ahead of him. The British always did that when trouble loomed, sending their fami-lies away, cities and towns emptied of women and children. He had sent them to the safety of the countryside during the war Sophie had described to him, the bombs and the great fires that had swept through the cities, the ancient buildings engulfed in

flames, towering walls collapsing into the street as though made of
cardboard. She had told him of the village and of how different it
was from villages in India, of a cottage called Ranmore, and how
the church bells rang out and the way they sounded, calling the
villagers to prayer. He knew everything about it.

A small breeze passed over him and he began to dream, imagining himself crossing the black water, flying over it like a bird, the
vast sea meeting the earth, and him soaring, soaring, over England's
green and pleasant land. On he flew, across the cities and out into
the countryside, looking down over the hills and fields until he saw a
church, bells pealing into the sky, and swooped down, circling, circling over the cottage. She was sitting in a chair, like the ones in the
orange garden, and she was wearing a dress in the palace blue, like the
tiles in the blue fountain. Down he went, diving through the thin air,
landing near to her. *I have found you*, he said, but he was a bird and his
words came out as a song, high and sweet, and she looked at him and
smiled. *It is me!* he sang, a pretty ditty that went *chirrup chirrup*, and she
watched him for a while. *It is me! It is me!* he said, hopping around as
though the grass was burning his feet, but she was looking away now,
far off into the distance. He sang to her again but she did not notice
him. Instead, she got up and went inside.

☙❀❧

"Jagaan." Jag opened his eyes, his aunt's face peering down at him.
"Jagaan. It is morning again."

He sat up a little, propping his weight on his elbows. How many
mornings? Two, he thought. He had counted two. Or perhaps he
had been dreaming. He pulled himself up, his muscles heavy, and
stood as though trying his legs, testing his balance. He flexed his
shoulders, joints and sinews cracking, and loosened his neck.

"How are you feeling?" she asked.

"Yes," Jag said, nodding to himself. "Much better. I am sorry I
have slept so long."

"It is good for you. You needed it. You will eat something now?"

"Yes. I will."

"Geeta is making *dosas* with curried vegetables." She came to him and arranged his twisted shirt. "She makes the best *dosas* you have ever tasted. Thin and golden and crisp, and so light." Jag smiled. "Komal made the vegetables. They are not as good as mine, but we will pretend."

Jag laughed, his aunt slapping his hand playfully, telling him to shush. She laughed along with him for a while, then her face darkened. She took his hand between her palms, looking at it, stroking the back of it gently as she breathed softly to herself.

Jag didn't want her to cry. He had seen too much crying during those terrible bleak months when he had felt so alone, and the sound of it had been one of the hardest things to bear. His aunt put his hand to her lips. She kissed it and returned it to him. Only then did she look up.

"Jagaan," she said.

"Yes, Aunty?"

"We will sit together this morning, just you and I."

"Yes, Aunty. I would like that."

"And we shall talk of all the things we have to talk about. You must have many questions to ask me."

Jag looked at her. He had no questions. His mind was a blank, like it had been washed clean, as though the sleep had taken every thought in him and carried it away. His aunt noticed his vacant expression, a tiny shift in his eyes, almost imperceptible. Those eyes, she thought. They were unlike any that she had ever seen: deep green, like jewels.

◠◡◠

Geeta and Komal served Jag's breakfast in silence, then slipped away to the kitchen where they could be heard faintly, talking softly, moving pots, sluicing water, pounding grains in the quern.

"This is the best food I have ever tasted," Jag said.

"We are very lucky," his aunt told him. "We are mostly traders in Kim Street. Deepak brings us vegetables and will never accept any payment. Your uncle makes shoes for him, for his family, and he never takes payment either. We look after each other, all the trade families. It is the way it has always been, but many have left now. Who knows who will come and take their places?"

"Where is my uncle?"

"I will come to that. You do not need to worry about him. He is safe."

"Perhaps Navinder will become a tailor," Jag said.

"That would suit Deepak very well indeed. He is worried that now he will have to start paying for his shirts. He is a generous man with his vegetables, but not so generous in matters of money."

"You can't eat money," Jag said. "That is one of the things that I have learned. What use is money when there is no food to buy? His vegetables are far more valuable."

"It is a good lesson," his aunt said. "Your mother always swore that when she had a son, he would be properly educated. He would learn to read the great books and become a great man."

"Yes," Jag said. "My father talked about her often."

"And did her wish come true?"

"Partly," Jag said. "I was educated, as she wanted, but only time will tell if I live to honor her as she deserves."

"So you can read the English?"

"Yes." Jag smiled, a little proud of himself. "I can read the English."

His aunt nodded in a small way. "Have you finished your breakfast?" His plate was empty, the thin platter wiped clean. She took it from him and went downstairs.

Jag flexed his back, sitting upright, hands on his folded knees, and belched. He was awake now, fully awake for the first time in days. It was a relief, to be out of that weary, transcended state. He would go out today maybe, ask his aunt about it first, but he needed to be outside, to feel something other than the cocoon of these four walls. Perhaps he had spent too long out in the open, living in it, sleeping under the sky. He would have to get used to being indoors again, to adjust to a new life, and he wondered if a day would come when all this felt like normality.

Mrs. Gupta returned from the kitchen, entering the room as though it were a tomb. Jag stood up at once, the veil of worry across his aunt's face sinking his stomach. She was holding something in her hands, an envelope, already open, her fingers turning it over.

"Jagaan," she said. "There is something I have to tell you about. But first, I want you to sit down."

He did as he was told, and his aunt sat near to him, straight-backed, the usually soft line of her figure unnaturally stiff. Jag settled himself as best he could, his eyes shifting constantly to her hand.

"Jagaan. A letter came for you a month ago," she said. "We didn't understand what it was or why it had been sent here. We didn't know where you were. We never expected to see you." She dropped her face in shame. "Your uncle opened it." She held it out to him. "I am sorry." Her head remained bowed as she felt the envelope taken from her.

Jag looked down and saw his name, the shape it formed when written in English. He did not recognize the writing. Lifting the flap, he opened the envelope, then stopped, mystified. Inside was a scrap of paper, folded small, like the notes he had once pressed into the gaps in the stone slabs beneath the huge marble urns in the Moghul gardens. His fingers reached in for it, tissue thin, tiny flecks of gold at its edges, and he saw his name again, the address of his aunt's house, the handwriting different from the envelope—different, and unmistakable. His heart caught in his chest. Sophie. She had remembered, and she had written to him. He felt over-joyed, swallowing hard, his hands trembling. He wanted to leap into the air and yell at the top of his voice. He wanted to crouch in a corner, curl into a ball, and weep, because he had missed her so badly. Carefully he unfolded the delicate paper, fearing that it might disintegrate if he even breathed too hard.

The state of her writing threw him into confusion, her hand unsteady, the once elegant curve of her tails scratched sharply into the paper, the dots and crosses fast and untidy.

My darling Jag,

You have a son. He was born on 23 May 1948 in St. Bride's mission in Cuttack, Orissa. They made me give him up. I don't know what to do except to send this. We have a son. Find him.

Sophie

Nothing moved. Not the air in the room or the dust motes that hung there. Not the sun in the sky or the earth below it. Jag felt his blood lie still, his heart stop beating, his skin shrink from his flesh, his whole being sucked from the room into a vast vacuum of stillness. His mouth went dry, his throat filled with stones. He began to shake, uncontrollably, as though thrown into a tub of ice water. His aunt put her arms around him, holding him tightly, feeling him rigid beneath his shirt, his rapid swallows, his juddering breaths.

"Be still," she whispered to him. "You have nothing to be afraid of."

Jag felt his head splitting open. The room began to sway. He pulled in deep breaths, hard and fast. *You have a son.* He wrenched himself away from his aunt, standing up, flailing, two clay oil lamps knocked to the floor. His hands clasped his head, bending, straightening, striding to the window, his breathing suddenly heavy. He turned from the window and bent down, doubled over as though in pain, his face contorted, hand pressed to his mouth now, perhaps to stop himself screaming.

He stood up, feet unsteady. "I have to go," he said, then began to pace up and down as if trapped, wanting to push the walls down and run. "I have to leave."

His aunt got up and took hold of him, grasping his arms firmly. "Jagaan! Look at me!"

He turned his face away. Sophie. His Sophie. She had borne a child, *his* child, and he had not even known about it. Now he realized why the gods had made the doctor disappear. He was not meant to follow the doctor. He had been destined to come here all along.

"Jagaan!" His aunt pulled at him hard. "*Listen* to me!"

"I can't stay," he said.

"You must," she told him. "You uncle has already gone. He took the advocate with him and the barber. They left two weeks ago." Jag stared at her, his mouth opening mutely. "What did you *think?*" she said softly, reaching to his face. "Did you think we would leave a child of our family to the mercy of strangers?" She smiled at him, a painful smile filled with happiness and sorrow. "They have gone to claim him," she said. She steadied him as he sank to his haunches, the breath knocked out of him. "It's all right," she said softly. "They will bring your son home."

～❦・1959

Francis Xavier

Nursing Home, Delhi

39

The rains over, Delhi emerged renewed from the damp fog of winter's chill. The thick smell of wood smoke and dung fires lifted, the air now clear and blue and laced with the scent of hibiscus and frangipani where slumbering borders had miraculously sprung back into life. Sophie leaned back in her chair and lifted her face to the sun, its springtime warmth soothing against her skin. Her father had insisted upon moving her to the nursing home some weeks earlier, with its charming gardens and manicured lawns, neat paths cutting through them, wide enough to take small exercise on the supportive arm of a nurse, comfortable white wicker chairs set out here and there beneath the wide veranda.

"You are looking so much better, memsa'b."

"Thank you, John." Sophie smiled from behind her dark glasses, the two of them taking tea in the shade. The pleasant surroundings had come as a blessing after the starkness of the hospital, and her father had been quite right. She had still been suffering from the shock of it all, and just because her scars had begun to heal hadn't meant that she was well again.

She had known that it was gone from the moment she woke up from the second surgery, feeling the emptiness beneath a haze of morphine. It had all happened so fast, the onslaught of blood, the nurse's confusion, the way she had been rushed to the theater again. No one had said anything to her afterward, yet she knew. It had been written on their faces, a cloak of sympathy creased so deeply into every touch, every bravely born smile. It was over for her now, all choice removed, and she must come to terms with it, like she had with so many other things. Who knows what this life will deal to us? she thought. Perhaps her mother had been right, her sins so great that she would be made to atone for them for the rest of her days. And atone for them she had, in spades. Sophie moved a little in her chair, adjusting one of the cushions, smarting briefly from a sharp twinge in her abdomen, still tender.

They had taken good care of her here, but she would not be sorry to leave. It was as though part of her had expired, left for dead in a devastated drawing room on that terrible morning when the world fell in around her. The part of her that remained, the part that had survived this, felt strangely alive now, as though it too had woken from a winter slumber, like the flowers in the garden. Everything was different now. She wasn't afraid any more.

"I won't be coming back to the house," she said.

"No, memsa'b."

"But I think you probably knew that already."

"Yes, memsa'b."

"Have you received any news about Mr. Grainger?"

"No, memsa'b."

"No word at all still?"

"Nothing, mem."

No one had seen hide nor hair of Lucien. At least, that had been the official line, although it had been obvious that someone must have assisted him in his disappearance. The police had been too busy dealing with the matter laid out so unequivocally before them: Tony Hinchbrook, a smoking gun in his hand that he had attempted to turn upon himself before it was wrestled from him.

On her arrival at the hospital, the first priority had been to attend to Sophie's injuries, and by the time the details began to emerge—the terrible fight John had heard behind the barricaded door, the smashing of furniture, the way she had been screaming—Lucien was already gone.

The passenger lists showed that he had taken a flight to Karachi.

Where he had gone from there, nobody knew. The police inspector had said that he had probably got on a ship, and they wouldn't have a hope of finding out which one, his file quickly closed and swept under the carpet. It was not police business, as far as he was concerned, a woman caught having relations with a guard and being beaten by her husband. She should count herself lucky. If he ever caught his wife with another man, he would have killed the fellow as well, and her too.

"There have been some rumors," John said. "The cook from number eight heard them talking at one of the memsa'b's dinners. He said that he had heard that Mr. Grainger had gone to South America, to Argentina. He wanted to borrow some money, but I don't think they sent him any. One of the memsa'bs was very angry about it."

"I see," Sophie said. They would have sent him the money, of course. That was the way of it with that set, closing ranks, disposing of problems quietly and efficiently behind a diplomatic smokescreen. Tony Hinchbrook too had been removed, extracted from police custody by the powers-that-be at the British Consulate. They would clear up their own mess, they insisted, and the chief of police was only too happy to oblige, once his department's expenses had been disbursed, of course, his own pockets comfortably filled. Hinchbrook had been flown back to London, to be dealt with by the Home Secretary, his name quietly erased from the lips of all who remained in New Delhi. These things happened now and then, dreadful scandals that had to be cleaned up posthaste to minimize the embarrassment.

It was rare that a situation ever blew up in their faces like this. Usually they were containable, passed over as unpleasant gossip that could be overlooked provided nobody went about parading their sordid little peccadilloes. June Smythson carrying on with their bearer, for instance, or Jim Bevan's penchant for the company of young Indian men. One did whatever one had to, to bear a dystopian, transient life of foreign cities and unfamiliar customs, of rigid etiquette and high manners frozen in aspic. It was another world, a tiny microcosm of stagnant ideals and old-fashioned thinking. Sophie would not miss it, not for one second. It had been like living in a sealed jam jar: no air, no space, the view to the outside just an unreliable distortion of reality.

"We will have new people coming to the house soon?"

"Yes, John. I expect so."

"We will all miss you very much."

"Thank you, John. That is kind of you. Dr. George will be coming to tie up any loose ends. I have decided to go back with him to Ooty for a while. If you could have my things packed up by the weekend, I would very much appreciate it. All I want is my clothes and personal effects. The things from my dressing table and so forth. There won't be terribly much. Two trunks should do it, don't you think?"

"Yes, memsa'b."

"If it runs to any more than that, then you'll have to cull some of it. I'll leave it to you to decide what stays and what goes, but I don't want to be bogged down with a lot of pointless clutter. It doesn't do."

"Yes, memsa'b. What about Mr. Grainger's things?"

"Do whatever you like with them."

"But won't he be wanting them?"

"I really don't know, John. And I'm not sure that I care either. I suppose you could ask Mrs. Hinchbrook if she knows where he would like them sent." She slipped John a dry smile. "She seemed to know more about my husband's whereabouts than I ever did."

"Yes," John said. "And she is currently knowing the whereabouts of the husband at number eleven."

Sophie regarded him closely for a moment. "I'm sorry about all this fuss, John. Heaven only knows how it looks to you, all these lies and tawdry behavior. You must think us all savages."

"I don't think anything, memsa'b."

"Of course you do." She gave a resigned tut. "And you are very kind to keep those thoughts to yourself. I want to thank you for that and for all you have done for me."

"You do not need to thank me, memsa'b."

Sophie sighed to herself. "What a terrible mess."

"Do not feel bad, memsa'b. It is not good for you."

"No," she said. "What's done is done. The future is what matters now. Not the past."

"And you will have a good future, memsa'b."

"Thank you, John. I do hope so."

"There is no need for you to hope." John smiled at her and pointed to the wide blue sky. "It is written."

They sat and drank tea for a while, John helping himself to a biscuit. He would miss the memsahib, but he would not miss all the trouble, the fighting and arguing and the husband's bad temper and keeping him out with the car until four o'clock in the morning. Still, he liked working in the British houses. They paid much more than the Indians. He finished his biscuit and thought about taking another. Perhaps the next people would be better. They had been talking about it at the house, him, the cook, the gardener, and the maid. They would all say that they were being paid fifty rupees a month more than they were. The new people would be bound to match it without question, and Mrs. Grainger would not be around to enlighten them.

"So you are going to Ooty, mem?"

"Yes."

"Very nice. Very...*picturesque*." John nodded approvingly, as though he knew the place well, although he had never been. His family had come from the Punjab, part of the mass migration into Delhi that had taken place a decade before, and he had never left the city after that. "Very clean air," he added.

"Do you know it?"

"Oh, no, memsa'b. But I have heard about it, from Dr. George."

"You are to take good care of him when he arrives and make sure that he eats properly."

"Yes, memsa'b. Dilip knows what he likes."

"This has all been very upsetting for him."

"It has been upsetting for everyone, mem. Bhavat Singh, one of the other guards, was most upset. He was very shocked about the whole thing. I think he was very good friends with the man who died."

"With Jagaan Ramakrishnan?"

"Oh yes, mem. He saw to it himself that his things were sent back to his family and that he was paid the wages he was owed. Every month he was sending money to his family. I think they relied on it very much. Bhavat Singh went to a lot of trouble. He has a son of about the same age. Perhaps that is why he felt so sorry about it."

Sophie felt her face tighten. "What?"

John put his cup down and looked at her cautiously. "Memsa'b?" All the color had drained from her face. "Are you all right, memsa'b?"

Sophie felt herself liquefy. Her hands started to tremble, her breathing suddenly difficult.

"Memsa'b?"

"The dead man." She pressed a hand to her throat. "Are you telling me that he had a son?"

"Yes, mem." John shifted awkwardly in his seat. He had said something bad, and he had no idea what it was. She looked like she had been struck by lightning.

"Who told you this?" she asked quietly.

"The other guard, Bhavat Singh."

"And did he tell you how old the son is?"

"No, memsa'b." John tried to think quickly. "But I can ask him."

"Did he say where the boy was?"

"Amritsar," John said. "He had been sending his wages there every month."

Sophie folded in her seat, closing her eyes, murmuring *oh my God, oh my God*, over and over.

"Nurse!" John got up from the table and rushed inside. "Nurse! Come quickly!"

40

George Schofield sat on the edge of the empty bed, sheets stripped, shafts of sunlight streaming through the windows. He watched his daughter gather the last of her toiletries into her case, the scar across her cheekbone less red where the stitches had knitted neatly together. He would have killed him, killed him with his bare hands had he been given the chance, but Lucien had been long gone by the time he received the news. For a while, a whisper had circulated that he had been seen in South America, in Buenos Aires, but the rumor was never substantiated. Even if it had been, what was he going to do about it? Fly off to another continent and go searching for him so that he could beat him to within an inch of his life? The thought had crossed his mind.

George had been furious when he discovered that Lucien had fled, that they had let him escape like that from right under their noses. He didn't mince his words with the police, nor indeed with the men from the embassy. The police didn't give a damn. It had even been intimated by the chief inspector that his daughter had brought the trouble upon herself. The men from the embassy were less insensitive to Dr. Schofield's rage and assured him that Lucien would be utterly ruined, a *persona non grata*, unable to show his face anywhere. His career was over, and should he ever turn up, he would of course be arrested and detained, although the chances of that ever happening were pretty much nonexistent. Dr. Schofield thought of Lucien often, a dozen times a day or more, fantasizing about having him in his grasp. It was the first thing he had prayed for in years, hoping to God that he would get his comeuppance and that when it came to him it would be terrible. He envisaged him a bloated mess, living in poverty and squalor in some god-forsaken place, riddled with disease and taken to a slow, painful death. He wished the worst things imaginable upon him, things that he never thought himself capable of thinking, taking from it some small compensation, all the anger and hatred he had gathered through his life concentrated on that one man. He took a few deep breaths. One of these days he would have to let these feelings go, before they poisoned him.

Sophie clicked her case shut and sat in the chair beside him.

"Are you sure about this?" he asked her.

"Yes," she said. "I have never been more certain of anything in my life."

"Then let me come with you."

"I'm sorry, Dad. I want to do this on my own."

He let out a weighty sigh. "I wish you'd change your mind."

"I can't." She shrugged and smiled at him. "You do understand that, don't you?" Her father nodded at her. "I have to go. My son is there. I am sure of it."

"What if it is not him?"

"Dad. We've talked about this already."

"He could have got married and had a child by his wife."

"There is no wife."

"The man said he had a wife and that she was dead."

"He was lying," Sophie said. "Of course he's going to say that he had a dead wife. How else was he going to explain a son?"

"You're chasing dreams, Sophie." Dr. Schofield took his daughter's hand. "I can understand it, with everything that's happened. It's been a terrible shock for you, but this will just lead to more heartache."

"I don't care. If I don't go, I will never know. Don't you see? This is my only chance. St. Bride's has gone. There are no records. You can't seriously expect me to just sit here and do nothing?"

"Then let me come with you."

"No."

"Or at least take one of the staff."

"I am perfectly capable of getting on a train, and they're not my staff any more."

"Sophie, Sophie." Dr. Schofield sighed to himself. "How much more pain are you going to put yourself through?"

"Pain?" She smiled at him. "You think this is pain? This isn't pain, Dad. It's hope, real hope. Do you have any idea what it has been like for me to live like this, knowing that I had a son that I gave away, simply because he wasn't convenient? Can you imagine what it's like to deal with that, day after day, or the loathing I feel for the terrible thing I did?" Her father studied the floor, nodding silently. "And what if I do find him? For all I know, he may not even realize that I exist. He might think he's somebody else's child. And even if he did know me, he might walk right up to me and spit in my face. Do you think I haven't thought about these things?"

"You must have," Dr. Schofield said.

"Of course I have. It makes me sick, down to the pit of my stomach."

"What if you get there and he is not your child?"

"I'll cross that bridge when I come to it." She broke off, her mouth set into a hard line. "If he is not my son, then I shall tell him what a brave man his father was, and that he sacrificed his life in order to save a man who was not worthy to breathe the same air as him."

"Sophie..."

"And then I will offer the family anything that I can give, and more, because nothing I ever do can ever make up for the loss they have suffered."

"Sophie. Don't upset yourself."

She leaned forward in her seat, face in her hands, rocking gently, as though trying to comfort herself. Dr. Schofield watched her, feeling impotent, unable to reach out and touch her. This fate was as much his doing as hers. Would it have been so very bad if they had kept the baby? Yes, he thought quietly. Yes, it would have.

"I have to go," she said. "I have to go and find out, otherwise I shall never be able to live with myself. It is already hard enough. Nothing could be worse than this." She lifted her head. "And if he is not my son, then so be it, and I promise I will let it go."

"All right," her father said. "All right." He heaved a long sigh. "I of all people should know what you're like when your mind is made up. I admire you for it."

Sophie looked at him. "I wonder who I get that from."

"Give your father a hug," he said. "I am feeling old today."

Sophie and her father sat in silence, waiting for the doctor to arrive and give her the all-clear. More than two months had passed since she had been brought to the hospital unconscious. At first the doctors had thought she had been involved in a car accident, such were her injuries. Then the police had arrived and two men from the British Embassy shortly thereafter. A junior envoy had been sent via special flight down to Coimbatore, to fetch Dr. Schofield. It was mid-morning, and he had been at the clinic, attending to his general practice and thinking about cutting down the eucalyptus tree that had grown too close to the house.

He remembered it so clearly, the way he had been thinking about something so banal while his daughter lay battered and broken in a hospital bed over a thousand miles away. He had been taken to the airport and flown up in a matter of hours, the official dispatched to escort him saying precious little on the way. The doctors were waiting for him at the hospital, two of them, primed to prepare him for what he was about to see. She had a broken cheekbone, a fractured jaw, and a ruptured spleen that had taken seven pints of blood. And she had lost the baby. Had they realized that she was pregnant when she had been brought in, they might have stood a better chance, but she had hemorrhaged badly, and they had had no choice other than to take it all away.

Dr. Schofield folded his hands in his lap and dipped his head. "I saw him, you know," he said.

"Who?"

"The guard. I thought I recognized him, but I couldn't place it."

Sophie stared at her father, her breath becoming still. "What did he say?"

"Nothing. He ran into me one evening, literally, after the Christmas party. I had gone outside to smoke a cigarette and I wandered over to the guardhouse. The other guard in there gave me a cup of chai in a dirty cup, and I drank it, then went outside and bumped straight into him. And that was it." Dr. Schofield shook his head, as though he still couldn't quite believe it. "He didn't say a word and I only caught a glimpse of him, but there was something about him, something I just *knew*. I was never able to place it. It was as though I recognized him, although I know that can't be so. Such a strange thing."

The doctor walked in through the open door, smiling broadly. "Ah!" he said. "I see that you are all ready to go."

"Yes." Sophie smiled back at him.

"I expect you'll be glad to get out of here."

"A little," she said. "Although I have never felt so well looked after in all my life."

"And you are feeling all right today?"

"Perfectly fine," she said.

"Good." He handed her a small paper bag. "No headaches?"

"No."

"And your abdomen? Is it very tender still?"

"A bit, but it's fine. Really. Getting better every day."

"Good. There are some extra painkillers in here for you should you need them."

"Thank you, Doctor. You've all been wonderful."

"And thank you for being a model patient. We'll miss you."

Dr. Schofield stood up. "I owe you a great debt of gratitude." He shook the doctor's hand. "And remember what I said, now. If ever you feel like a change of scenery, we'd love to see you down in Ooty. The door will always be open to you."

"I may very well do that," the doctor said, then, to Sophie, "Send us a postcard when you get there."

"I will." Sophie picked up her case. "Although you may have to wait a little while."

The night train crawled slowly northward through the slumbering landscape. Sophie lay in her bunk, drifting in and out of a half-sleep, her body cradled by the rocking motion of the carriage, its wheels shunting rhythmically from track to track. She pulled the sheet up around her shoulders, her hand wandering to her cheek, fingers gently massaging the skin. She hoped it wouldn't frighten him. It looked much better now, and the scar would fade, given time.

She quieted her thoughts and tried to sleep. She must not be tired when she got there. She must be strong and clear-minded. But what if he was not there? Even worse, what if he was not her son? She pushed the thought out of her mind. It was him. She was sure of it. She had never felt more sure of anything. It was as though she could hear him calling to her. But what if she were to get there and be turned away? For all she knew, his family might never have been told about her, and even if they had, they could deny everything. They could call the police, and then what would she do? She squeezed her eyes tightly shut and turned over in her bunk.

Whatever happened, she would have to be prepared for it, and she was right to arrive unannounced. If they knew she was coming, they might take him away or hide him somewhere. Would she not do the same thing if she were in their position? They had raised him, her son, and she could be anybody. She was just a girl who had let herself get into trouble, then given her baby away, and what kind of woman was that? Was she poor? No. Would the child have starved to death or been beaten by its mother? No. Was it a girl child that nobody wanted? No. There could be no excuse for what she had done, no words that might present her in a more flattering light. There would be nothing she could say, except to tell them that she wanted her son, and that if she had to fight for him, then so be it. She must think about these things now and prepare herself for the worst. Whatever fate might await her, it would be nothing compared to what she had already gone through.

She pulled the sheet tightly around herself and tried to sleep, to preserve her strength. By morning, the train would be on the outskirts of Amritsar.

41

An untidy line of black and yellow auto rickshaws spurted into life outside the station, belching fumes from thin-pitched engines, scrambling toward the curb, toward the red-shirted porters and weary travelers. Sophie passed a pair of coins to the porter and allowed herself to be ushered into a fume-filled cabin, her case thrust in with her.

"Namaste," the driver called over his shoulder.

"Namaste," said Sophie. "*Mein Kim Street do dhoonh rahai hoo?*"

"Kim Street?" The driver gave a bemused frown and pulled out into the traffic. "*Kim Street kahaan hai?*"

"I was rather hoping you'd know," Sophie said.

"You English?" He smiled into the cracked rear-view mirror.

"Yes."

"First time Amritsar?"

"Yes."

"You want I show you Amritsar? It very beautiful city. Most beautiful Golden Temple in whole of India. You come Amritsar, you must see Golden Temple. I take you all around and I show you…"

Sophie barely heard a word, his voice chattering on as she sat back in her juddering seat, looking out of the window. She breathed deeply, the air ripe, and found herself searching the figures on the crowded streets. Men, women, children, babies. Every age, every generation, scattered all around, living their lives. A boy, of a similar age perhaps, in white pajamas, wearing a cap, steadying a broad wooden crate on his head, piled high with flat loaves of bread. She craned through the open window, trying to see his face. He turned a corner suddenly and was gone. Not him, she thought. Her son would be taller, like his father, and fairer-skinned. A group of children dashed out from a narrow alleyway, one clutching a ball, the others running wildly behind him, shouting and laughing. She twisted in her seat and watched after them out of the small, scratched window behind her. Run and play, she thought. I hope my son runs and plays all day long and laughs like a happy child. She sat forward and stared into the traffic.

Does he know his father is dead? Do they know what happened? They must do. Surely the other guard, the man called Bhavat Singh, would have written to the place where he had been sending his money, every transaction neatly recorded in the flimsy notebook they had found in with Jag's things. Bhavat Singh. A name she had come to know so well for a man she had never met. More than once she had started to write to him from the nursing home to thank him, but the words would not come. John had said that he had been Jag's friend, and Sophie had held on to that thought, that perhaps he had not been so terribly alone in his vigil.

It was a few moments before Sophie realized the tuk-tuk had stopped, the spluttering engine sending pungent fumes into the cabin again.

"Kim Street," the driver said.

"Here?" Sophie peered out.

"Yes, memsahib."

She paid the fare and stepped into the glaring sunshine, case in hand, standing at the mouth of the street as the tuk-tuk lurched away, spitting blue smoke.

A mishmash of tightly packed open-fronted shops, their stalls spilling out into the street, lined the way set out before her, the road between them an untidy traffic of people and bullock carts, a man pulling at a bad-tempered camel. Sophie walked the street slowly, picking her way through the shouting tradesmen and haggling customers, unaware of the eyes that picked her out in the crowds, watching her, a stranger in their midst. There were no outward signs to help her. None that she could read anyway. No numbers, no names.

She wandered past a tatty café, pans bubbling on a smoking stove set on the edge of the pavement, moving on past the next three stalls selling piles of cottons and brightly colored *phulkaari* shawls with intricately embroidered flowers. She stopped outside a hardware stall, looking absentmindedly at the teetering stacks of pots and pans. A man appeared.

"Very good quality, memsahib." He gestured proudly at his wares. "Very good price. You tell me what you want. I give you very good price."

"Sorry," Sophie said. "I was only…excuse me." She pulled her scarf over her head and walked away.

A little further along, a tailor sat at his sewing machine, a middle-aged Sikh with a red turban and experienced fingers that worked quickly beneath the dull, beating needle. She stood and watched him for a little while as he finished his seam and pulled the cuff away, testing the thread. He looked up at her, nodding briefly in deference.

"Namaste," she said, bowing back to him. "*Mein sath number seven Kim Street dhoondh rahai hoon?*" He looked at her curiously. "I am looking for the family who lives there," she said. "They have a boy, of about ten years." She measured a height with her hand, a vague guess, as most people seemed not to know how old they were, and she was not sure of the size of a ten-year-old anyway. He put down the unfinished shirt and got up, gesturing her to sit. "No, thank you," she said. "I did not mean to disturb your work. I just wondered if you might…"

"Please," he said, scraping the wooden stool toward her. "You sit." Reluctantly Sophie gave in to his insistence. "You sit. I come." And with that, the tailor went off, disappearing behind a slow, ambling cow as he crossed the street.

Sophie sat and waited, a few minutes at first, stretching to almost half an hour. If he didn't come back soon, she would have to move on, but then there would be nobody to watch over his stall, and what if someone were to walk in and help themselves? She sighed and looked at her wristwatch.

From behind the pillar outside his shop, Deepak Kapoor remained concealed while he took a good look at the woman sitting in the shade of the tailor's green canopy.

"She is asking about Parvesh Gupta's family?"

"Yes," said Navinder. "That's the address she had, and she asked about the boy." He looked over his shoulder in irritation. "Where is that fellow?"

"English?"

"I think so." Navinder joined Deepak in the shadows and looked out across the street again. "She has good-quality clothes."

"She is very skinny."

"She has a scar on her face too. She tried to hide it behind her scarf, but I saw it."

"A scar?"

"Yes. It looks like a knife scar."

"Hmm." Deepak hummed to himself curiously. "I wonder what she has in that little suitcase?"

"Maybe she is a tourist."

"Maybe it is full of valuables."

"He's here!" shouted the boy, out of breath, full of smiles. Deepak patted his son roughly on the head.

"Good. Now go and unpack some more onions and tidy up those brinjals at the front." The boy returned to the stall and set back to work.

"What's going on?" asked the barber. "I have a queue of customers waiting for me."

"Look." Deepak pointed across the street. "You see that

woman sitting in Navinder's stall? She is asking about Parvesh Gupta's family. She asked about the boy too." The barber slid behind the pillar and craned his head. "What do you think?" The barber stared at the woman. "You think maybe it is someone come to make trouble?"

"Why would anyone want to come and make trouble?" said the barber.

"No," said Navinder. "I think she is a nice respectable person. She was very polite."

"But what does she want with Parvesh Gupta?"

"Perhaps she has come to ask him to make her a nice pair of shoes!"

"Hey, boy!" Deepak shouted to his son. "Run over to Gupta shoemaker and tell him there is a visitor looking for him. Tell him to hurry." The men looked back across the street while the boy dashed away.

"Why not just take her there?" said the barber. "I could walk her across to him."

"Are you not in your right thinking?" Deepak stabbed his finger in admonishment. "What if she is somebody that Parvesh Gupta doesn't want Mrs. Gupta to know about? Huh? Did you even think of that?" He looked back over to the woman and felt a twinge of admiration for the respectable family shoemaker who so diligently kept himself to himself, the sly fox.

Sophie looked at her watch again. It was no good. She would have to abandon the tailor's shop and hope that nobody robbed him blind. She stood up and replaced the stool in its rightful position beside the sewing machine. Picking up her case, she turned to leave, and came face to face with two men. For a moment she felt panicked, and took a protective step backward into the street.

"Please." The barber offered her a small bow, palms pressed

together. "You are looking for the family at number seven Kim Street?" The other man was just staring at her, as though looking straight through her, his face showing no sign of greeting.

"Yes," she said tentatively, looking from one man to the other.

"This is Parvesh Gupta," said the barber. "He is head of the family at number seven."

"Oh!" Sophie's eyes darted back to the man. She felt her face tightening, her heart pounding. The way he was staring at her, just *staring*. It emptied her. "I…" she started, then faltered. "I…I would…"

Parvesh Gupta took a step toward her and said quietly, "I know who you are."

❦

In the stillness of the room, Mrs. Gupta stood before Sophie, her hands coming over her mouth as she folded in two and wept. Parvesh Gupta helped her to sit and comforted her, whispering to her gently, holding her hand.

No words had passed between them and Sophie. Parvesh Gupta had walked in silence as he led her to their home at the far end of the street, the ground floor occupied by his business, making and selling shoes, the deep scent of the raw materials perfuming the air richly. At the back of the workshop, a kitchen, and beyond that a narrow flight of stairs leading up and into two rooms above. The first, cool and dim, was furnished with two web-strung charpoys, protected from the high temperatures of the hot season by the small windows cut thickly into the walls. The second room, brighter, contained two more beds, scattered with mirror-work cushions, with patterned rugs on the floor, threadbare in places. This was where Mrs. Gupta had stood, so still, as though she had been waiting there since the beginning of time, standing there in her yellow sari.

Sophie did as she was bid and sat on the floor, covering her legs with her shawl, curling them up beside her hips. There they remained, the three of them, sitting in silence. No food was offered. No water. It was as though they hardly dared to breathe. Sophie concentrated on the hands folded into her lap, her skin a little tanned, a few lines appearing here and there that would no doubt deepen as the years caught up with her. She stole a glance at Mrs. Gupta and saw that she was looking directly back at her, unblinking. Sophie tried to smile, but couldn't. She looked back into her lap. Why didn't he say something? Were they just going to sit here like this for ever, in this abominable silence? Sophie kept quiet. It would not be her place to speak first. It was not her house. She would just have to wait until he chose to break the silence.

Another hour passed. Parvesh Gupta said something to his wife, then pulled himself up from the floor. He went to the window, looking out on to the street below for a while before leaving the room, his footsteps creaking on the wooden stairs.

Sophie heard herself sigh. She picked up her head, easing the tension in her neck, and noticed for the first time the shallow shelves set into the wall above her. A few books lay stacked on their faces, three red clay oil pots with clean, unlit tapers. A glass jar containing pale grains of raw incense. A small wooden box, a photograph propped against it. Sophie straightened, hands against the floor as she lifted herself toward it. Her breath halted. She turned quickly to Mrs. Gupta and found her to be staring at her again, watching closely her every move.

"*Kya mein?*" Sophie asked quietly. Mrs. Gupta looked into her hands and nodded.

Sophie raised herself to her knees, her hand reaching up, oh so slowly, and taking down the photograph. And there he was, his gaze fixed squarely into the center of the camera's lens, pale eyes looking straight at her, tourmalines lost to the monochrome. It was a photographer's portrait, a picture taken for the sake of memento. She turned it over and read the inscription on the back. The name of the photography studio, the date, May 1952, seven years ago. How old would he have been? She turned it over again and looked

at him, searching him. Twenty-four, maybe twenty-five? She had
never asked him how old he was, having been told that age did
not matter to the Indians. *Why did I never ask how old you were?*
She found herself smiling at him. She touched the image with her
fingertip, then looked up at Mrs. Gupta. "Thank you," she whispered. "*Shukriya.*" Her head dipped.

Mrs. Gupta stood up and went to the shelf. She took down the
small wooden box and opened it, taking something from it and
pressing it into Sophie's palm, closing her hand around it.

"It was the only thing Jagaan had left when he found us," she
said quietly. "He had never shown it to anyone, not in all the
months it took him to get here. He was afraid that if anyone knew
about it, it would be stolen from him."

Sophie opened her hand. Her gold locket glinted back at her,
the one she had worn as a girl before dropping it from a high
window into the hands of the boy she loved.

The sob shook her whole body, the wave of grief crashing
over her, closing in above her head, taking her down with it. She
pressed her face into her hands and heard herself wailing, a sound
so terrible that it might have come from every spirit lost to the
darkness between heaven and hell. Tears poured from her eyes,
her mouth, her nose. She felt Mrs. Gupta's arms come around her,
holding her tightly, rocking her into her chest, wiping her tears
with the soft hem of her sari.

"Shhh," she said. "Do not cry." She continued to dry Sophie's
tears. "Shhh. Do not let your son see you like this." Sophie nodded
into her hands, her breath stuttering. She reached down and took
the woman's hand and gripped it hard.

Mrs. Gupta looked at her. From outside came a few distant
shouts, a brief burst of children's laughter. "School is finished,"
Mrs. Gupta said. Sophie nodded again and swallowed hard,
almost choking on her own breath, feeling suddenly that she
might be sick. Mrs. Gupta rose from the floor and pulled her to
her feet, then stood before her and took slow, deep breaths, not

once taking her eyes from Sophie's: *breathe in, two, three, four, five, six, and exhale.*

Sophie steadied herself, wiped her face, and sniffed hard. Shaking her head briskly, she returned Mrs. Gupta's gaze and began to breathe along with her. In, and out, and in again, until she felt herself calmed.

"He will be here soon," Mrs. Gupta told her. "His name is Joy."

☙ ❧

Parvesh Gupta stood guard outside his stall, watching every young figure as it ran toward him before rushing past along the street. Joy was fast on his feet. That boy could outrun anyone. A customer interrupted his concentration. Parvesh hushed him in annoyance and told him to wait. The customer took umbrage and began to complain. Parvesh sighed and turned to him, about to explain why he was busy. In that moment, a flash of white cotton dashed past the corner of his eye.

Parvesh rushed after him, catching the cloth of his white pajamas, snapping him back. The customer called his exasperation, threw the sandals back on to the stall, and marched off indignantly.

"Wait!" Parvesh held on to the boy's arm.

Joy looked at him and hoped he wasn't about to send him off on an errand. He was starving, and the only thing he cared about right now was whether there were any chapattis left over in the kitchen. With any luck, Mausi would have made a batch of pakoras and put a few out for him, to stave off his hunger until suppertime. He stared at his uncle, his hope sinking a little as he saw the grave look on his face. It was something serious, he could tell. Perhaps some busybody had gone and told them about the accident, so now he would be in big trouble, even though he hadn't been the one who did it. It wasn't even his ball. If he had a cricket ball, he wouldn't be stupid enough to let an idiot like Manoj bowl it straight through a window, never to be seen again. They had turned on their heels and scattered like cockroaches under a light before anyone came out to catch them, and there was no way that any of them were going to knock on the door of the house with the broken window to ask for it back.

"What's the matter, Uncle?" Joy tried to look innocent.

"Joy," his uncle said, putting his hands on the boy's shoulders. Joy felt his guts become leaden. There was only one other time when his uncle had done that to him. It could mean only one thing. Somebody was dead.

"Yes, Uncle?"

Parvesh Gupta took a deep breath. "Your mother has been found."

Joy's mouth opened, but nothing came out. He stared at his uncle, his eyes widening.

"She is here," Parvesh said. "She is upstairs, waiting for you."

Joy stood stock still, his head turning slowly, looking into the back of the shop. He wrenched himself out from under his uncle's hands and ran.

***

Sophie broke away from Mrs. Gupta, turning suddenly at the noise, fast footsteps thundering up the wooden staircase, a boy bursting into the room. He stopped, thin body breathing hard beneath his loose white shirt, staring at her with wide green eyes. She looked at him, her heart turning over, but before she could speak, before she could smile, he rushed forward and grabbed hold of her so hard that the force of it unsteadied her. His face pressed fast into her chest. Sophie wrapped her arms around him, bending into him, holding him to her. She felt his heart beating fast like a bird through his thin shirt. She felt his breath, short and hot, dampening her blouse. She closed her eyes.

"My son," she whispered into his soft dark hair. "My Joy."

He pulled away from her, staring up into her face, his expression filled with wonder, and with worry. "Are you staying?"

Sophie glanced uncertainly at Mrs. Gupta, who was watching silently from the corner of the room, a sad smile on her lips. Mrs. Gupta nodded.

"Yes," Sophie said to him. "I am staying. I will never leave you again."

"I knew you were coming," said Joy. "My father promised me. He said he would find you even if it took him a hundred years."

Sophie smiled at him, glad that her tears had been spent before he could see them.

"I know," she said gently, holding him close. "I'm sorry I took so long."

42

D
r. Schofield picked up the package and inspected the handwriting. It was from Sophie, and she had written: PHOTO-
GRAPHS, DO NOT BEND across the front, boldly underlined.
He slit it open with a paper knife. Inside were two photographic
mounts, covered over with a face of textured black card, and a
note, left flat and unfolded, as though it had just fallen from her
fingertips. Dr. Schofield began to read, a smile coming over him.
*You said you wanted me to send you a photograph to display proudly at
the clinic.* He continued down the page, his smile drifting away,
before setting the letter aside. He chose the larger of the two black
cards and opened it, a gasp on his lips as he looked at her, smiling
into the camera, the boy at her side, about a dozen people grouped
closely around them. An older couple, of his age perhaps. A young
man of about twenty, looking very serious. A pair of apparent
newlyweds, with a baby. A Sikh family, unrelated he guessed but
smiling nonetheless. And Sophie, right there among them. He
shook his head in amazement and stared at them all, posing so
proudly for this unlikely family portrait. She looked so happy. It
had been a long time since he had seen that smile, the one that had
lit him up inside when she was a girl.

The door to his study opened.

"Coffee," said Mrs. Nayar, her tray clattering to the table. She
hovered next to his desk. The package had arrived this morning
when the doctor was at his clinic, and she and Salil had been
bursting to see what was in it. They had taken it into the kitchen

and propped it on the table against a jam jar so that they could talk about it all day, speculating about it before the doctor came home. He had been in his study now for over half an hour and still no news.

Dr. Schofield glanced up at her and smiled enigmatically before handing her the photograph to see for herself. Mrs. Nayar looked at it, her brow rumpling for a moment as she stared into the image more closely. Her eyes slid inquiringly toward Dr. Schofield.

"Yes," Dr. Schofield said. "Go and show Salil."

Mrs. Nayar rushed off to the kitchen and Dr. Schofield took up the other black card, holding it closed for a moment, preparing himself for what lay inside. *The other is a picture of Joy's father, Jagaan Ramakrishnan. It is the only photograph that exists of him, so this is a copy.* Dr. Schofield took a deep breath and opened it.

He recognized him in an instant. The boy from the camp. The face the same, but older. It knocked the wind from him. He pulled the spectacles from his face, dropping them to his desk, and let out an endless sigh.

15 AUGUST 1970

California

15 August 1970
Carpinteria, CA

My darling Jag,

It is 15 August again, the day when I sit quietly and write to you. I talk to you for hours. I tell you everything. My hopes and dreams, my darkest fears, my life and what it has become.

Our son graduated this summer. He smiled at me with such happiness, my face hidden behind the camera, and I saw you so clearly. Such a beautiful day it was. You would have been so proud of him. He went out afterward, to celebrate with his friends, and I came home and lit a candle for you and put it on the shelf where we keep your memories.

He is in love with a girl. He has not told me as much, but I know. They have been going steady for almost a year now, and they look at each other as we once did. She is half Japanese and delicate like a doll. Joy is taller than ever and brave-looking and he towers over her. He has your eyes. Sometimes I can hardly bear to look into them, such is their weight. It reminds me of you, and I have to be careful because sometimes I see him and I want to cry, or to hold on to him and pretend that he is you. I have to remember that he is not you, and that you are waiting for us in a distant place where all love is the same.

We talk about you often. I tell him my legend, and he tells me his. We never tire of it. It brings you closer to us. I piece together your journey and write every word so it will never be forgotten, even after I am long gone. I tell the tale of the boy who was raised in a palace and fell in love with a girl he was not supposed to fall in love with, and how he spent the rest of his life searching for her, to restore his family.

Your aunt calls me daughter. We visited her in the spring, and she could scarcely believe how much Joy had grown. She is seventy-four now and has more grandchildren than she knows what to do with. You are the hero of the family, she says, and she gathers the little ones around her and tells them of your adventures. We traveled down to Ooty afterward, and Joy's grandfather paraded him proudly and insisted he become a proper member of the club now that he is twenty-one. My father tells him the stories of how you worked together in the camp hospital. He is getting old now, and he likes to talk about the past. He says that the day he met his grandson was the happiest day of his life.

Joy wants to make his home here in America. It is a good place for him. It seems that everyone here has come from somewhere else. Like us, they arrived full of hope and filled with dreams of a life not yet lived. We are happy here, in this land of people from other places where nobody cares who we are or where we came from. He has been offered an internship at a hospital in San Francisco. It will be the making of him. He is coming home this weekend and is bringing Lucy with him. He says they have some news.

Oh, how I miss you. I took out the letter this morning and read it, as I always do on this day. We keep it in a small silver box with the locket I gave you, and it sits on the shelf of memories with your picture. The paper is falling apart and the stains have faded, but I touch them still and bring my finger to my lips, as if wanting to taste your blood, so that you might live within me. Sometimes I see a bird high above, riding the thermals, circling, circling, and I think of it as you, watching over us.

At midnight I will go outside and look at the stars and pray that you can hear me. The black water has no memory, they say. It traverses the earth without soul or conscience, gathering nothing on its way, waves crashing into the shore before sloping back and turning over, heading out again. I am at peace here, looking out over the sea of no memories, watching the water that never sleeps while I think of you. I shall see you again one day, my love, and our spirits shall be as one, passing silently through the walls of a palace in the sky.

READING GROUP GUIDE

1. Why would it have been considered unthinkable for Sophie to have kept her baby in 1948? What has changed since then?

2. Do you think Sophie's mother realizes her role in the destruction of her family?

3. Was George Schofield a weak man? Should he have done more to protect Sophie from her mother's rages?

4. Jagaan defies his father and rejects the ancient traditions regarding marriage in India. Do you think this contributed to his father's death?

5. As an adult, how has Sophie been affected by her relationship with her mother? Does this influence her choice of husband? Or do you think she married Lucian for other reasons? If yes, what were they?

6. How would the First Maharani and her retinue of ladies-in-waiting have felt about women like Mrs. Ripperton and Sophie?

7. Is it human nature to plaster over the cracks of an unsuccessful marriage rather than to admit defeat? Why stay in a

bad marriage rather than divorce? Was it merely a trend of the times?

8.   Race and religion are at the root of many of the conflicts in the story. Is it natural for different races to be suspicious of one another?

9.   How would the Diplomatic Wives have reacted to modern views toward women's equality and the high-profile female politicians of today?

10.   How did women handle postnatal depression in the days before its recognition and treatment? Did it carry a stigma?

11.   Are there similarities between Jagaan and Lucien?

12.   India's partition was implemented in August 1947. What has been the legacy of that decision?

13.   Which is morally less acceptable: a philandering husband or an unfaithful wife?

14.   By 1970, Sophie is living as a single woman in California. What is the likelihood that she would want to find love again? Would her experience with Lucien have put her off relationships all together?

15.   Should Jagaan have been more forthright when he discovered Sophie was back in India? How did cultural differences affect his thinking?

16.   What would it be like to live in *purdah*, in an all-female environment, shielded from the outside world? Did the women of the *zenana* mind?

17. Did Lucien deliberately misrepresent himself to Sophie prior to their marriage?

18. Was it selfish for Sophie to take her son away from his family in India to make a fresh start in America? Would you have done the same thing?

A CONVERSATION
WITH THE AUTHOR

Q. Where did you get the idea for *Under the Jeweled Sky*?

A. *Under the Jeweled Sky* was inspired by memories of the women I would eavesdrop on, the hushed voices and grave expressions passed over teacups. My mother and her friends had grown up in the days before such things were openly spoken of. But it was all there: domestic violence, unwanted pregnancies, addiction, ruin, and occasional salvation.

Among the whispers I overheard as a child was the story of the love affair that ended in tragedy and scandal and, separately, the tale of the baby who was birthed in secret and left at an orphanage in Delhi. Adults think that small children are not listening, or that if they are, they are too young to take anything in. But this is not so. I remember everything.

Q. Why did you set the story in the 1940s and 1950s?

A. *Under the Jeweled Sky* unravels the fragile construct of a dysfunctional British family and watches its slow disintegration in the wake of World War II, the subsequent partition of India, and a scandal with terrible consequences. The tangle of politics and diplomacy during both periods seemed like a fitting backdrop to the disordered lives of the characters, with layers of deceit and half-truths and nothing being quite what it seems.

Q. How did you learn about the details of what India was like back then?

A. One strand of the novel is partially set in a maharaja's palace. Although the palace and its location is anonymous and fictional, I did have an inside track into life inside an Indian palace. In her twenties, my mother was hired as the private nurse to the Maharaja of Indore's mother-in-law. She arrived there from Bombay and was shown to her quarters—an enormous suite in a grand building set across the grounds from the main palace. A car was sent for her every morning, but she preferred to walk. So off she would go, strolling through the grounds while the car followed along a few yards behind, driving at a snail's pace in case she should change her mind. Her breakfast would be served to her on a solid silver service, with a footman standing by should she want for anything.

From what she has told me, I am not sure that she handled it particularly well. She said that she didn't want any fuss, which was quite the wrong way to go about things in a palace. There was also an incident when she was caught preparing her own boiled egg, which didn't go down well at all. The cook was quite overcome with grief, and my mother never ventured to lift a finger again. I have to say, I rather like the thought of that.

Q. How did your personal history inform the novel?

A. My mother was born in Assam in 1928. The daughter of an unproclaimed liaison, she came to England thirty years later, never meaning to stay, and met my father. I was born in London in 1964, four years before Enoch Powell's "Rivers of Blood" speech. Mixed marriages were still a rarity then. I knew that I had a grandfather and that he had a farm in Africa, in Southern Rhodesia as it was then known, but I never met him. He existed only as a single photograph in my mother's album. My father was an orphan, dumped on the steps of a Barnardo's Home at the age of five. With so little information about who I was and where my family came from, it's little wonder I became a writer.

Some years on, I pestered my mother about why she had never gone to Africa to visit her father. My mother got very cross and eventually said that for a brown face to turn up on her father's doorstep "just wouldn't do." Those were her exact words.

It was my father who took me aside one day and whispered that my mother and her sister were born outside of marriage. They were the children of a British tea-planter, born to his Indian concubine, and the shame of it had followed my mother like a shadow her whole life. I have no doubt she thought the world would come tumbling down if anyone found out, for that is what she had been conditioned to believe.

My mother and her sister, aged five and seven, were taken from their mother and sent to a remote convent to be educated before being trained as nurses. My mother was just eleven when she last saw her father. She has no idea what happened to her mother. On the day she left school, she was taken into the mother superior's office and told that the woman she thought to be her aunt, her father's sister, was actually his wife.

As the years wore on, my mother began to talk to me, as though unburdening herself of every memory, good or bad. We pored over maps, trawled through old pictures and keepsakes, and trudged around India. She cried a lot, too, which was hard. Recently, she gave me a box of letters and photographs that I had never seen before. I don't think anyone else had either.

About twenty years ago, when she was in her sixties, my mother disclosed to her sister that she had told her family about their past. Her sister was furious, having kept the secret from her own children. My mother shrugged off her anger and told her we all thought it was marvelous and very romantic. Although it wasn't romantic, of course. It was tragic and heartbreaking and had left two women's lives with a backdrop of unspeakable sorrow.

My mother imparted her stories to me over many, many years. She told me things she had never told anyone—not just her secrets, but those of her friends, my "aunties." I came to know things that their own children didn't know, and probably still don't. Nobody talked about these things. They still don't.

I promised my mother I would remember her stories and pass them on to my own children so they might always have a sense of belonging. All my aunties are now dead; my mother is the only survivor. Any sense of shame about the past has long since fallen away. She has learned to be proud of who she is and where she came from, just as we are.

ABOUT THE AUTHOR

Born to an Indian mother and an English
jazz musician father, Alison McQueen
grew up in London and worked in
advertising for twenty-five years before
retiring to write full time. Alison lives in
Northamptonshire, England, with her husband and two daughters.

Photo credit: Jayne West